ARCA

@IDWpublishing
IDWpublishing.com

EDITORS:
Mark Doyle & Maggie Howell

ASSISTANT EDITOR:
Jake Williams

PRODUCTION DESIGN:
Nathan Widick

978-1-68405-998-0   26   25   24   23   1   2   3   4

Nachie Marsham, Publisher
Blake Kobashigawa, SVP Sales, Marketing & Strategy
Mark Doyle, VP Editorial & Creative Strategy
Tara McCrillis, VP Publishing Operations
Anna Morrow, VP Marketing & Publicity
Alex Hargett, VP Sales
Jamie S. Rich, Executive Editorial Director
Scott Dunbier, Director, Special Projects
Greg Gustin, Sr. Director, Content Strategy
Kevin Schwoer, Sr. Director of Talent Relations
Lauren LePera, Sr. Managing Editor
Keith Davidsen, Director, Marketing & PR
Topher Alford, Sr. Digital Marketing Manager
Patrick O'Connell, Sr. Manager, Direct Market Sales
Shauna Monteforte, Sr. Director of Manufacturing Operations
Greg Foreman, Director DTC Sales & Operations
Nathan Widick, Director of Design
Neil Uyetake, Sr. Art Director, Design & Production
Shawn Lee, Art Director, Design & Production
Jack Rivera, Art Director, Marketing

Ted Adams and Robbie Robbins, IDW Founders

For international rights, contact licensing@idwpublishing.com.

ARCA

WRITER
VAN JENSEN

INTERIOR & COVER ARTIST
JESSE LONERGAN

COLORIST
PATRICIO DELPECHE

LETTERER
NATHAN WIDICK

Arca created by Van Jensen and Jesse Lonergan

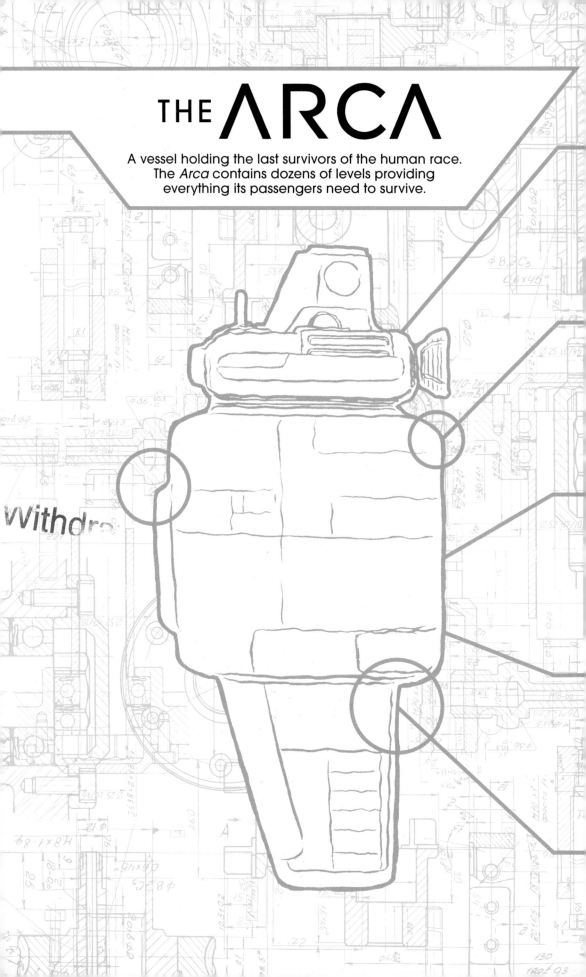

THE ARCA

A vessel holding the last survivors of the human race. The *Arca* contains dozens of levels providing everything its passengers need to survive.

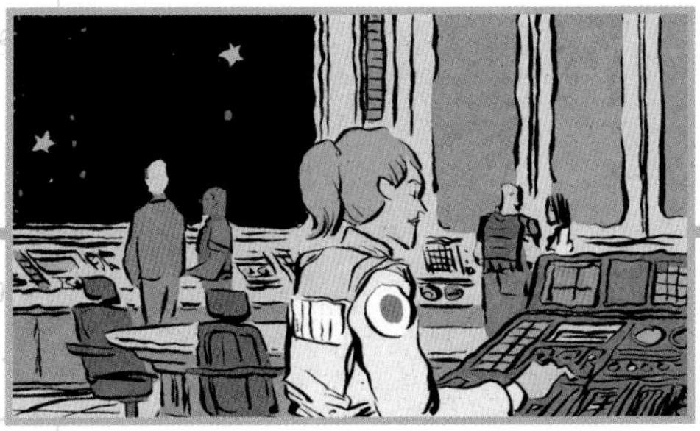
Control Center

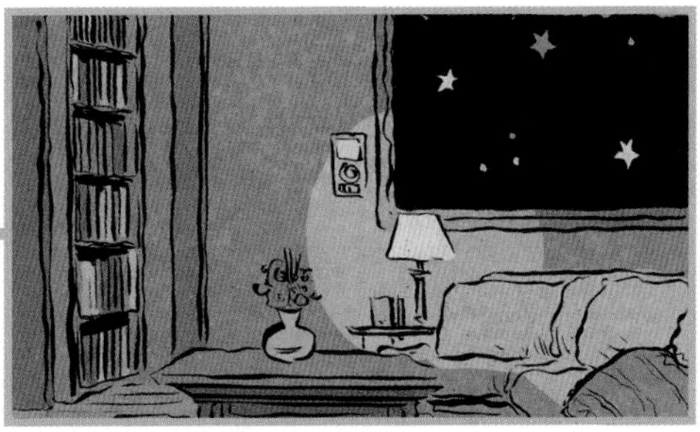
Citizen Residences

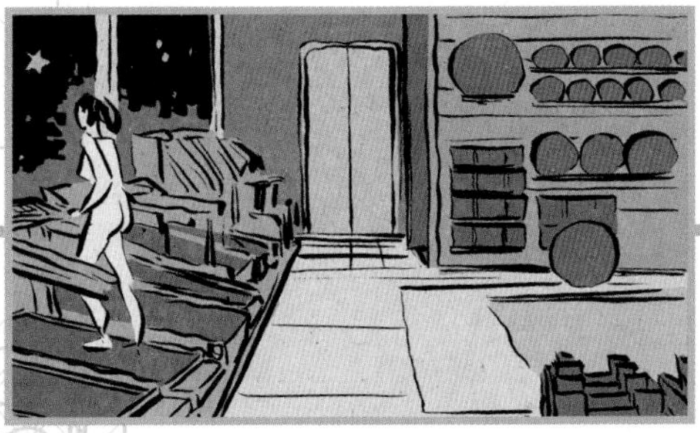
Gymnasium

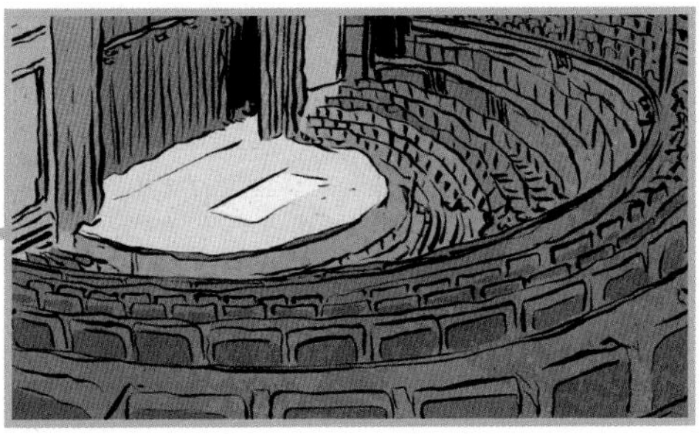
Amphitheater and Entertainment

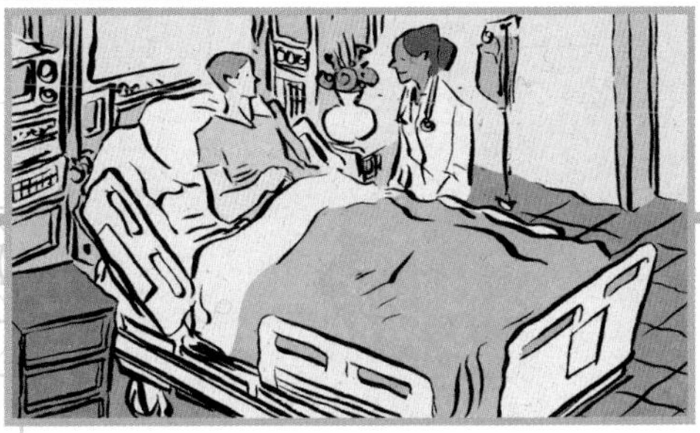
Medical Bay

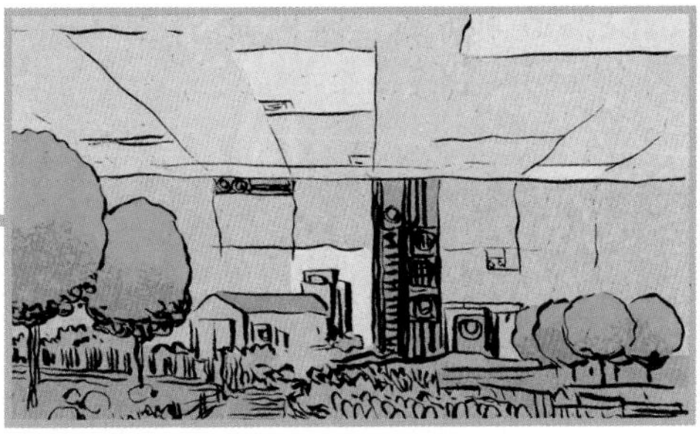
The Farm

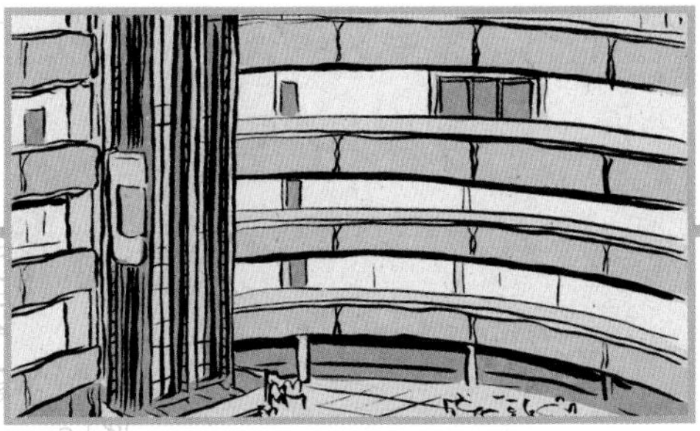
Central Atrium

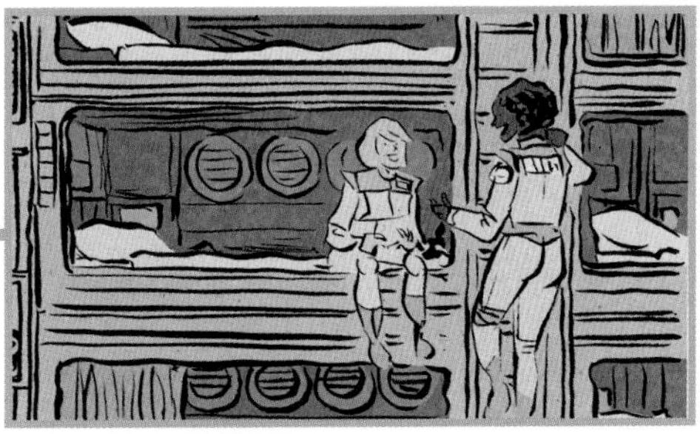
Settler Residences

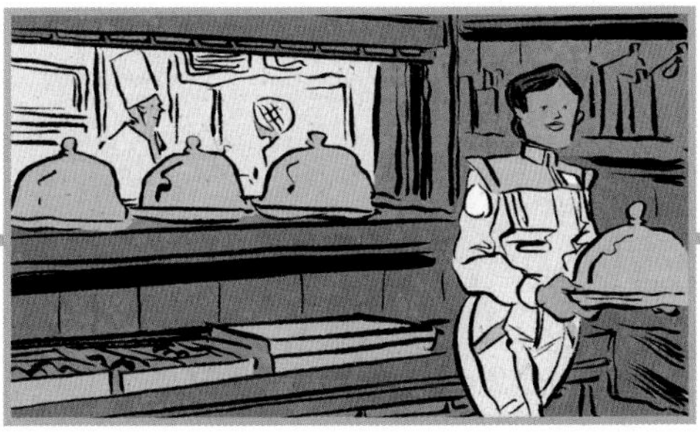
Kitchens

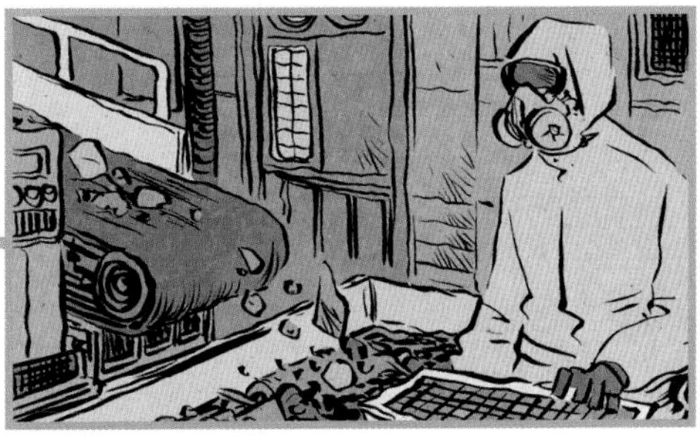
Waste Management

THE SURVIVORS

The *Arca* is home to hundreds, and they are divided into three key groups.

CITIZENS

Citizens are those who planned and funded the *Arca* before the Earth became uninhabitable. They reside in the upper levels and enjoy many of the luxuries of the life they left behind when society collapsed.

Denton Graves
Geneticist and leader of the *Arca*.

Nahyan Al Said
Preserver of humanity's literature.

Luella Brazier
Roboticist and designer of *Arca's* mechanical systems.

Bud Black
Founder of a mixed martial arts fighting league.

Holly Fox
Heiress and philanthropist.

David Fox (deceased)
Scion of an old money family.

Pharaoh X
Famed musician and cultural icon.

HELPERS

Helpers are armed security personnel who serve to maintain order aboard the *Arca* and respond to any emergencies. Their loyalty belongs to the Citizens.

Jacob Mason
Head of security aboard the *Arca*.

SETTLERS

Settlers are children and teenagers who tend to the chores of the *Arca* and the needs of the Citizens. At age 18, they graduate and retire from their chores. Each Settler serves in one of four divisions:

AIDES

Personal assistants to the Citizens, serving them in whatever needs they have.

Effie
Aide serving Denton Graves and nearing her 18th birthday.

Mat
Aide and Effie's closest friend.

MECHANICAL

Skilled in technical tasks, repairing and maintaining the many systems of the *Arca*.

Key
Tasked with maintaining the *Arca's* broadcast systems.

SANITATION

Cleaning crews who tidy the *Arca*, oversee laundry, and manage recycling and composting.

Bet
Manager of the vast composting operation in the lowest levels.

FOOD

Growers and raisers who tend to the gardens and livestock pens, harvesting, and slaughtering, as well as cooking meals.

Don
Grower and fighter in competitions held for the Citizens' entertainment.

Have you built your ship of death, O have you?
O build your ship of death, for you will need it.

D.H. Lawrence

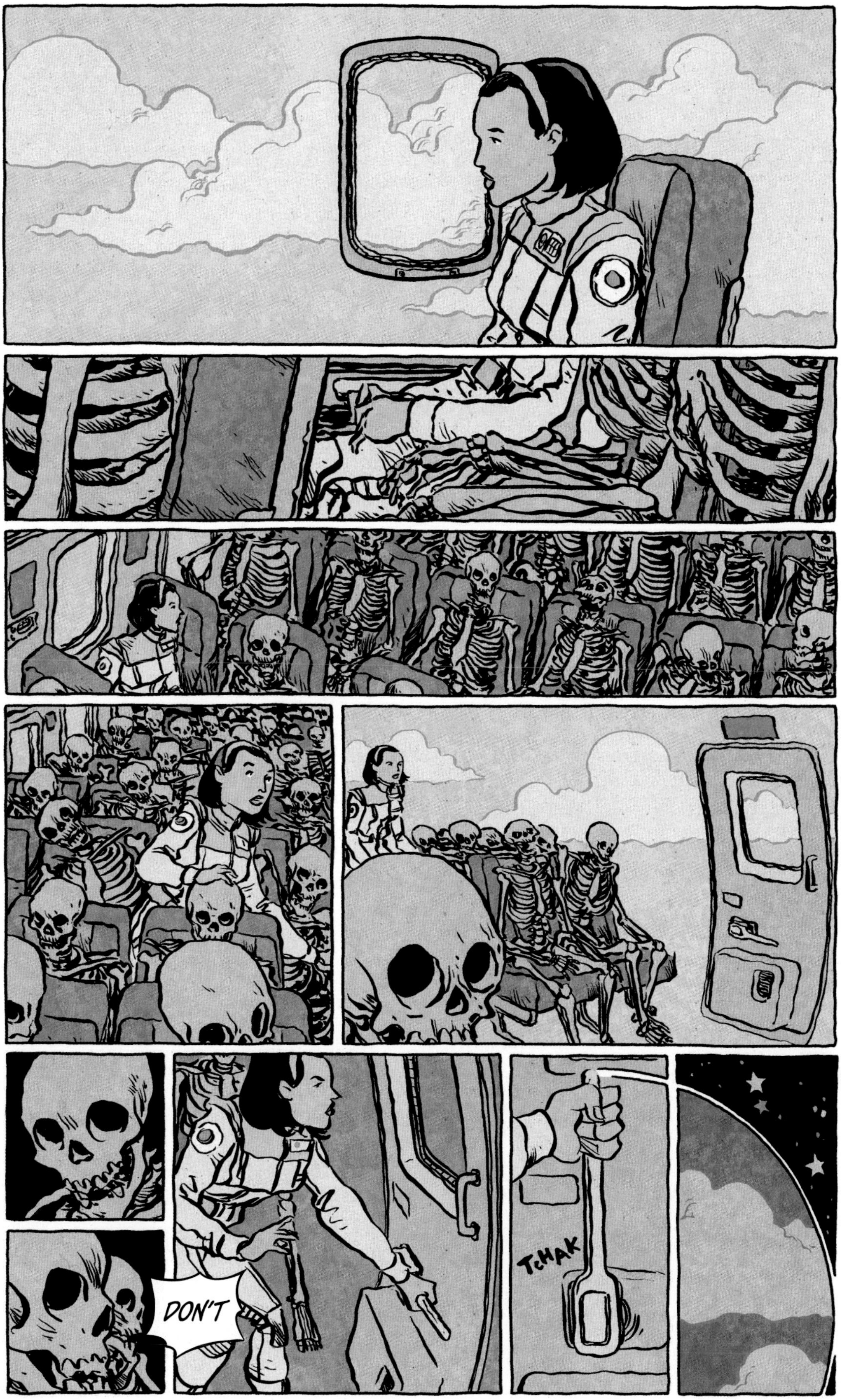
DON'T
TCHAK

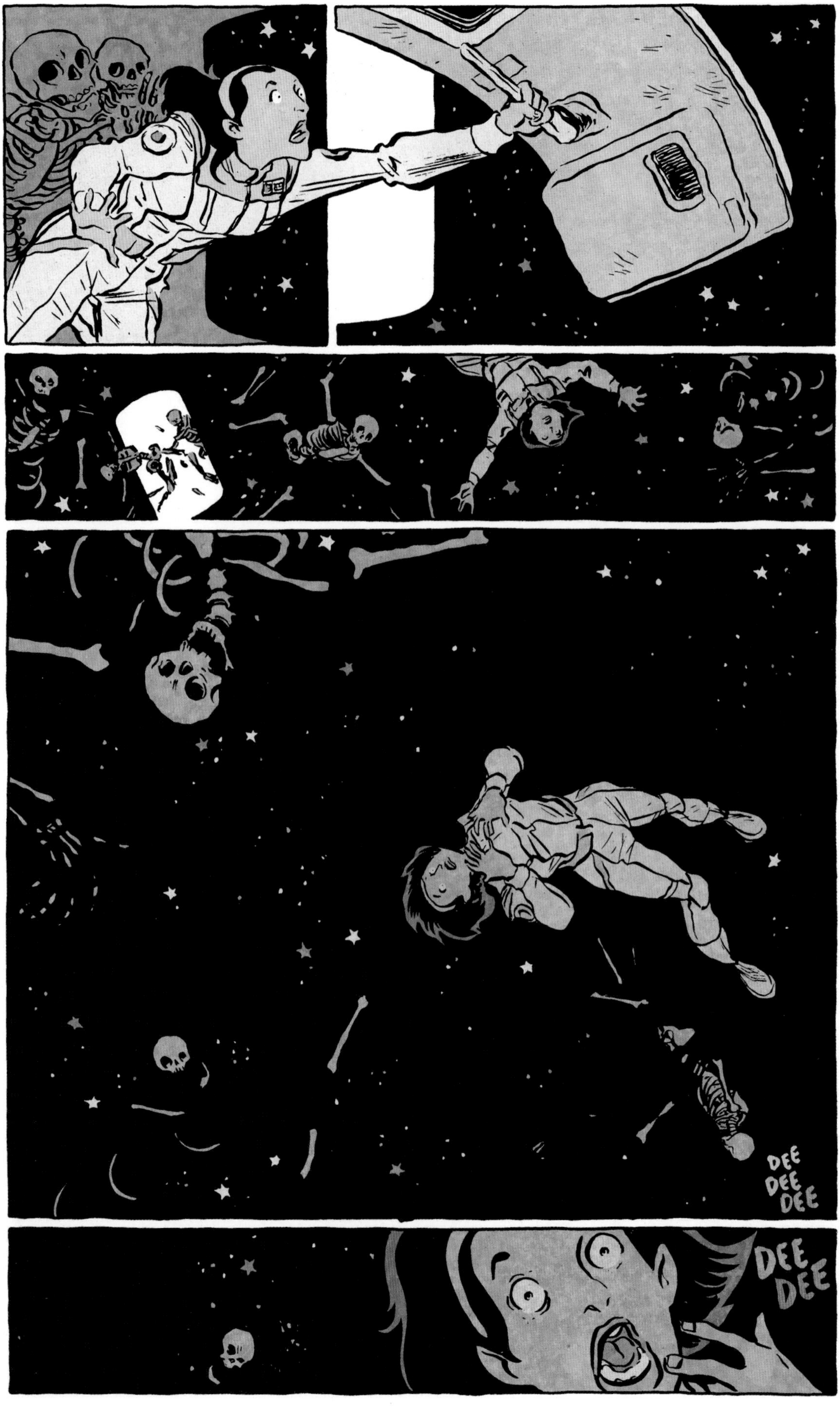
DEE
DEE
DEE
DEE
DEE

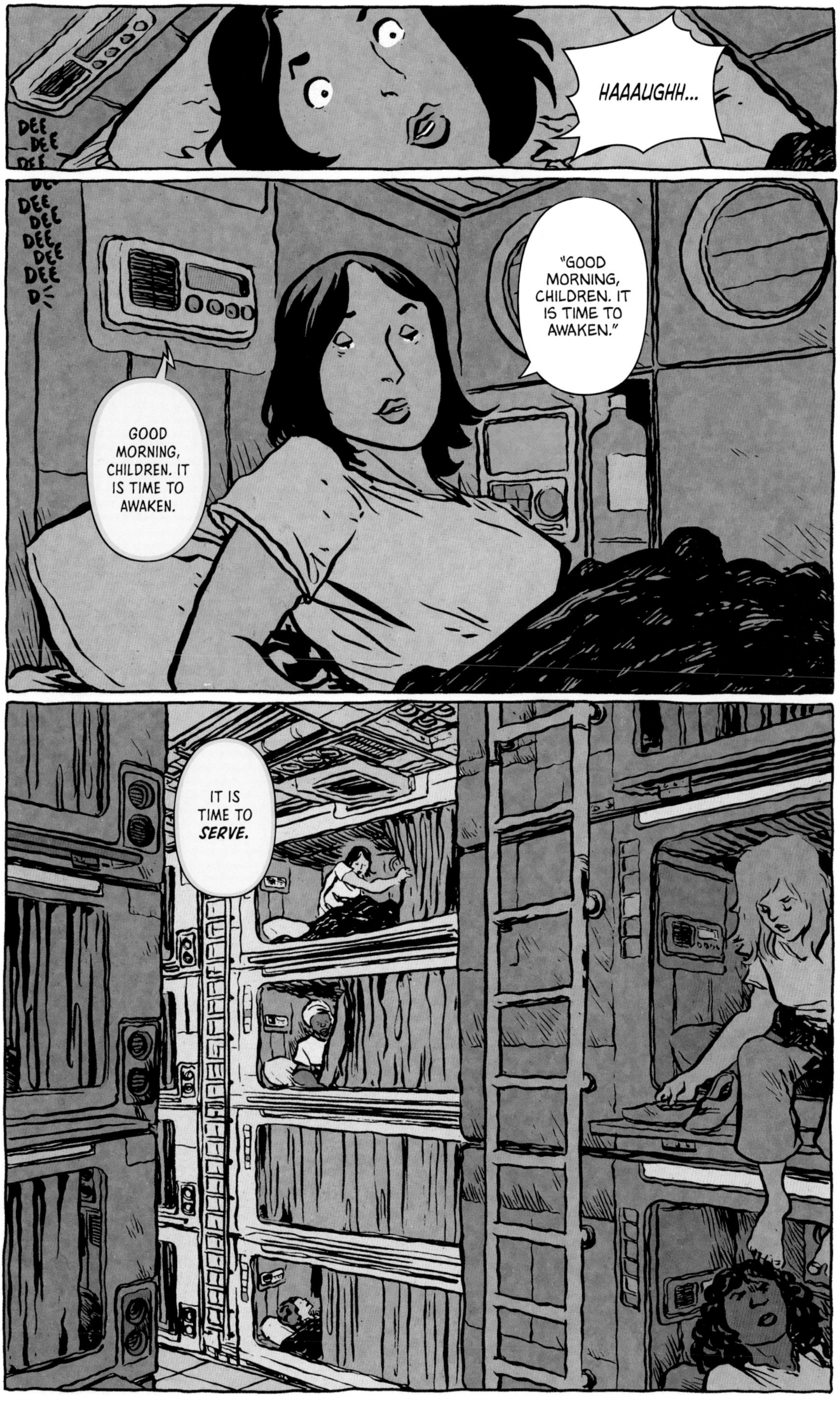
DEE DEE DEE
HAAAUGHH...
DEE DEE DEE DEE DEE D
"GOOD MORNING, CHILDREN. IT IS TIME TO AWAKEN."
GOOD MORNING, CHILDREN. IT IS TIME TO AWAKEN.
IT IS TIME TO *SERVE.*

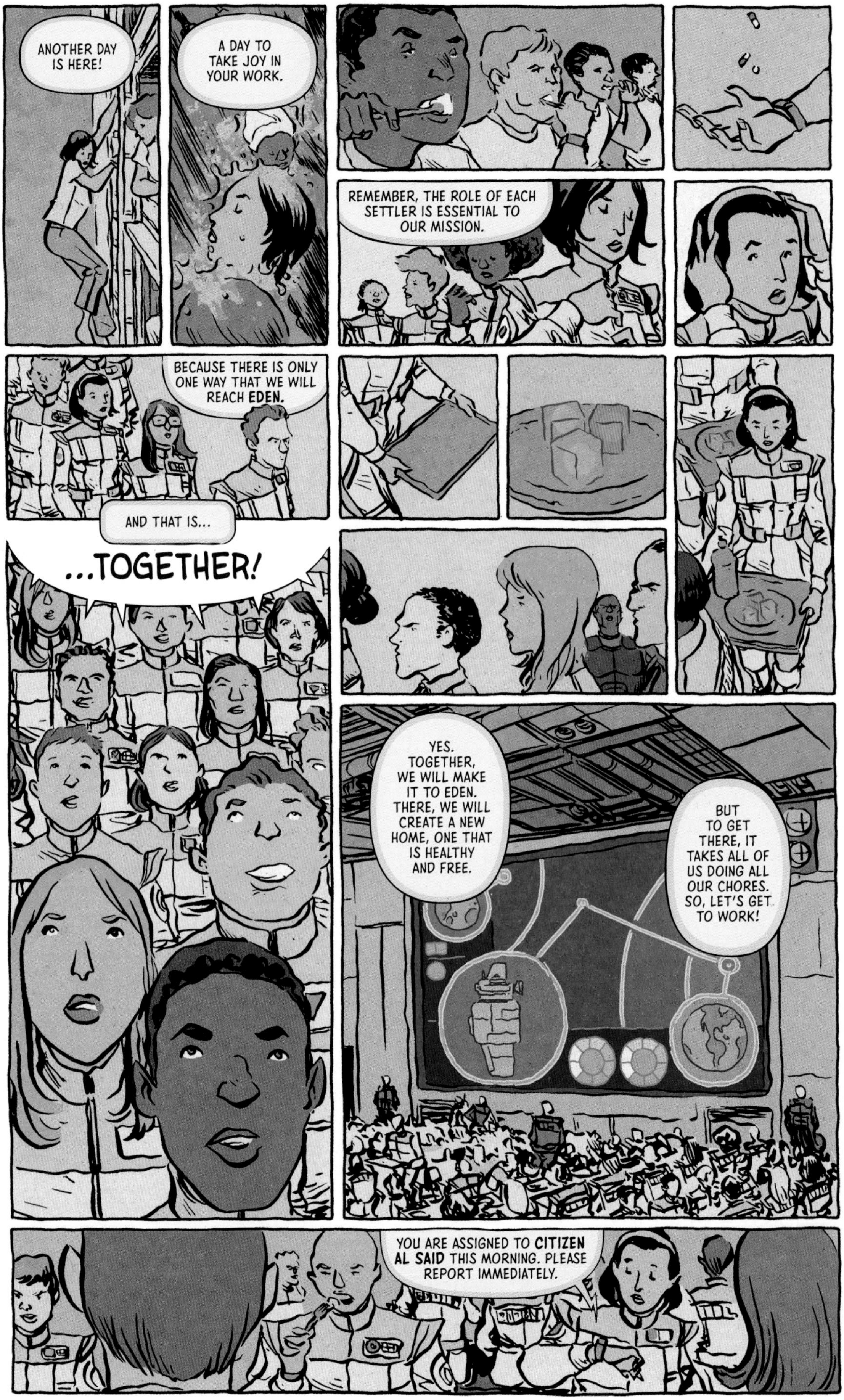
ANOTHER DAY IS HERE!
A DAY TO TAKE JOY IN YOUR WORK.
REMEMBER, THE ROLE OF EACH SETTLER IS ESSENTIAL TO OUR MISSION.
BECAUSE THERE IS ONLY ONE WAY THAT WE WILL REACH EDEN.
AND THAT IS...
...TOGETHER!
YES. TOGETHER, WE WILL MAKE IT TO EDEN. THERE, WE WILL CREATE A NEW HOME, ONE THAT IS HEALTHY AND FREE.
BUT TO GET THERE, IT TAKES ALL OF US DOING ALL OUR CHORES. SO, LET'S GET TO WORK!
YOU ARE ASSIGNED TO CITIZEN AL SAID THIS MORNING. PLEASE REPORT IMMEDIATELY.

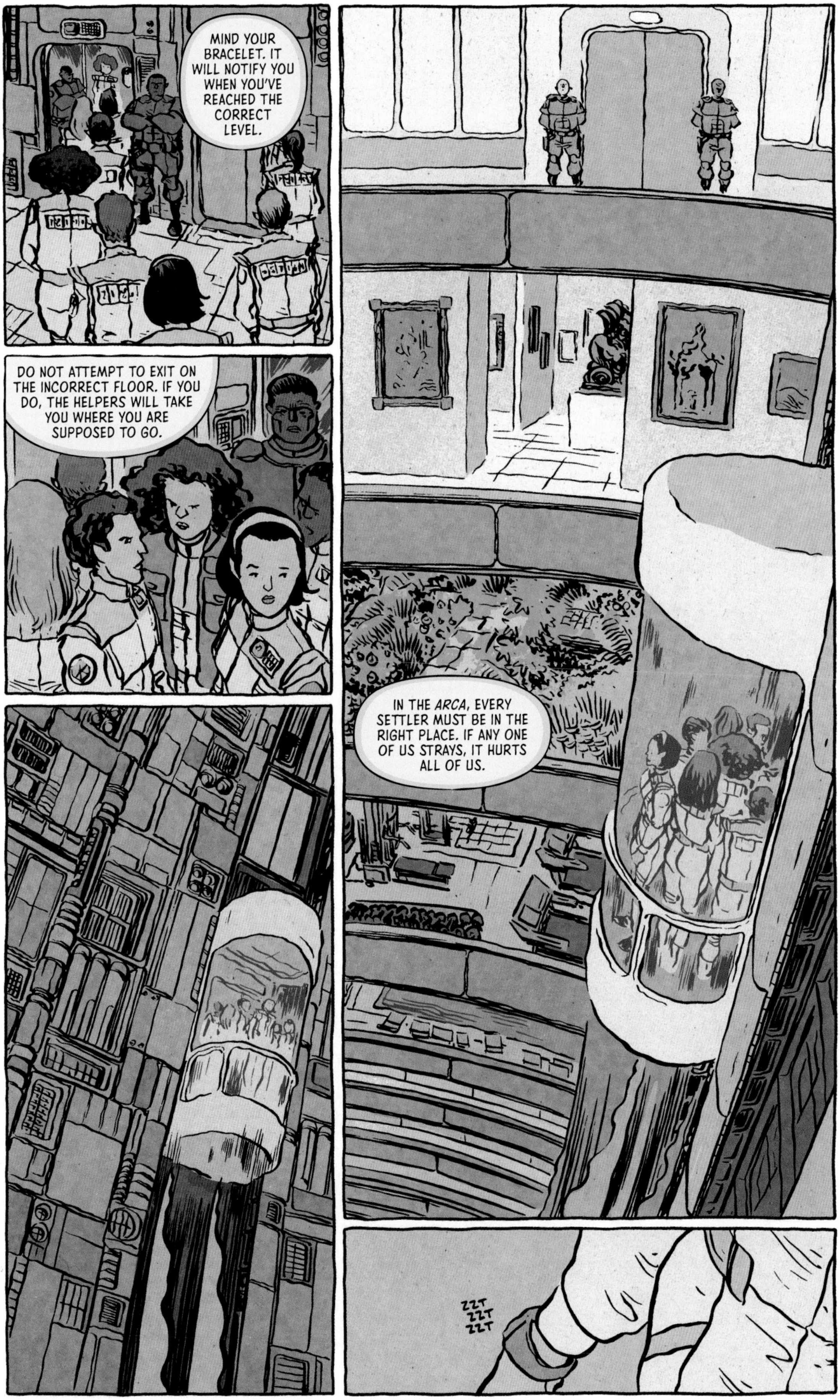
MIND YOUR BRACELET. IT WILL NOTIFY YOU WHEN YOU'VE REACHED THE CORRECT LEVEL.
DO NOT ATTEMPT TO EXIT ON THE INCORRECT FLOOR. IF YOU DO, THE HELPERS WILL TAKE YOU WHERE YOU ARE SUPPOSED TO GO.
IN THE *ARCA*, EVERY SETTLER MUST BE IN THE RIGHT PLACE. IF ANY ONE OF US STRAYS, IT HURTS ALL OF US.
ZZT ZZT ZZT

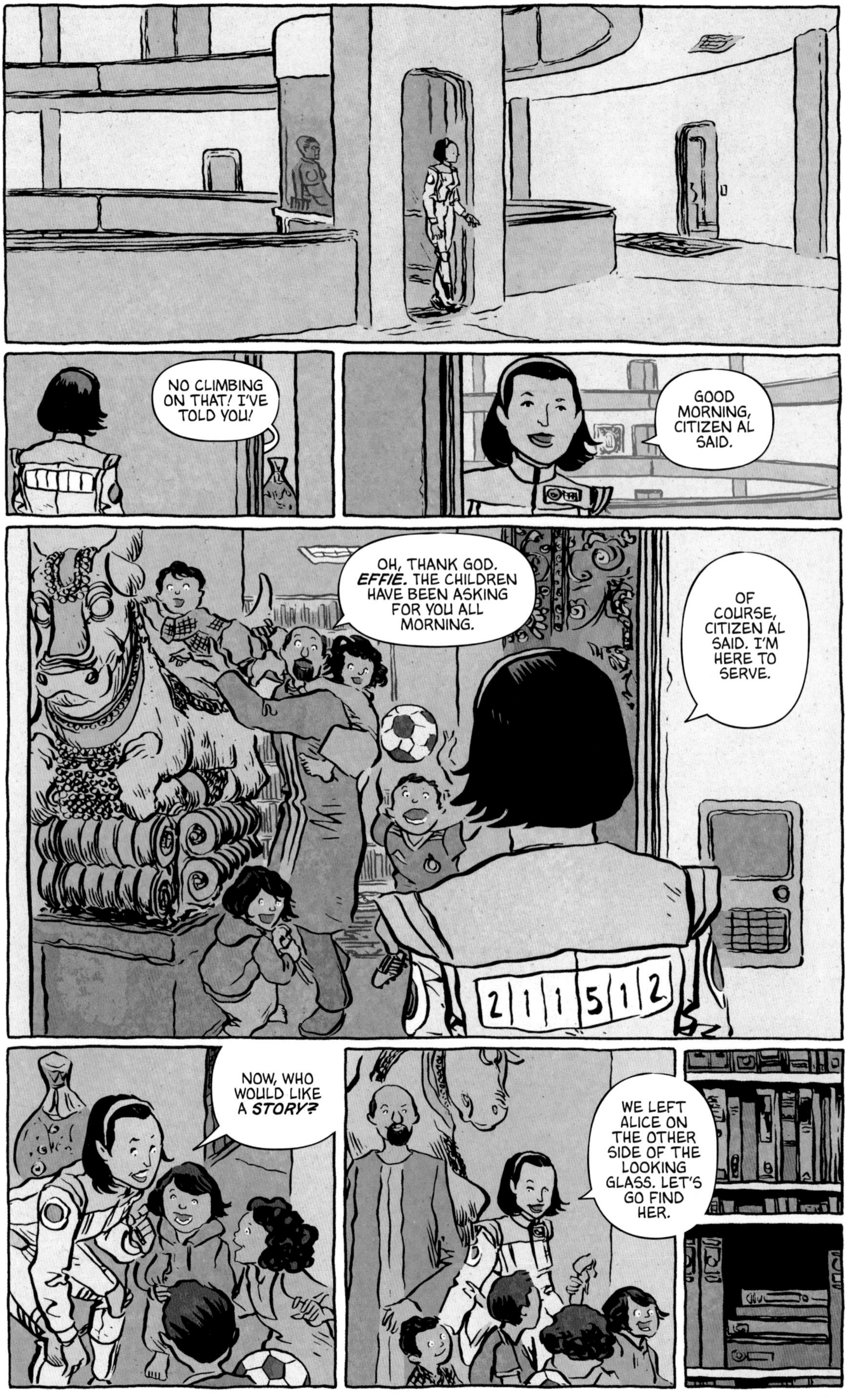
NO CLIMBING ON THAT! I'VE TOLD YOU!
GOOD MORNING, CITIZEN AL SAID.
OH, THANK GOD. *EFFIE.* THE CHILDREN HAVE BEEN ASKING FOR YOU ALL MORNING.
OF COURSE, CITIZEN AL SAID. I'M HERE TO SERVE.
211512
NOW, WHO WOULD LIKE A *STORY?*
WE LEFT ALICE ON THE OTHER SIDE OF THE LOOKING GLASS. LET'S GO FIND HER.

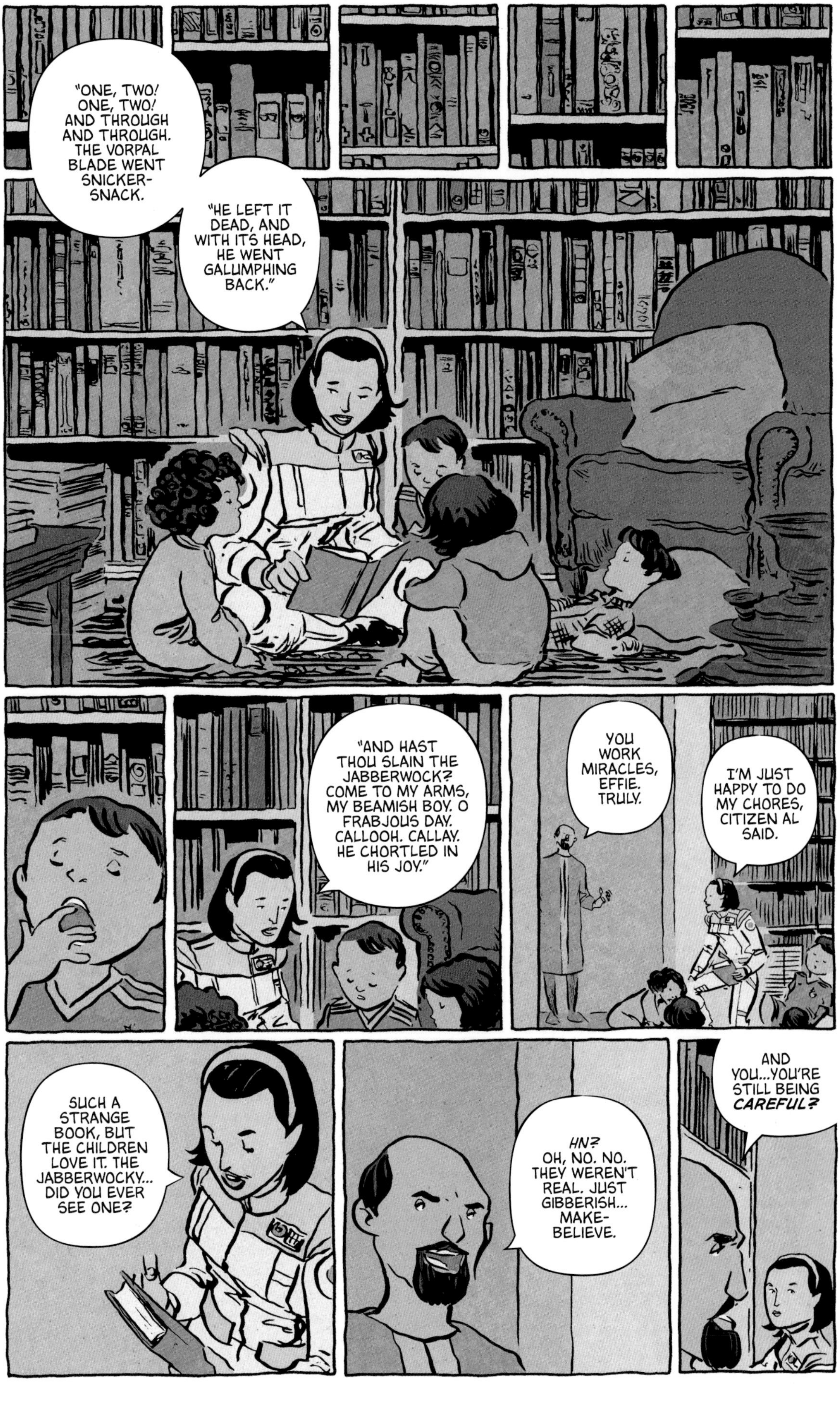
"ONE, TWO! ONE, TWO! AND THROUGH AND THROUGH. THE VORPAL BLADE WENT SNICKER-SNACK.
"HE LEFT IT DEAD, AND WITH ITS HEAD, HE WENT GALUMPHING BACK."
"AND HAST THOU SLAIN THE JABBERWOCK? COME TO MY ARMS, MY BEAMISH BOY. O FRABJOUS DAY. CALLOOH. CALLAY. HE CHORTLED IN HIS JOY."
YOU WORK MIRACLES, EFFIE. TRULY.
I'M JUST HAPPY TO DO MY CHORES, CITIZEN AL SAID.
SUCH A STRANGE BOOK, BUT THE CHILDREN LOVE IT. THE JABBERWOCKY... DID YOU EVER SEE ONE?
HN? OH, NO. NO. THEY WEREN'T REAL. JUST GIBBERISH... MAKE-BELIEVE.
AND YOU...YOU'RE STILL BEING ***CAREFUL?***

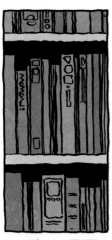

"HE STEPPED DOWN, TRYING NOT TO LOOK LONG AT HER, AS IF SHE WERE THE SUN, YET HE SAW HER, LIKE THE SUN, EVEN WITHOUT LOOKING."

AHH. AHH-NAA ...KARR...

YOU...YOU WERE *READING.* YOU AREN'T SUPPOSED TO BE ABLE...

HOW DO YOU KNOW HOW TO READ?

WHEN YOU LOOK AT BOOKS, YOU TALK OUT LOUD. I WAS JUST LISTENING. I THOUGHT MAYBE I COULD FIGURE IT OUT, TOO.

I'M SORRY, CITIZEN AL SAID. YOU LOVE YOUR BOOKS SO MUCH. I THOUGHT THEY MUST BE SPECIAL.

THEY *ARE* SPECIAL, EFFIE. ALL OF US CITIZENS BROUGHT SOME TREASURE FROM EARTH. THESE BOOKS ARE MY TREASURE.

I COULD TEACH YOU TO READ THEM. BUT THERE IS ONE THING YOU MUST *NEVER* DO...

OUR SECRET IS *SAFE,* CITIZEN AL SAID. NO ONE KNOWS THAT I CAN READ.

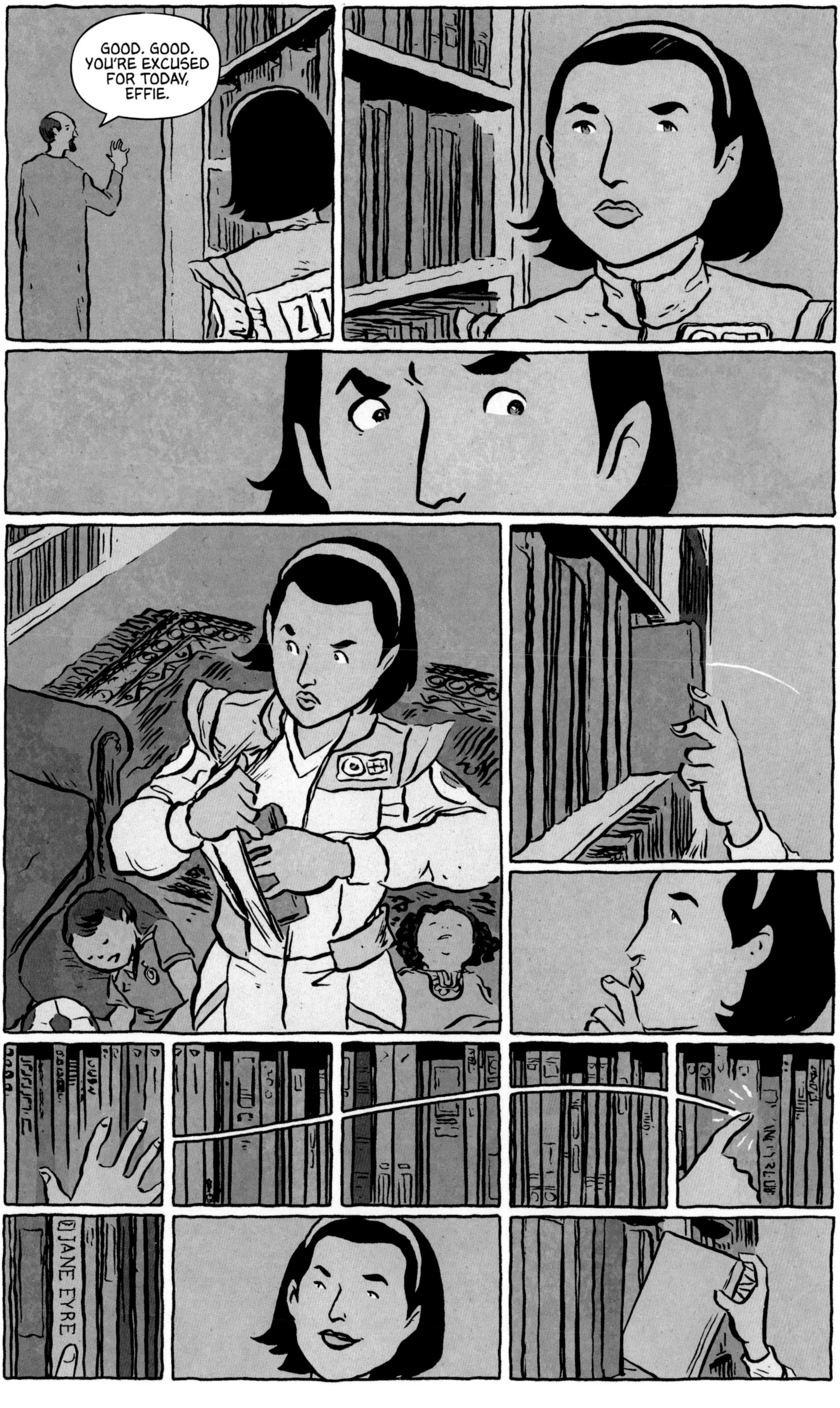
GOOD. GOOD. YOU'RE EXCUSED FOR TODAY, EFFIE.
21
JANE EYRE

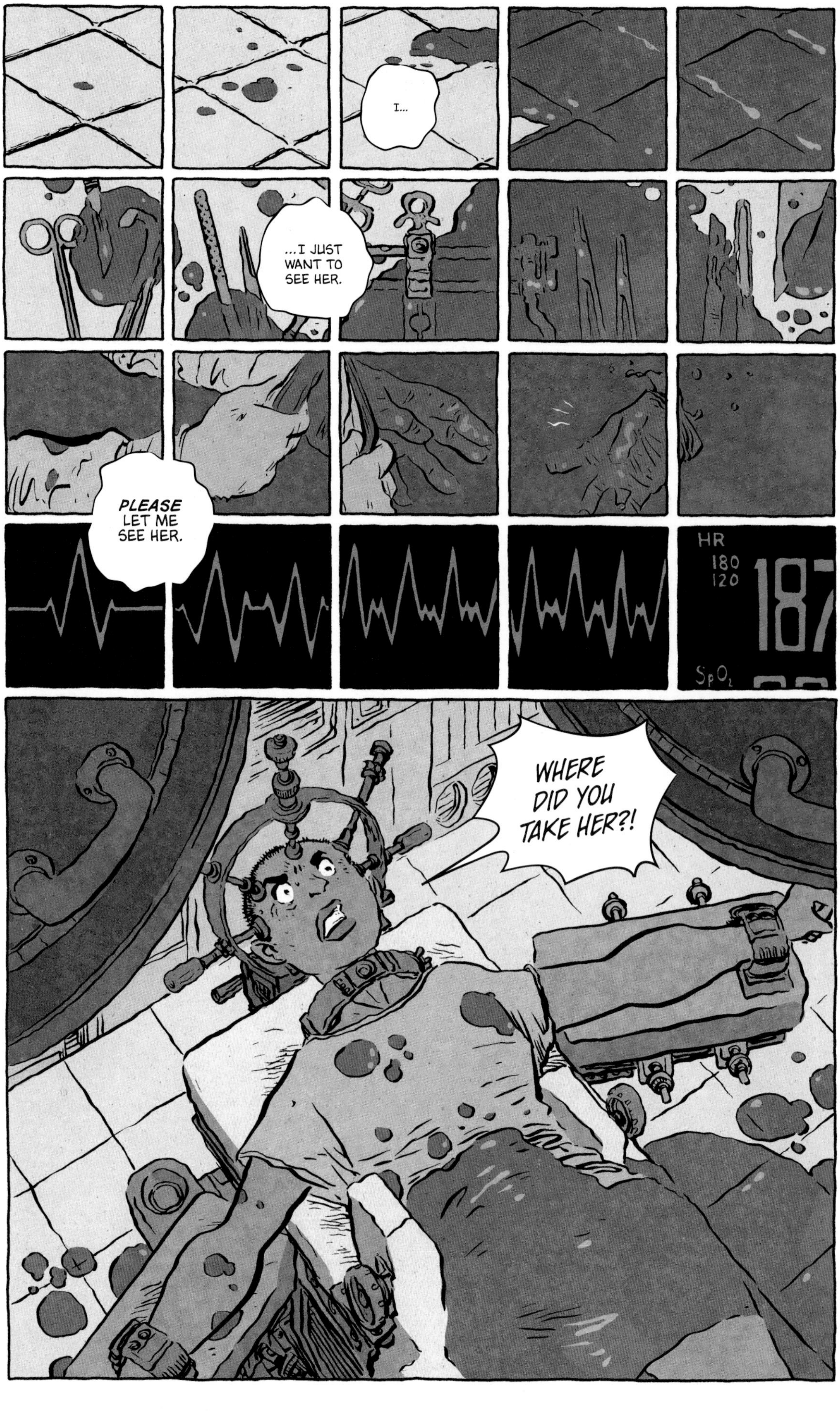
I...
...I JUST WANT TO SEE HER.
PLEASE LET ME SEE HER.
HR
180
120
187
SpO2
WHERE DID YOU TAKE HER?!

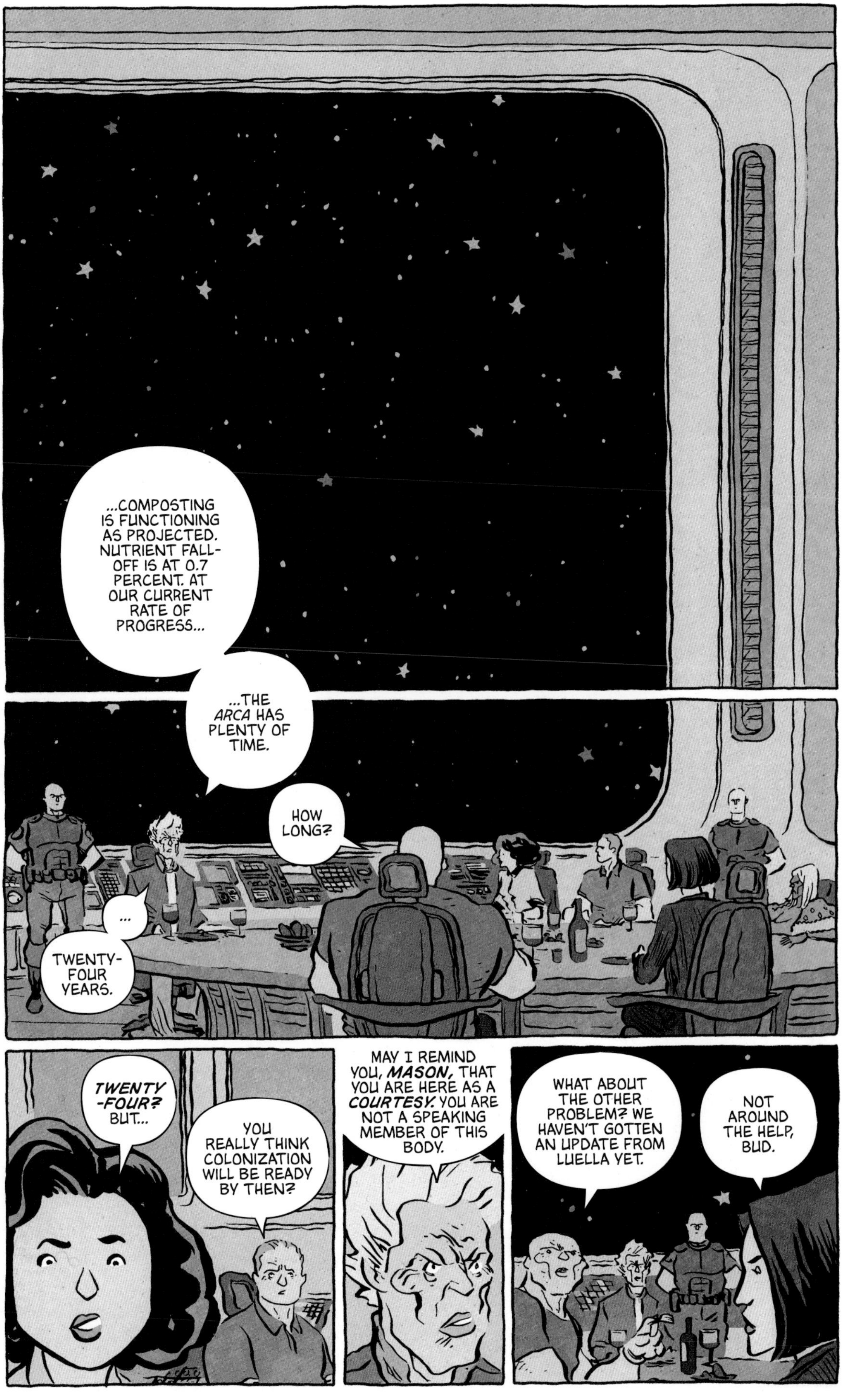
...COMPOSTING IS FUNCTIONING AS PROJECTED. NUTRIENT FALL-OFF IS AT 0.7 PERCENT. AT OUR CURRENT RATE OF PROGRESS...
...THE *ARCA* HAS PLENTY OF TIME.
HOW LONG?
...
TWENTY-FOUR YEARS.
TWENTY-FOUR? BUT...
YOU REALLY THINK COLONIZATION WILL BE READY BY THEN?
MAY I REMIND YOU, ***MASON,*** THAT YOU ARE HERE AS A ***COURTESY.*** YOU ARE NOT A SPEAKING MEMBER OF THIS BODY.
WHAT ABOUT THE OTHER PROBLEM? WE HAVEN'T GOTTEN AN UPDATE FROM LUELLA YET.
NOT AROUND THE HELP, BUD.

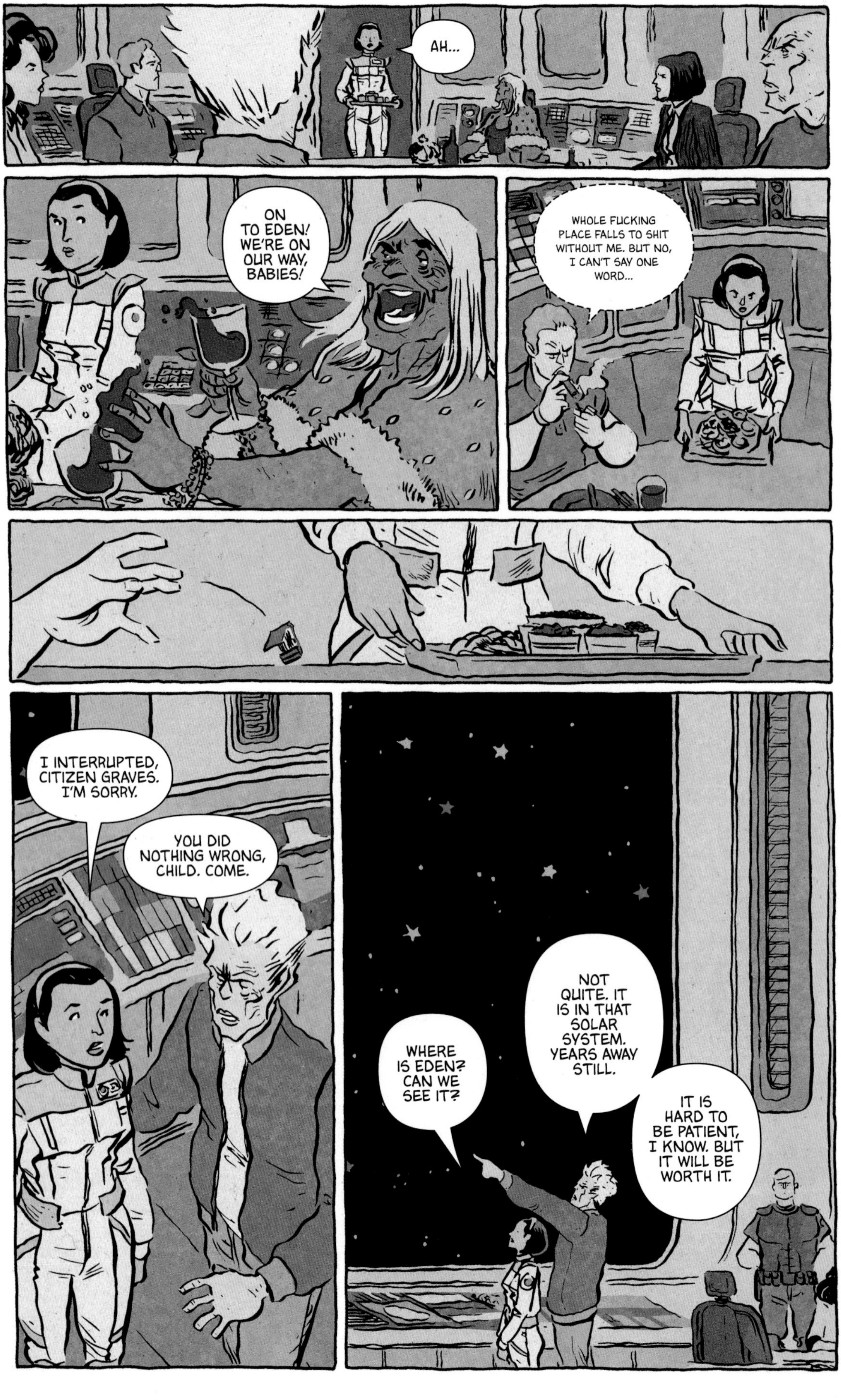
AH...
ON TO EDEN! WE'RE ON OUR WAY, BABIES!
WHOLE FUCKING PLACE FALLS TO SHIT WITHOUT ME. BUT NO, I CAN'T SAY ONE WORD...
I INTERRUPTED, CITIZEN GRAVES. I'M SORRY.
YOU DID NOTHING WRONG, CHILD. COME.
WHERE IS EDEN? CAN WE SEE IT?
NOT QUITE. IT IS IN THAT SOLAR SYSTEM. YEARS AWAY STILL.
IT IS HARD TO BE PATIENT, I KNOW. BUT IT WILL BE WORTH IT.

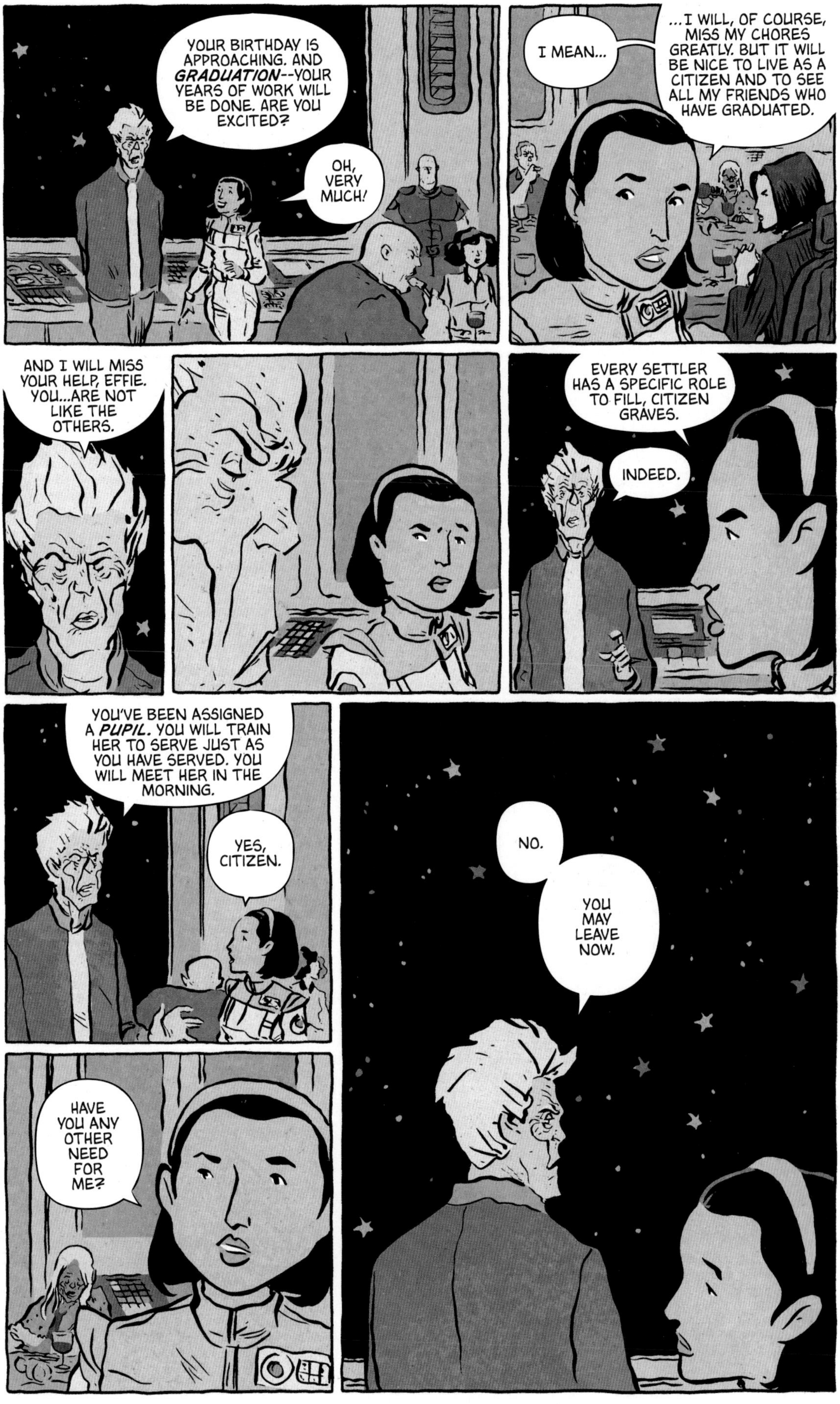
YOUR BIRTHDAY IS APPROACHING. AND GRADUATION--YOUR YEARS OF WORK WILL BE DONE. ARE YOU EXCITED?
OH, VERY MUCH!
I MEAN...
...I WILL, OF COURSE, MISS MY CHORES GREATLY. BUT IT WILL BE NICE TO LIVE AS A CITIZEN AND TO SEE ALL MY FRIENDS WHO HAVE GRADUATED.
AND I WILL MISS YOUR HELP, EFFIE. YOU...ARE NOT LIKE THE OTHERS.
EVERY SETTLER HAS A SPECIFIC ROLE TO FILL, CITIZEN GRAVES.
INDEED.
YOU'VE BEEN ASSIGNED A PUPIL. YOU WILL TRAIN HER TO SERVE JUST AS YOU HAVE SERVED. YOU WILL MEET HER IN THE MORNING.
YES, CITIZEN.
HAVE YOU ANY OTHER NEED FOR ME?
NO.
YOU MAY LEAVE NOW.

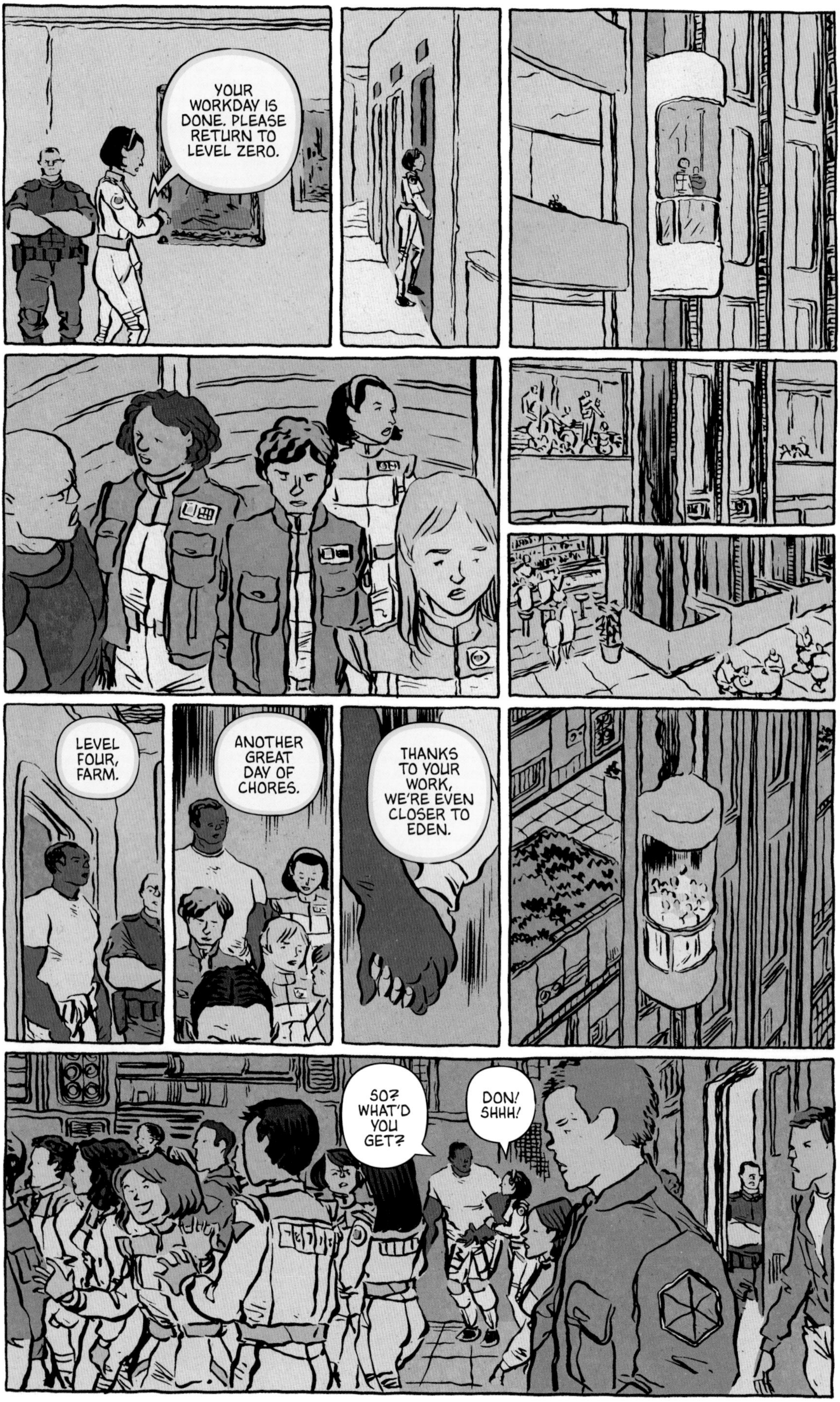
YOUR WORKDAY IS DONE. PLEASE RETURN TO LEVEL ZERO.
LEVEL FOUR, FARM.
ANOTHER GREAT DAY OF CHORES.
THANKS TO YOUR WORK, WE'RE EVEN CLOSER TO EDEN.
SO? WHAT'D YOU GET?
DON! SHHH!

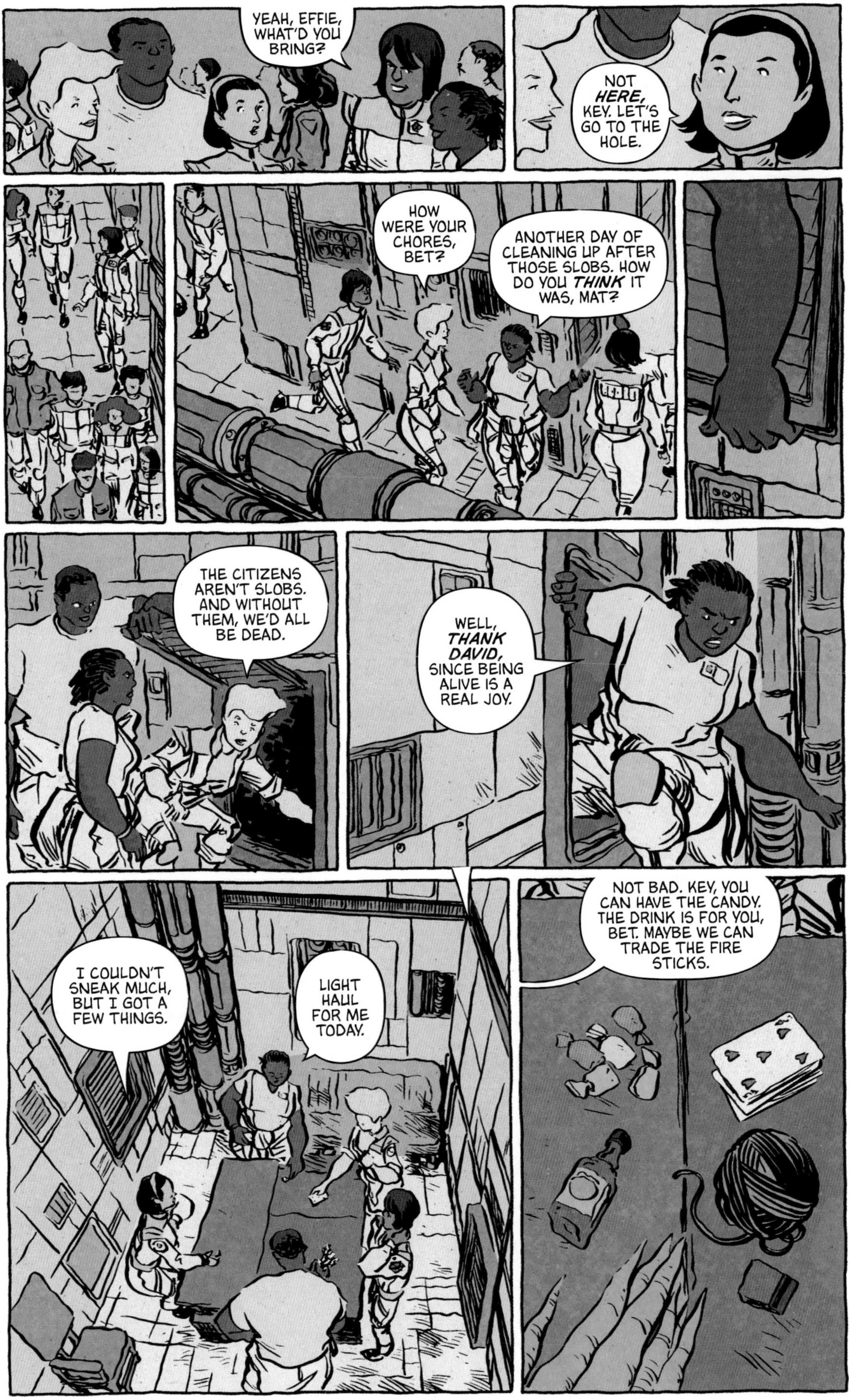
YEAH, EFFIE, WHAT'D YOU BRING?
NOT *HERE,* KEY. LET'S GO TO THE HOLE.
HOW WERE YOUR CHORES, BET?
ANOTHER DAY OF CLEANING UP AFTER THOSE SLOBS. HOW DO YOU *THINK* IT WAS, MAT?
THE CITIZENS AREN'T SLOBS. AND WITHOUT THEM, WE'D ALL BE DEAD.
WELL, *THANK DAVID,* SINCE BEING ALIVE IS A REAL JOY.
I COULDN'T SNEAK MUCH, BUT I GOT A FEW THINGS.
LIGHT HAUL FOR ME TODAY.
NOT BAD. KEY, YOU CAN HAVE THE CANDY. THE DRINK IS FOR YOU, BET. MAYBE WE CAN TRADE THE FIRE STICKS.

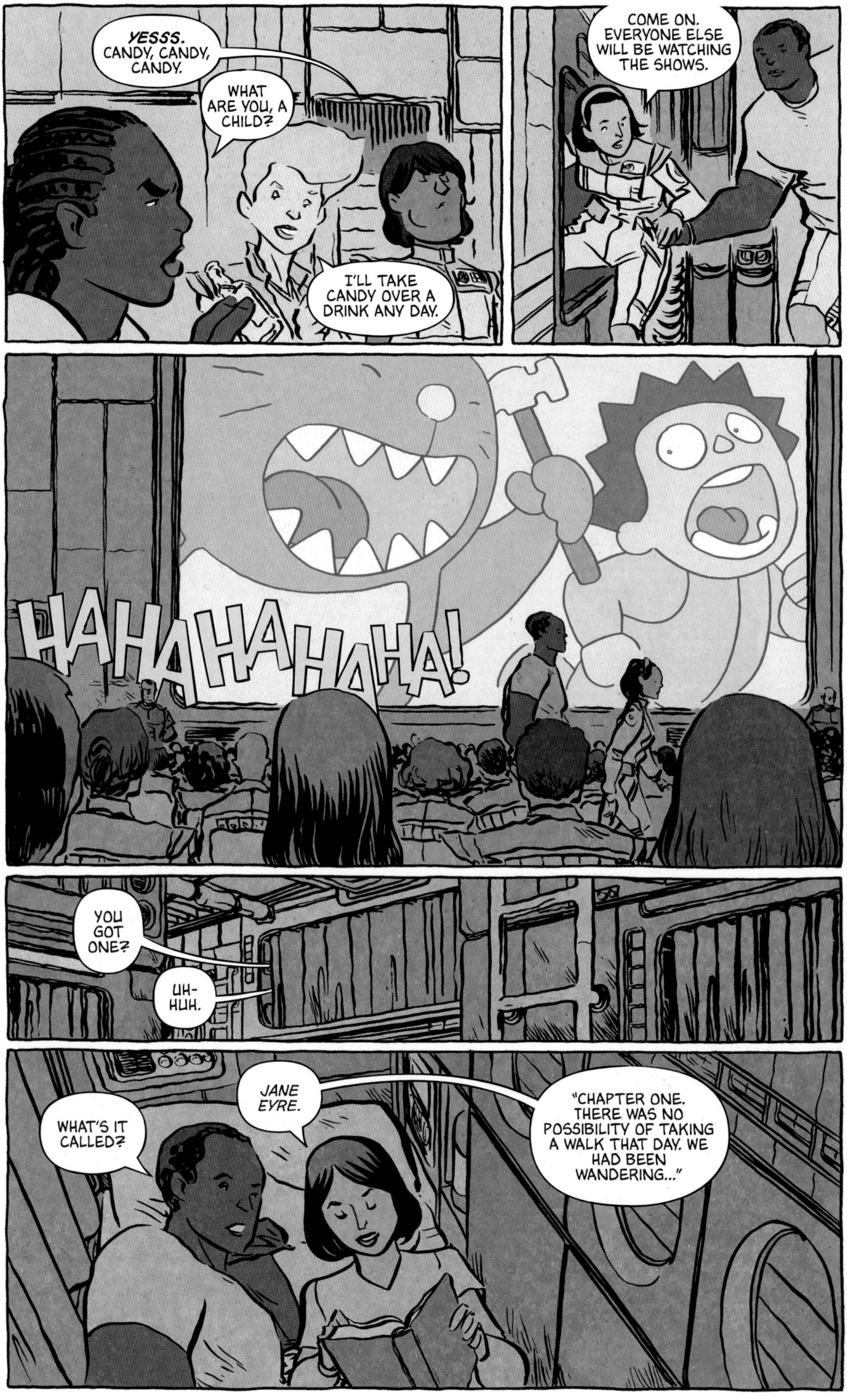
YESSS. CANDY, CANDY, CANDY.
WHAT ARE YOU, A CHILD?
I'LL TAKE CANDY OVER A DRINK ANY DAY.
COME ON. EVERYONE ELSE WILL BE WATCHING THE SHOWS.
HAHAHAHAHAHA!
YOU GOT ONE?
UH-HUH.
WHAT'S IT CALLED?
JANE EYRE.
"CHAPTER ONE. THERE WAS NO POSSIBILITY OF TAKING A WALK THAT DAY. WE HAD BEEN WANDERING..."

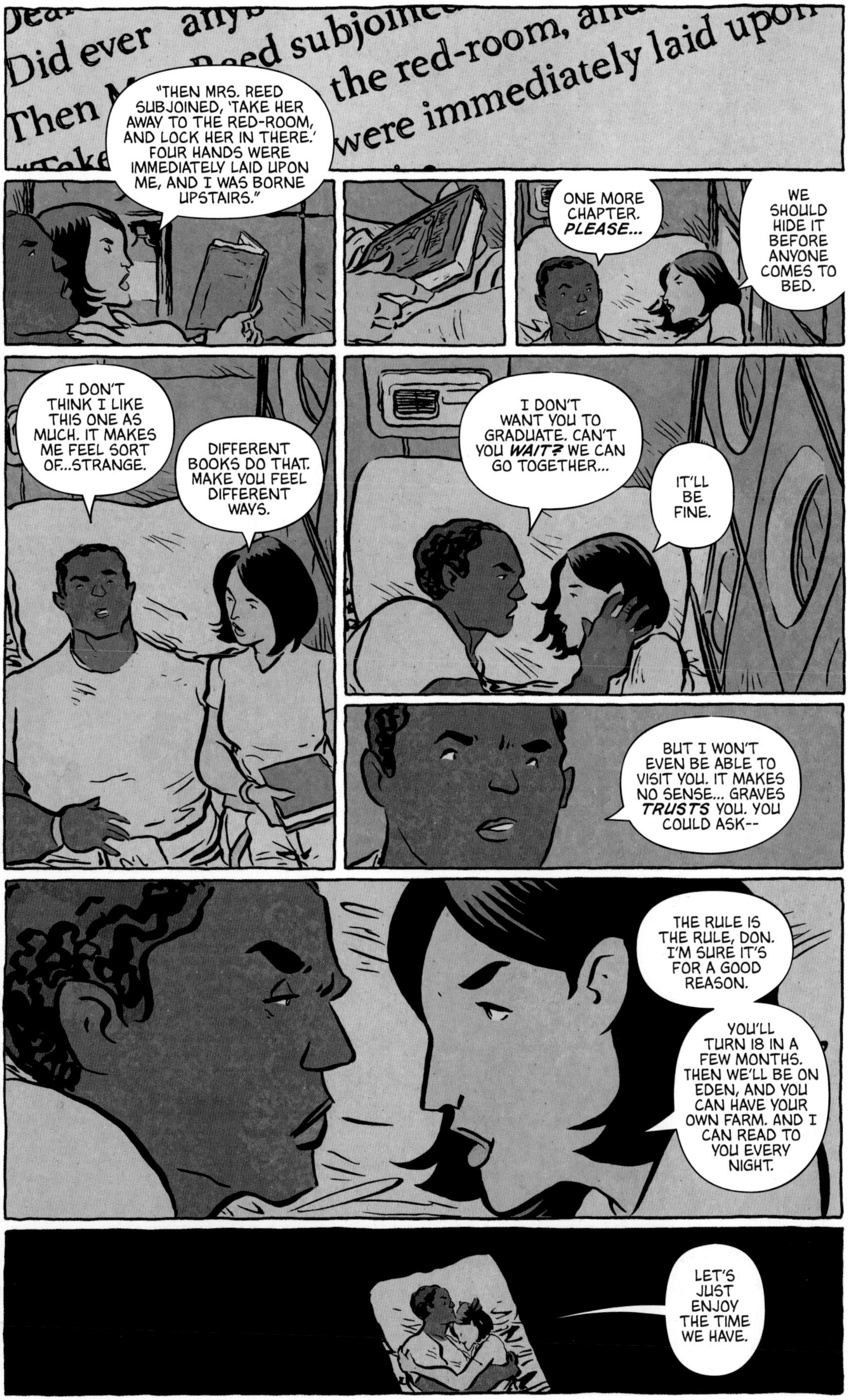
Did ever
Then M
the red-room, and
were immediately laid upon
"THEN MRS. REED SUBJOINED, 'TAKE HER AWAY TO THE RED-ROOM, AND LOCK HER IN THERE.' FOUR HANDS WERE IMMEDIATELY LAID UPON ME, AND I WAS BORNE UPSTAIRS."
ONE MORE CHAPTER. PLEASE...
WE SHOULD HIDE IT BEFORE ANYONE COMES TO BED.
I DON'T THINK I LIKE THIS ONE AS MUCH. IT MAKES ME FEEL SORT OF...STRANGE.
DIFFERENT BOOKS DO THAT. MAKE YOU FEEL DIFFERENT WAYS.
I DON'T WANT YOU TO GRADUATE. CAN'T YOU WAIT? WE CAN GO TOGETHER...
IT'LL BE FINE.
BUT I WON'T EVEN BE ABLE TO VISIT YOU. IT MAKES NO SENSE... GRAVES TRUSTS YOU. YOU COULD ASK--
THE RULE IS THE RULE, DON. I'M SURE IT'S FOR A GOOD REASON.
YOU'LL TURN 18 IN A FEW MONTHS. THEN WE'LL BE ON EDEN, AND YOU CAN HAVE YOUR OWN FARM. AND I CAN READ TO YOU EVERY NIGHT.
LET'S JUST ENJOY THE TIME WE HAVE.

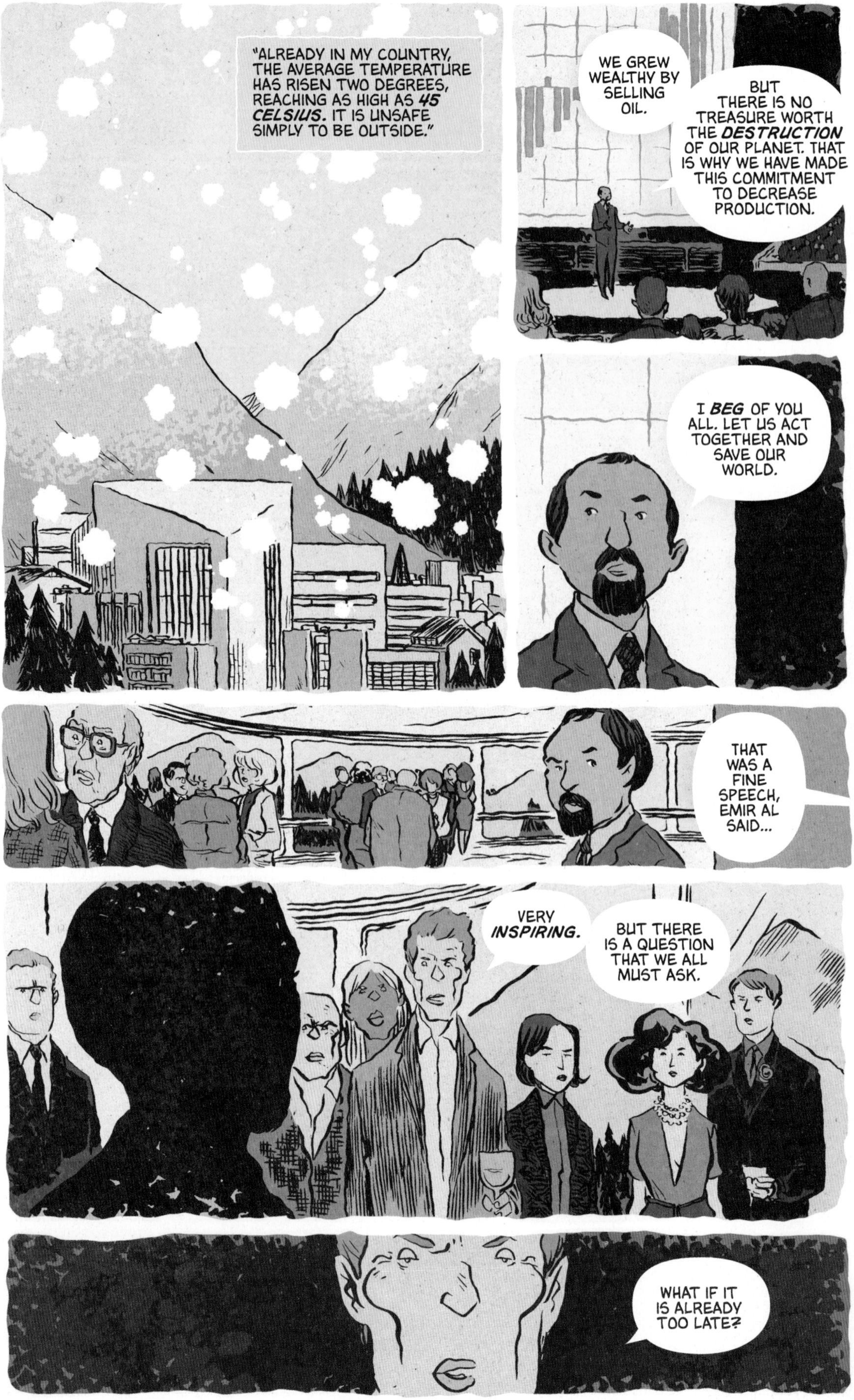
"ALREADY IN MY COUNTRY, THE AVERAGE TEMPERATURE HAS RISEN TWO DEGREES, REACHING AS HIGH AS *45 CELSIUS.* IT IS UNSAFE SIMPLY TO BE OUTSIDE."
WE GREW WEALTHY BY SELLING OIL.
BUT THERE IS NO TREASURE WORTH THE *DESTRUCTION* OF OUR PLANET. THAT IS WHY WE HAVE MADE THIS COMMITMENT TO DECREASE PRODUCTION.
I *BEG* OF YOU ALL. LET US ACT TOGETHER AND SAVE OUR WORLD.
THAT WAS A FINE SPEECH, EMIR AL SAID...
VERY *INSPIRING.*
BUT THERE IS A QUESTION THAT WE ALL MUST ASK.
WHAT IF IT IS ALREADY TOO LATE?

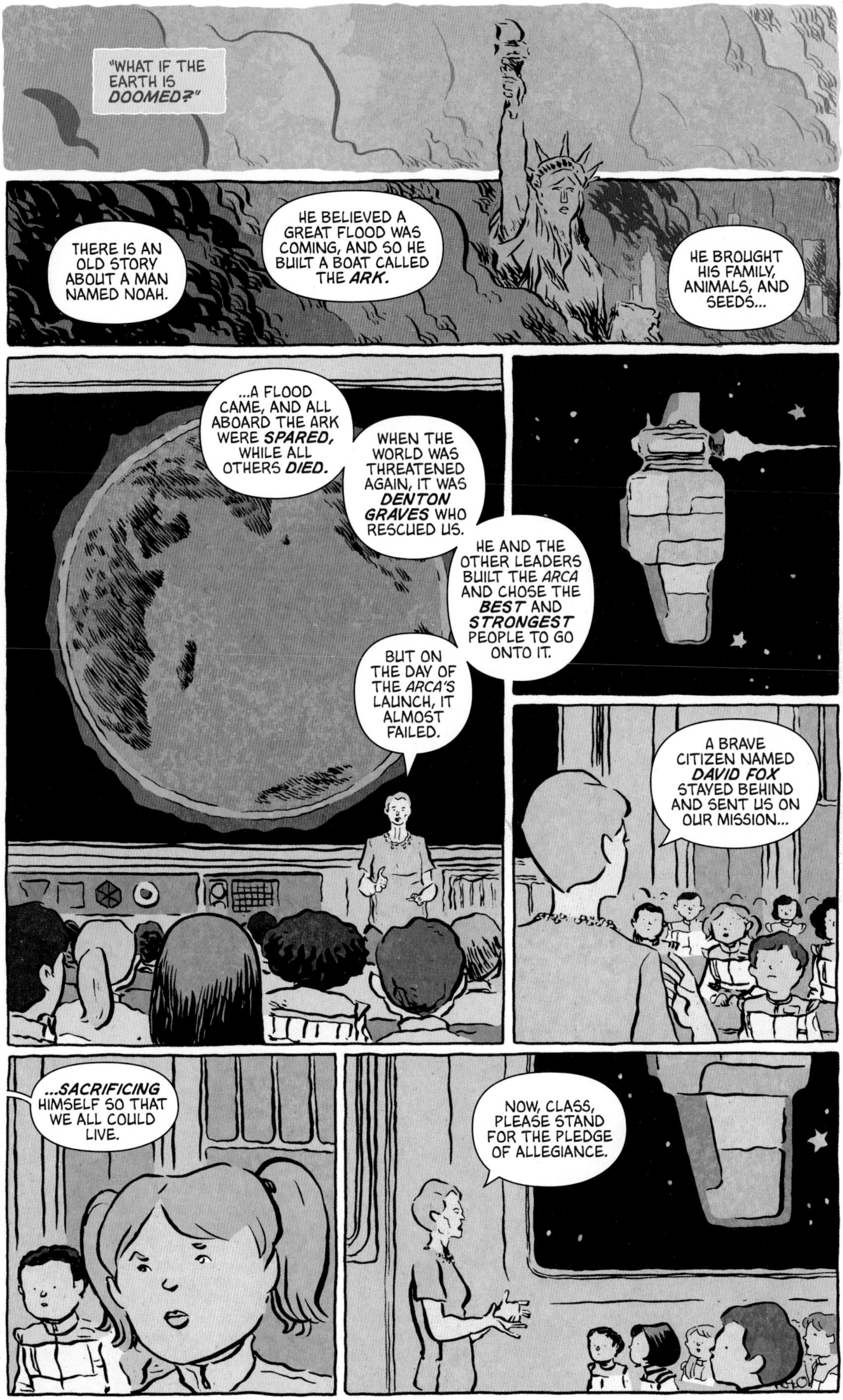
"WHAT IF THE EARTH IS DOOMED?"
THERE IS AN OLD STORY ABOUT A MAN NAMED NOAH.
HE BELIEVED A GREAT FLOOD WAS COMING, AND SO HE BUILT A BOAT CALLED THE ARK.
HE BROUGHT HIS FAMILY, ANIMALS, AND SEEDS...
...A FLOOD CAME, AND ALL ABOARD THE ARK WERE SPARED, WHILE ALL OTHERS DIED.
WHEN THE WORLD WAS THREATENED AGAIN, IT WAS DENTON GRAVES WHO RESCUED US.
HE AND THE OTHER LEADERS BUILT THE ARCA AND CHOSE THE BEST AND STRONGEST PEOPLE TO GO ONTO IT.
BUT ON THE DAY OF THE ARCA'S LAUNCH, IT ALMOST FAILED.
A BRAVE CITIZEN NAMED DAVID FOX STAYED BEHIND AND SENT US ON OUR MISSION...
...SACRIFICING HIMSELF SO THAT WE ALL COULD LIVE.
NOW, CLASS, PLEASE STAND FOR THE PLEDGE OF ALLEGIANCE.

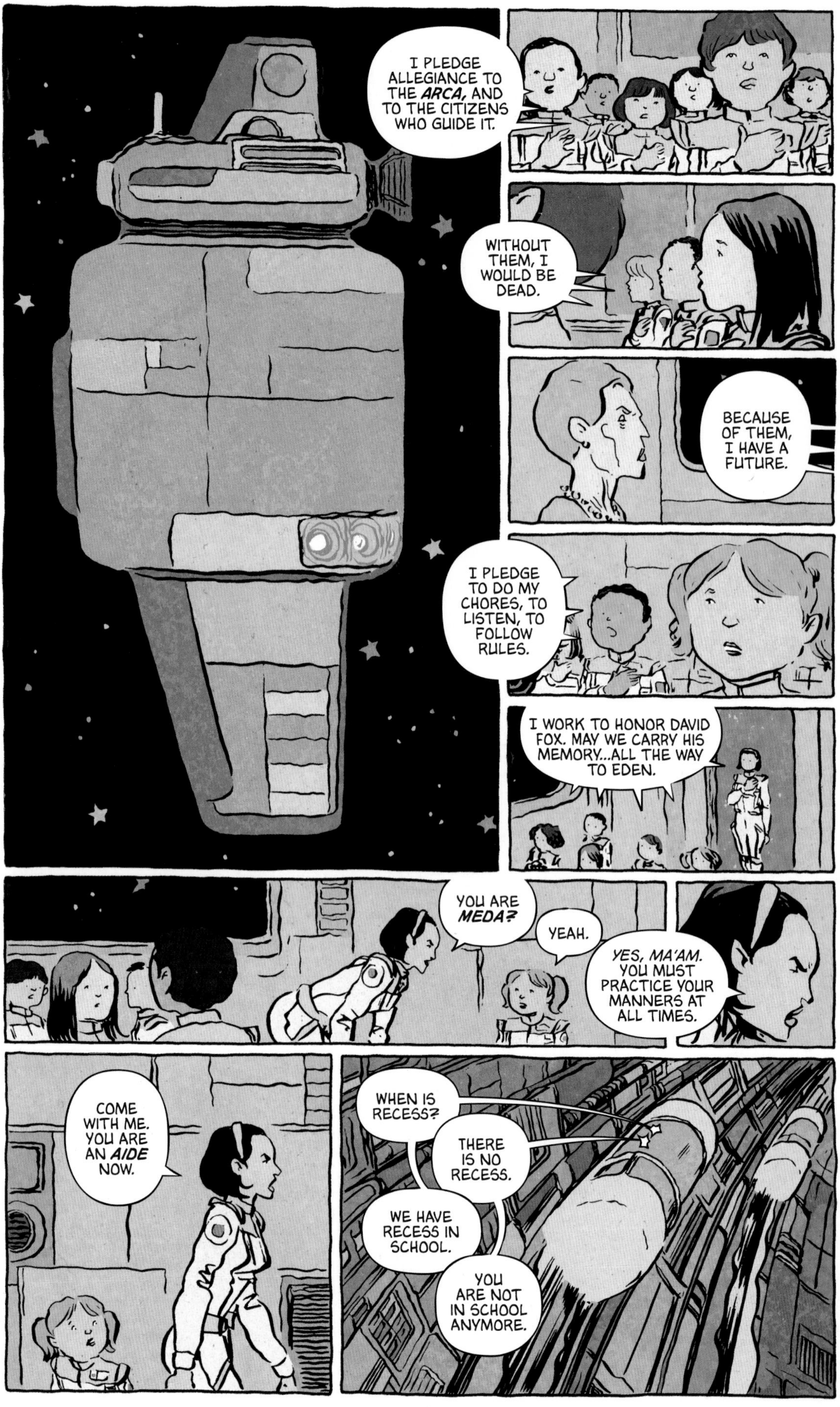

I PLEDGE ALLEGIANCE TO THE *ARCA,* AND TO THE CITIZENS WHO GUIDE IT.
WITHOUT THEM, I WOULD BE DEAD.
BECAUSE OF THEM, I HAVE A FUTURE.
I PLEDGE TO DO MY CHORES, TO LISTEN, TO FOLLOW RULES.
I WORK TO HONOR DAVID FOX. MAY WE CARRY HIS MEMORY...ALL THE WAY TO EDEN.
YOU ARE *MEDA?*
YEAH.
YES, MA'AM. YOU MUST PRACTICE YOUR MANNERS AT ALL TIMES.
COME WITH ME. YOU ARE AN *AIDE* NOW.
WHEN IS RECESS?
THERE IS NO RECESS.
WE HAVE RECESS IN SCHOOL.
YOU ARE NOT IN SCHOOL ANYMORE.

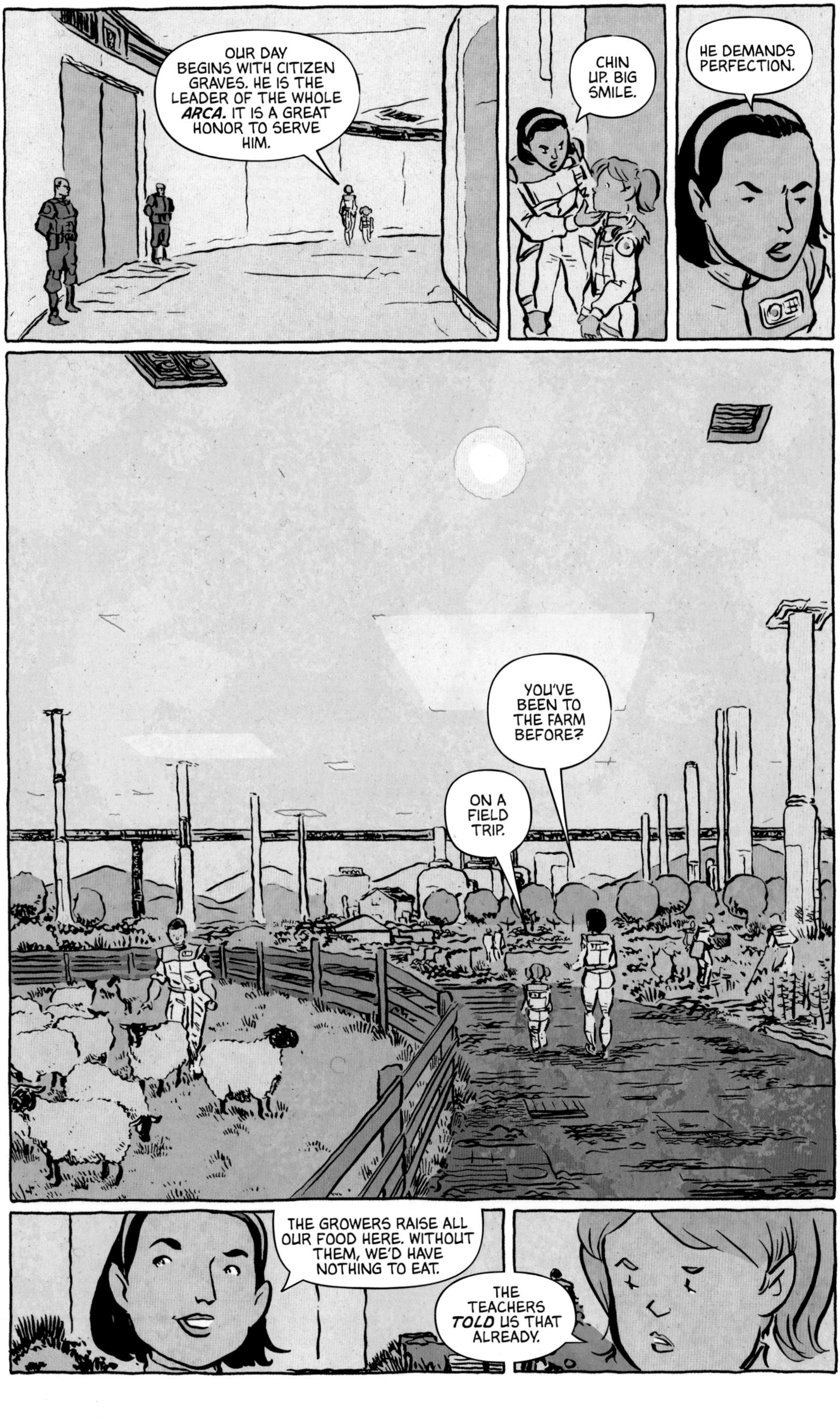
OUR DAY BEGINS WITH CITIZEN GRAVES. HE IS THE LEADER OF THE WHOLE *ARCA.* IT IS A GREAT HONOR TO SERVE HIM.
CHIN UP. BIG SMILE.
HE DEMANDS PERFECTION.
YOU'VE BEEN TO THE FARM BEFORE?
ON A FIELD TRIP.
THE GROWERS RAISE ALL OUR FOOD HERE. WITHOUT THEM, WE'D HAVE NOTHING TO EAT.
THE TEACHERS *TOLD* US THAT ALREADY.

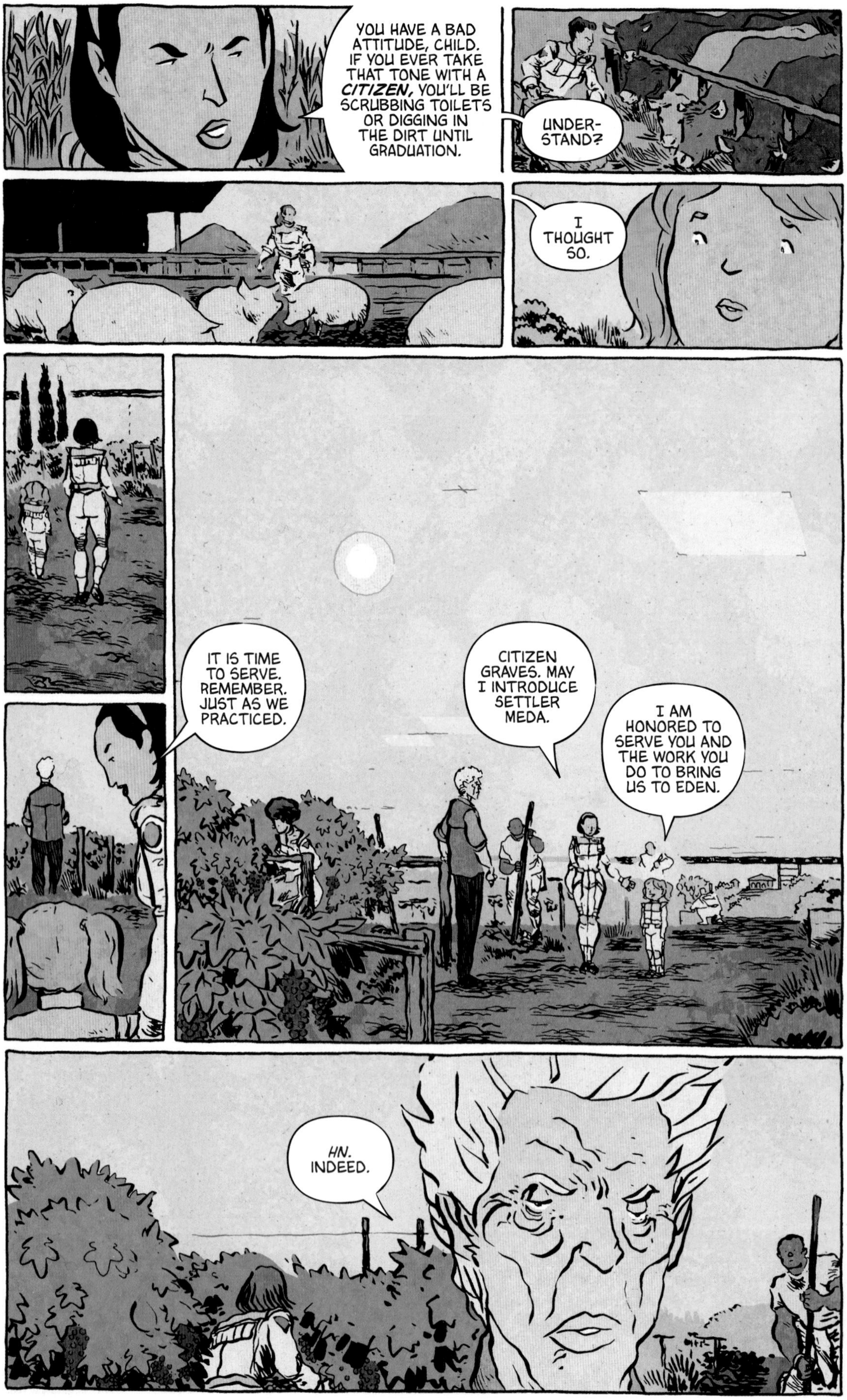
YOU HAVE A BAD ATTITUDE, CHILD. IF YOU EVER TAKE THAT TONE WITH A *CITIZEN,* YOU'LL BE SCRUBBING TOILETS OR DIGGING IN THE DIRT UNTIL GRADUATION.
UNDER-STAND?
I THOUGHT SO.
IT IS TIME TO SERVE. REMEMBER. JUST AS WE PRACTICED.
CITIZEN GRAVES. MAY I INTRODUCE SETTLER MEDA.
I AM HONORED TO SERVE YOU AND THE WORK YOU DO TO BRING US TO EDEN.
HN. INDEED.

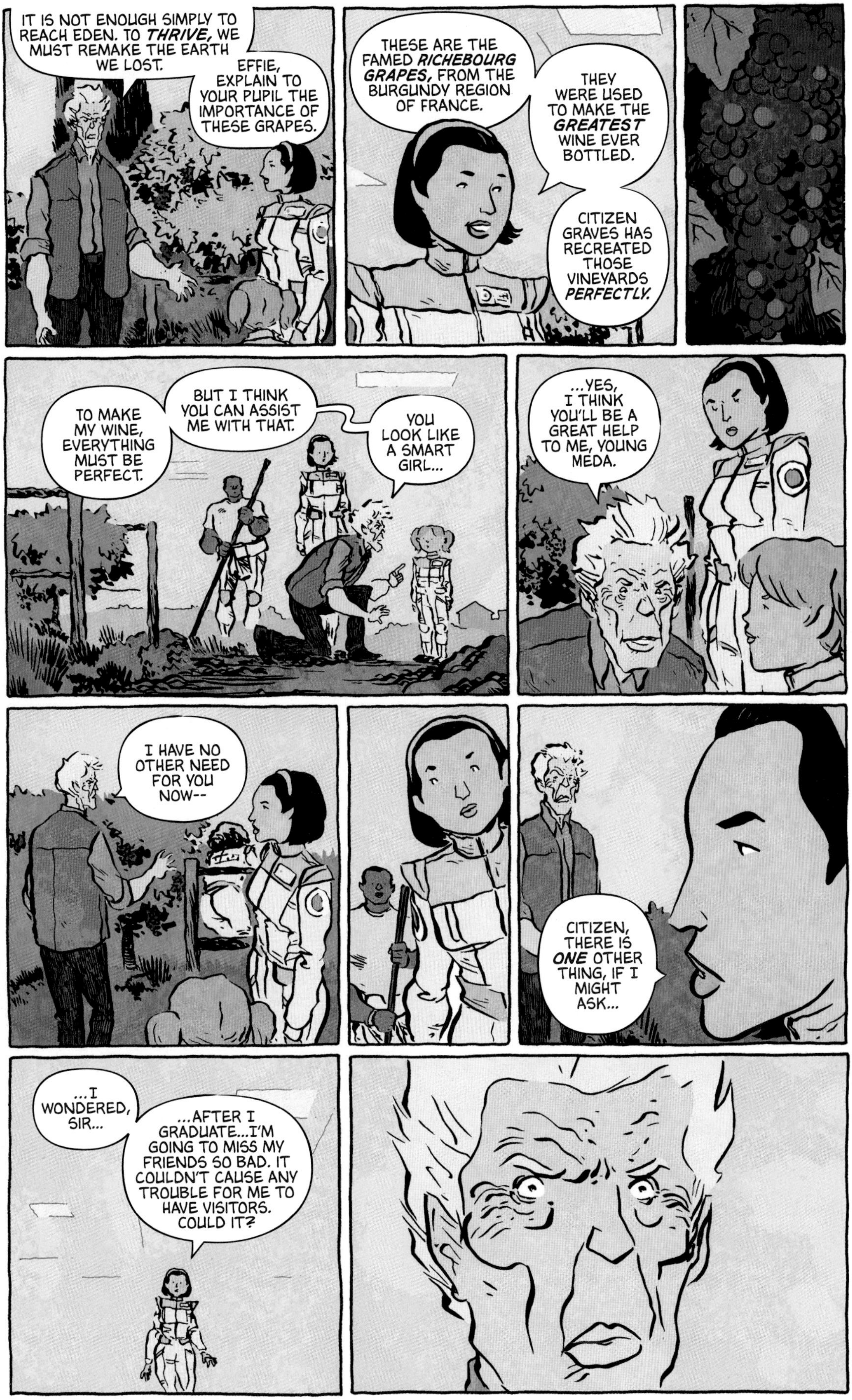
IT IS NOT ENOUGH SIMPLY TO REACH EDEN. TO THRIVE, WE MUST REMAKE THE EARTH WE LOST.
EFFIE, EXPLAIN TO YOUR PUPIL THE IMPORTANCE OF THESE GRAPES.
THESE ARE THE FAMED RICHEBOURG GRAPES, FROM THE BURGUNDY REGION OF FRANCE.
THEY WERE USED TO MAKE THE GREATEST WINE EVER BOTTLED.
CITIZEN GRAVES HAS RECREATED THOSE VINEYARDS PERFECTLY.
TO MAKE MY WINE, EVERYTHING MUST BE PERFECT.
BUT I THINK YOU CAN ASSIST ME WITH THAT.
YOU LOOK LIKE A SMART GIRL...
...YES, I THINK YOU'LL BE A GREAT HELP TO ME, YOUNG MEDA.
I HAVE NO OTHER NEED FOR YOU NOW--
CITIZEN, THERE IS ONE OTHER THING, IF I MIGHT ASK...
...I WONDERED, SIR...
...AFTER I GRADUATE...I'M GOING TO MISS MY FRIENDS SO BAD. IT COULDN'T CAUSE ANY TROUBLE FOR ME TO HAVE VISITORS. COULD IT?

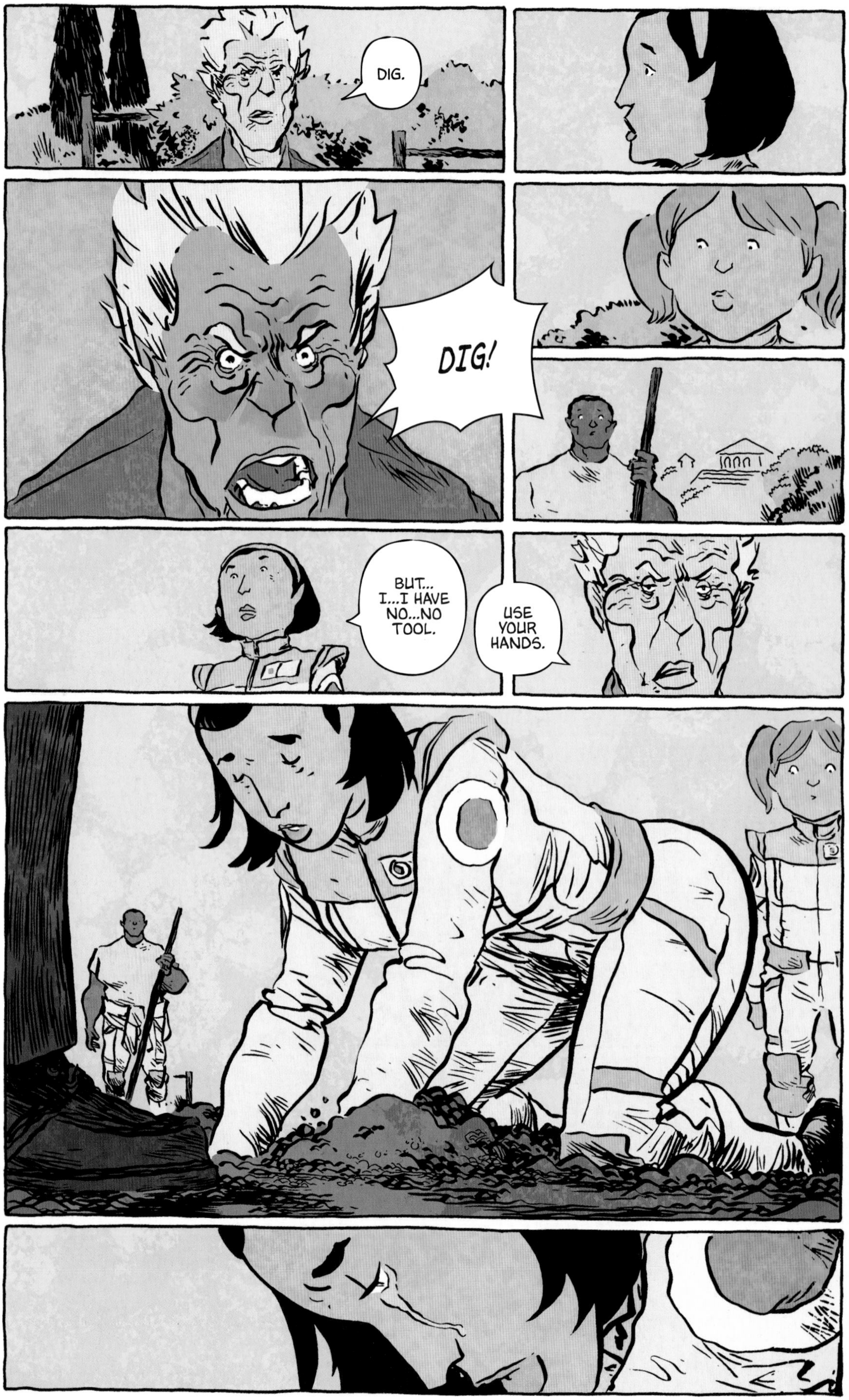
DIG.
DIG!
BUT... I...I HAVE NO...NO TOOL.
USE YOUR HANDS.

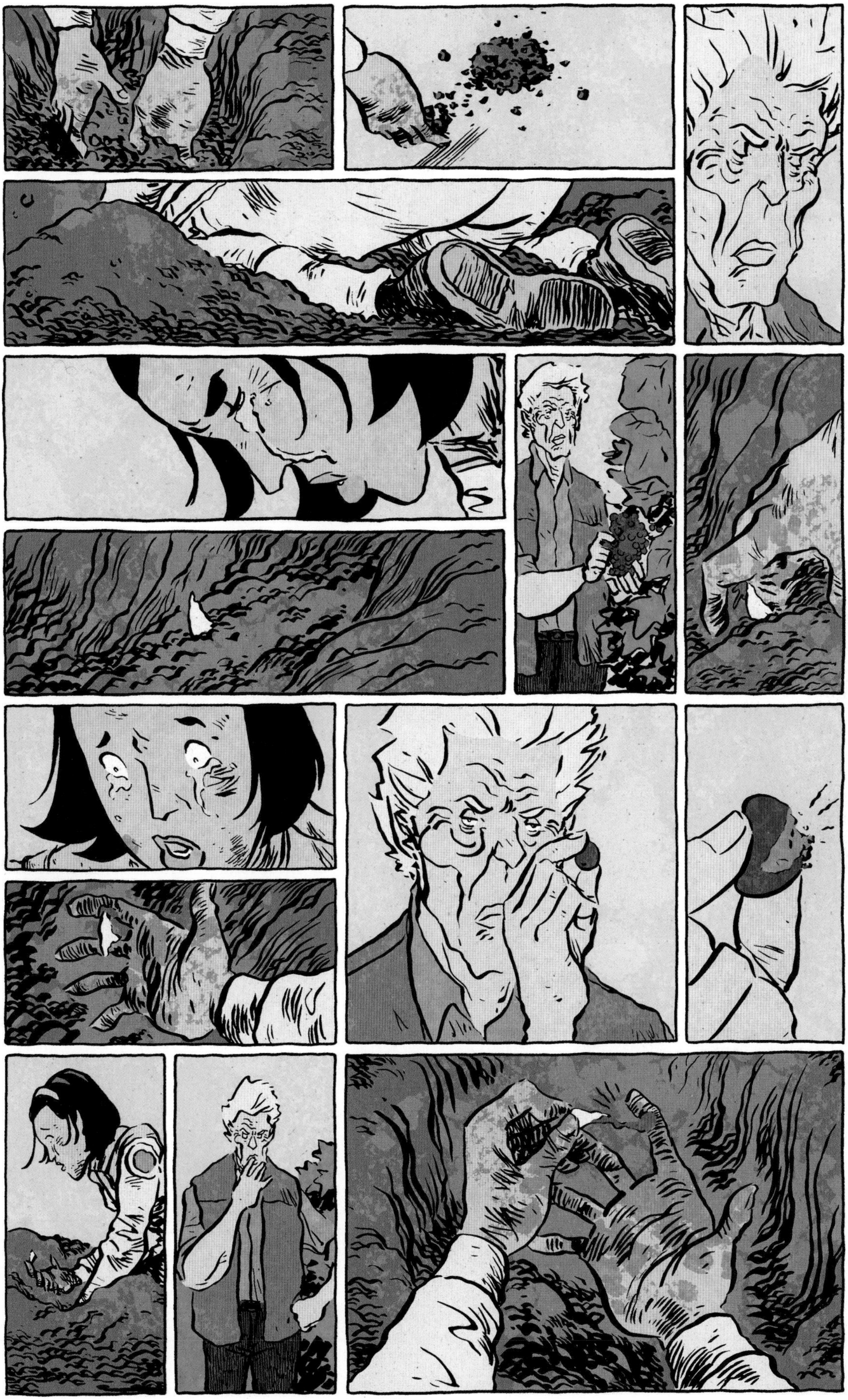

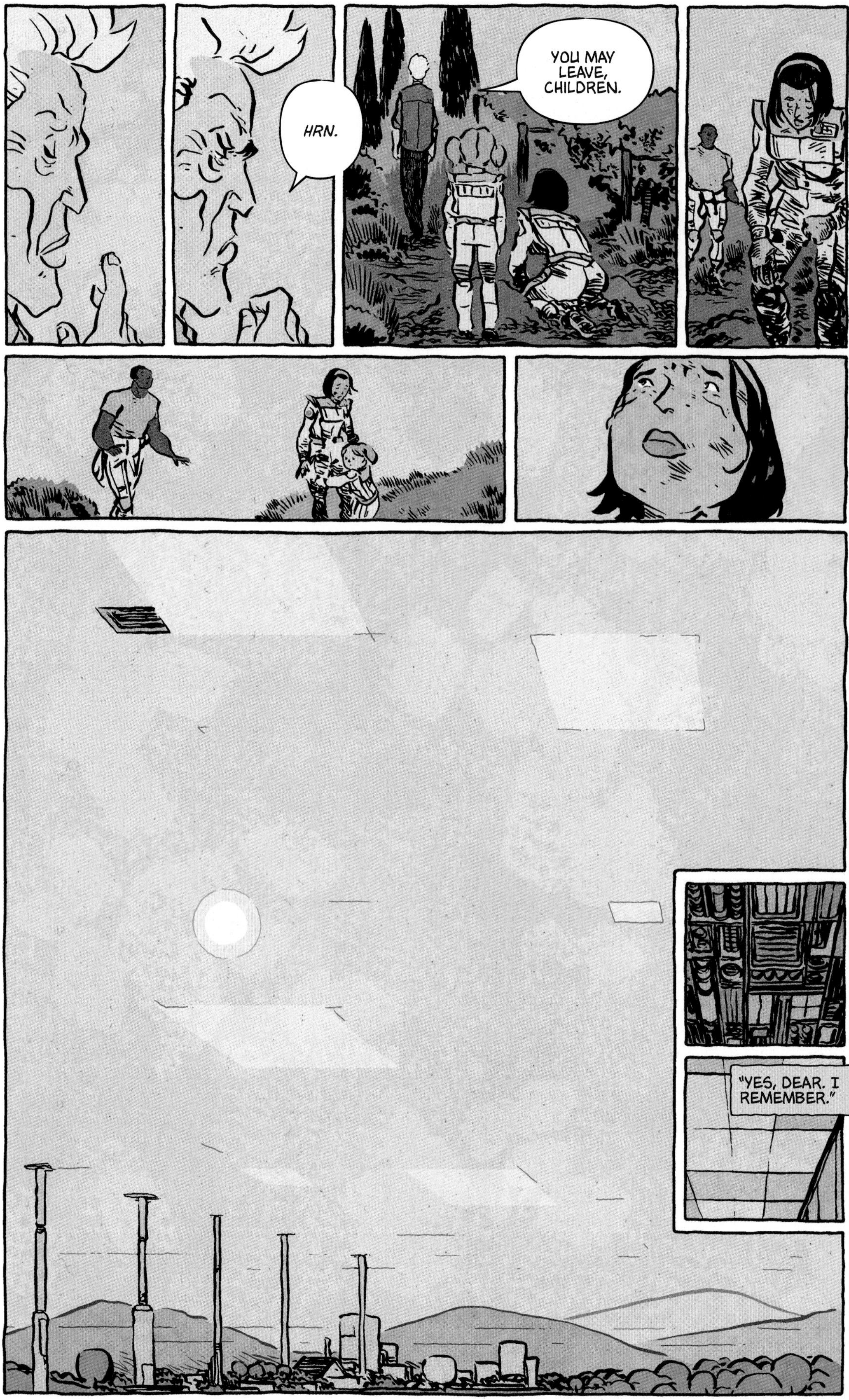
HRN.
YOU MAY LEAVE, CHILDREN.
"YES, DEAR. I REMEMBER."

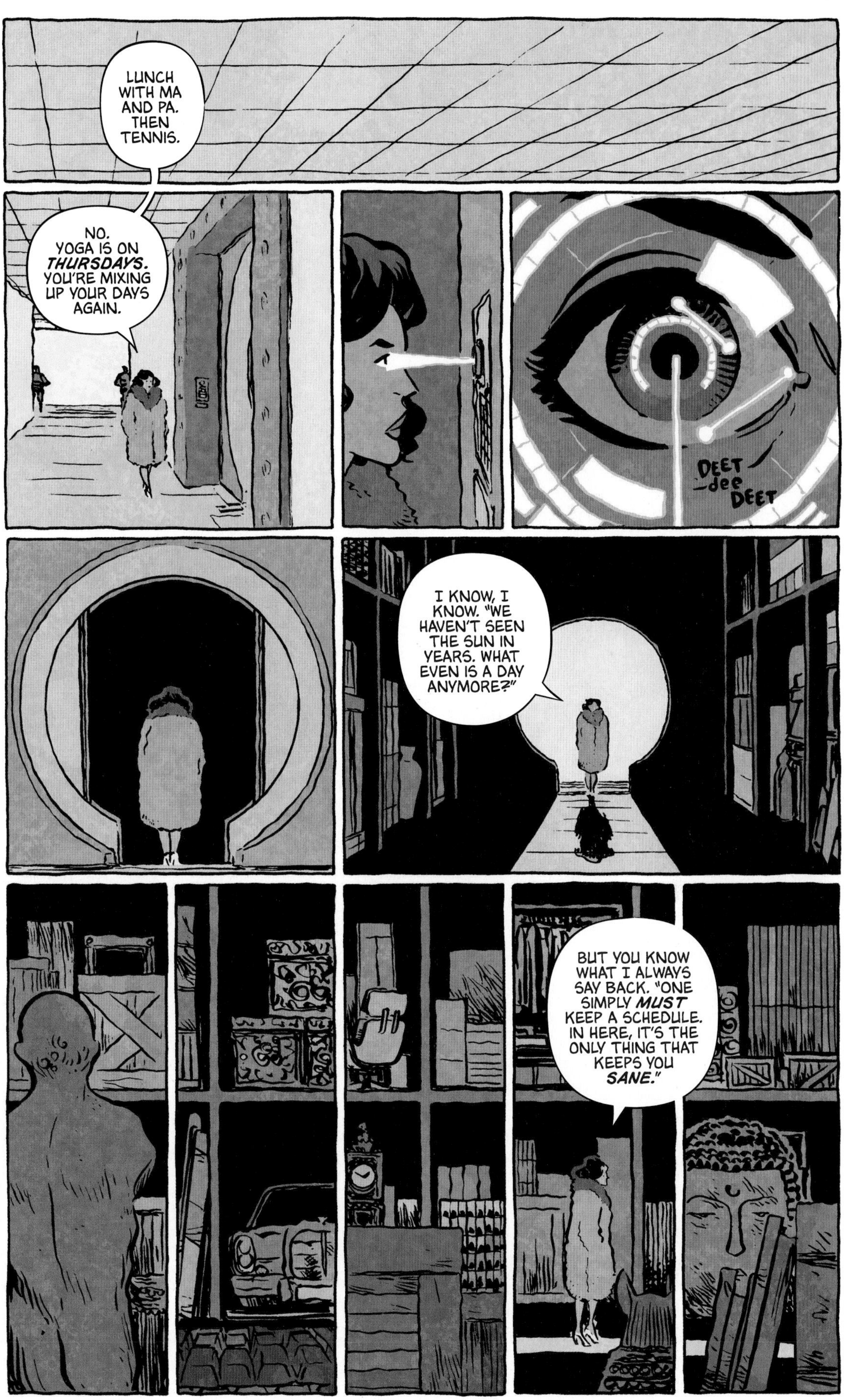
LUNCH WITH MA AND PA. THEN TENNIS.
NO. YOGA IS ON *THURSDAYS.* YOU'RE MIXING UP YOUR DAYS AGAIN.
DEET dee DEET
I KNOW, I KNOW. "WE HAVEN'T SEEN THE SUN IN YEARS. WHAT EVEN IS A DAY ANYMORE?"
BUT YOU KNOW WHAT I ALWAYS SAY BACK. "ONE SIMPLY *MUST* KEEP A SCHEDULE. IN HERE, IT'S THE ONLY THING THAT KEEPS YOU *SANE.*"

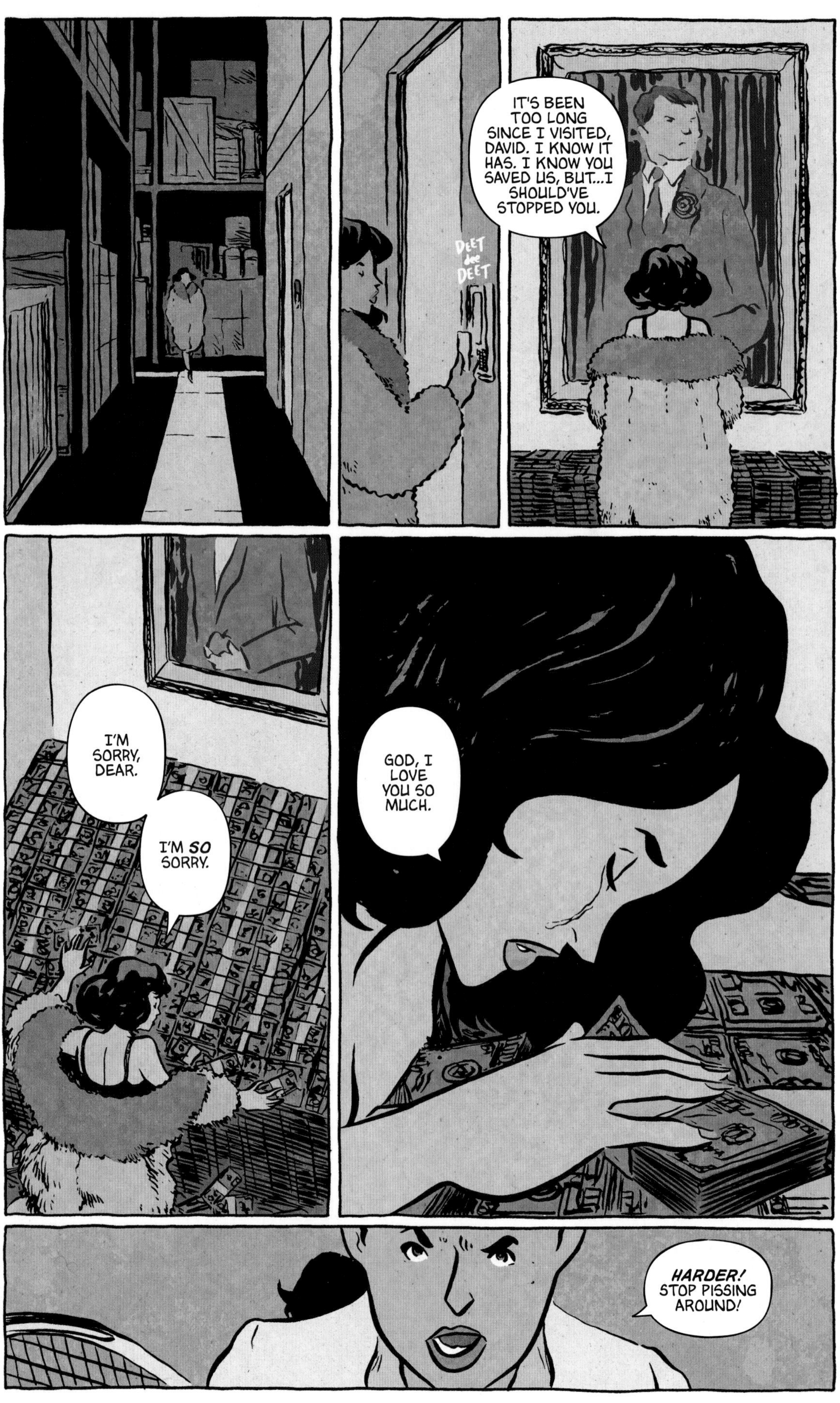

DEET dee DEET
IT'S BEEN TOO LONG SINCE I VISITED, DAVID. I KNOW IT HAS. I KNOW YOU SAVED US, BUT...I SHOULD'VE STOPPED YOU.
I'M SORRY, DEAR.
I'M SO SORRY.
GOD, I LOVE YOU SO MUCH.
HARDER! STOP PISSING AROUND!

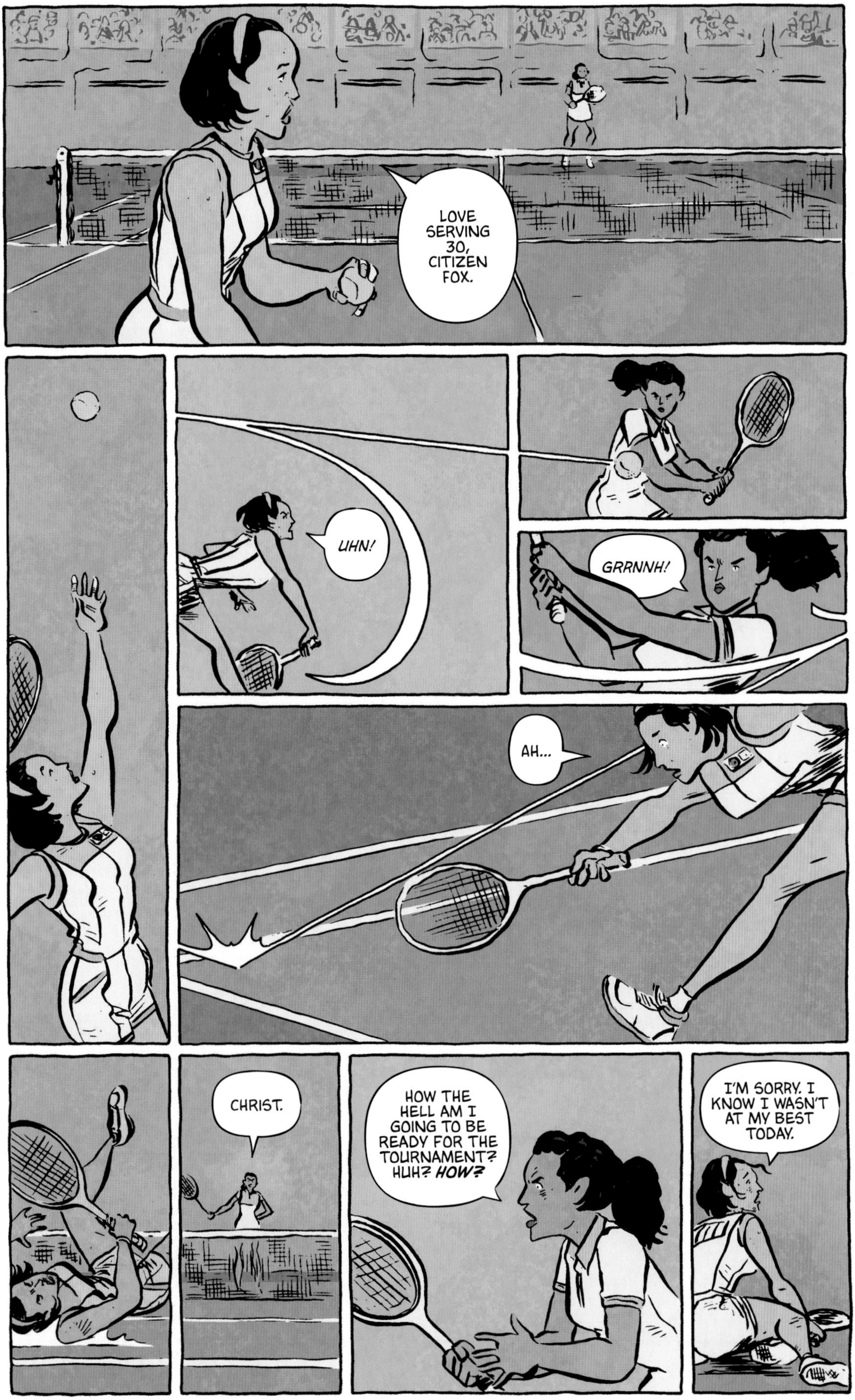
LOVE SERVING 30, CITIZEN FOX.
UHN!
GRRNNH!
AH...
CHRIST.
HOW THE HELL AM I GOING TO BE READY FOR THE TOURNAMENT? HUH? *HOW?*
I'M SORRY. I KNOW I WASN'T AT MY BEST TODAY.

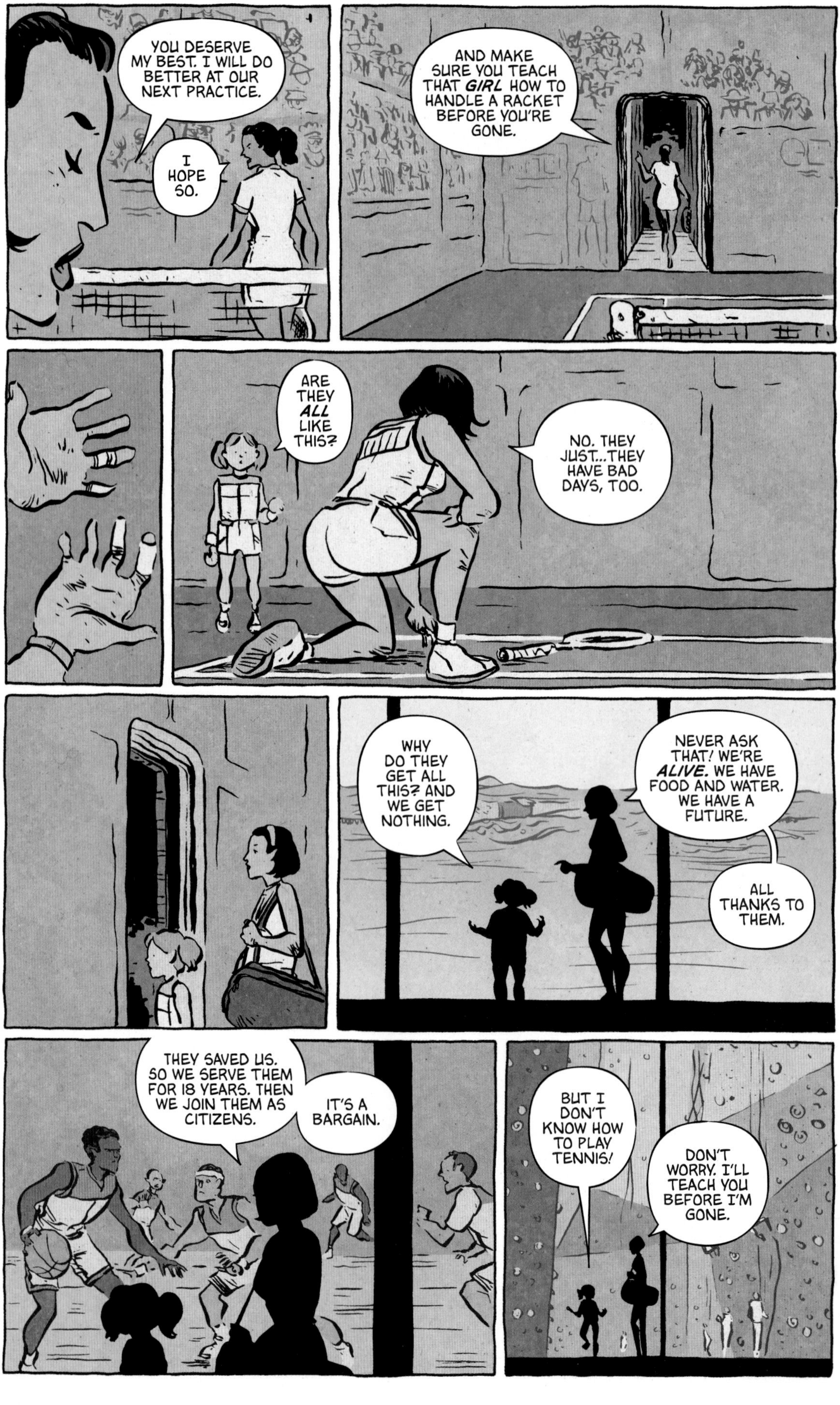
YOU DESERVE MY BEST. I WILL DO BETTER AT OUR NEXT PRACTICE.
I HOPE SO.
AND MAKE SURE YOU TEACH THAT *GIRL* HOW TO HANDLE A RACKET BEFORE YOU'RE GONE.
ARE THEY *ALL* LIKE THIS?
NO. THEY JUST...THEY HAVE BAD DAYS, TOO.
WHY DO THEY GET ALL THIS? AND WE GET NOTHING.
NEVER ASK THAT! WE'RE *ALIVE.* WE HAVE FOOD AND WATER. WE HAVE A FUTURE.
ALL THANKS TO THEM.
THEY SAVED US. SO WE SERVE THEM FOR 18 YEARS. THEN WE JOIN THEM AS CITIZENS.
IT'S A BARGAIN.
BUT I DON'T KNOW HOW TO PLAY TENNIS!
DON'T WORRY. I'LL TEACH YOU BEFORE I'M GONE.

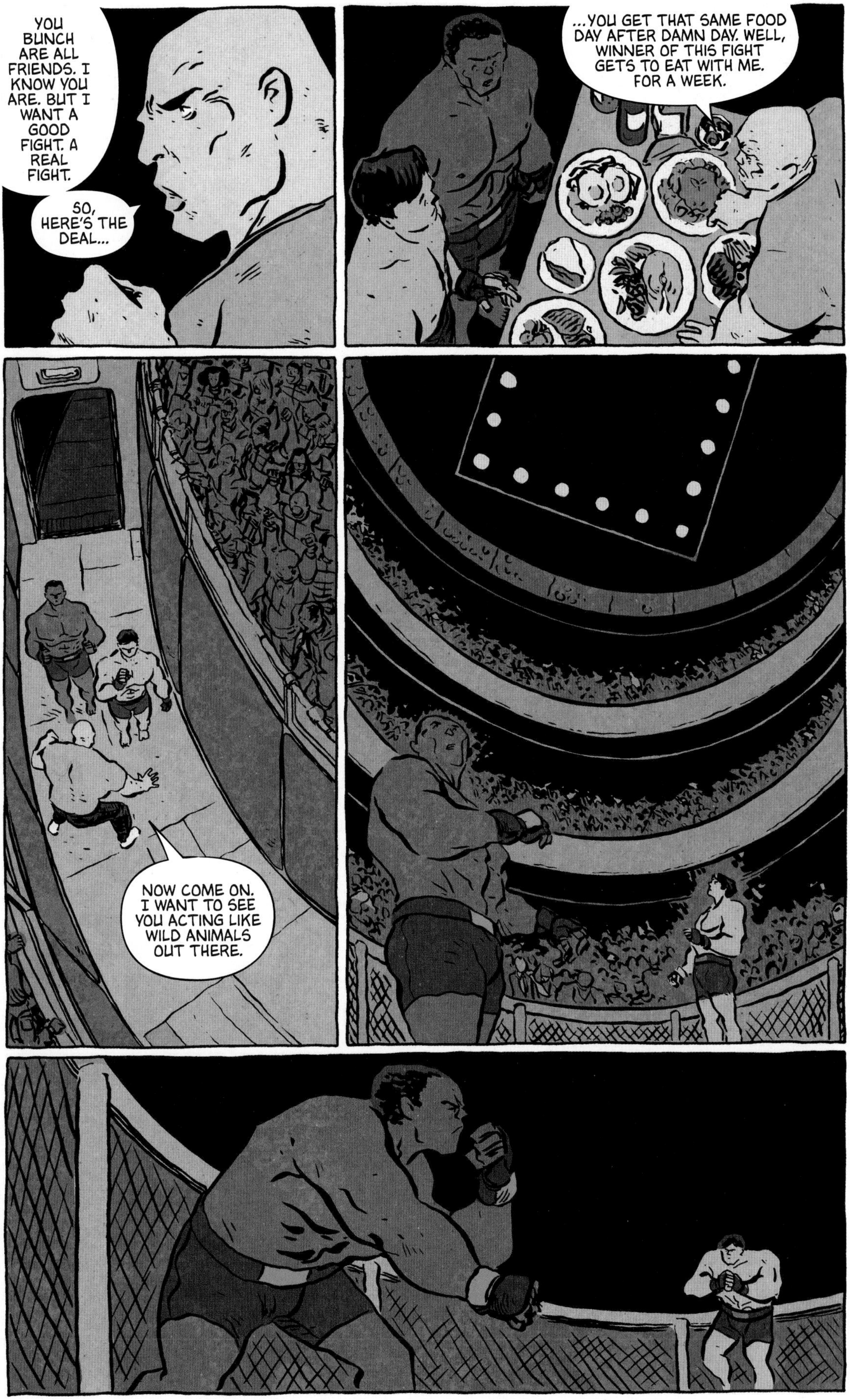
YOU BUNCH ARE ALL FRIENDS. I KNOW YOU ARE. BUT I WANT A GOOD FIGHT. A REAL FIGHT.
SO, HERE'S THE DEAL...
...YOU GET THAT SAME FOOD DAY AFTER DAMN DAY. WELL, WINNER OF THIS FIGHT GETS TO EAT WITH ME. FOR A WEEK.
NOW COME ON. I WANT TO SEE YOU ACTING LIKE WILD ANIMALS OUT THERE.

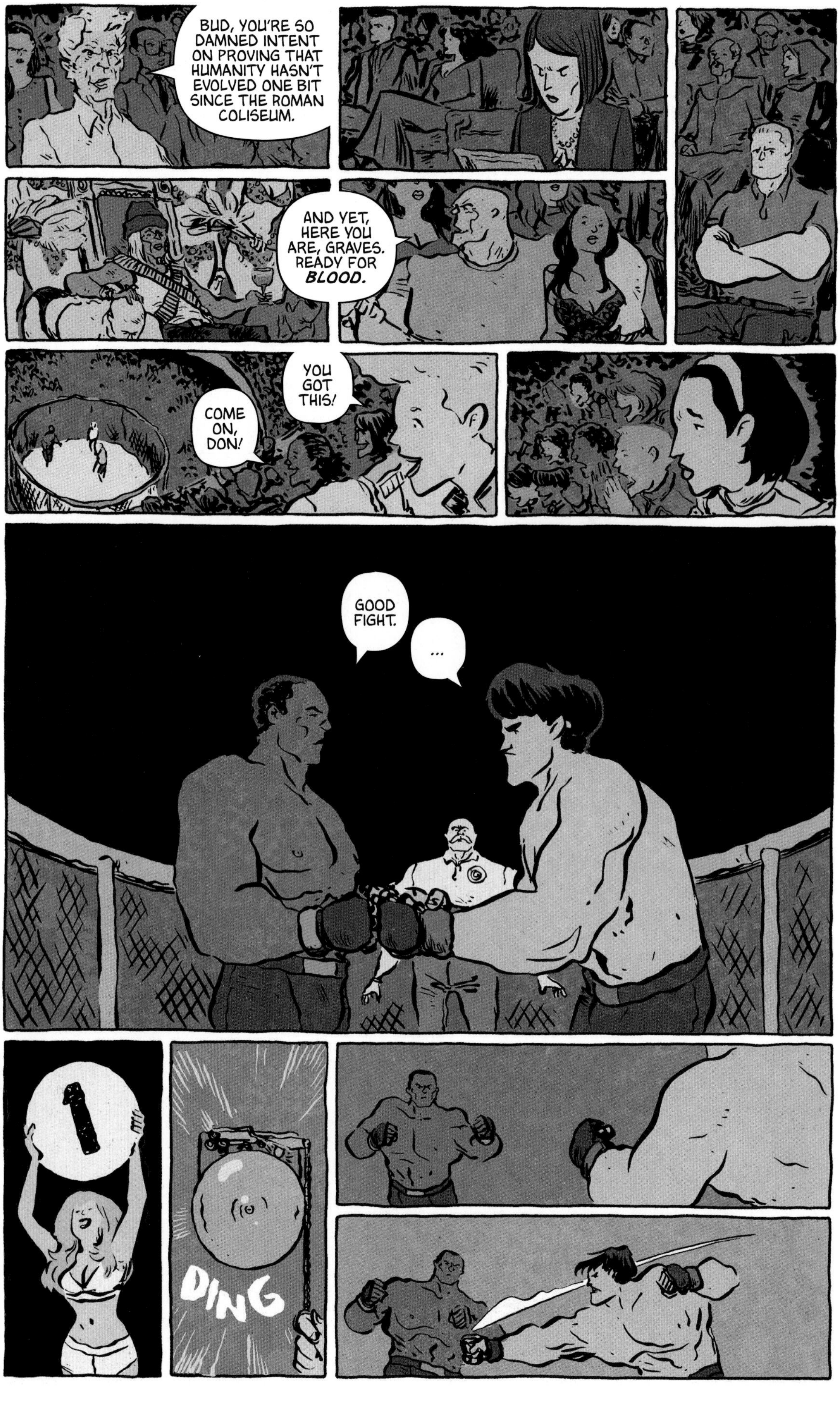
BUD, YOU'RE SO DAMNED INTENT ON PROVING THAT HUMANITY HASN'T EVOLVED ONE BIT SINCE THE ROMAN COLISEUM.
AND YET, HERE YOU ARE, GRAVES. READY FOR *BLOOD.*
YOU GOT THIS!
COME ON, DON!
GOOD FIGHT.
...
DING

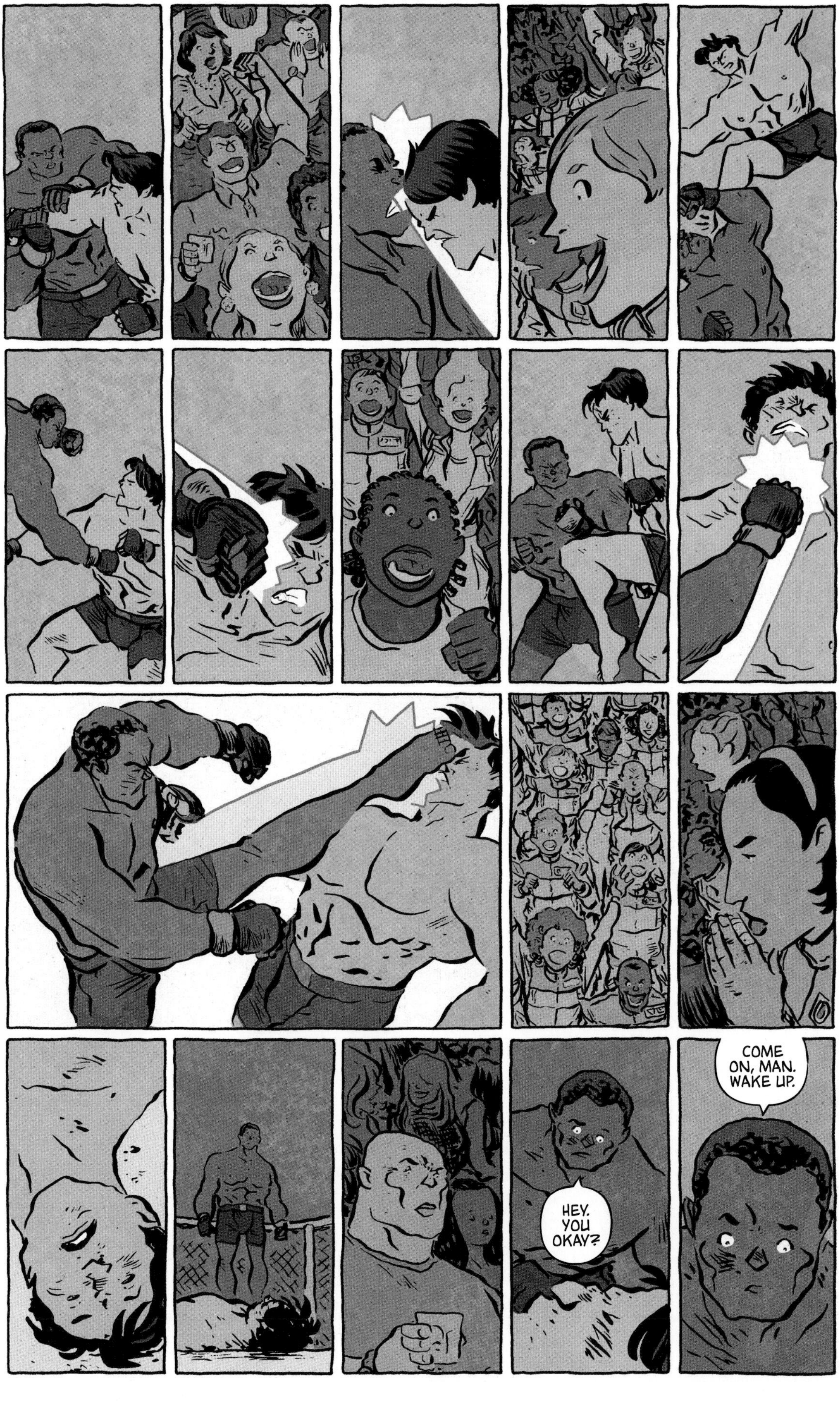
HEY. YOU OKAY?
COME ON, MAN. WAKE UP.

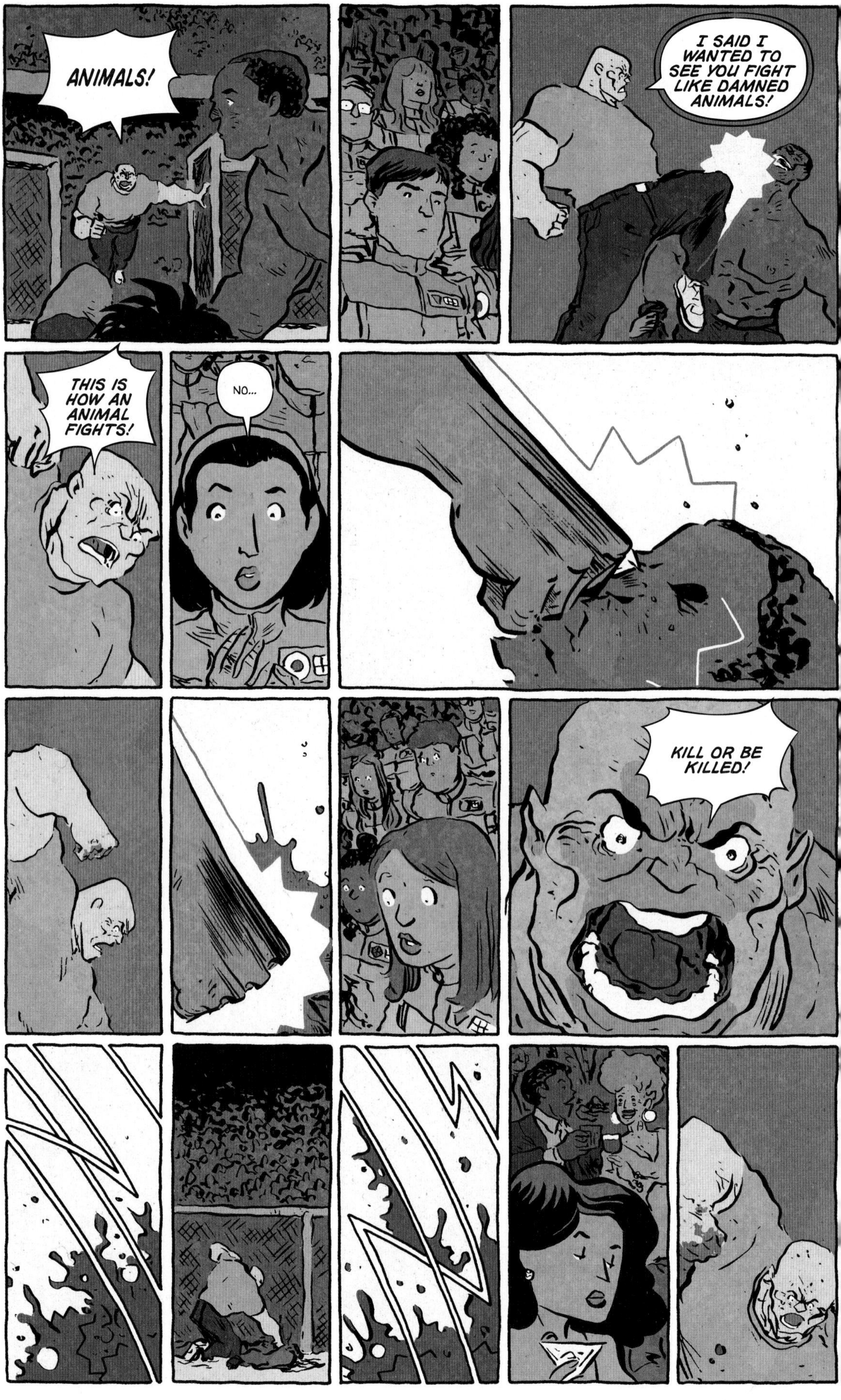
ANIMALS!
I SAID I WANTED TO SEE YOU FIGHT LIKE DAMNED ANIMALS!
THIS IS HOW AN ANIMAL FIGHTS!
NO...
KILL OR BE KILLED!

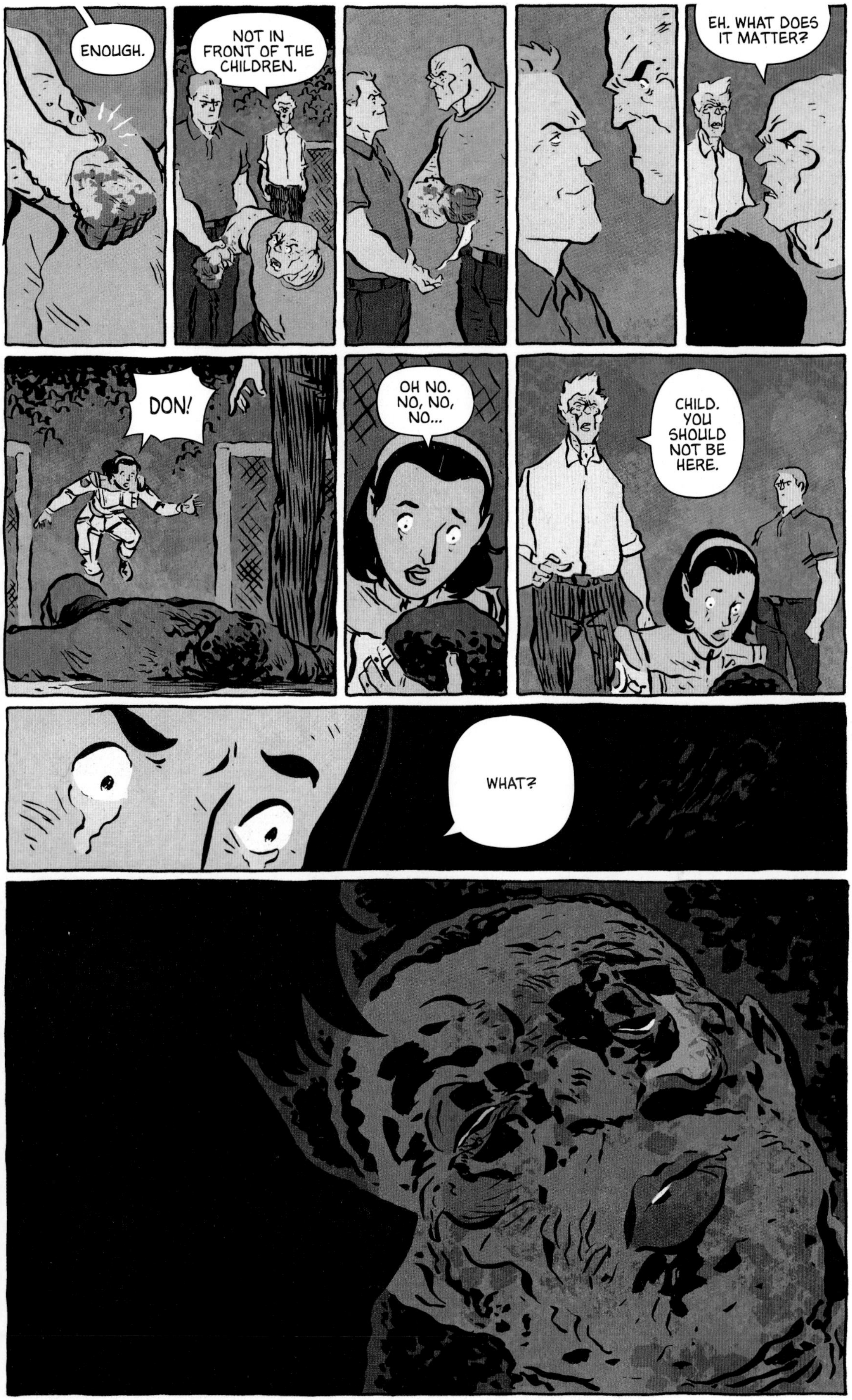
ENOUGH.
NOT IN FRONT OF THE CHILDREN.
EH. WHAT DOES IT MATTER?
DON!
OH NO. NO, NO, NO...
CHILD. YOU SHOULD NOT BE HERE.
WHAT?

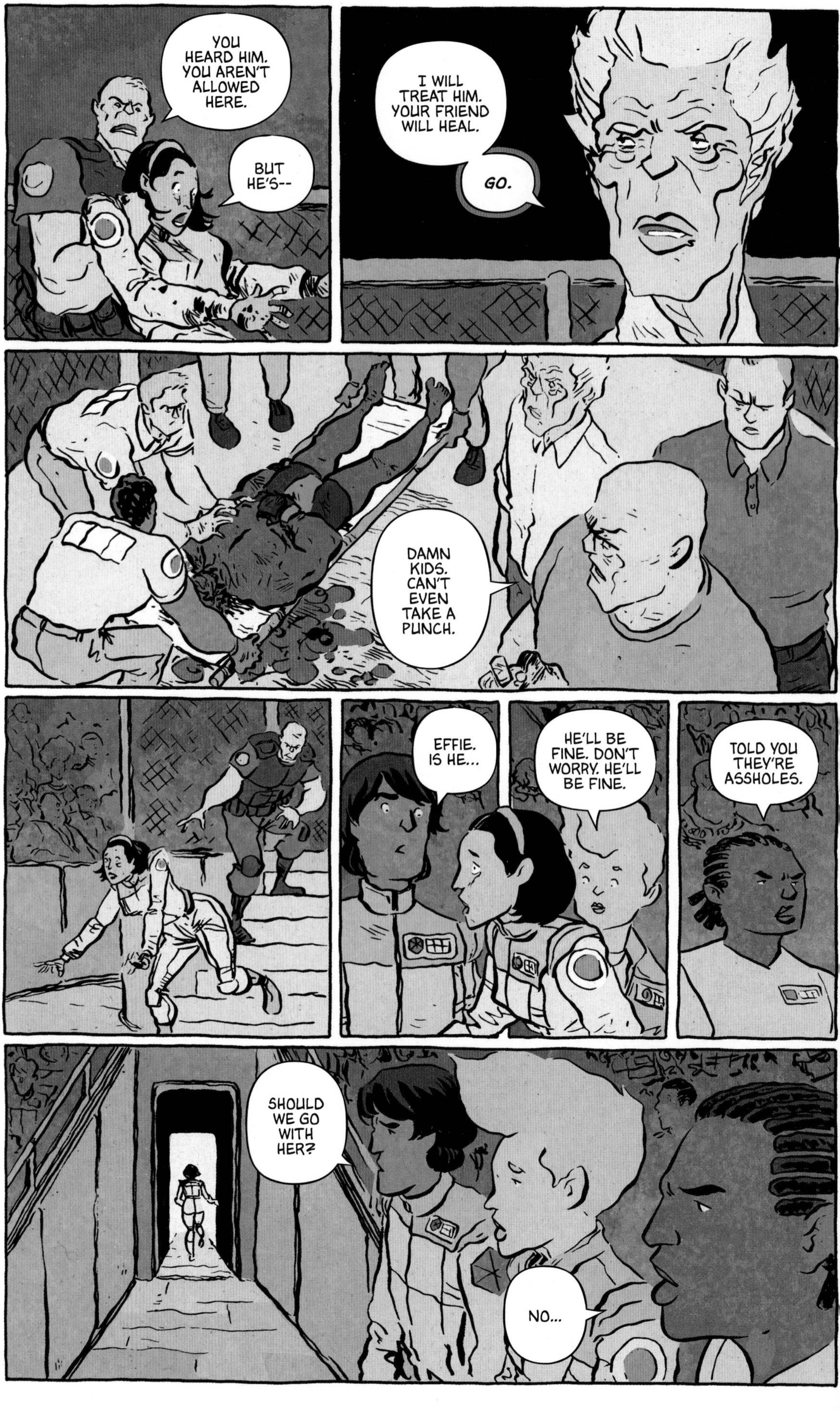
YOU HEARD HIM. YOU AREN'T ALLOWED HERE.
BUT HE'S--
I WILL TREAT HIM. YOUR FRIEND WILL HEAL.
GO.
DAMN KIDS. CAN'T EVEN TAKE A PUNCH.
EFFIE. IS HE...
HE'LL BE FINE. DON'T WORRY. HE'LL BE FINE.
TOLD YOU THEY'RE ASSHOLES.
SHOULD WE GO WITH HER?
NO...

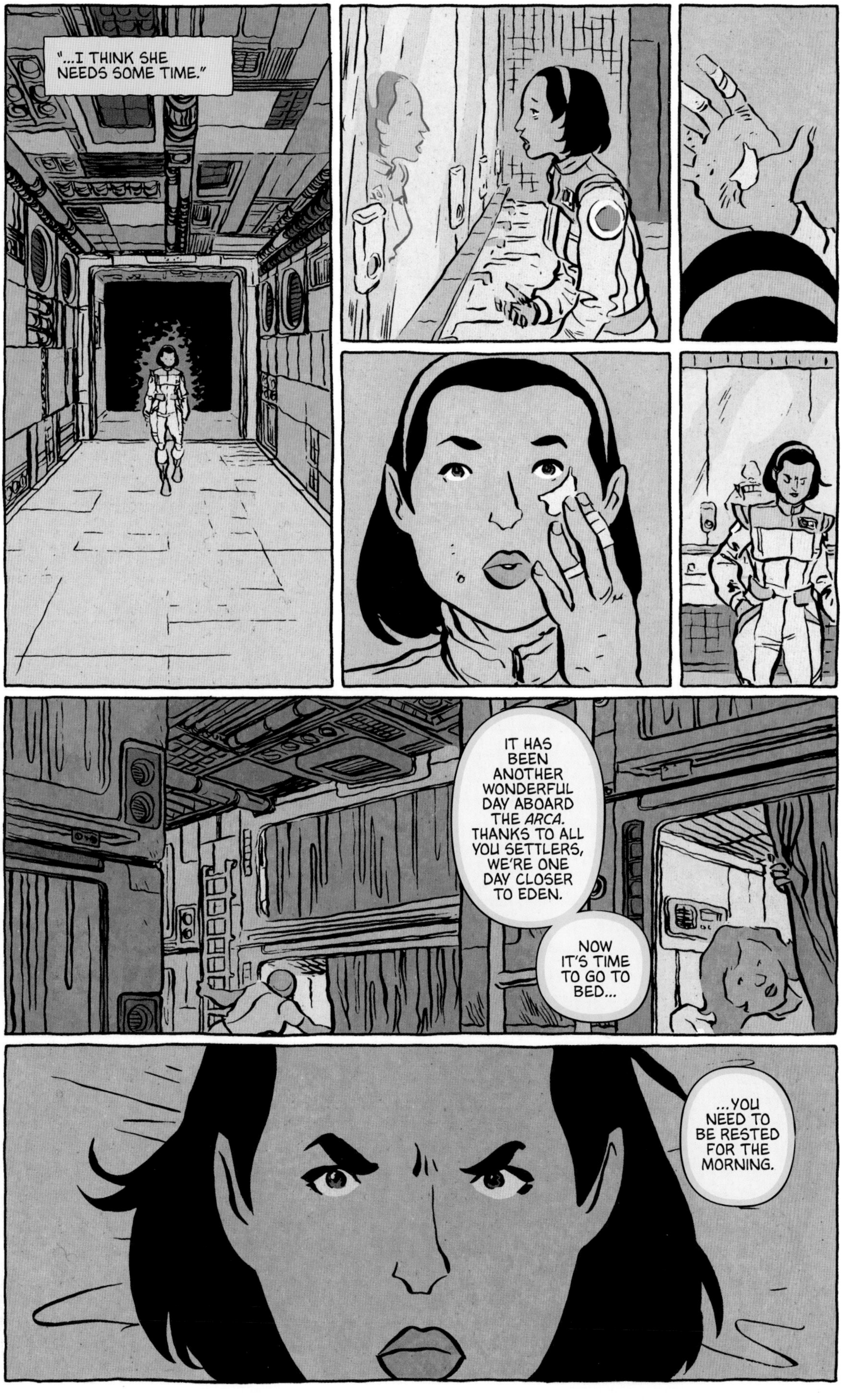
"...I THINK SHE NEEDS SOME TIME."
IT HAS BEEN ANOTHER WONDERFUL DAY ABOARD THE *ARCA*. THANKS TO ALL YOU SETTLERS, WE'RE ONE DAY CLOSER TO EDEN.
NOW IT'S TIME TO GO TO BED...
...YOU NEED TO BE RESTED FOR THE MORNING.

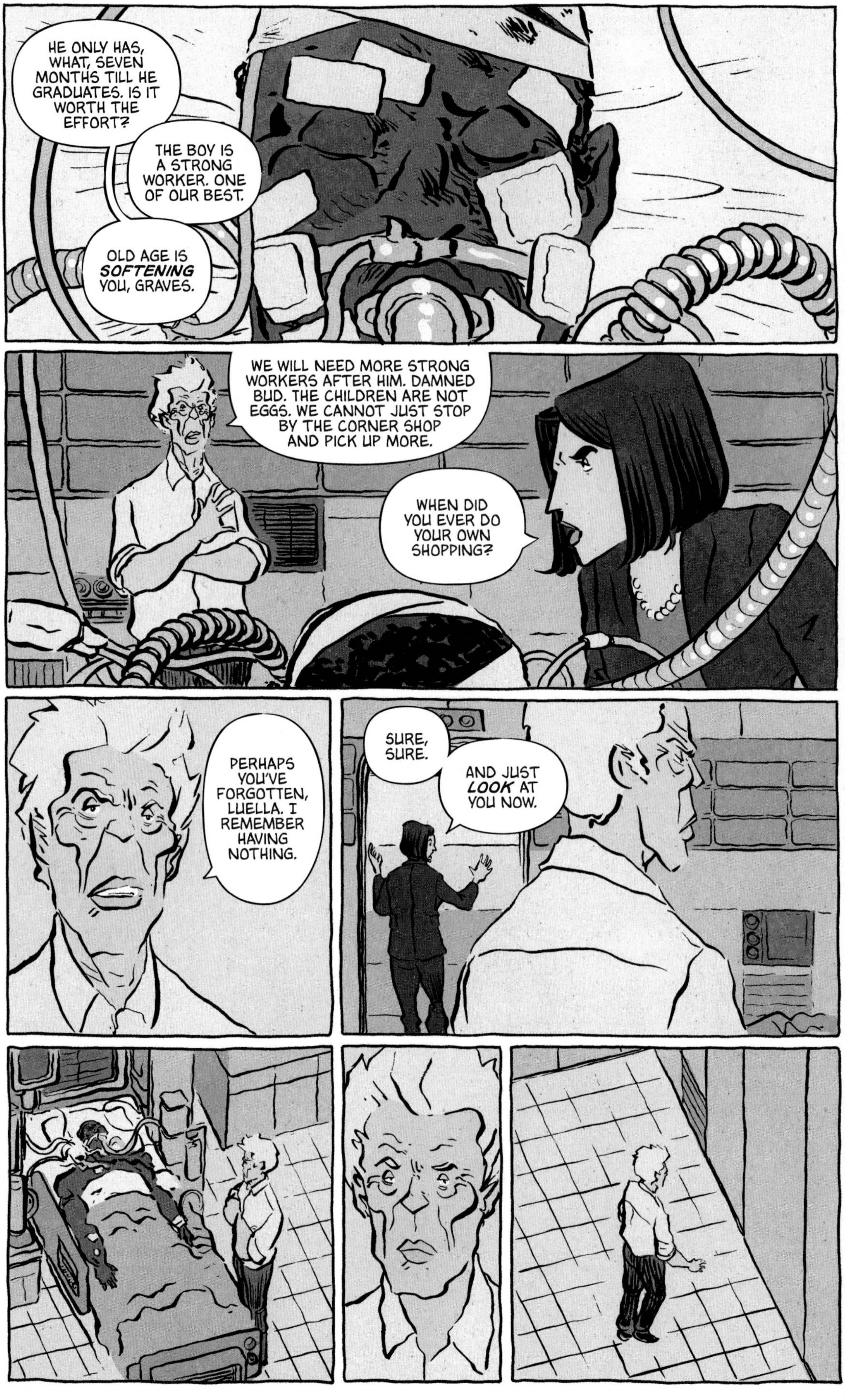

HE ONLY HAS, WHAT, SEVEN MONTHS TILL HE GRADUATES. IS IT WORTH THE EFFORT?
THE BOY IS A STRONG WORKER. ONE OF OUR BEST.
OLD AGE IS *SOFTENING* YOU, GRAVES.
WE WILL NEED MORE STRONG WORKERS AFTER HIM. DAMNED BUD. THE CHILDREN ARE NOT EGGS. WE CANNOT JUST STOP BY THE CORNER SHOP AND PICK UP MORE.
WHEN DID YOU EVER DO YOUR OWN SHOPPING?
PERHAPS YOU'VE FORGOTTEN, LUELLA. I REMEMBER HAVING NOTHING.
SURE, SURE.
AND JUST *LOOK* AT YOU NOW.

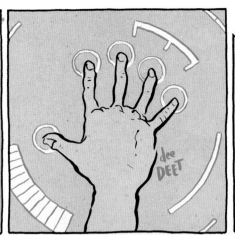

DID YOU HEAR? BUYING GROCERIES IN A STORE...

HOW MANY TIMES DID WE GET CAUGHT SHOPLIFTING?

WELL, *YOU* GOT CAUGHT. I CREATED THE DISTRACTION SO YOU COULD LOAD YOUR POCKETS.

THAT ONE SHOP OWNER GRABBED YOU AND SCREAMED, "WHERE ARE YOUR PARENTS?"

AND YOU JUST SMILED AND SAID, "JOKE'S ON YOU. THEY'RE DEAD!"

YOU ALWAYS WERE THE FUNNY ONE.

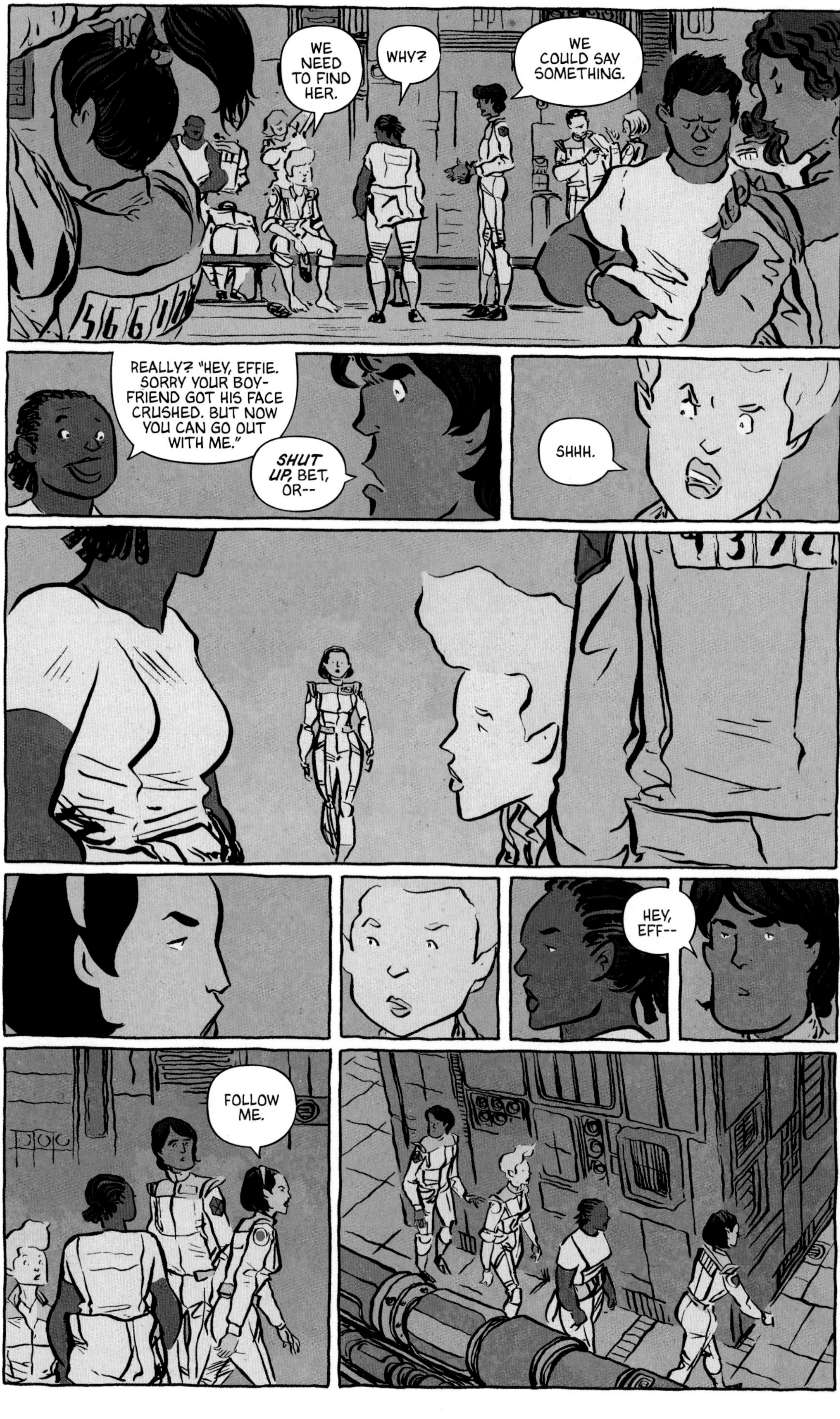
WE NEED TO FIND HER.
WHY?
WE COULD SAY SOMETHING.
REALLY? "HEY, EFFIE. SORRY YOUR BOY-FRIEND GOT HIS FACE CRUSHED. BUT NOW YOU CAN GO OUT WITH ME."
SHUT UP, BET, OR--
SHHH.
HEY, EFF--
FOLLOW ME.

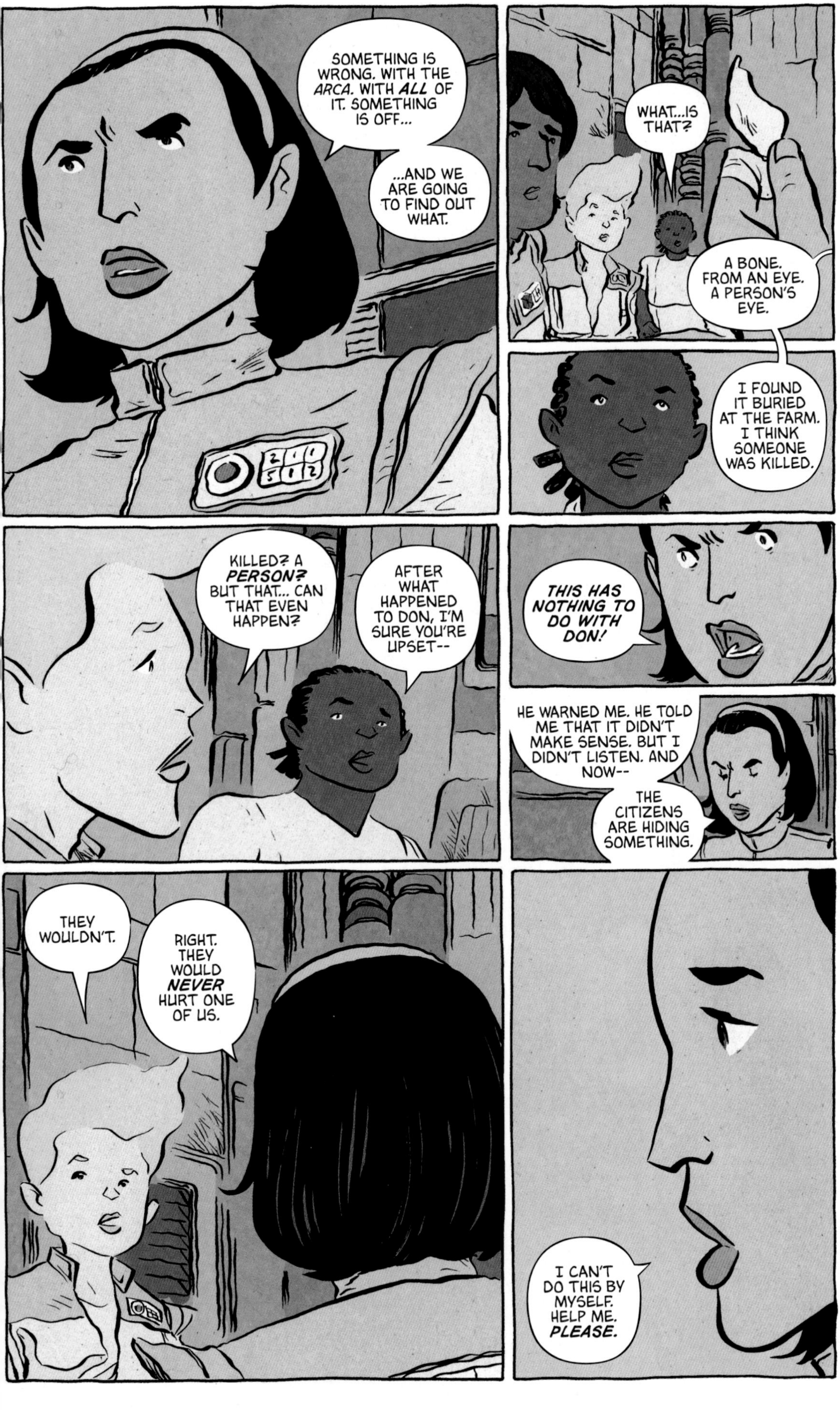
SOMETHING IS WRONG. WITH THE *ARCA.* WITH ***ALL*** OF IT. SOMETHING IS OFF...
...AND WE ARE GOING TO FIND OUT WHAT.
WHAT...IS THAT?
A BONE. FROM AN EYE. A PERSON'S EYE.
I FOUND IT BURIED AT THE FARM. I THINK SOMEONE WAS KILLED.
KILLED? A ***PERSON?*** BUT THAT... CAN THAT EVEN HAPPEN?
AFTER WHAT HAPPENED TO DON, I'M SURE YOU'RE UPSET--
THIS HAS NOTHING TO DO WITH DON!
HE WARNED ME. HE TOLD ME THAT IT DIDN'T MAKE SENSE. BUT I DIDN'T LISTEN. AND NOW--
THE CITIZENS ARE HIDING SOMETHING.
THEY WOULDN'T.
RIGHT. THEY WOULD ***NEVER*** HURT ONE OF US.
I CAN'T DO THIS BY MYSELF. HELP ME. ***PLEASE.***

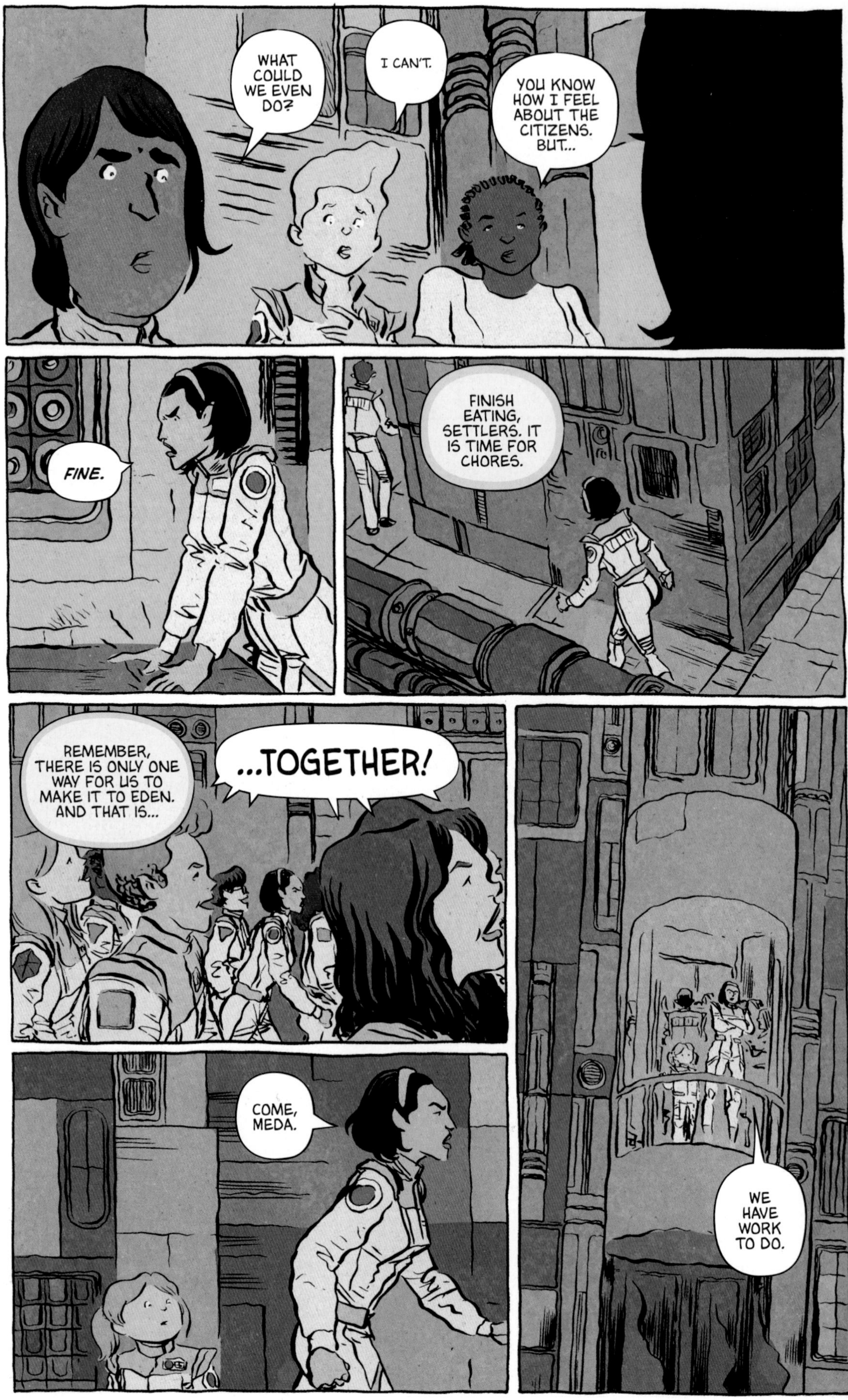
WHAT COULD WE EVEN DO?
I CAN'T.
YOU KNOW HOW I FEEL ABOUT THE CITIZENS. BUT...
FINE.
FINISH EATING, SETTLERS. IT IS TIME FOR CHORES.
REMEMBER, THERE IS ONLY ONE WAY FOR US TO MAKE IT TO EDEN. AND THAT IS...
...TOGETHER!
COME, MEDA.
WE HAVE WORK TO DO.

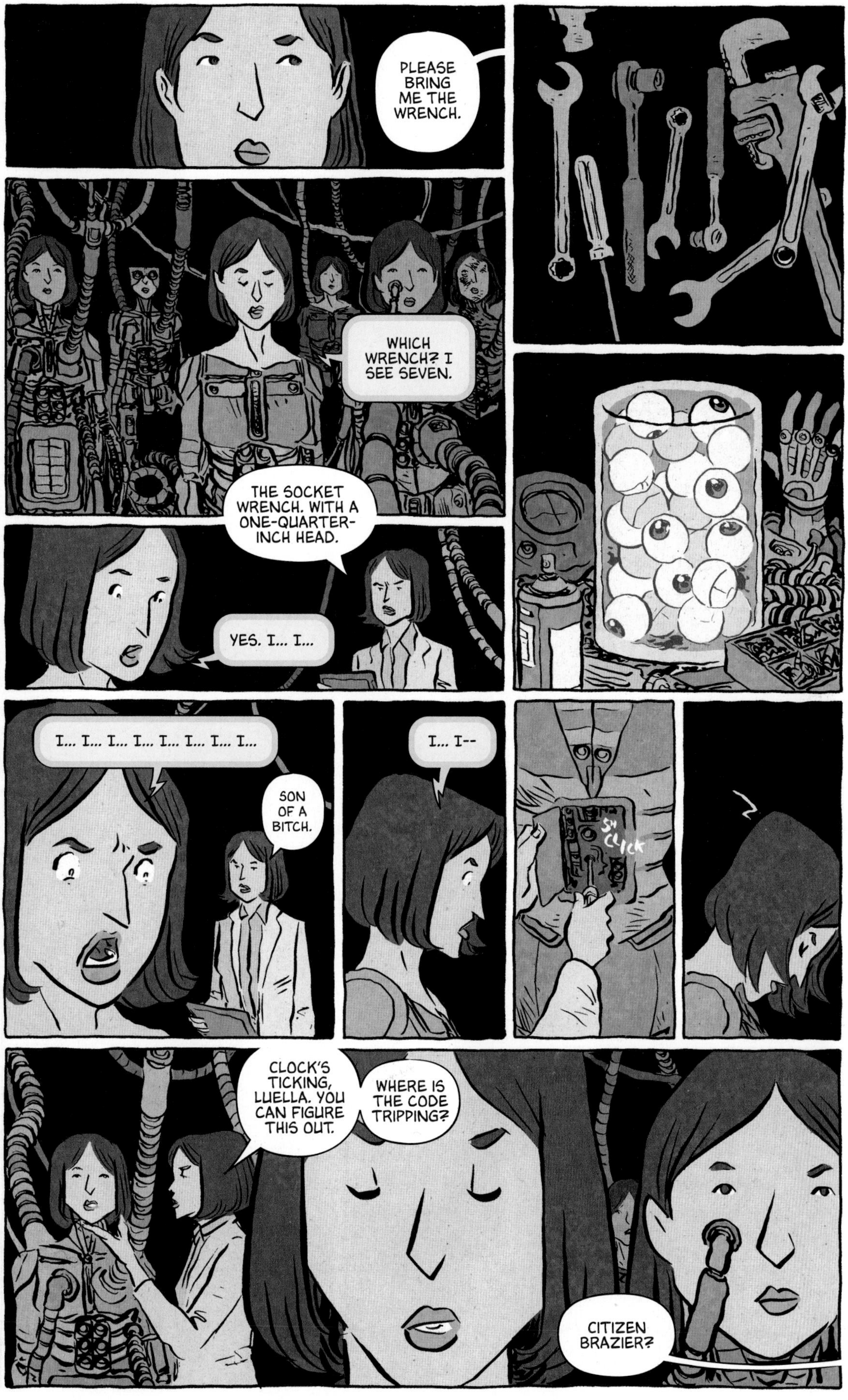
PLEASE BRING ME THE WRENCH.
WHICH WRENCH? I SEE SEVEN.
THE SOCKET WRENCH. WITH A ONE-QUARTER-INCH HEAD.
YES. I... I...
I... I... I... I... I... I... I... I...
SON OF A BITCH.
I... I--
SHCLICK
CLOCK'S TICKING, LUELLA. YOU CAN FIGURE THIS OUT.
WHERE IS THE CODE TRIPPING?
CITIZEN BRAZIER?

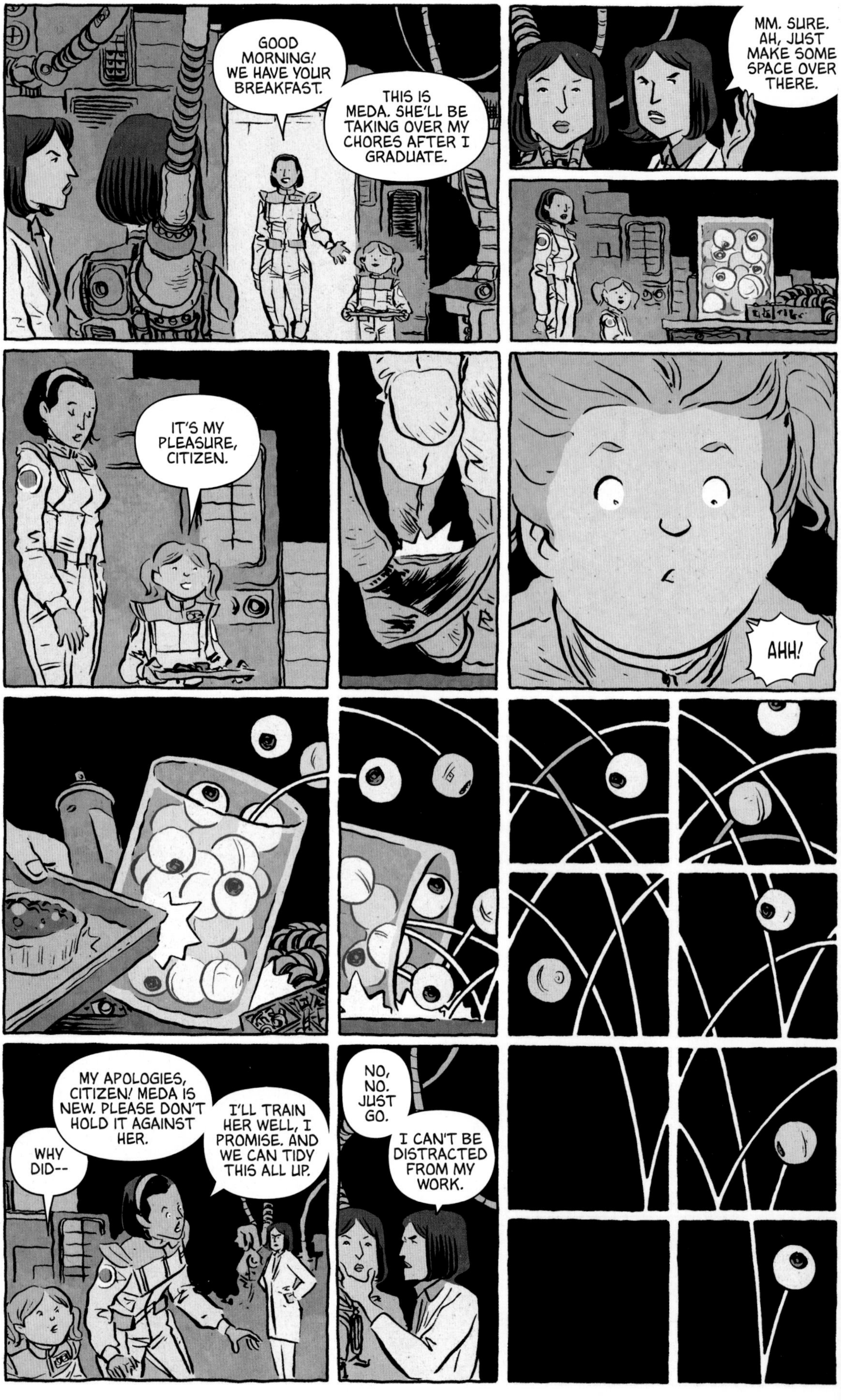
GOOD MORNING! WE HAVE YOUR BREAKFAST.
THIS IS MEDA. SHE'LL BE TAKING OVER MY CHORES AFTER I GRADUATE.
MM. SURE. AH, JUST MAKE SOME SPACE OVER THERE.
IT'S MY PLEASURE, CITIZEN.
AHH!
MY APOLOGIES, CITIZEN! MEDA IS NEW. PLEASE DON'T HOLD IT AGAINST HER.
WHY DID--
I'LL TRAIN HER WELL, I PROMISE. AND WE CAN TIDY THIS ALL UP.
NO, NO. JUST GO.
I CAN'T BE DISTRACTED FROM MY WORK.

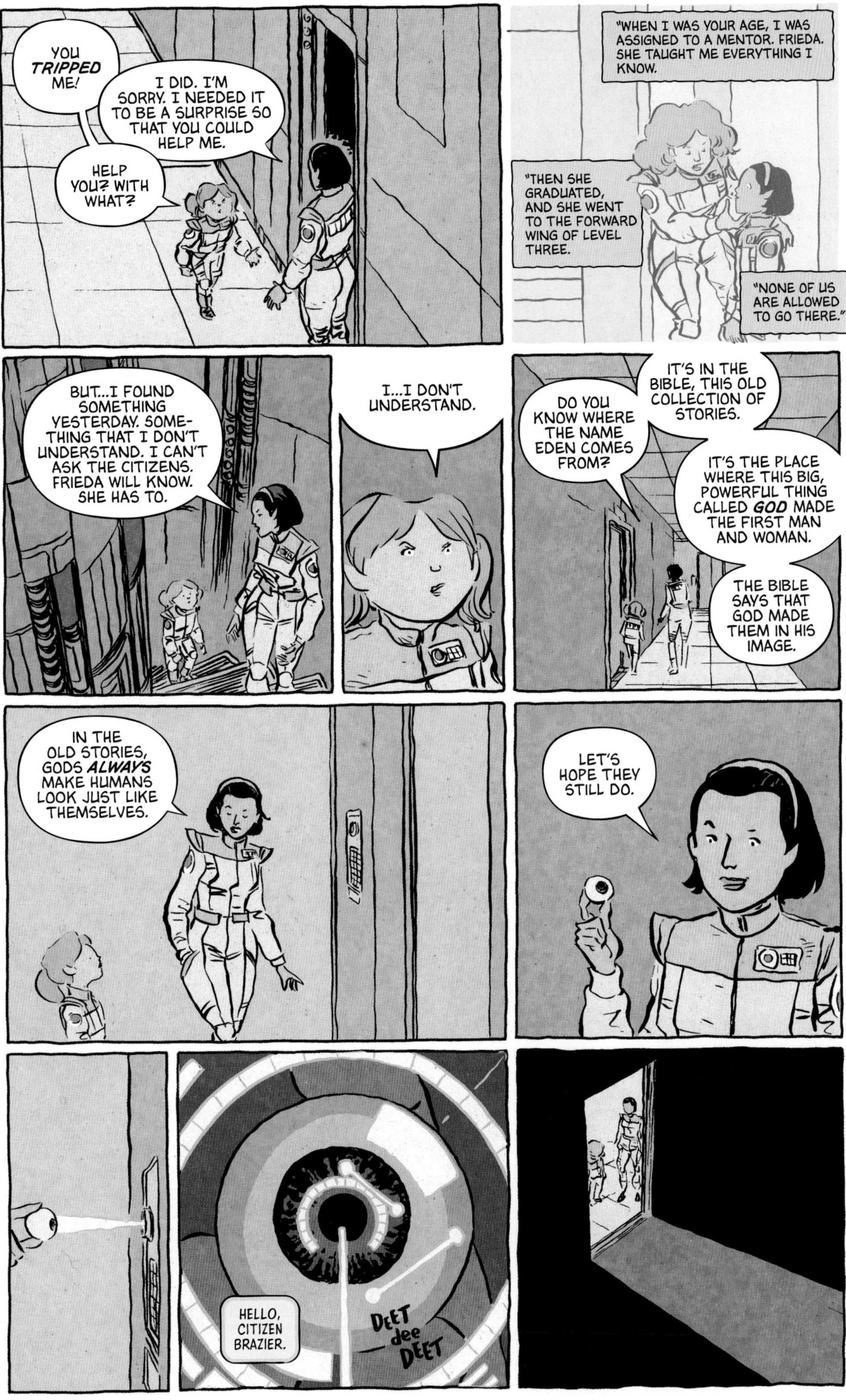

YOU *TRIPPED* ME!
I DID. I'M SORRY. I NEEDED IT TO BE A SURPRISE SO THAT YOU COULD HELP ME.
HELP YOU? WITH WHAT?
"WHEN I WAS YOUR AGE, I WAS ASSIGNED TO A MENTOR. FRIEDA. SHE TAUGHT ME EVERYTHING I KNOW.
"THEN SHE GRADUATED, AND SHE WENT TO THE FORWARD WING OF LEVEL THREE.
"NONE OF US ARE ALLOWED TO GO THERE."
BUT...I FOUND SOMETHING YESTERDAY. SOMETHING THAT I DON'T UNDERSTAND. I CAN'T ASK THE CITIZENS. FRIEDA WILL KNOW. SHE HAS TO.
I...I DON'T UNDERSTAND.
DO YOU KNOW WHERE THE NAME EDEN COMES FROM?
IT'S IN THE BIBLE, THIS OLD COLLECTION OF STORIES.
IT'S THE PLACE WHERE THIS BIG, POWERFUL THING CALLED *GOD* MADE THE FIRST MAN AND WOMAN.
THE BIBLE SAYS THAT GOD MADE THEM IN HIS IMAGE.
IN THE OLD STORIES, GODS *ALWAYS* MAKE HUMANS LOOK JUST LIKE THEMSELVES.
LET'S HOPE THEY STILL DO.
HELLO, CITIZEN BRAZIER.
DEET dee DEET

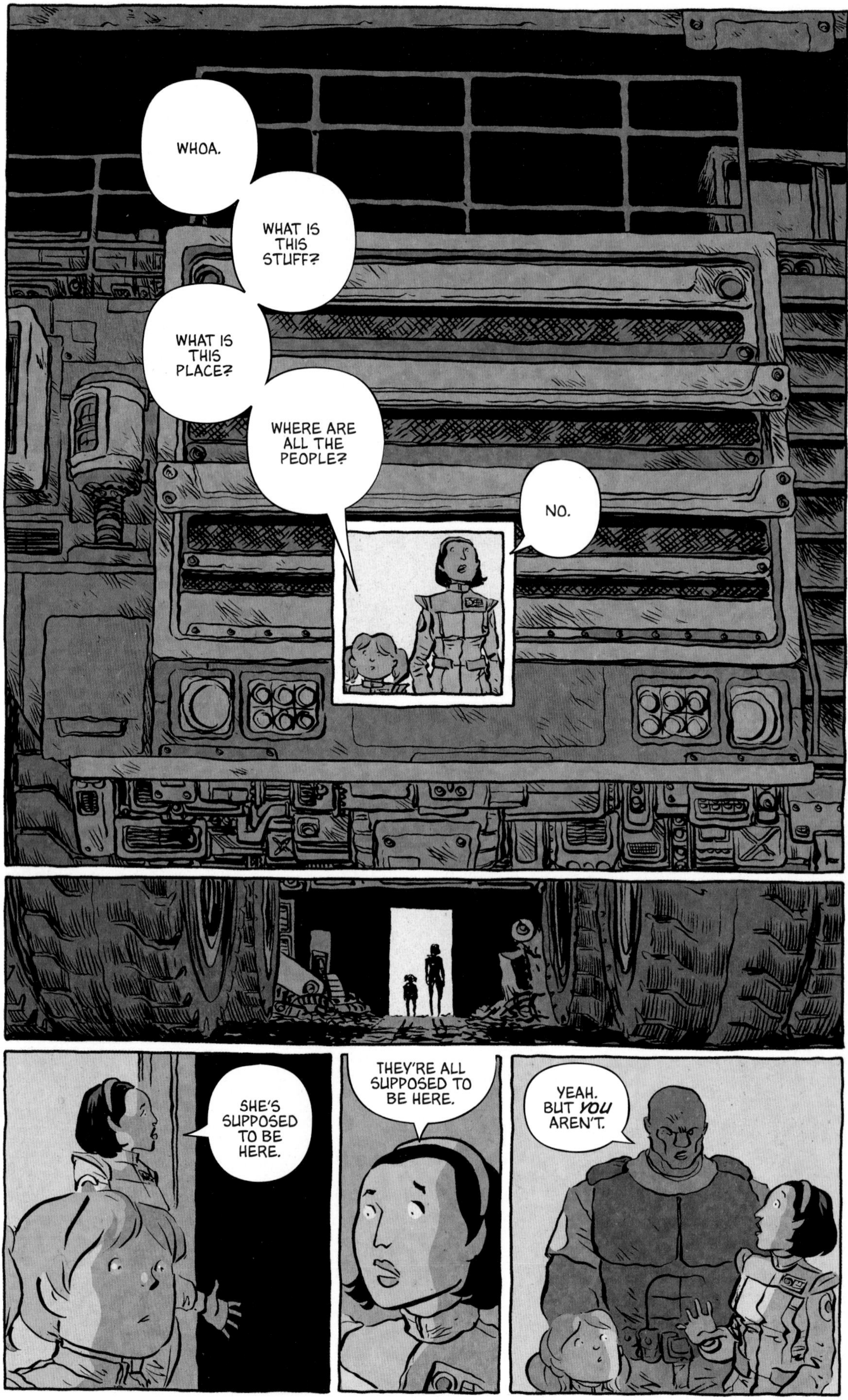

WHOA.
WHAT IS THIS STUFF?
WHAT IS THIS PLACE?
WHERE ARE ALL THE PEOPLE?
NO.
SHE'S SUPPOSED TO BE HERE.
THEY'RE ALL SUPPOSED TO BE HERE.
YEAH. BUT *YOU* AREN'T.

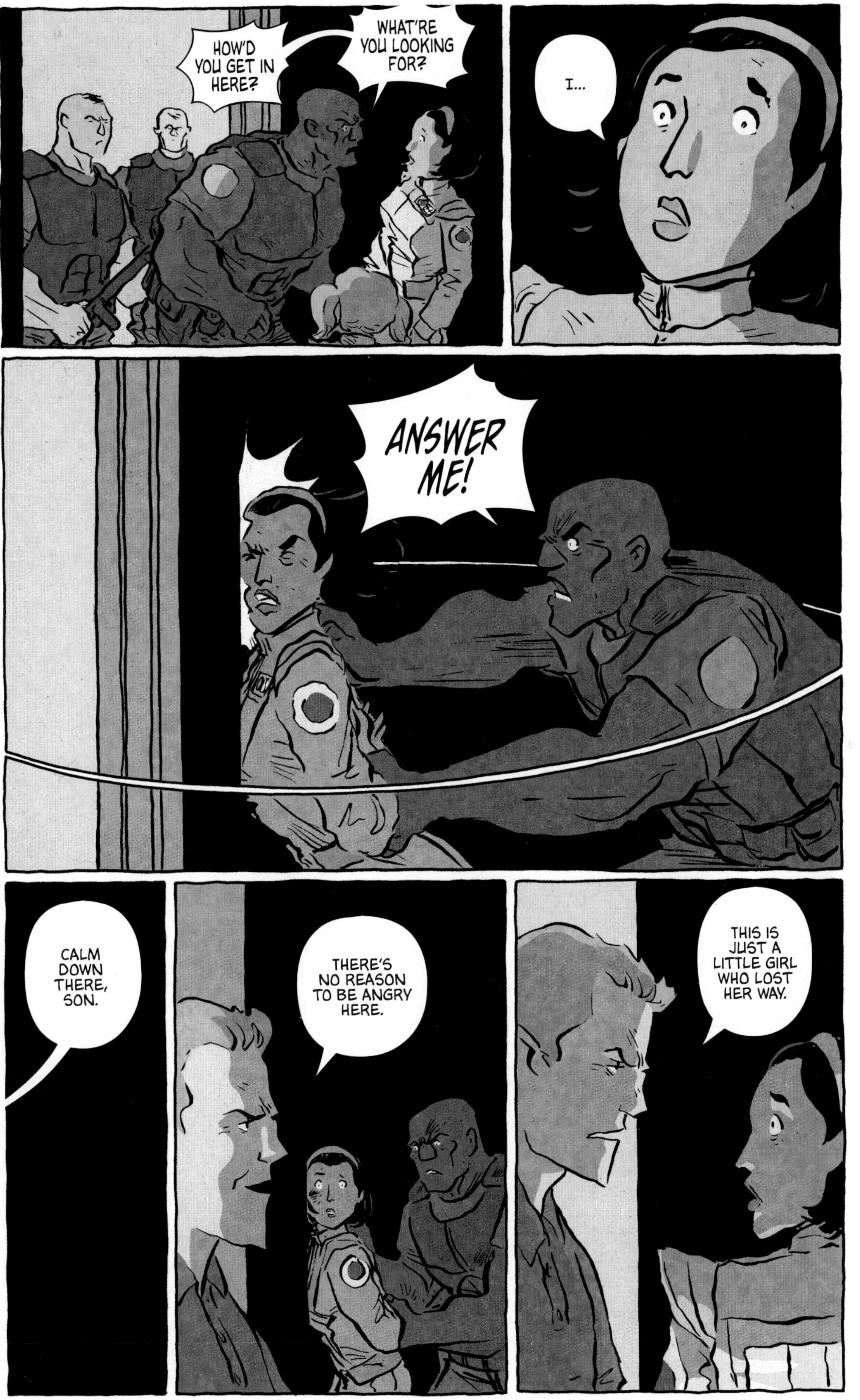
HOW'D YOU GET IN HERE?
WHAT'RE YOU LOOKING FOR?
I...
ANSWER ME!
CALM DOWN THERE, SON.
THERE'S NO REASON TO BE ANGRY HERE.
THIS IS JUST A LITTLE GIRL WHO LOST HER WAY.

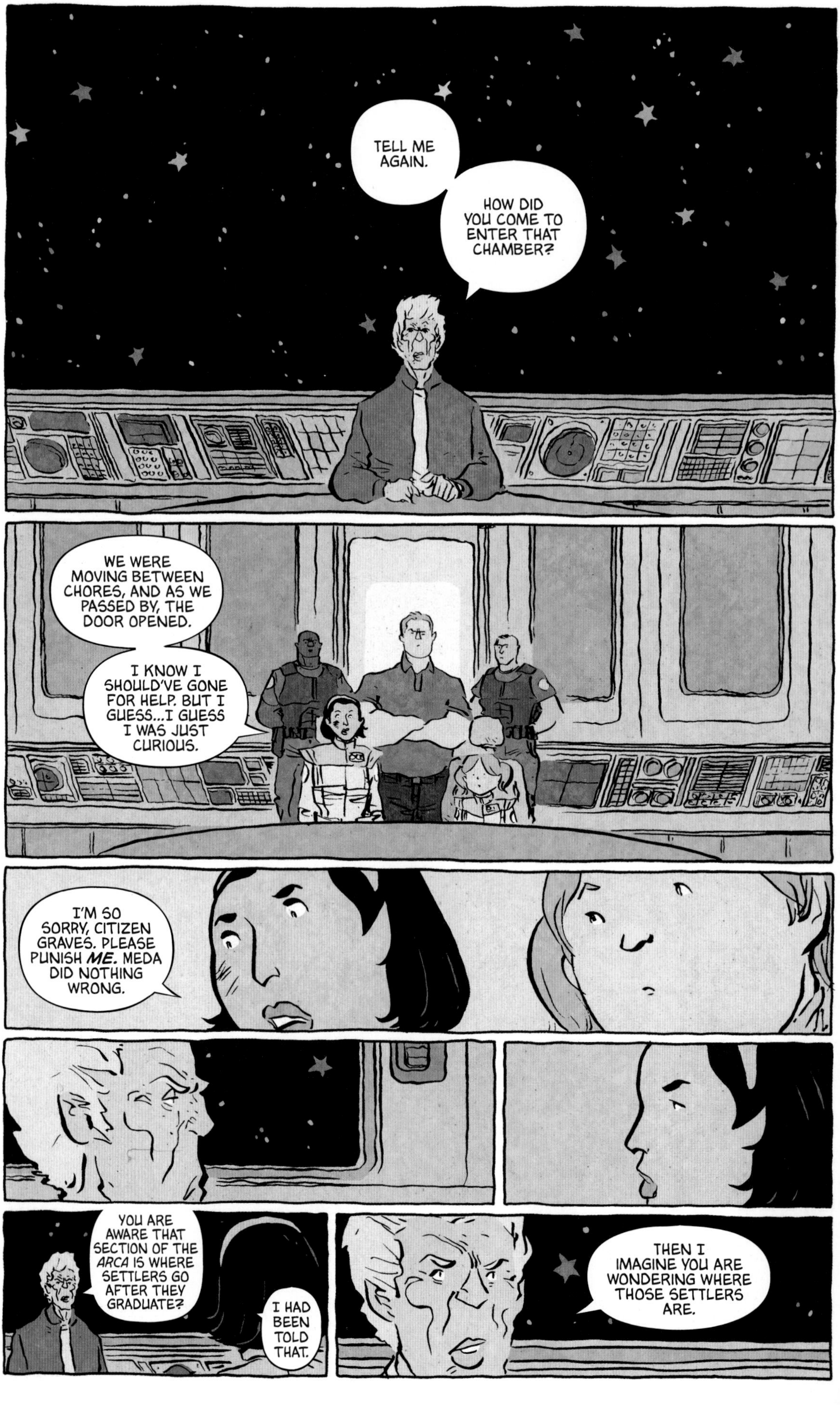
TELL ME AGAIN.
HOW DID YOU COME TO ENTER THAT CHAMBER?
WE WERE MOVING BETWEEN CHORES, AND AS WE PASSED BY, THE DOOR OPENED.
I KNOW I SHOULD'VE GONE FOR HELP. BUT I GUESS...I GUESS I WAS JUST CURIOUS.
I'M SO SORRY, CITIZEN GRAVES. PLEASE PUNISH *ME.* MEDA DID NOTHING WRONG.
YOU ARE AWARE THAT SECTION OF THE *ARCA* IS WHERE SETTLERS GO AFTER THEY GRADUATE?
I HAD BEEN TOLD THAT.
THEN I IMAGINE YOU ARE WONDERING WHERE THOSE SETTLERS ARE.

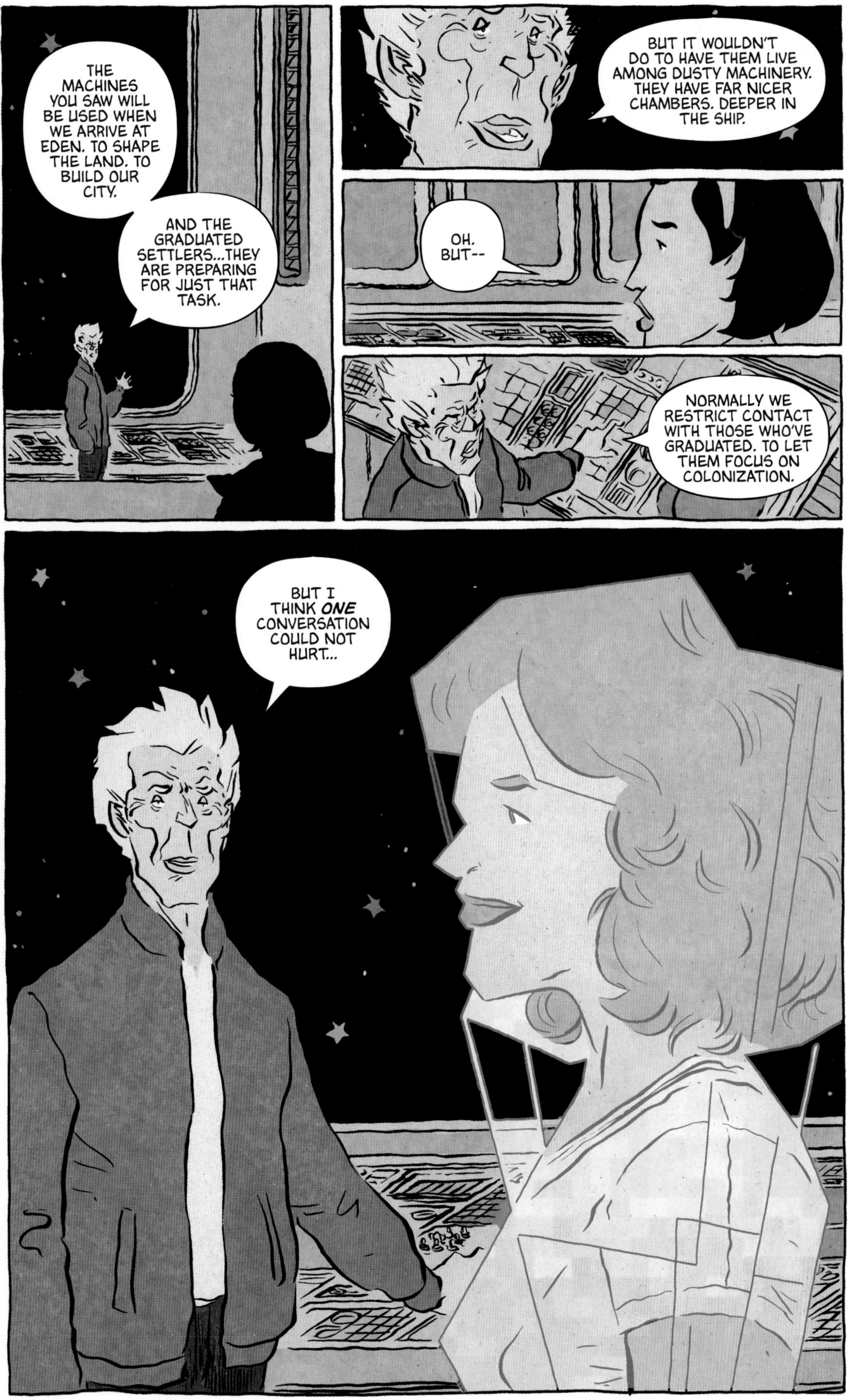
THE MACHINES YOU SAW WILL BE USED WHEN WE ARRIVE AT EDEN. TO SHAPE THE LAND. TO BUILD OUR CITY.
AND THE GRADUATED SETTLERS...THEY ARE PREPARING FOR JUST THAT TASK.
BUT IT WOULDN'T DO TO HAVE THEM LIVE AMONG DUSTY MACHINERY. THEY HAVE FAR NICER CHAMBERS. DEEPER IN THE SHIP.
OH. BUT--
NORMALLY WE RESTRICT CONTACT WITH THOSE WHO'VE GRADUATED. TO LET THEM FOCUS ON COLONIZATION.
BUT I THINK *ONE* CONVERSATION COULD NOT HURT...

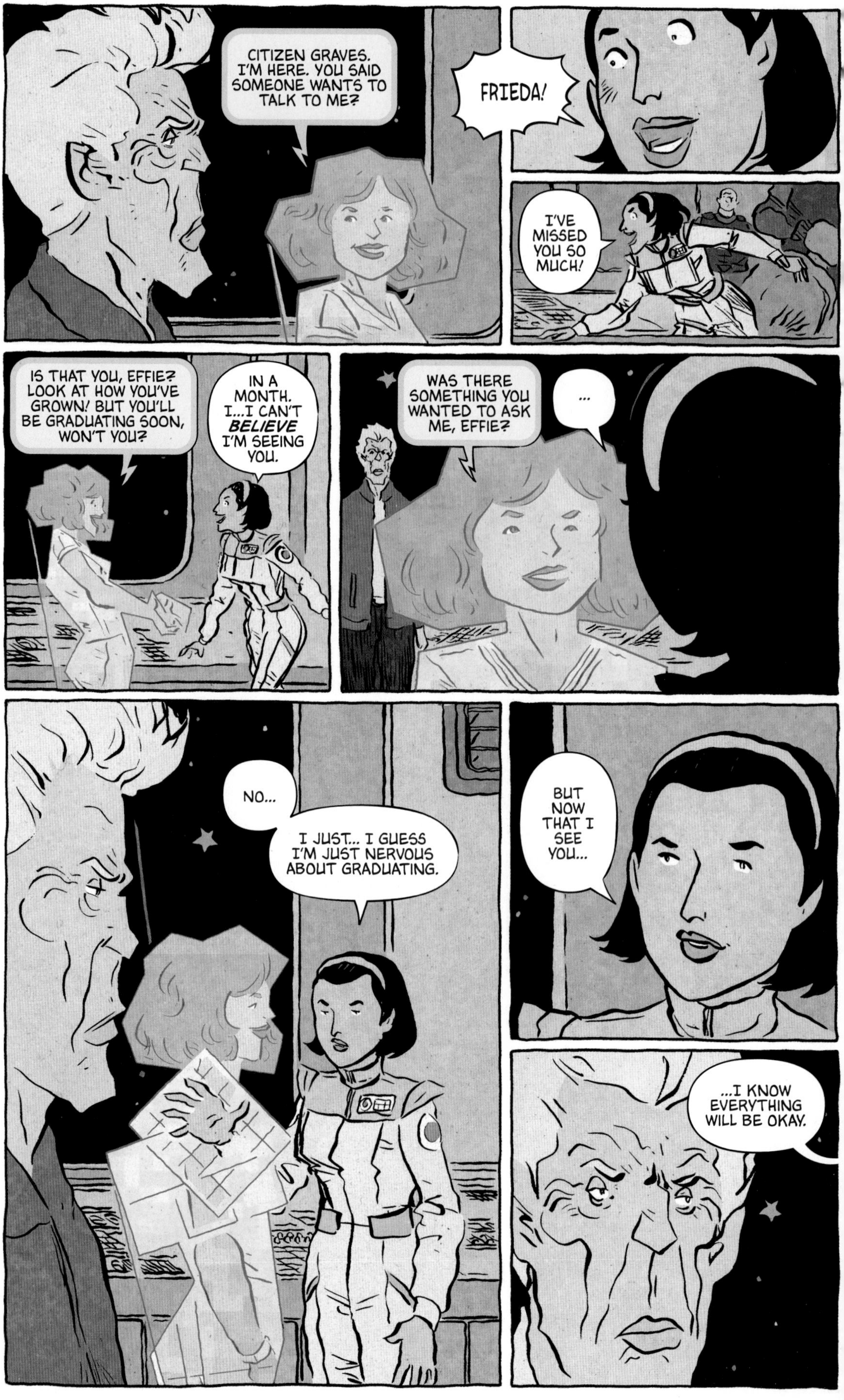
CITIZEN GRAVES. I'M HERE. YOU SAID SOMEONE WANTS TO TALK TO ME?
FRIEDA!
I'VE MISSED YOU SO MUCH!
IS THAT YOU, EFFIE? LOOK AT HOW YOU'VE GROWN! BUT YOU'LL BE GRADUATING SOON, WON'T YOU?
IN A MONTH. I...I CAN'T BELIEVE I'M SEEING YOU.
WAS THERE SOMETHING YOU WANTED TO ASK ME, EFFIE?
...
NO...
I JUST... I GUESS I'M JUST NERVOUS ABOUT GRADUATING.
BUT NOW THAT I SEE YOU...
...I KNOW EVERYTHING WILL BE OKAY.

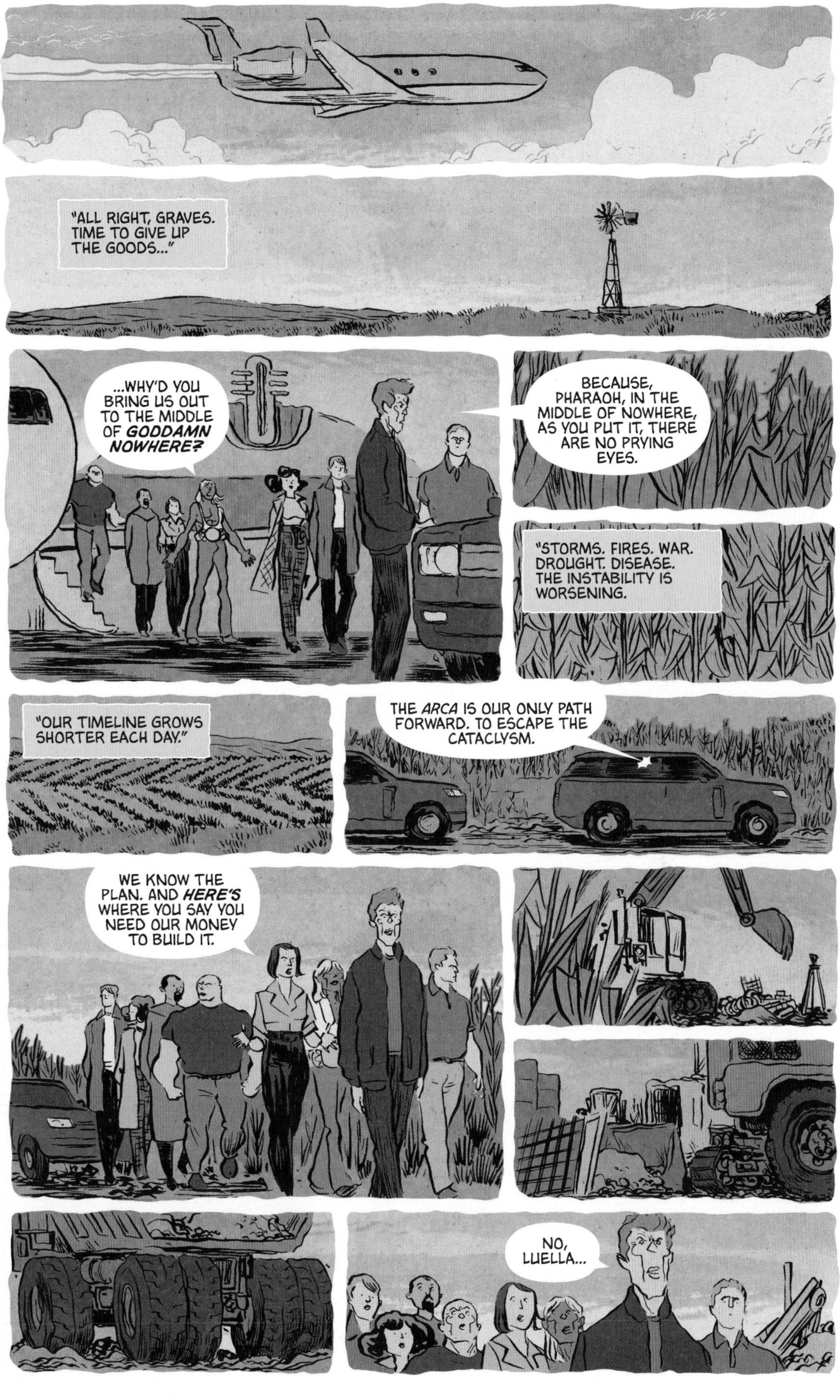
"ALL RIGHT, GRAVES. TIME TO GIVE UP THE GOODS..."
...WHY'D YOU BRING US OUT TO THE MIDDLE OF *GODDAMN NOWHERE?*
BECAUSE, PHARAOH, IN THE MIDDLE OF NOWHERE, AS YOU PUT IT, THERE ARE NO PRYING EYES.
"STORMS. FIRES. WAR. DROUGHT. DISEASE. THE INSTABILITY IS WORSENING.
"OUR TIMELINE GROWS SHORTER EACH DAY."
THE *ARCA* IS OUR ONLY PATH FORWARD. TO ESCAPE THE CATACLYSM.
WE KNOW THE PLAN. AND *HERE'S* WHERE YOU SAY YOU NEED OUR MONEY TO BUILD IT.
NO, LUELLA...

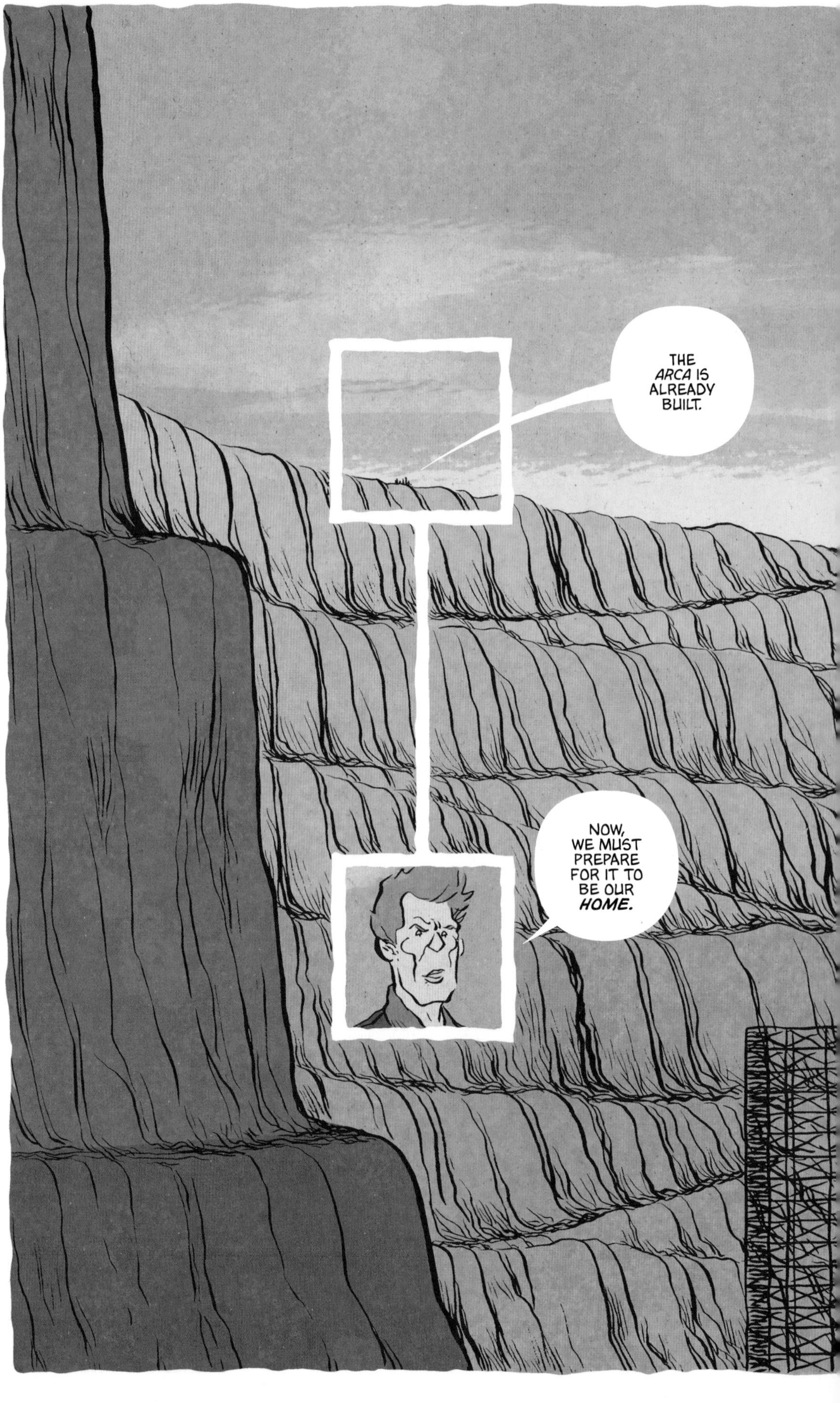
THE *ARCA* IS ALREADY BUILT.
NOW, WE MUST PREPARE FOR IT TO BE OUR ***HOME.***

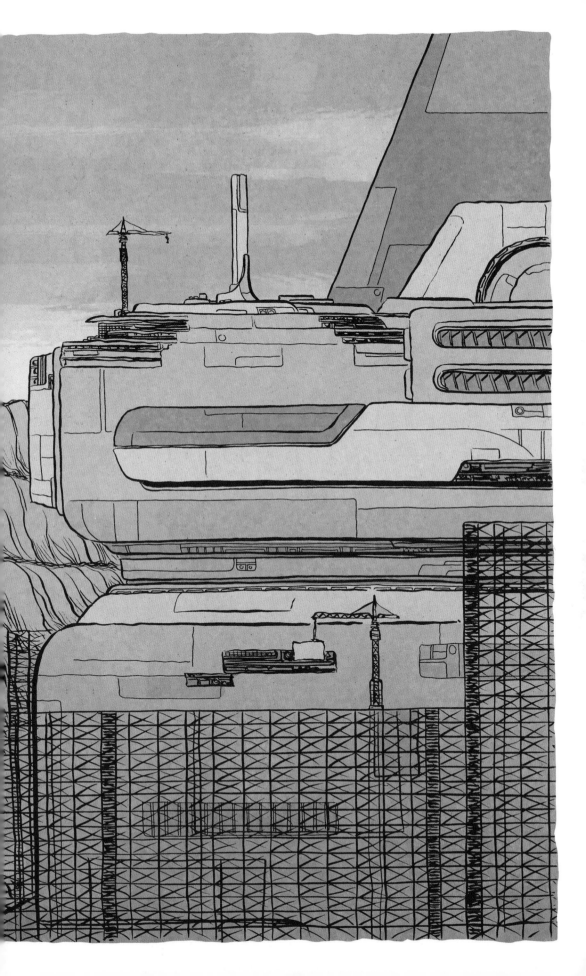

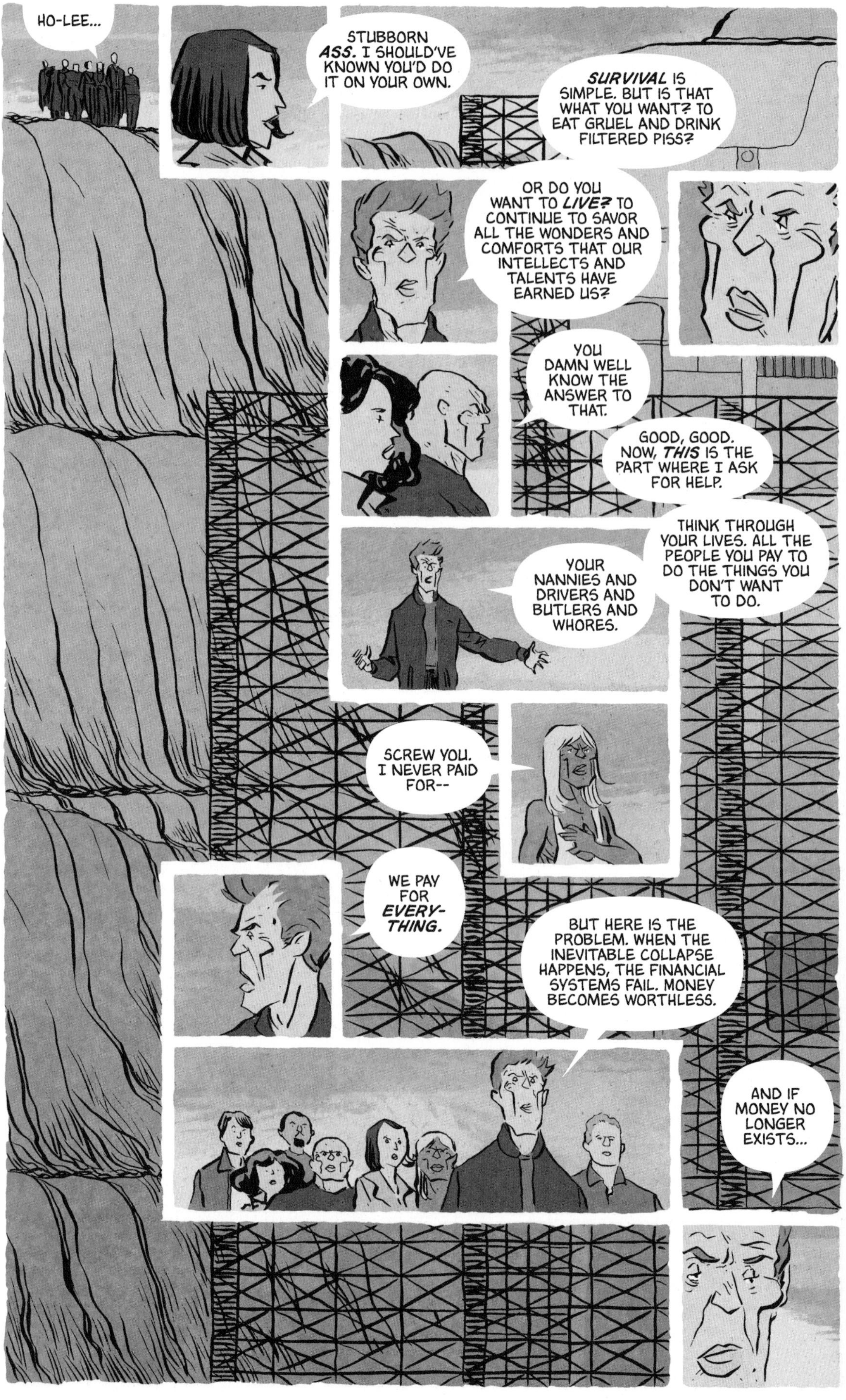
HO-LEE...
STUBBORN ASS. I SHOULD'VE KNOWN YOU'D DO IT ON YOUR OWN.
SURVIVAL IS SIMPLE. BUT IS THAT WHAT YOU WANT? TO EAT GRUEL AND DRINK FILTERED PISS?
OR DO YOU WANT TO LIVE? TO CONTINUE TO SAVOR ALL THE WONDERS AND COMFORTS THAT OUR INTELLECTS AND TALENTS HAVE EARNED US?
YOU DAMN WELL KNOW THE ANSWER TO THAT.
GOOD, GOOD. NOW, THIS IS THE PART WHERE I ASK FOR HELP.
THINK THROUGH YOUR LIVES. ALL THE PEOPLE YOU PAY TO DO THE THINGS YOU DON'T WANT TO DO.
YOUR NANNIES AND DRIVERS AND BUTLERS AND WHORES.
SCREW YOU. I NEVER PAID FOR--
WE PAY FOR EVERYTHING.
BUT HERE IS THE PROBLEM. WHEN THE INEVITABLE COLLAPSE HAPPENS, THE FINANCIAL SYSTEMS FAIL. MONEY BECOMES WORTHLESS.
AND IF MONEY NO LONGER EXISTS...

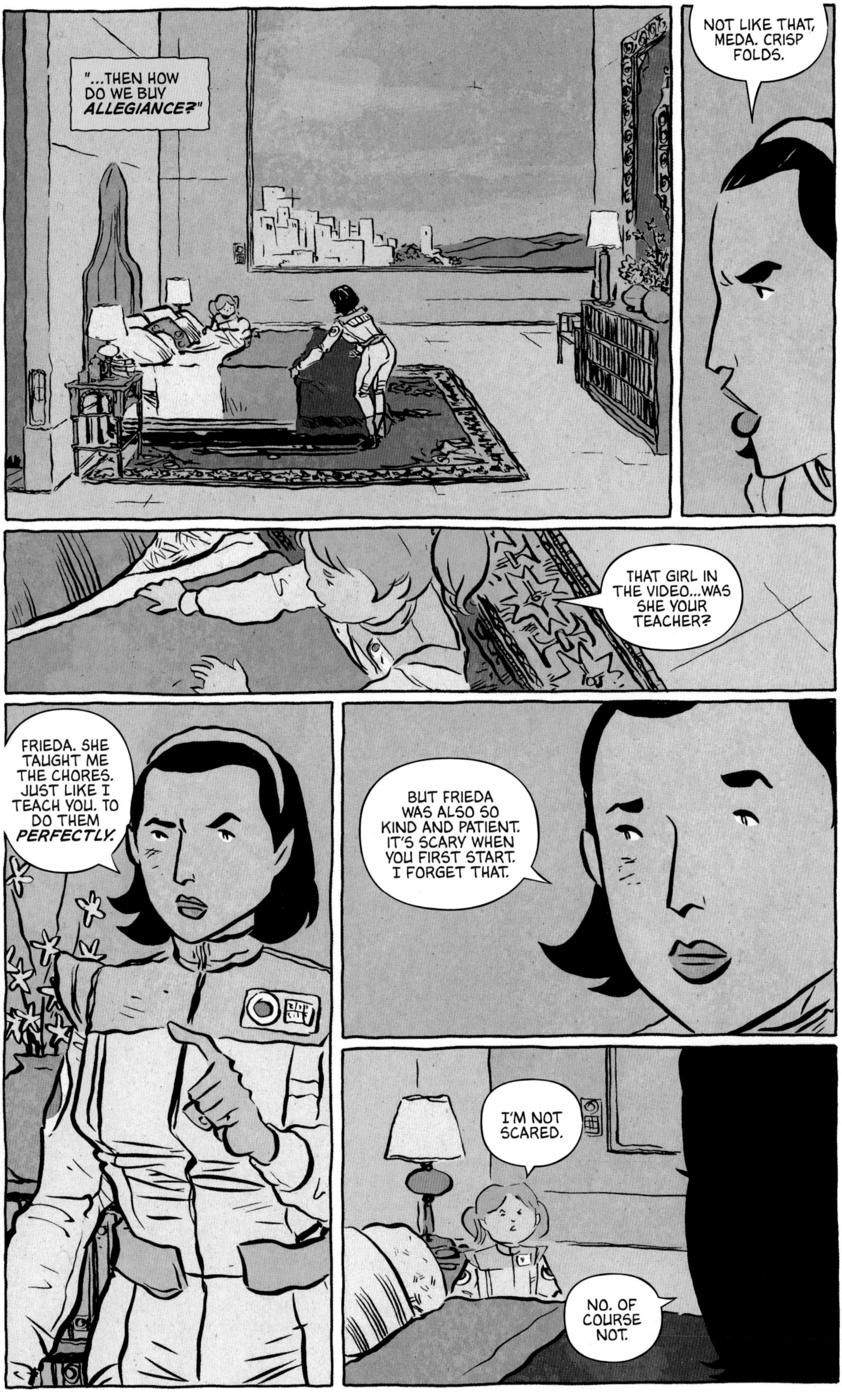
"...THEN HOW DO WE BUY *ALLEGIANCE?*"
NOT LIKE THAT, MEDA. CRISP FOLDS.
THAT GIRL IN THE VIDEO...WAS SHE YOUR TEACHER?
FRIEDA. SHE TAUGHT ME THE CHORES. JUST LIKE I TEACH YOU. TO DO THEM *PERFECTLY.*
BUT FRIEDA WAS ALSO SO KIND AND PATIENT. IT'S SCARY WHEN YOU FIRST START. I FORGET THAT.
I'M NOT SCARED.
NO. OF COURSE NOT.

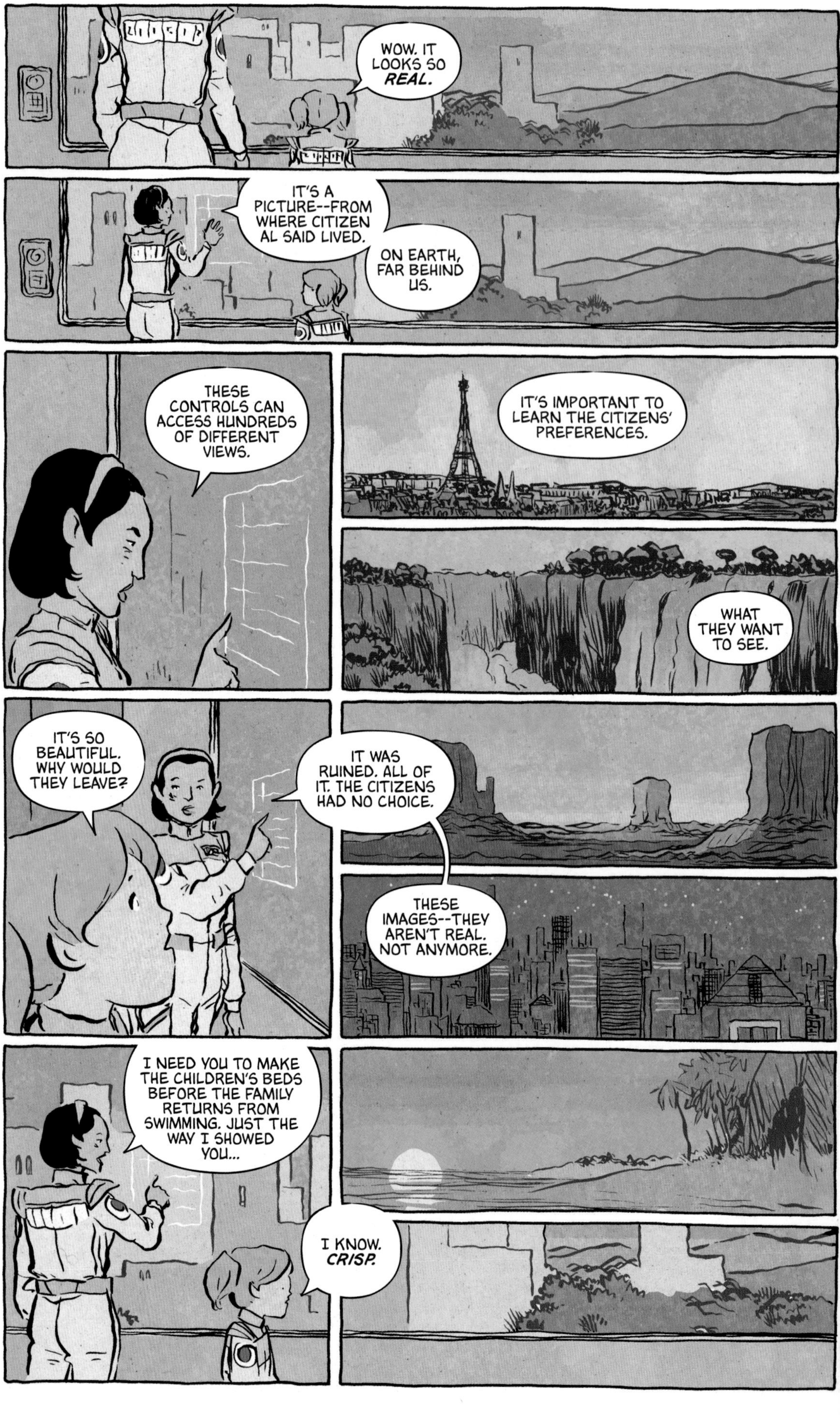

WOW. IT LOOKS SO *REAL.*
IT'S A PICTURE--FROM WHERE CITIZEN AL SAID LIVED.
ON EARTH, FAR BEHIND US.
THESE CONTROLS CAN ACCESS HUNDREDS OF DIFFERENT VIEWS.
IT'S IMPORTANT TO LEARN THE CITIZENS' PREFERENCES.
WHAT THEY WANT TO SEE.
IT'S SO BEAUTIFUL. WHY WOULD THEY LEAVE?
IT WAS RUINED. ALL OF IT. THE CITIZENS HAD NO CHOICE.
THESE IMAGES--THEY AREN'T REAL. NOT ANYMORE.
I NEED YOU TO MAKE THE CHILDREN'S BEDS BEFORE THE FAMILY RETURNS FROM SWIMMING. JUST THE WAY I SHOWED YOU...
I KNOW. *CRISP.*

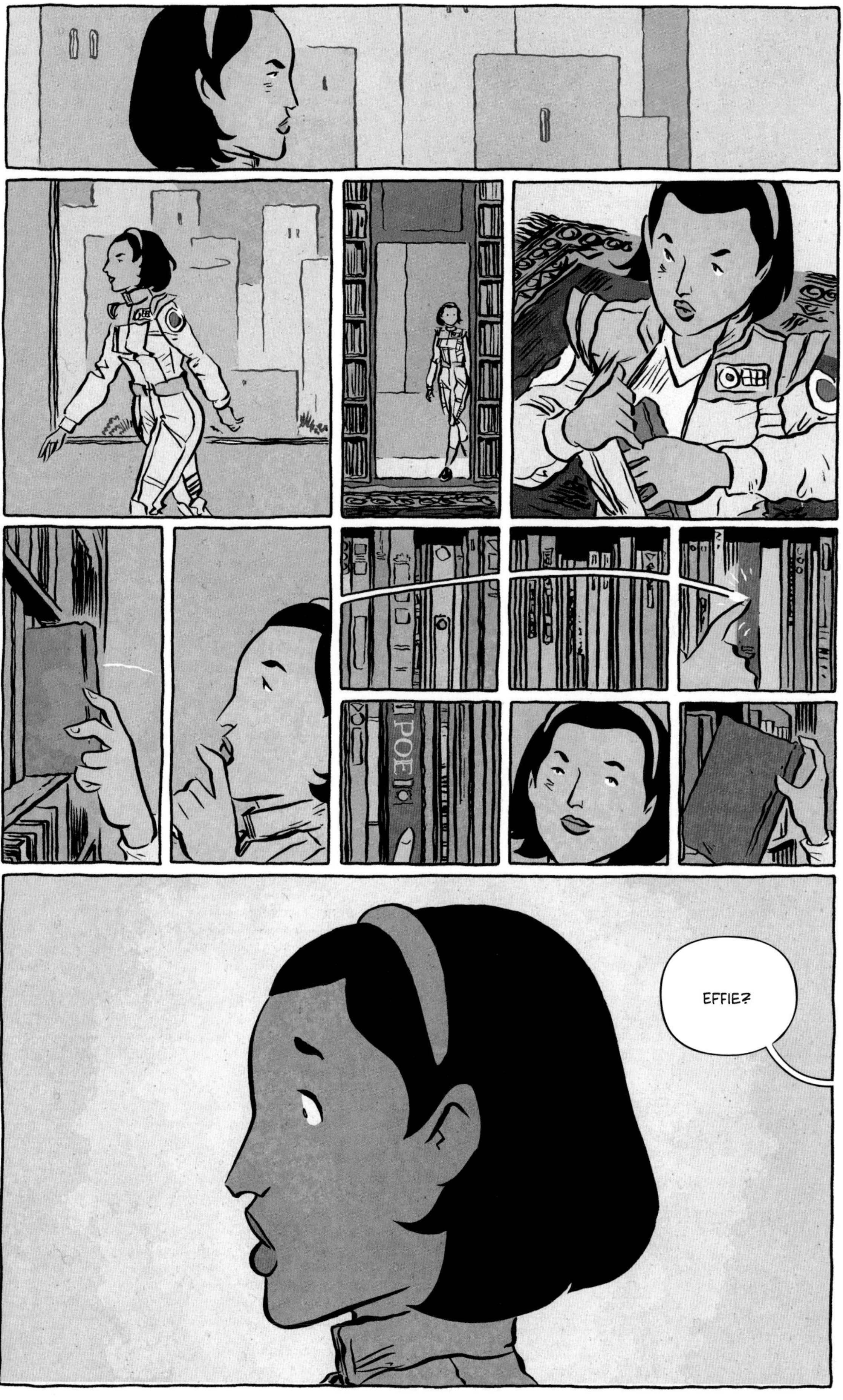
POE
EFFIE?

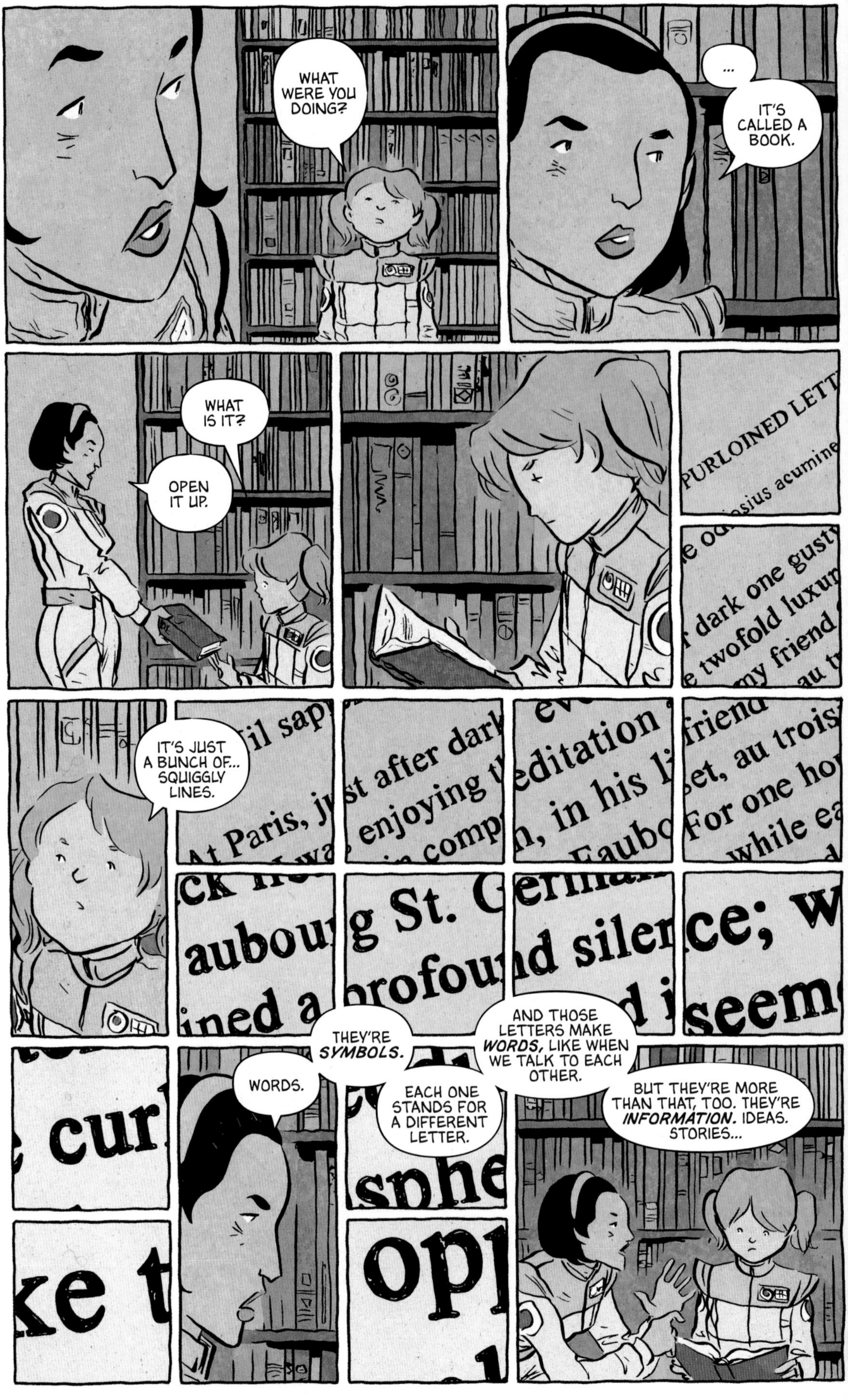
WHAT WERE YOU DOING?
...
IT'S CALLED A BOOK.
WHAT IS IT?
OPEN IT UP.
IT'S JUST A BUNCH OF... SQUIGGLY LINES.
WORDS.
THEY'RE *SYMBOLS.*
EACH ONE STANDS FOR A DIFFERENT LETTER.
AND THOSE LETTERS MAKE *WORDS,* LIKE WHEN WE TALK TO EACH OTHER.
BUT THEY'RE MORE THAN THAT, TOO. THEY'RE *INFORMATION.* IDEAS. STORIES...

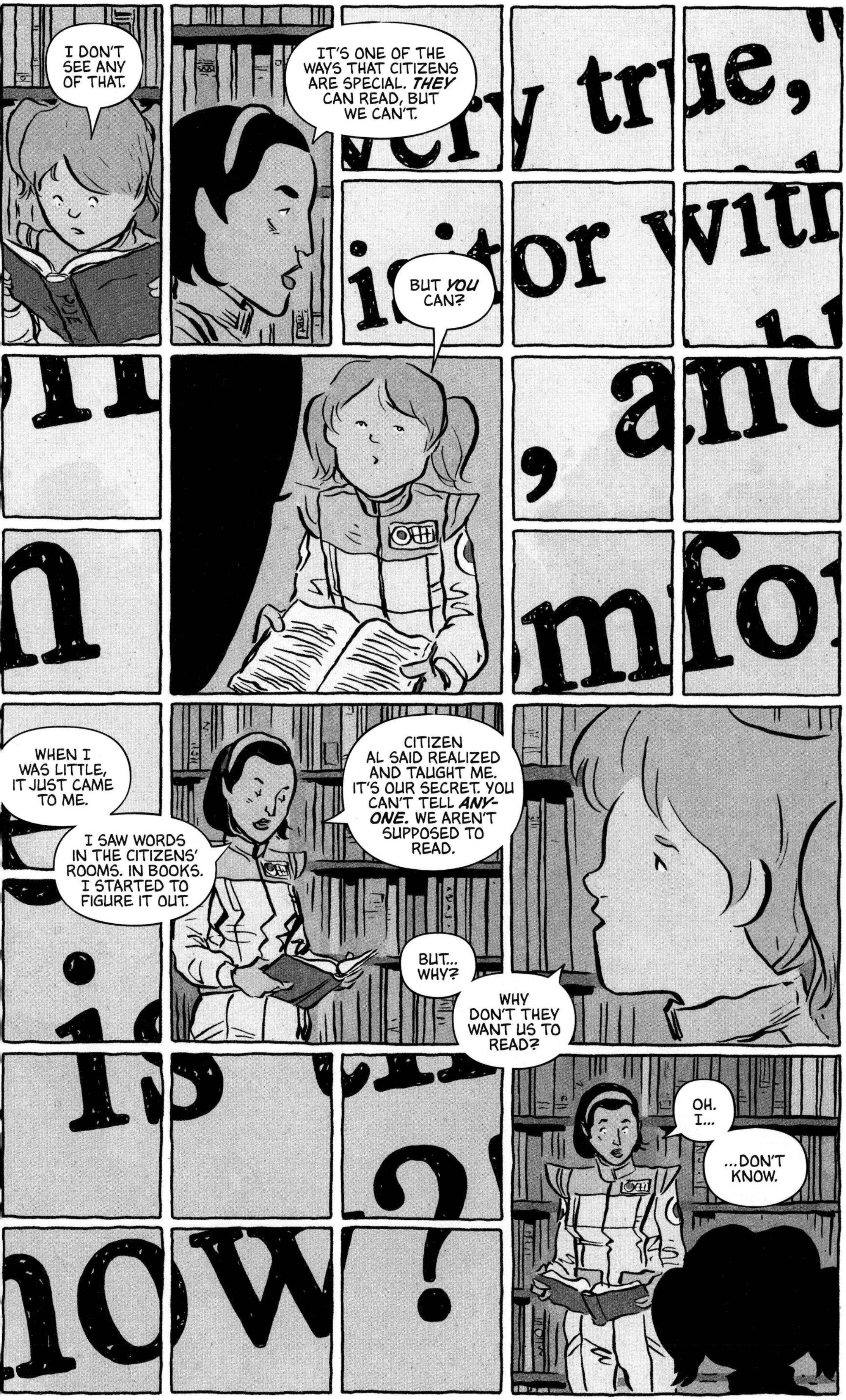
I DON'T SEE ANY OF THAT.
IT'S ONE OF THE WAYS THAT CITIZENS ARE SPECIAL. *THEY* CAN READ, BUT WE CAN'T.
very true,
or with
BUT *YOU* CAN?
, and
mfo
WHEN I WAS LITTLE, IT JUST CAME TO ME.
I SAW WORDS IN THE CITIZENS' ROOMS. IN BOOKS. I STARTED TO FIGURE IT OUT.
CITIZEN AL SAID REALIZED AND TAUGHT ME. IT'S OUR SECRET. YOU CAN'T TELL *ANYONE*. WE AREN'T SUPPOSED TO READ.
BUT... WHY?
WHY DON'T THEY WANT US TO READ?
OH. I...
...DON'T KNOW.
?
now?

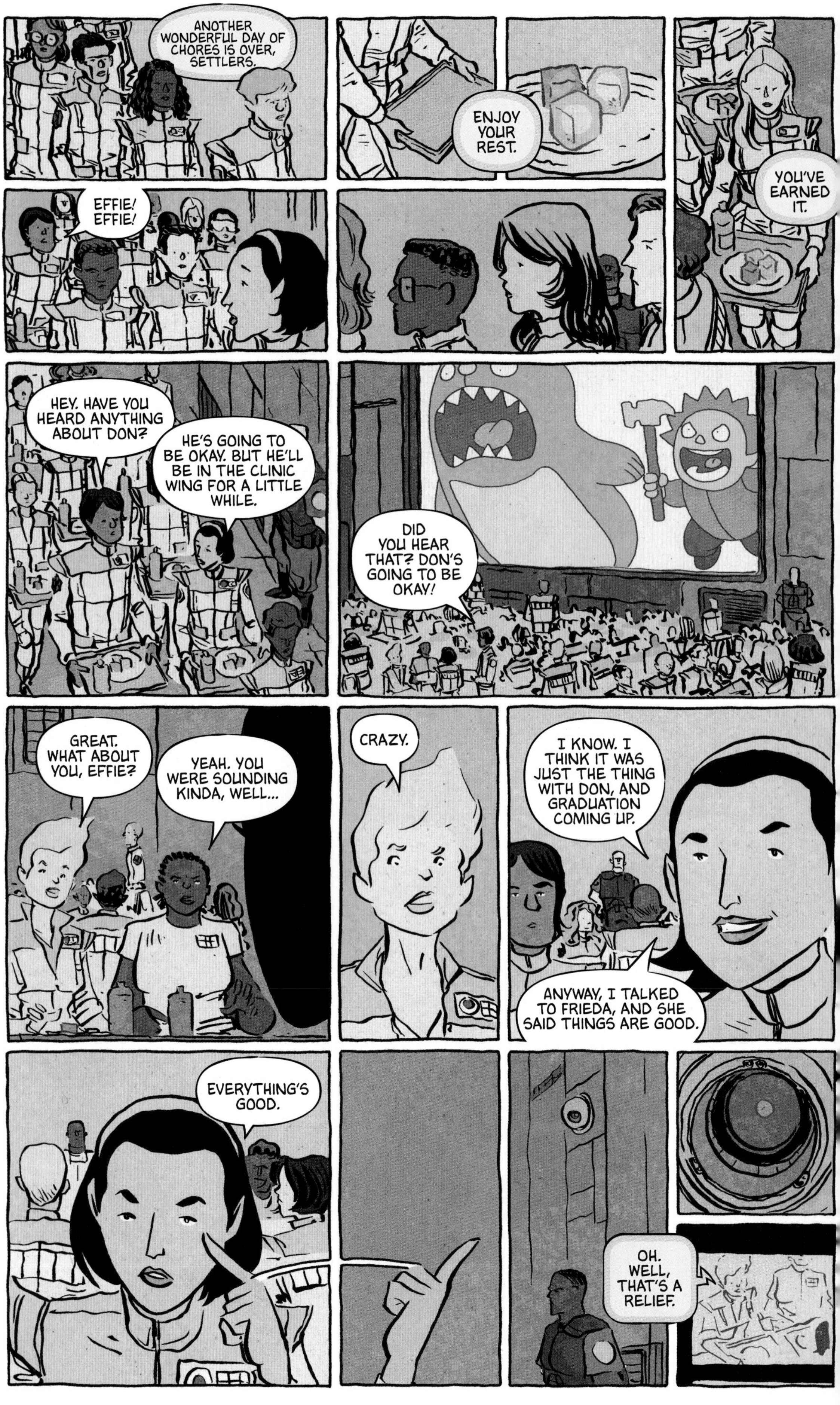

ANOTHER WONDERFUL DAY OF CHORES IS OVER, SETTLERS.
ENJOY YOUR REST.
YOU'VE EARNED IT.
EFFIE! EFFIE!
HEY. HAVE YOU HEARD ANYTHING ABOUT DON?
HE'S GOING TO BE OKAY. BUT HE'LL BE IN THE CLINIC WING FOR A LITTLE WHILE.
DID YOU HEAR THAT? DON'S GOING TO BE OKAY!
GREAT. WHAT ABOUT YOU, EFFIE?
YEAH. YOU WERE SOUNDING KINDA, WELL...
CRAZY.
I KNOW. I THINK IT WAS JUST THE THING WITH DON, AND GRADUATION COMING UP.
ANYWAY, I TALKED TO FRIEDA, AND SHE SAID THINGS ARE GOOD.
EVERYTHING'S GOOD.
OH. WELL, THAT'S A RELIEF.

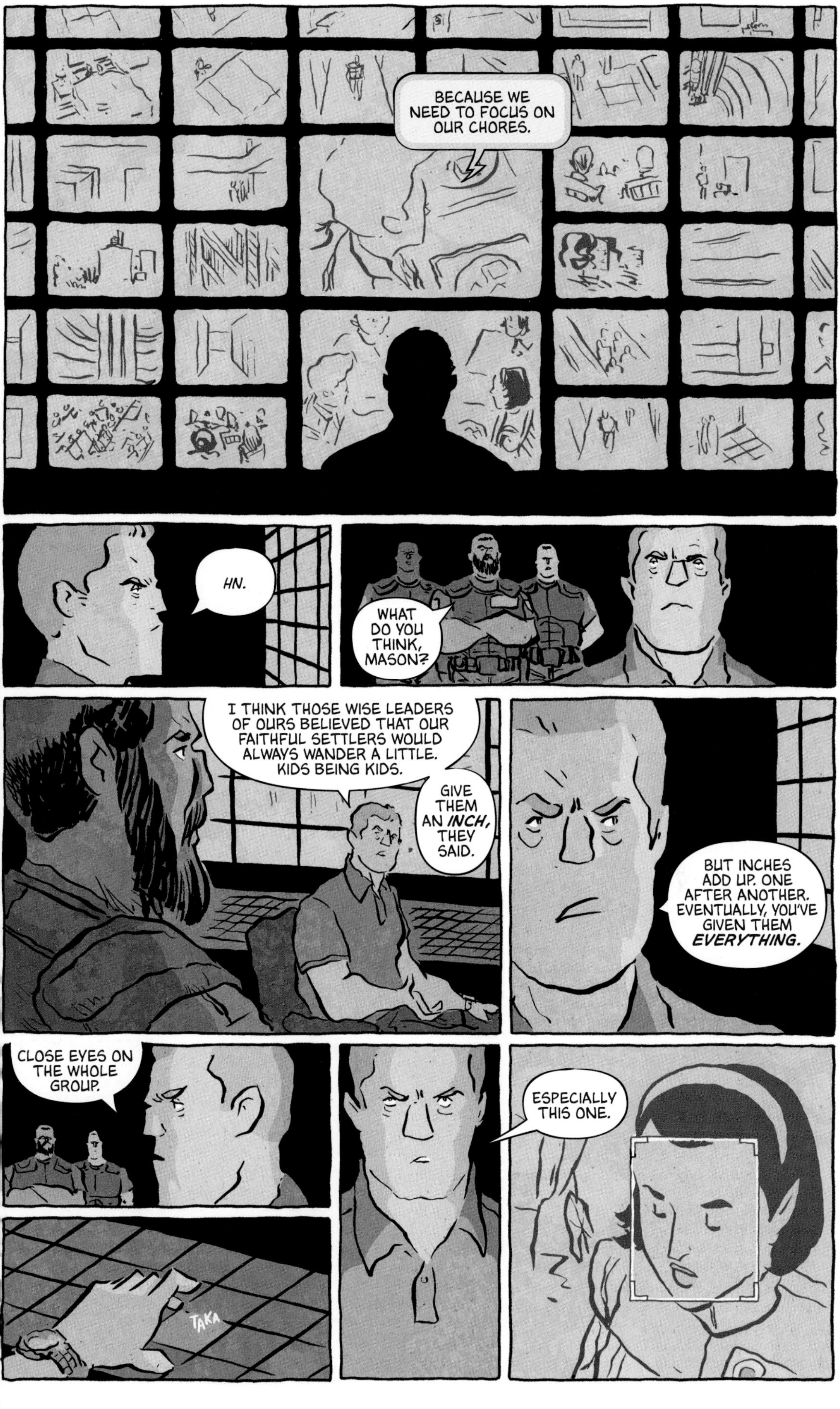
BECAUSE WE NEED TO FOCUS ON OUR CHORES.
HN.
WHAT DO YOU THINK, MASON?
I THINK THOSE WISE LEADERS OF OURS BELIEVED THAT OUR FAITHFUL SETTLERS WOULD ALWAYS WANDER A LITTLE. KIDS BEING KIDS.
GIVE THEM AN *INCH,* THEY SAID.
BUT INCHES ADD UP. ONE AFTER ANOTHER. EVENTUALLY, YOU'VE GIVEN THEM ***EVERYTHING.***
CLOSE EYES ON THE WHOLE GROUP.
TAKA
ESPECIALLY THIS ONE.

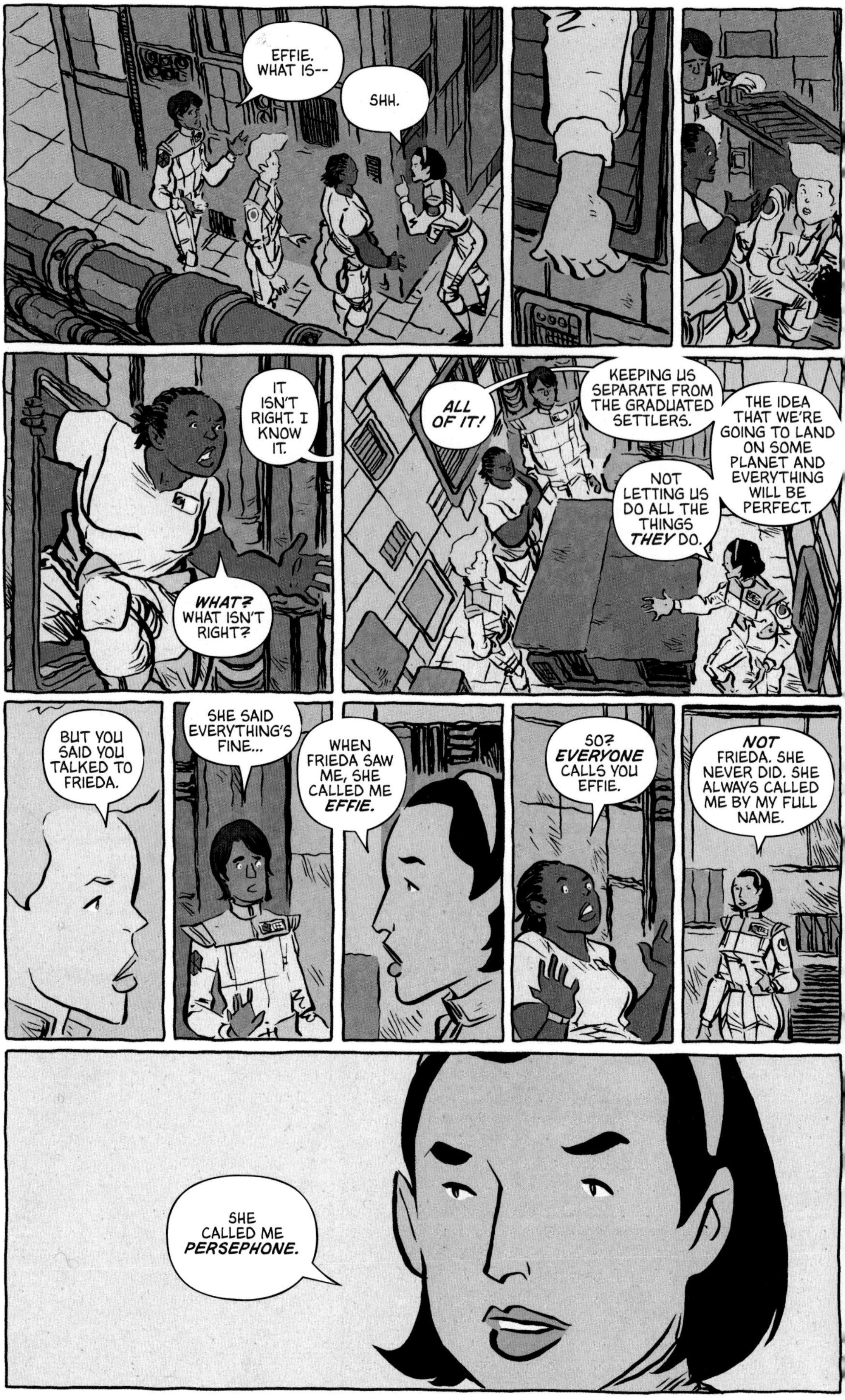
EFFIE. WHAT IS--
SHH.
IT ISN'T RIGHT. I KNOW IT.
WHAT? WHAT ISN'T RIGHT?
ALL OF IT!
KEEPING US SEPARATE FROM THE GRADUATED SETTLERS.
NOT LETTING US DO ALL THE THINGS THEY DO.
THE IDEA THAT WE'RE GOING TO LAND ON SOME PLANET AND EVERYTHING WILL BE PERFECT.
BUT YOU SAID YOU TALKED TO FRIEDA.
SHE SAID EVERYTHING'S FINE...
WHEN FRIEDA SAW ME, SHE CALLED ME EFFIE.
SO? EVERYONE CALLS YOU EFFIE.
NOT FRIEDA. SHE NEVER DID. SHE ALWAYS CALLED ME BY MY FULL NAME.
SHE CALLED ME PERSEPHONE.

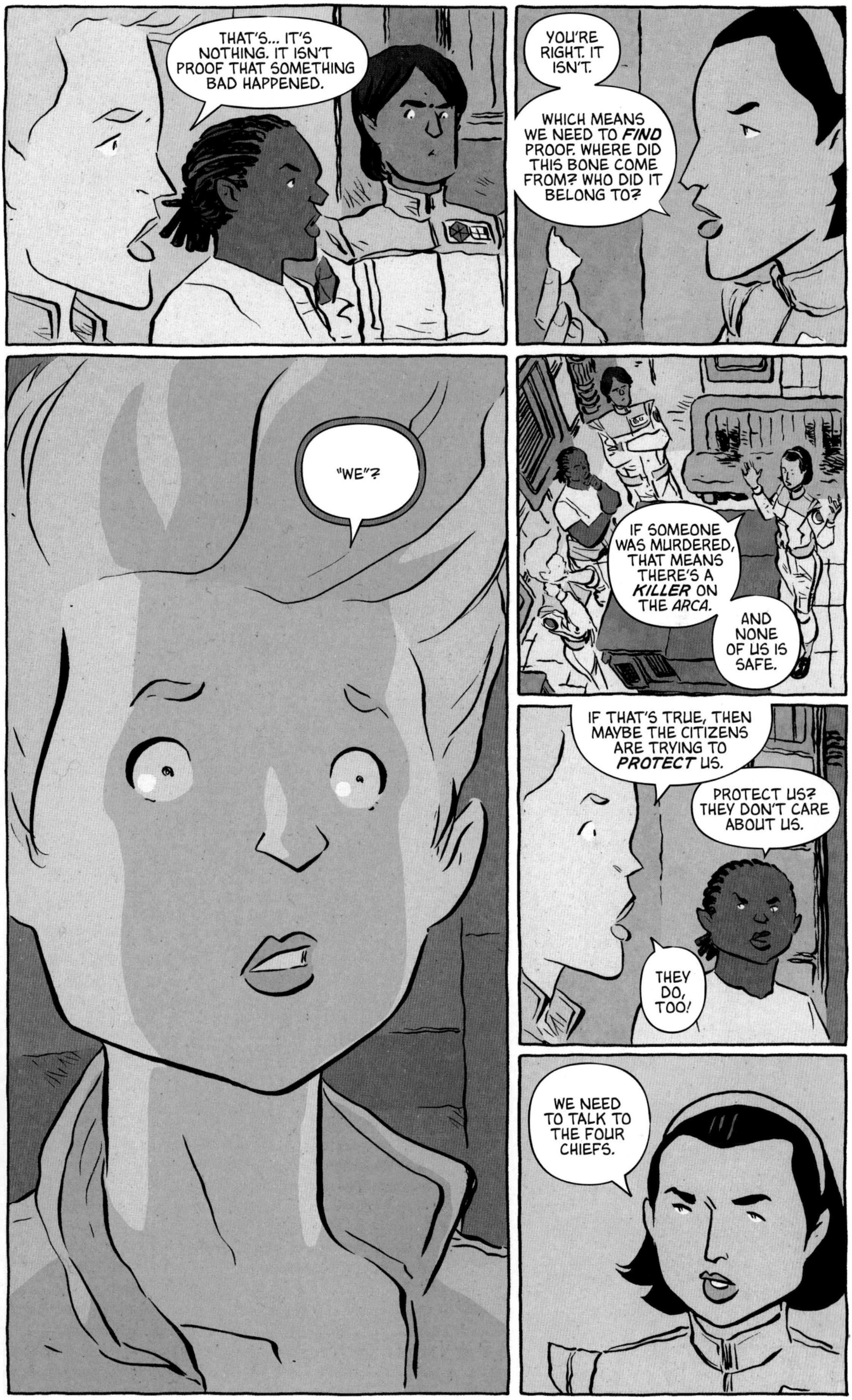
THAT'S... IT'S NOTHING. IT ISN'T PROOF THAT SOMETHING BAD HAPPENED.
YOU'RE RIGHT. IT ISN'T.
WHICH MEANS WE NEED TO *FIND* PROOF. WHERE DID THIS BONE COME FROM? WHO DID IT BELONG TO?
"WE"?
IF SOMEONE WAS MURDERED, THAT MEANS THERE'S A *KILLER* ON THE *ARCA*.
AND NONE OF US IS SAFE.
IF THAT'S TRUE, THEN MAYBE THE CITIZENS ARE TRYING TO *PROTECT* US.
PROTECT US? THEY DON'T CARE ABOUT US.
THEY DO, TOO!
WE NEED TO TALK TO THE FOUR CHIEFS.

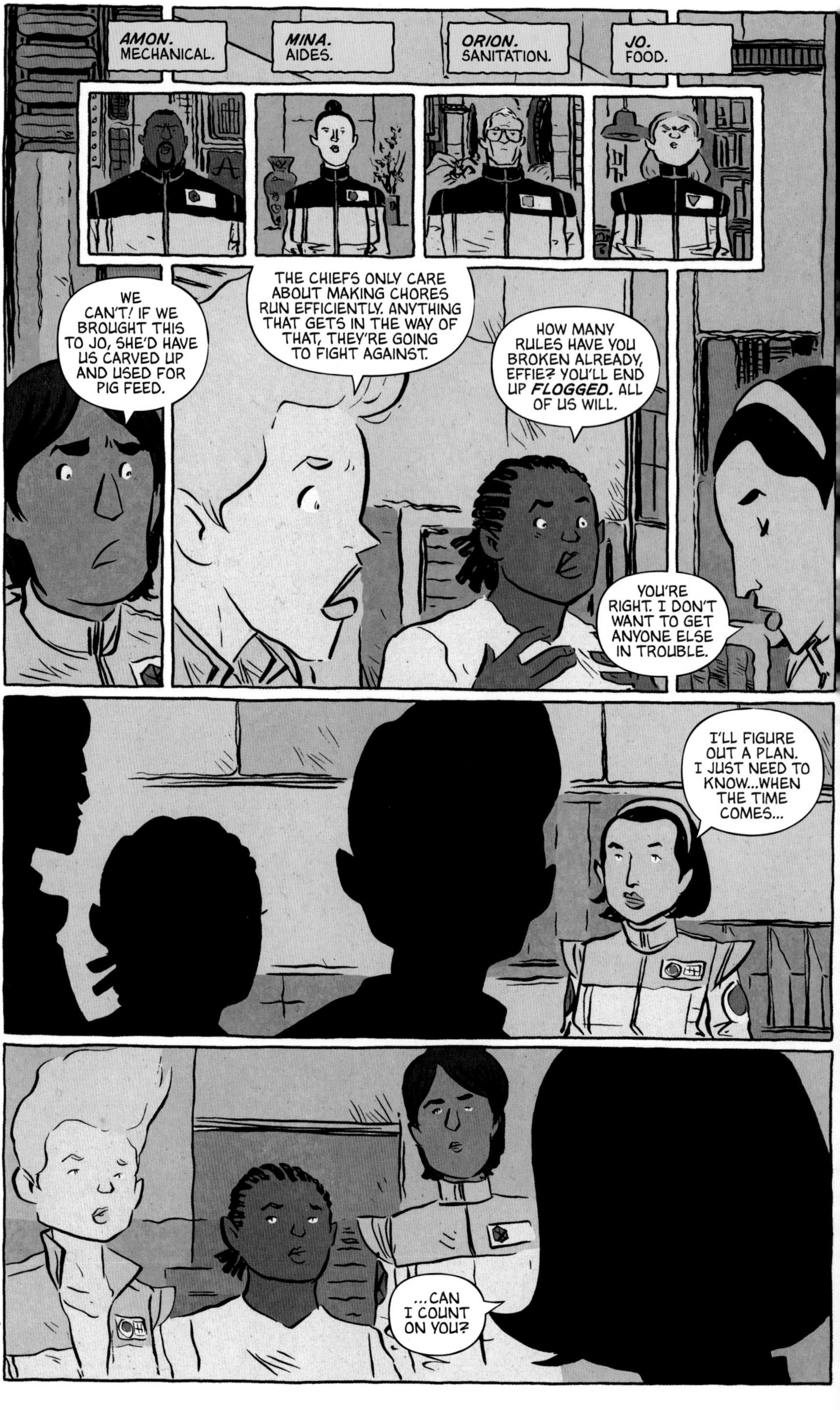
AMON. MECHANICAL.
MINA. AIDES.
ORION. SANITATION.
JO. FOOD.
WE CAN'T! IF WE BROUGHT THIS TO JO, SHE'D HAVE US CARVED UP AND USED FOR PIG FEED.
THE CHIEFS ONLY CARE ABOUT MAKING CHORES RUN EFFICIENTLY. ANYTHING THAT GETS IN THE WAY OF THAT, THEY'RE GOING TO FIGHT AGAINST.
HOW MANY RULES HAVE YOU BROKEN ALREADY, EFFIE? YOU'LL END UP FLOGGED. ALL OF US WILL.
YOU'RE RIGHT. I DON'T WANT TO GET ANYONE ELSE IN TROUBLE.
I'LL FIGURE OUT A PLAN. I JUST NEED TO KNOW...WHEN THE TIME COMES...
...CAN I COUNT ON YOU?

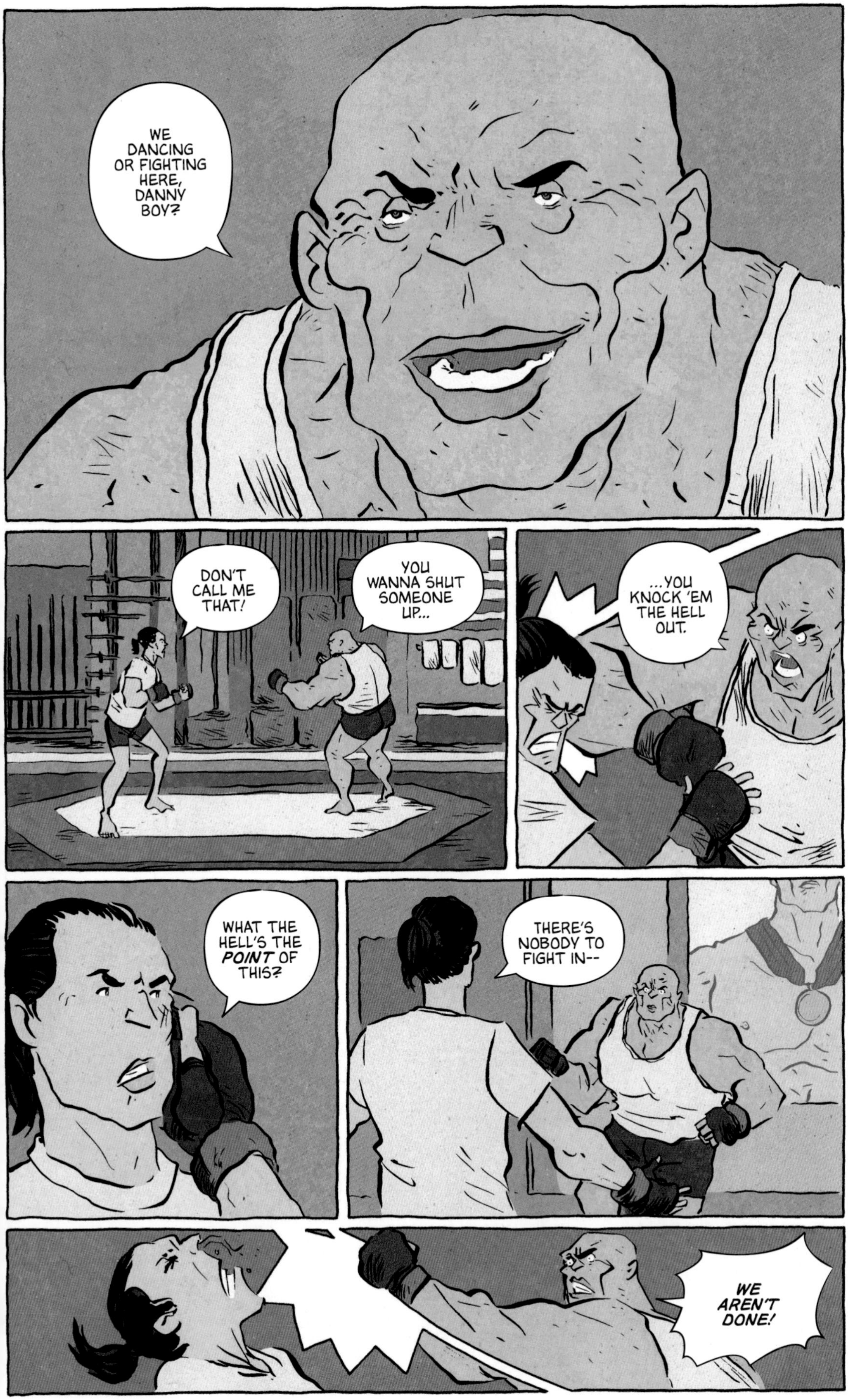
WE DANCING OR FIGHTING HERE, DANNY BOY?
DON'T CALL ME THAT!
YOU WANNA SHUT SOMEONE UP...
...YOU KNOCK 'EM THE HELL OUT.
WHAT THE HELL'S THE *POINT* OF THIS?
THERE'S NOBODY TO FIGHT IN--
WE AREN'T DONE!

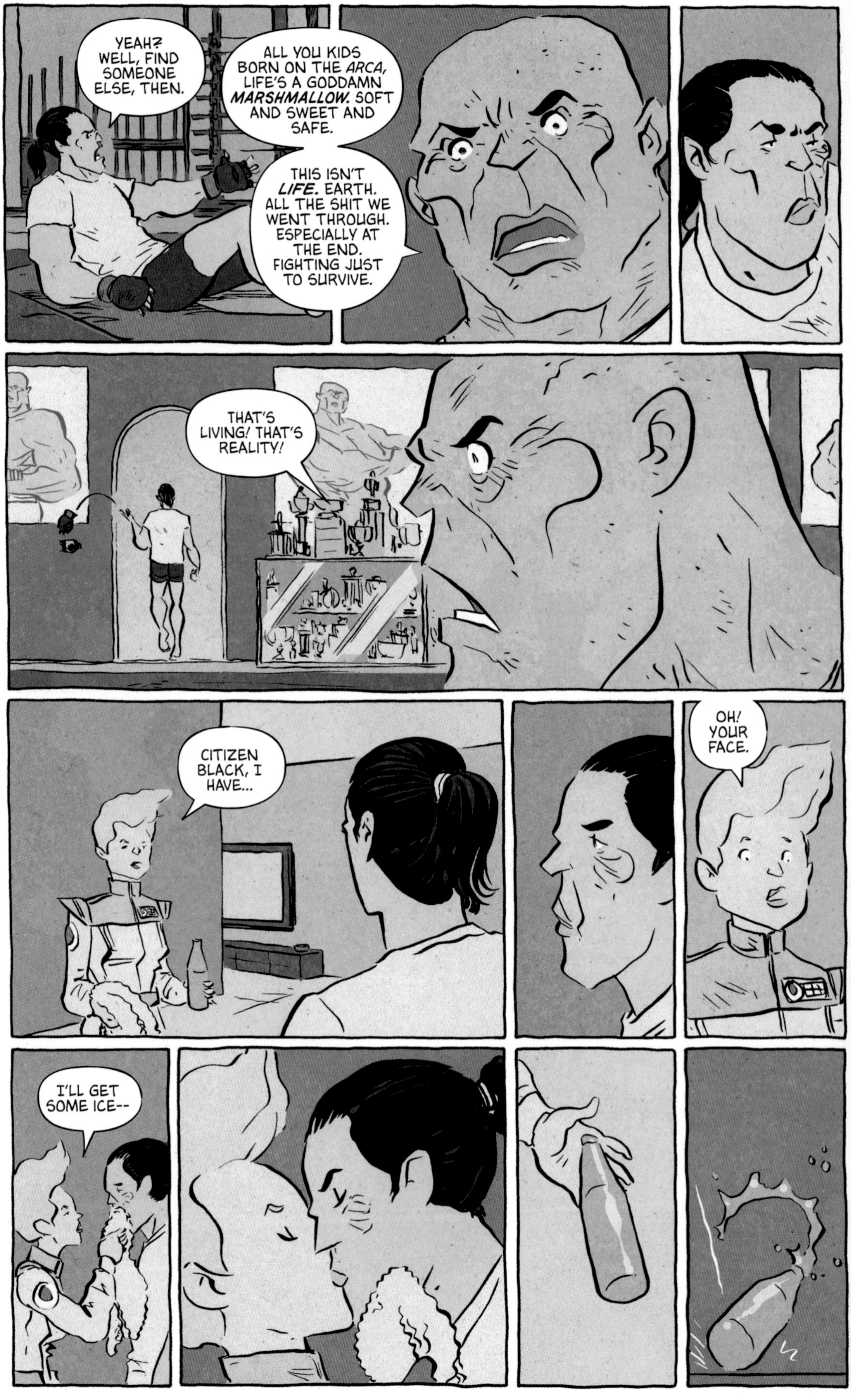

YEAH? WELL, FIND SOMEONE ELSE, THEN.
ALL YOU KIDS BORN ON THE *ARCA*, LIFE'S A GODDAMN ***MARSHMALLOW.*** SOFT AND SWEET AND SAFE.
THIS ISN'T ***LIFE.*** EARTH. ALL THE SHIT WE WENT THROUGH. ESPECIALLY AT THE END. FIGHTING JUST TO SURVIVE.
THAT'S LIVING! THAT'S REALITY!
CITIZEN BLACK, I HAVE...
OH! YOUR FACE.
I'LL GET SOME ICE--

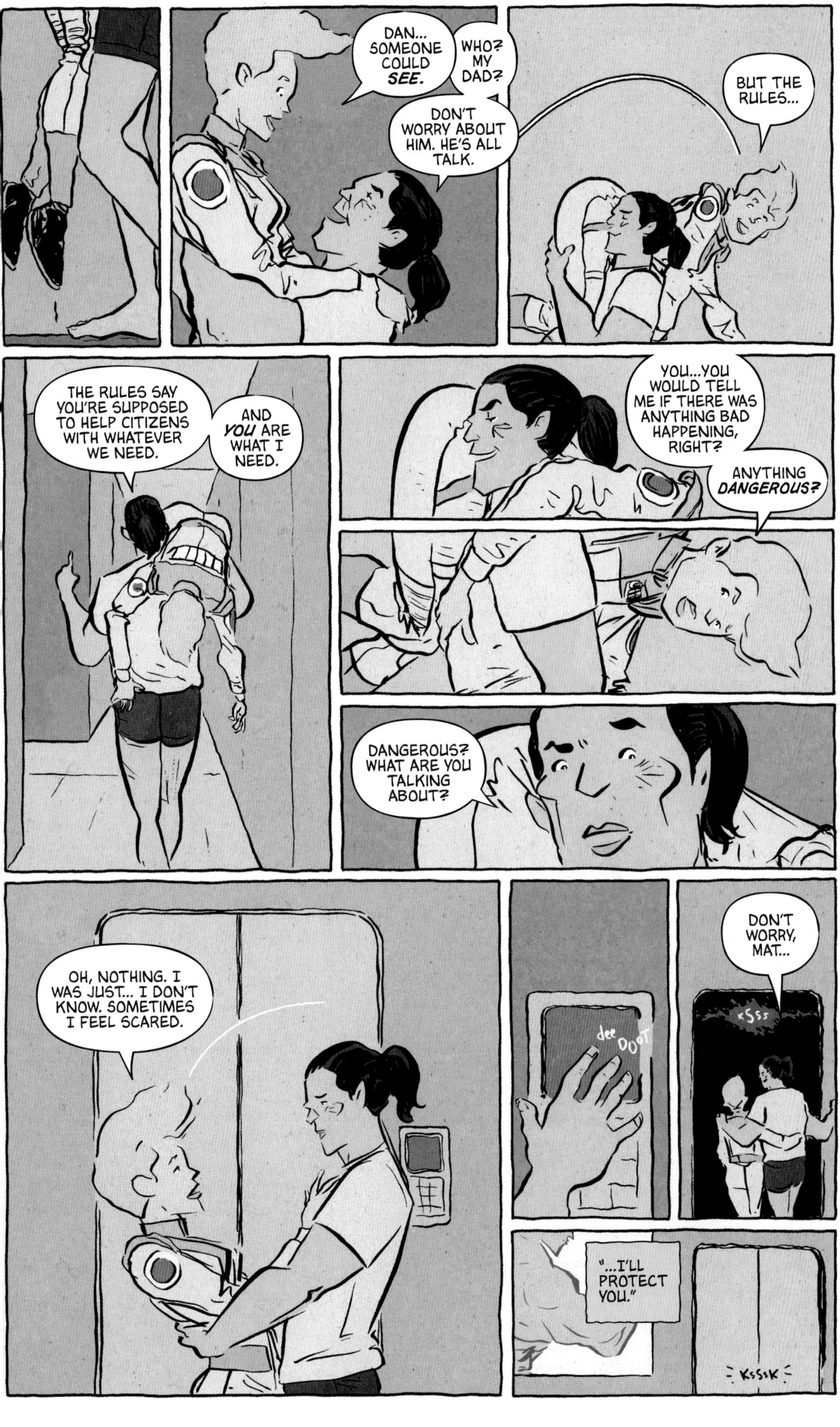
DAN... SOMEONE COULD *SEE.*
WHO? MY DAD?
DON'T WORRY ABOUT HIM. HE'S ALL TALK.
BUT THE RULES...
THE RULES SAY YOU'RE SUPPOSED TO HELP CITIZENS WITH WHATEVER WE NEED.
AND *YOU* ARE WHAT I NEED.
YOU...YOU WOULD TELL ME IF THERE WAS ANYTHING BAD HAPPENING, RIGHT?
ANYTHING *DANGEROUS?*
DANGEROUS? WHAT ARE YOU TALKING ABOUT?
OH, NOTHING. I WAS JUST... I DON'T KNOW. SOMETIMES I FEEL SCARED.
dee DOOT
DON'T WORRY, MAT...
KSSS
"...I'LL PROTECT YOU."
KSSSK

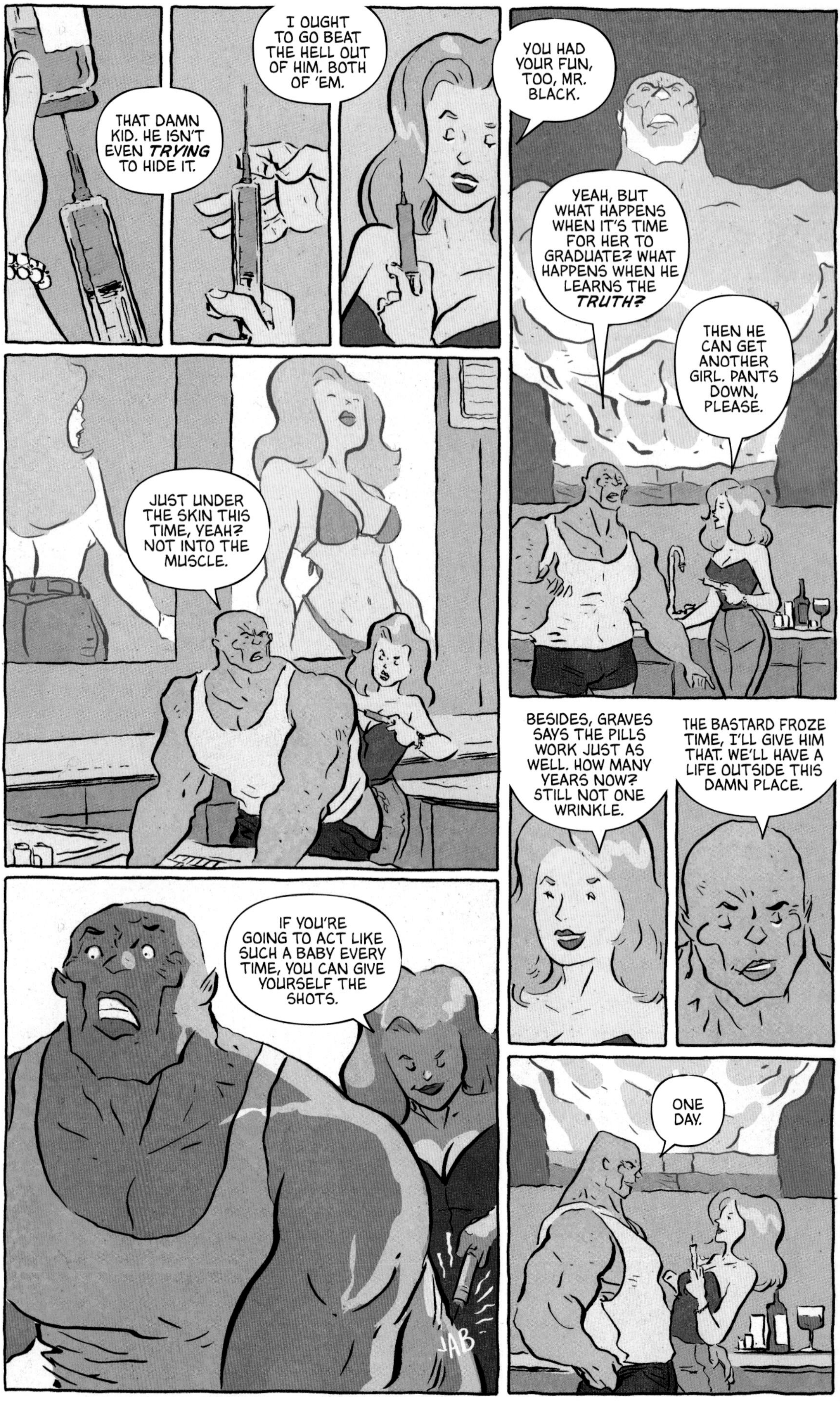
THAT DAMN KID. HE ISN'T EVEN *TRYING* TO HIDE IT.
I OUGHT TO GO BEAT THE HELL OUT OF HIM. BOTH OF 'EM.
YOU HAD YOUR FUN, TOO, MR. BLACK.
YEAH, BUT WHAT HAPPENS WHEN IT'S TIME FOR HER TO GRADUATE? WHAT HAPPENS WHEN HE LEARNS THE *TRUTH?*
THEN HE CAN GET ANOTHER GIRL. PANTS DOWN, PLEASE.
JUST UNDER THE SKIN THIS TIME, YEAH? NOT INTO THE MUSCLE.
BESIDES, GRAVES SAYS THE PILLS WORK JUST AS WELL. HOW MANY YEARS NOW? STILL NOT ONE WRINKLE.
THE BASTARD FROZE TIME, I'LL GIVE HIM THAT. WE'LL HAVE A LIFE OUTSIDE THIS DAMN PLACE.
IF YOU'RE GOING TO ACT LIKE SUCH A BABY EVERY TIME, YOU CAN GIVE YOURSELF THE SHOTS.
JAB
ONE DAY.

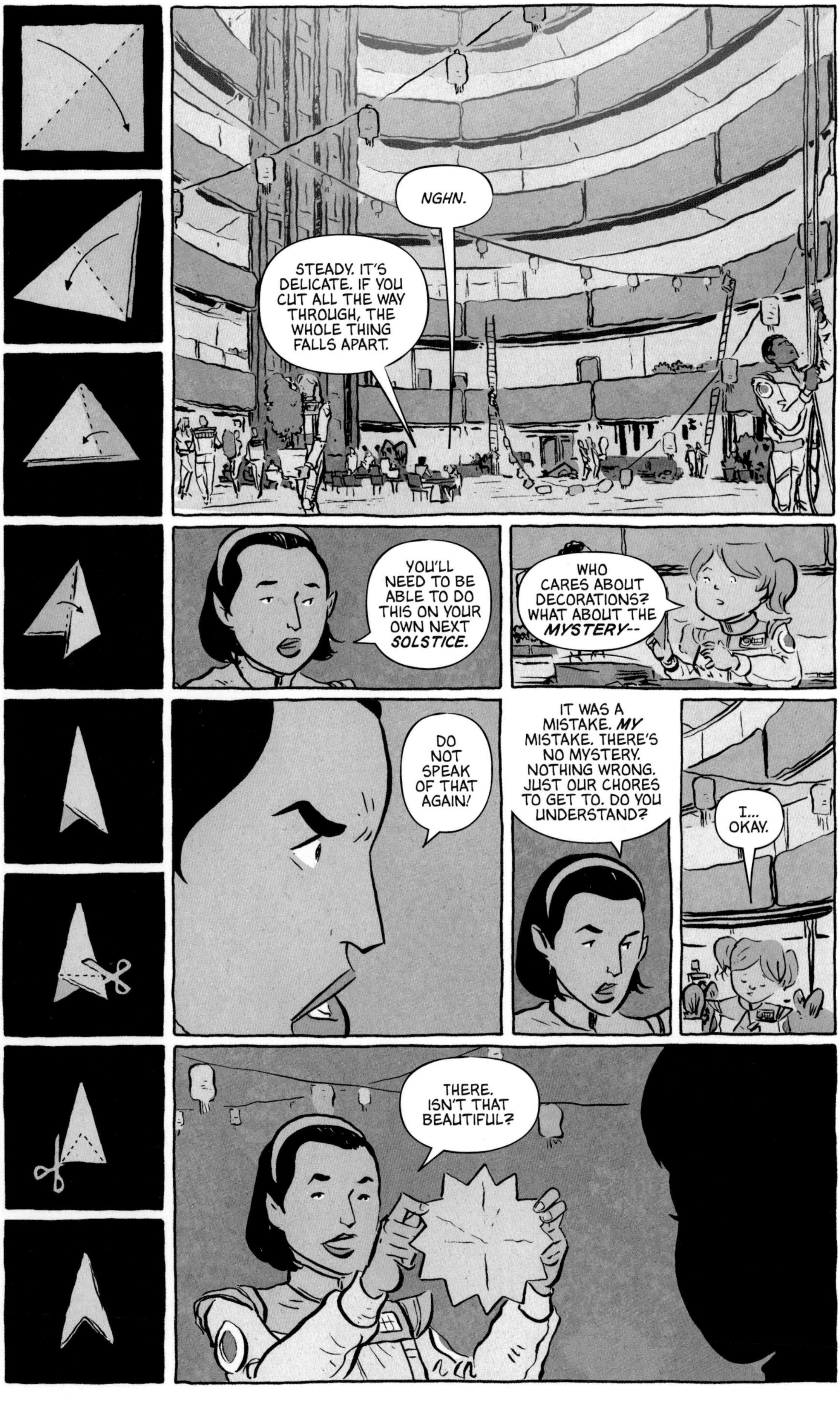
NGHN.
STEADY. IT'S DELICATE. IF YOU CUT ALL THE WAY THROUGH, THE WHOLE THING FALLS APART.
YOU'LL NEED TO BE ABLE TO DO THIS ON YOUR OWN NEXT SOLSTICE.
WHO CARES ABOUT DECORATIONS? WHAT ABOUT THE MYSTERY--
DO NOT SPEAK OF THAT AGAIN!
IT WAS A MISTAKE. MY MISTAKE. THERE'S NO MYSTERY. NOTHING WRONG. JUST OUR CHORES TO GET TO. DO YOU UNDERSTAND?
I... OKAY.
THERE. ISN'T THAT BEAUTIFUL?

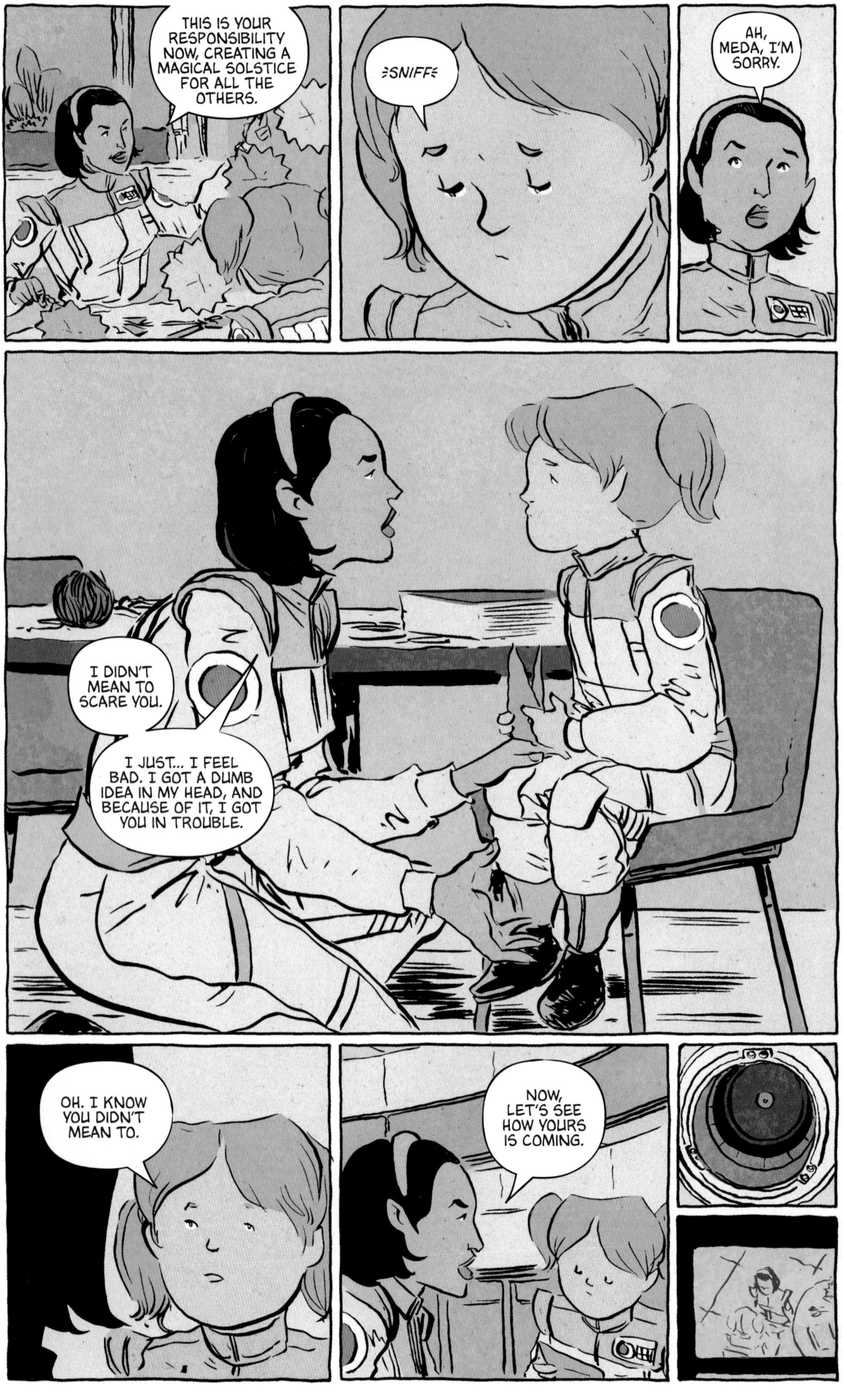
THIS IS YOUR RESPONSIBILITY NOW, CREATING A MAGICAL SOLSTICE FOR ALL THE OTHERS.
SNIFF
AH, MEDA, I'M SORRY.
I DIDN'T MEAN TO SCARE YOU.
I JUST... I FEEL BAD. I GOT A DUMB IDEA IN MY HEAD, AND BECAUSE OF IT, I GOT YOU IN TROUBLE.
OH. I KNOW YOU DIDN'T MEAN TO.
NOW, LET'S SEE HOW YOURS IS COMING.

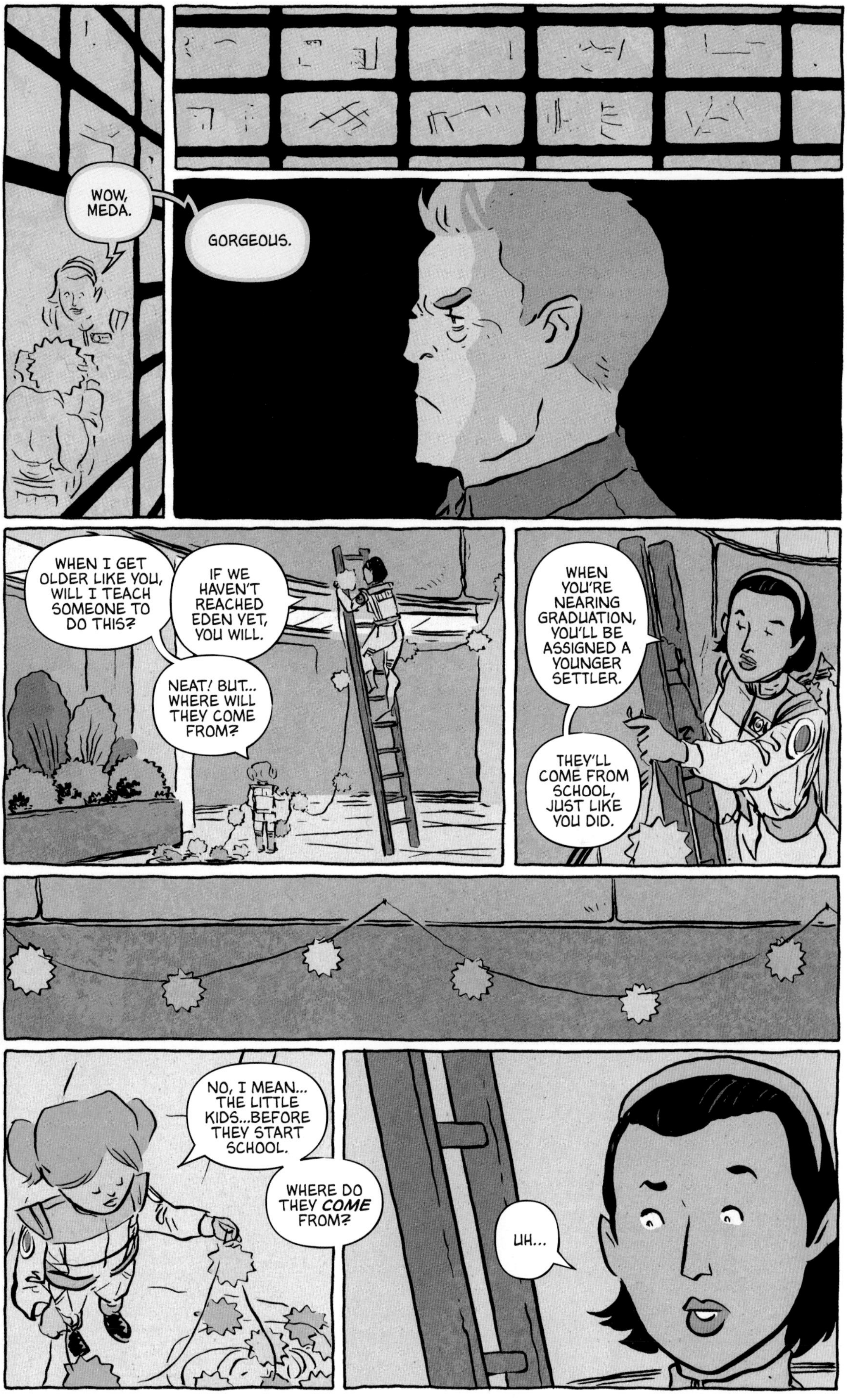
WOW, MEDA.
GORGEOUS.
WHEN I GET OLDER LIKE YOU, WILL I TEACH SOMEONE TO DO THIS?
IF WE HAVEN'T REACHED EDEN YET, YOU WILL.
NEAT! BUT... WHERE WILL THEY COME FROM?
WHEN YOU'RE NEARING GRADUATION, YOU'LL BE ASSIGNED A YOUNGER SETTLER.
THEY'LL COME FROM SCHOOL, JUST LIKE YOU DID.
NO, I MEAN... THE LITTLE KIDS...BEFORE THEY START SCHOOL.
WHERE DO THEY *COME* FROM?
UH...

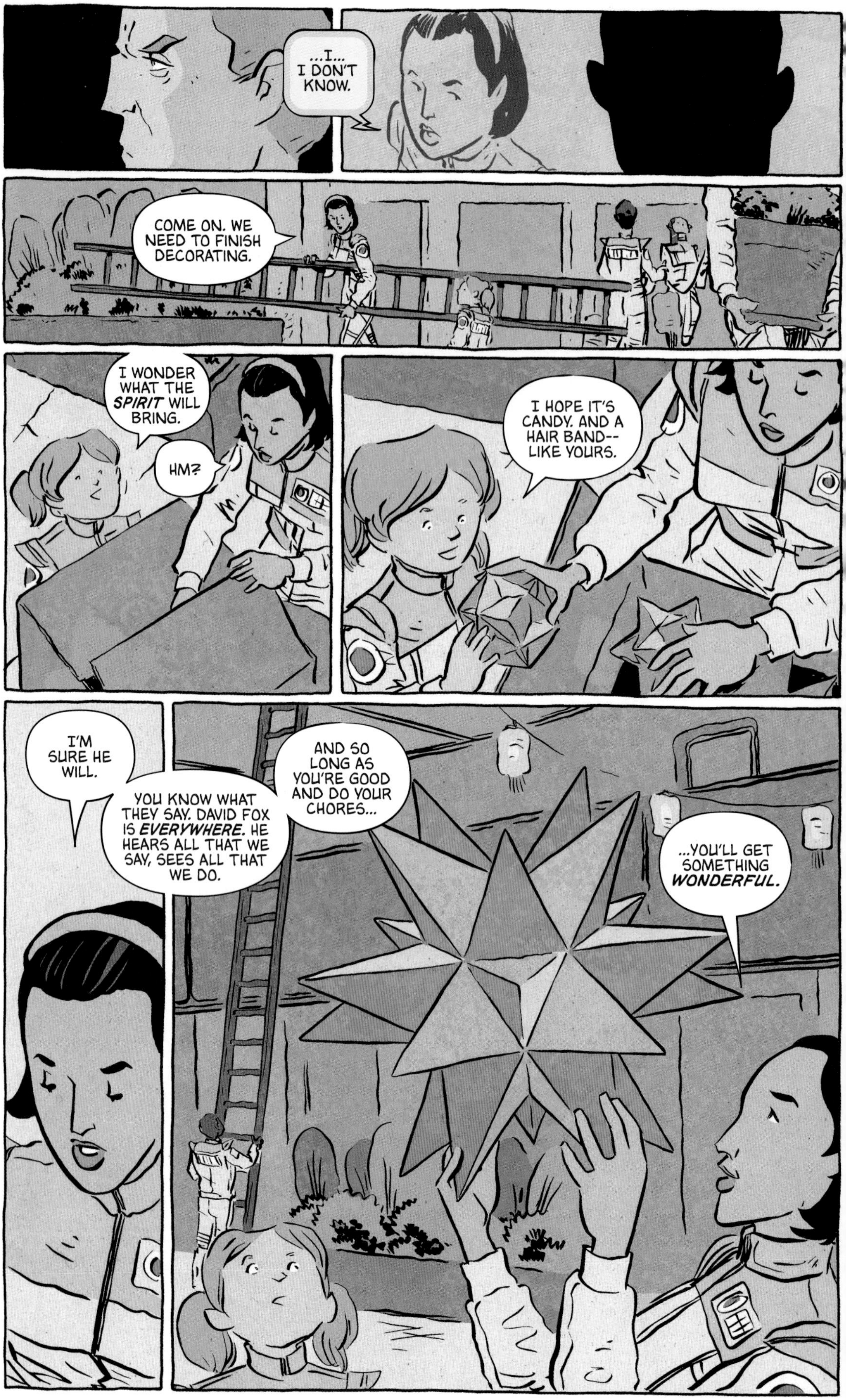
...I...
I DON'T KNOW.
COME ON. WE NEED TO FINISH DECORATING.
I WONDER WHAT THE *SPIRIT* WILL BRING.
HM?
I HOPE IT'S CANDY. AND A HAIR BAND--LIKE YOURS.
I'M SURE HE WILL.
YOU KNOW WHAT THEY SAY. DAVID FOX IS *EVERYWHERE.* HE HEARS ALL THAT WE SAY, SEES ALL THAT WE DO.
AND SO LONG AS YOU'RE GOOD AND DO YOUR CHORES...
...YOU'LL GET SOMETHING *WONDERFUL.*

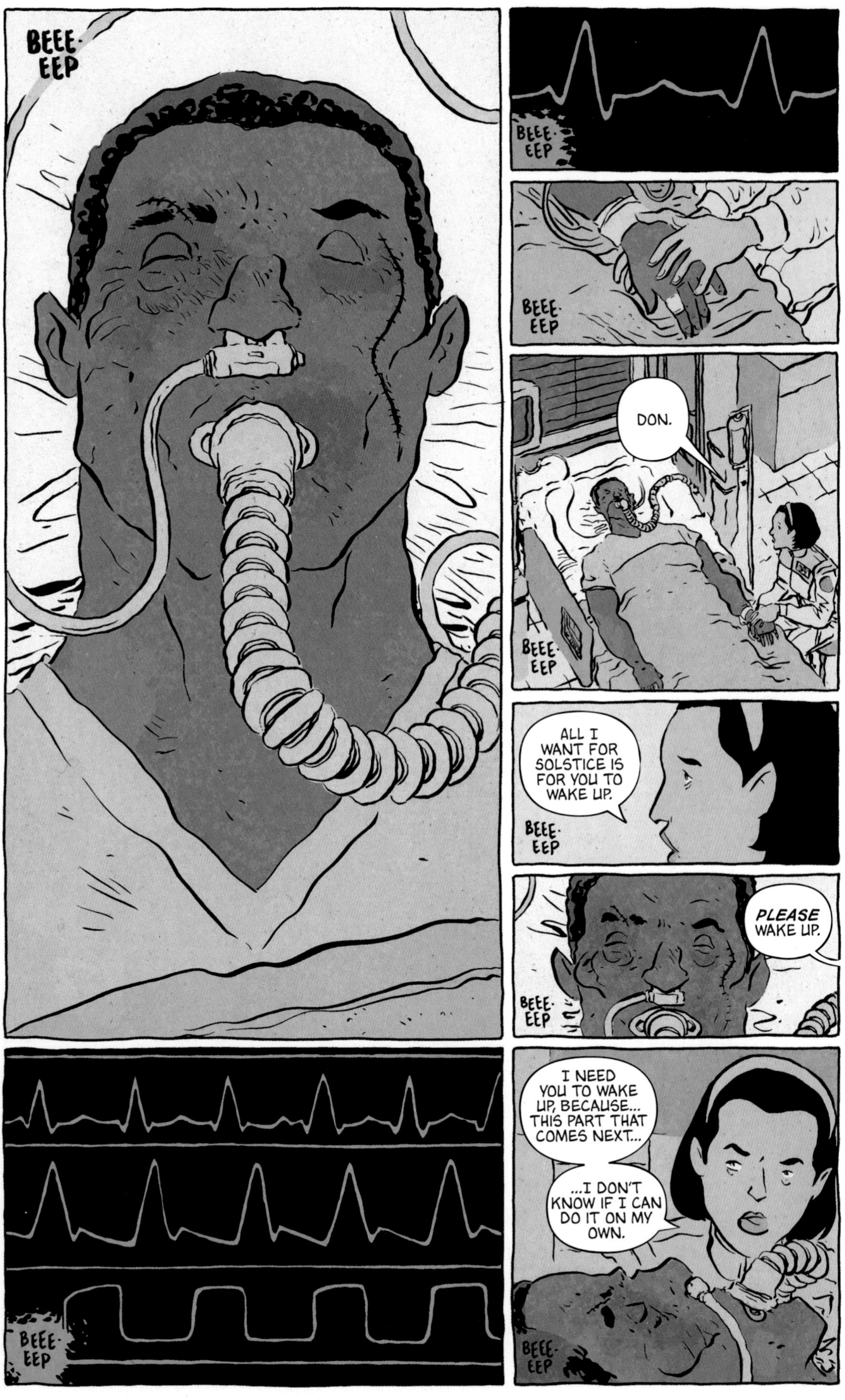

BEEE-EEP
BEEE-EEP
BEEE-EEP
DON.
BEEE-EEP
ALL I WANT FOR SOLSTICE IS FOR YOU TO WAKE UP.
BEEE-EEP
PLEASE WAKE UP.
BEEE-EEP
BEEE-EEP
I NEED YOU TO WAKE UP, BECAUSE... THIS PART THAT COMES NEXT...
...I DON'T KNOW IF I CAN DO IT ON MY OWN.
BEEE-EEP

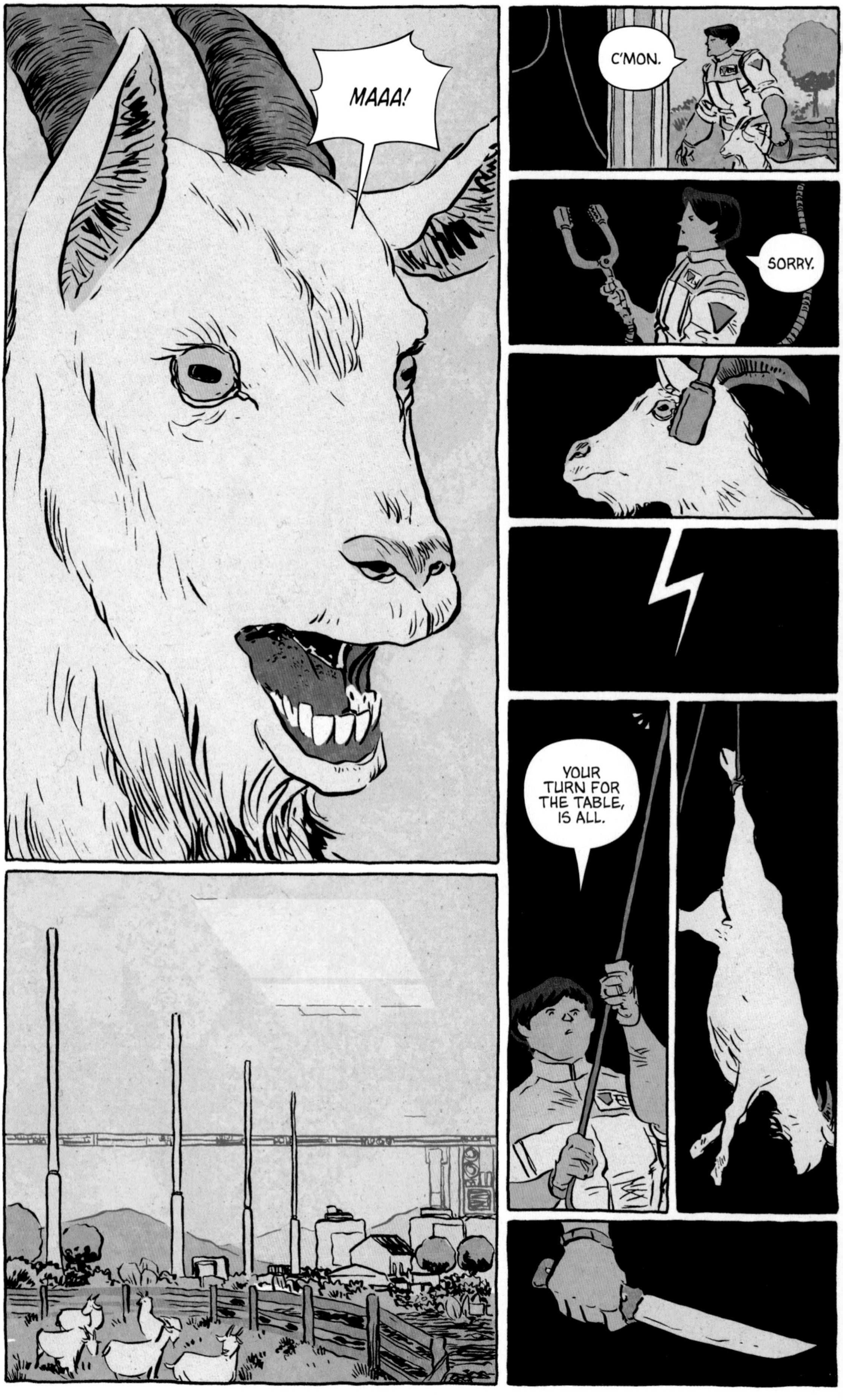
MAAA!
C'MON.
SORRY.
YOUR TURN FOR THE TABLE, IS ALL.

HELLO, SI.

EFF.

UNDERSTAND IF YOU'RE...SORE AT ME. FOR WHAT HAPPENED. TO YOUR BOYFRIEND.

NO. DON GETTING HURT WASN'T YOUR FAULT. IT WAS *THEIRS*.

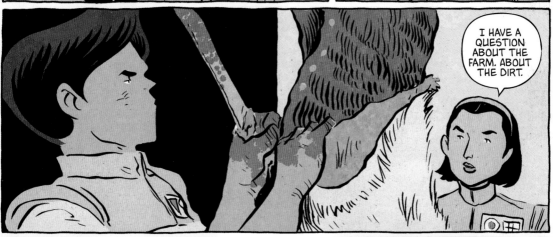

I HAVE A QUESTION ABOUT THE FARM. ABOUT THE DIRT.

DIRT IS DIRT.

LISTEN, I GOTTA GET THE MEAT READY FOR THE KITCHEN--

BUT HAVE YOU EVER FOUND ANYTHING IN THE DIRT? ANYTHING DIFFERENT?

ANYTHING LIKE *THIS*?

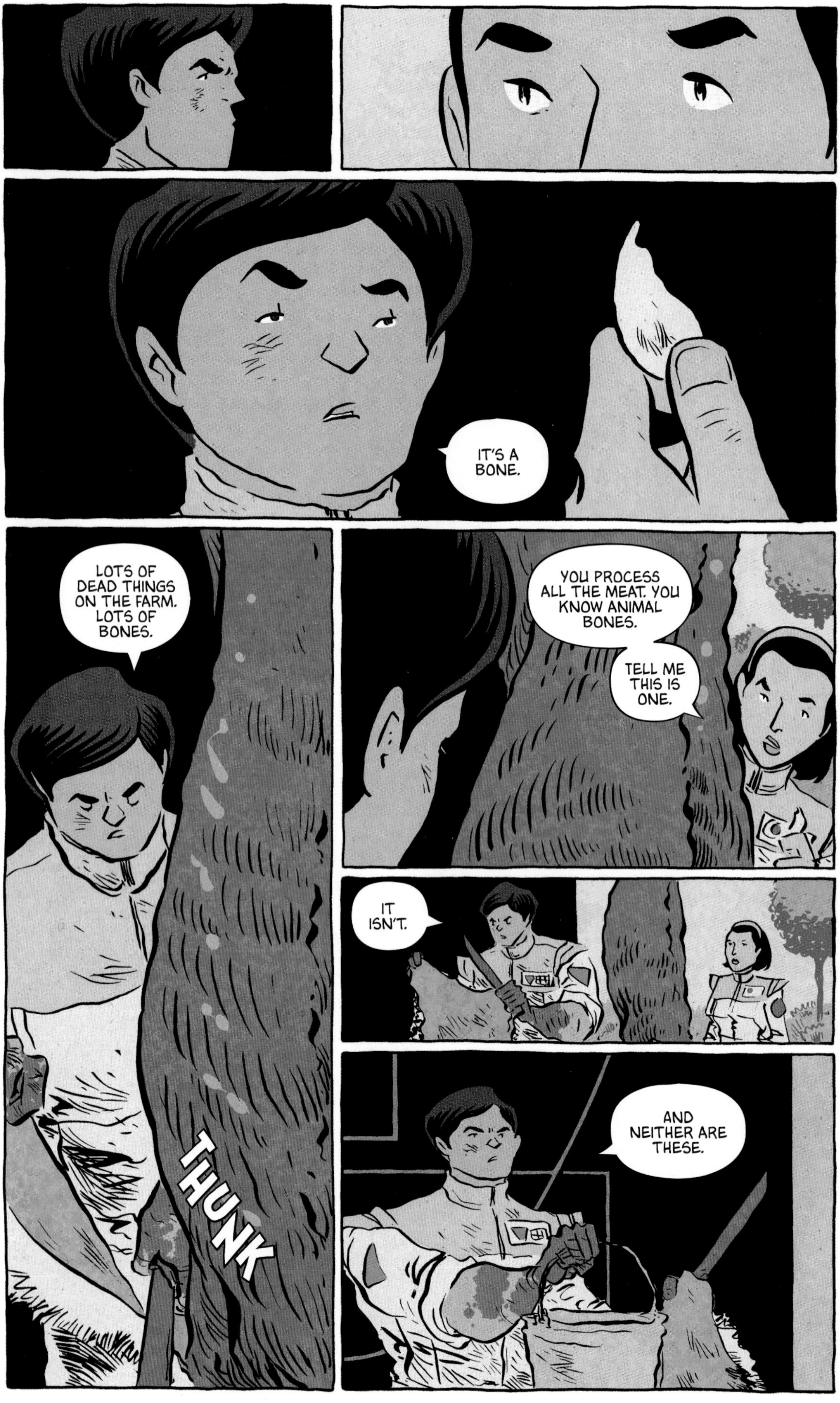
IT'S A BONE.
LOTS OF DEAD THINGS ON THE FARM. LOTS OF BONES.
THUNK
YOU PROCESS ALL THE MEAT. YOU KNOW ANIMAL BONES.
TELL ME THIS IS ONE.
IT ISN'T.
AND NEITHER ARE THESE.

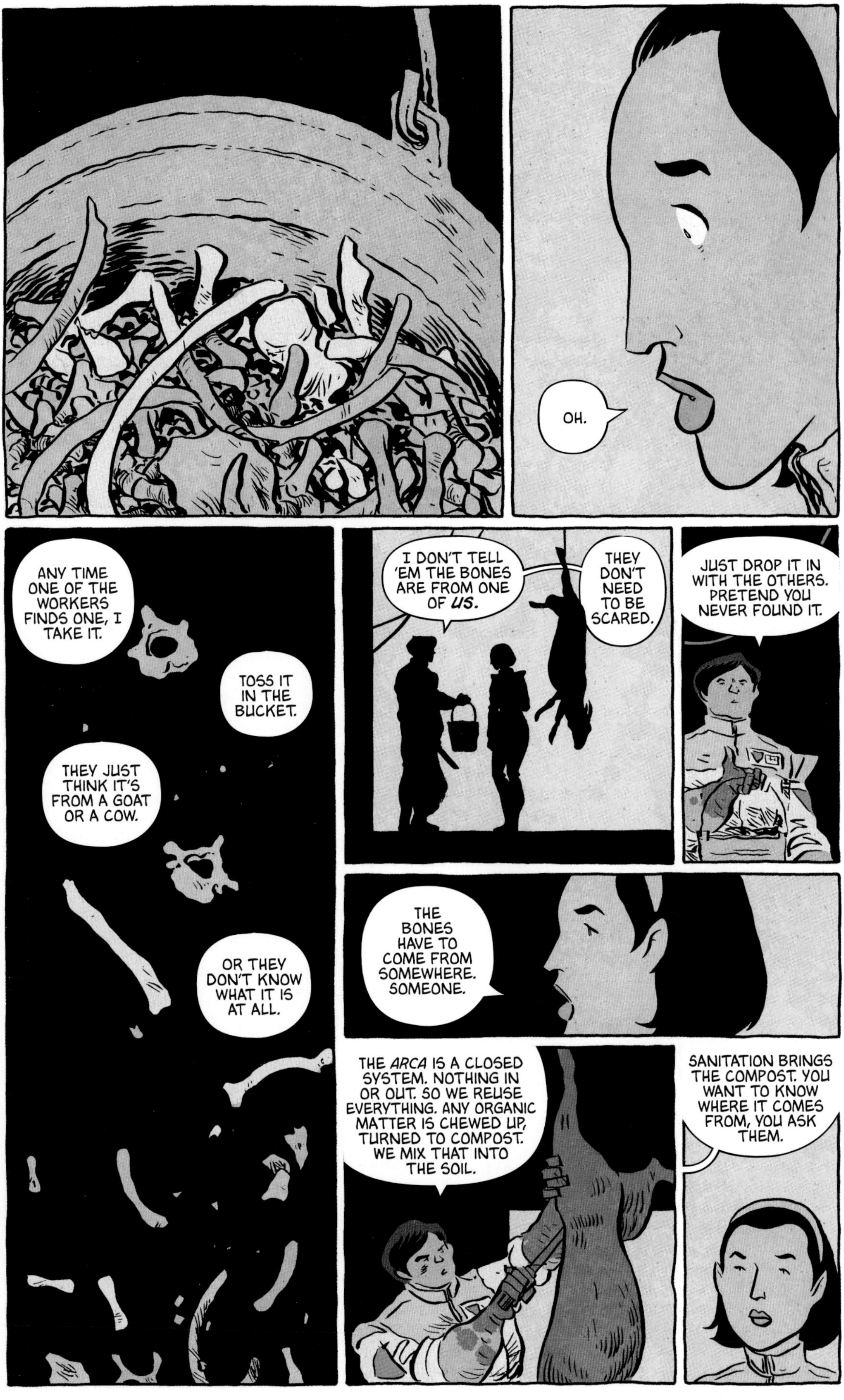

OH.
ANY TIME ONE OF THE WORKERS FINDS ONE, I TAKE IT.
TOSS IT IN THE BUCKET.
THEY JUST THINK IT'S FROM A GOAT OR A COW.
OR THEY DON'T KNOW WHAT IT IS AT ALL.
I DON'T TELL 'EM THE BONES ARE FROM ONE OF *US.*
THEY DON'T NEED TO BE SCARED.
JUST DROP IT IN WITH THE OTHERS. PRETEND YOU NEVER FOUND IT.
THE BONES HAVE TO COME FROM SOMEWHERE. SOMEONE.
THE *ARCA* IS A CLOSED SYSTEM. NOTHING IN OR OUT. SO WE REUSE EVERYTHING. ANY ORGANIC MATTER IS CHEWED UP, TURNED TO COMPOST. WE MIX THAT INTO THE SOIL.
SANITATION BRINGS THE COMPOST. YOU WANT TO KNOW WHERE IT COMES FROM, YOU ASK THEM.

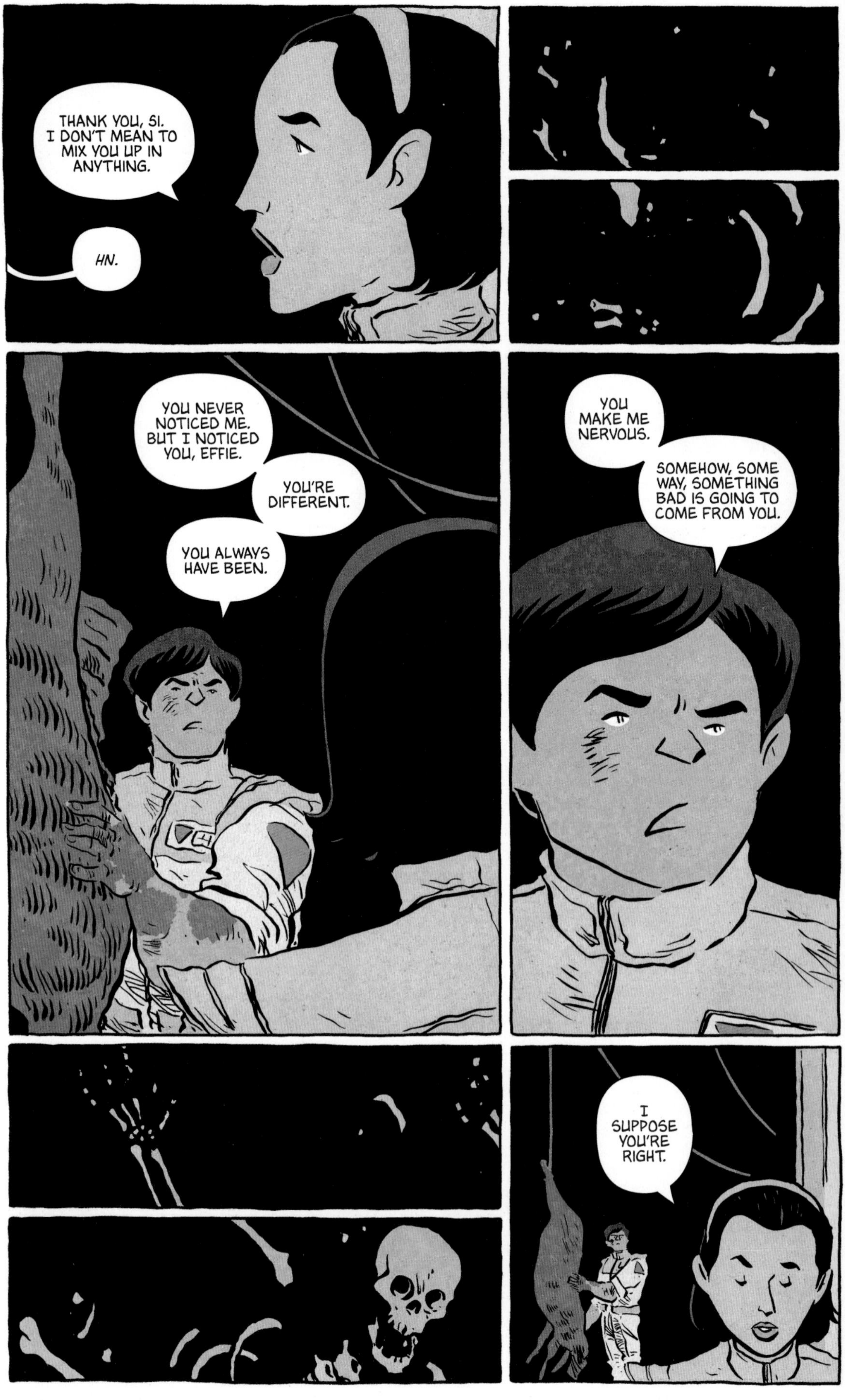
THANK YOU, SI. I DON'T MEAN TO MIX YOU UP IN ANYTHING.
HN.
YOU NEVER NOTICED ME. BUT I NOTICED YOU, EFFIE.
YOU'RE DIFFERENT.
YOU ALWAYS HAVE BEEN.
YOU MAKE ME NERVOUS.
SOMEHOW, SOME WAY, SOMETHING BAD IS GOING TO COME FROM YOU.
I SUPPOSE YOU'RE RIGHT.

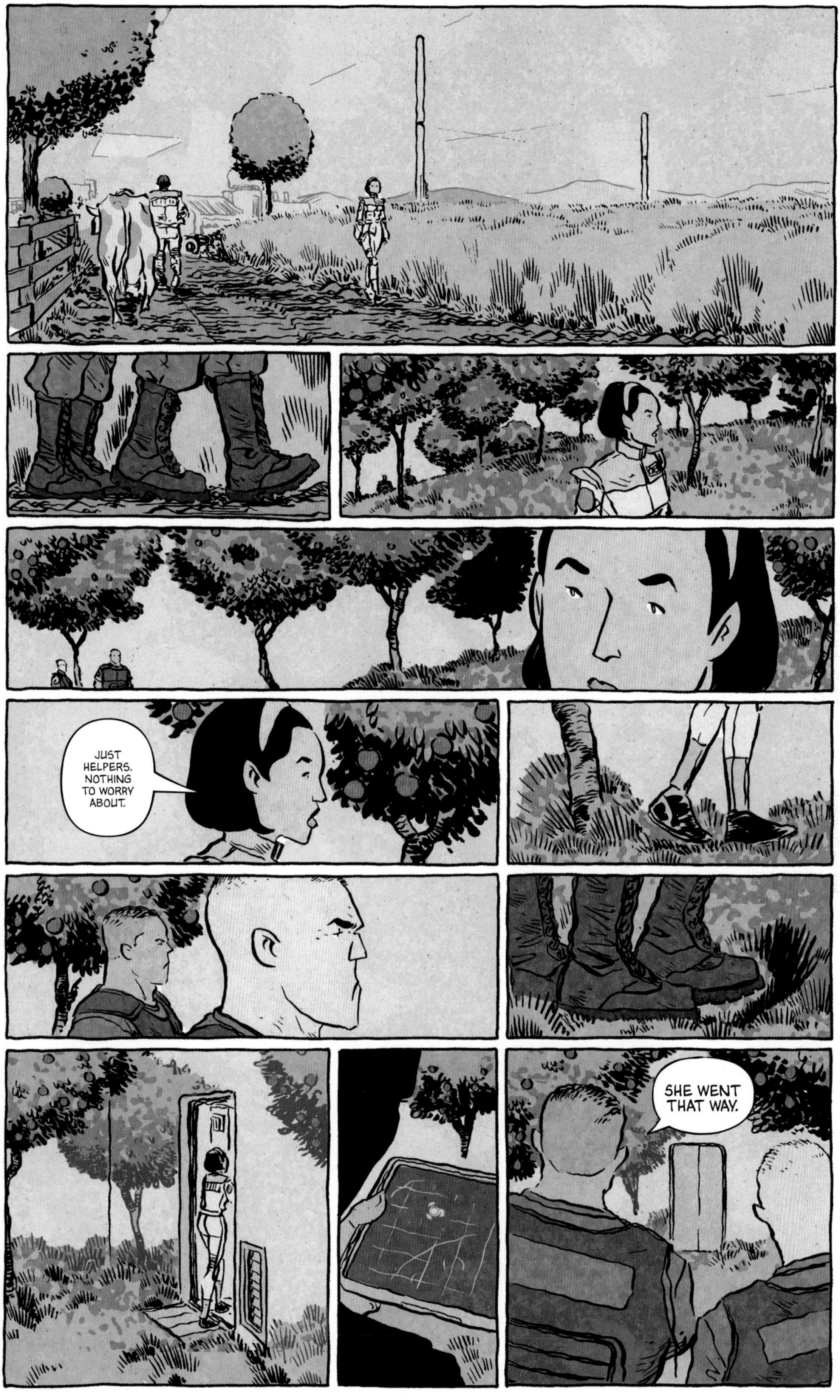
JUST HELPERS. NOTHING TO WORRY ABOUT.
SHE WENT THAT WAY.

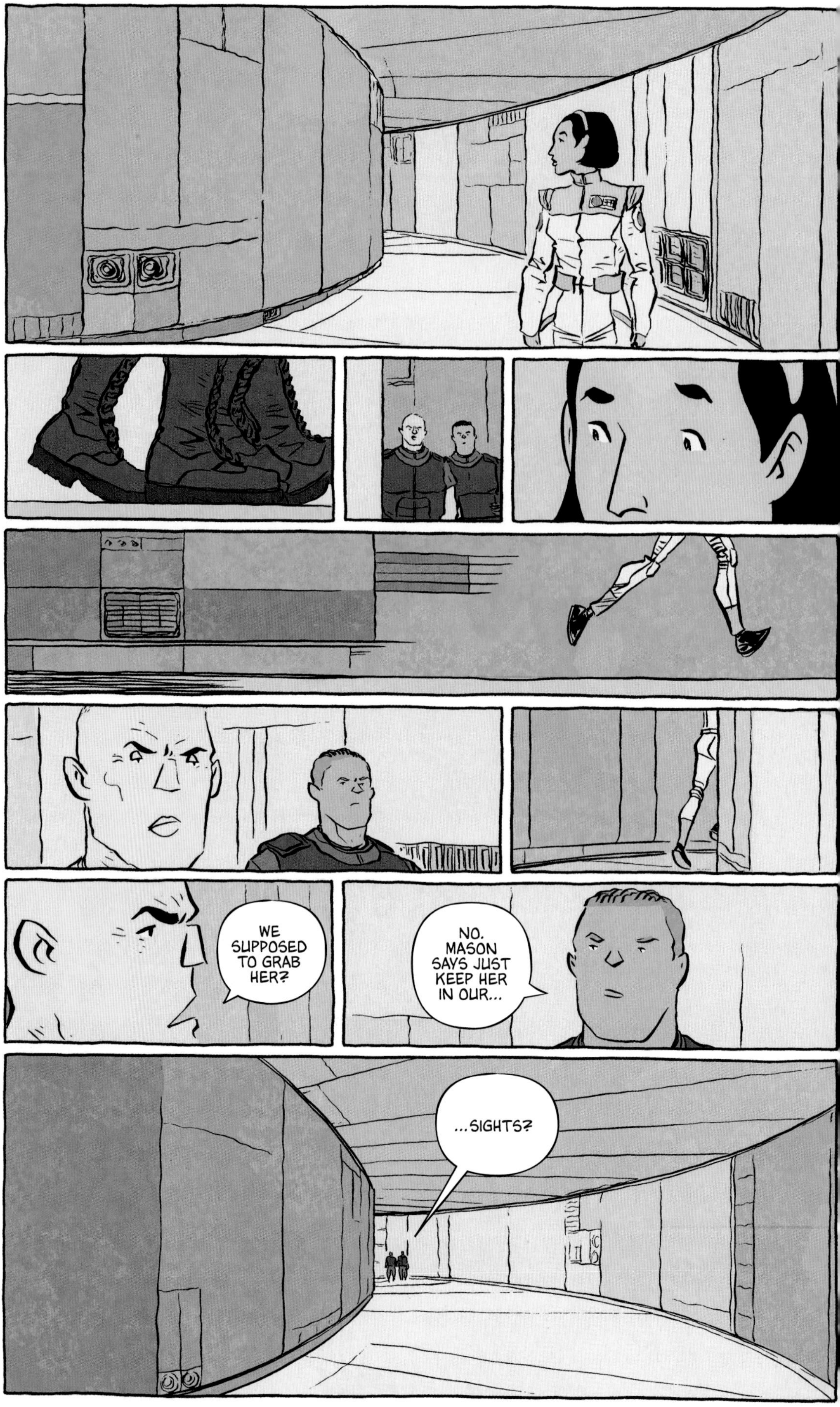
WE SUPPOSED TO GRAB HER?
NO. MASON SAYS JUST KEEP HER IN OUR...
...SIGHTS?

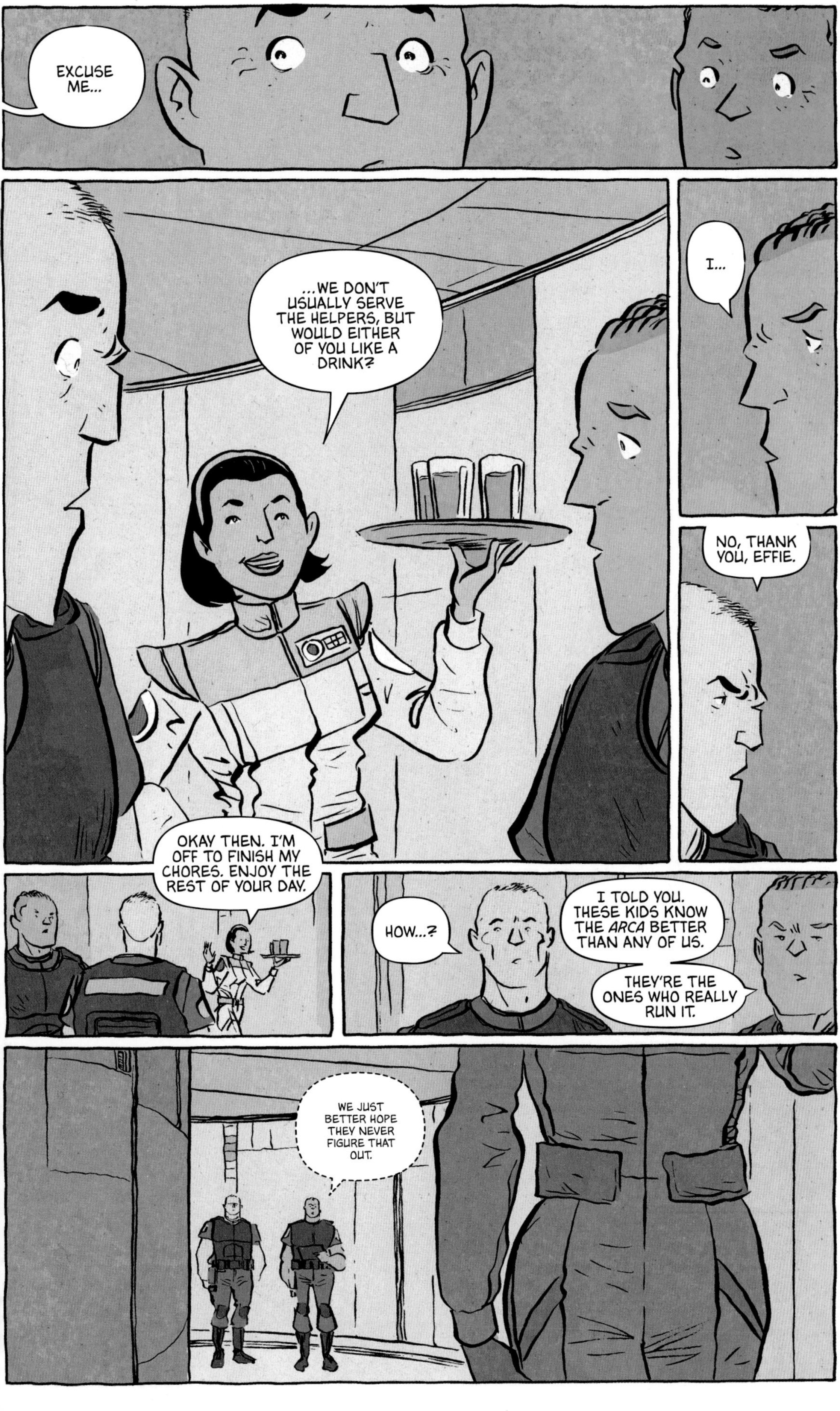
EXCUSE ME...
...WE DON'T USUALLY SERVE THE HELPERS, BUT WOULD EITHER OF YOU LIKE A DRINK?
I...
NO, THANK YOU, EFFIE.
OKAY THEN. I'M OFF TO FINISH MY CHORES. ENJOY THE REST OF YOUR DAY.
HOW...?
I TOLD YOU. THESE KIDS KNOW THE ARCA BETTER THAN ANY OF US.
THEY'RE THE ONES WHO REALLY RUN IT.
WE JUST BETTER HOPE THEY NEVER FIGURE THAT OUT.

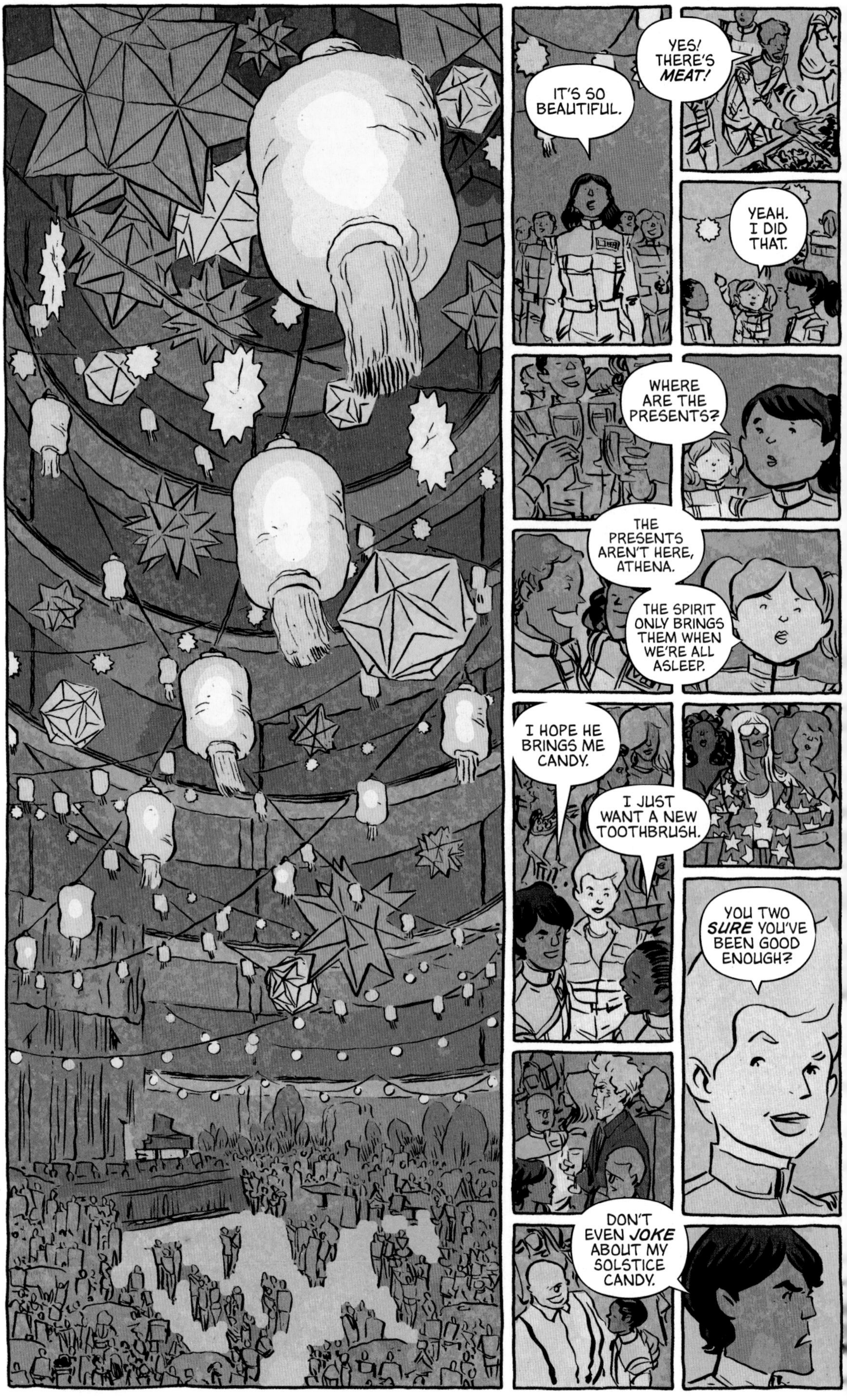
IT'S SO BEAUTIFUL.
YES! THERE'S *MEAT!*
YEAH. I DID THAT.
WHERE ARE THE PRESENTS?
THE PRESENTS AREN'T HERE, ATHENA.
THE SPIRIT ONLY BRINGS THEM WHEN WE'RE ALL ASLEEP.
I HOPE HE BRINGS ME CANDY.
I JUST WANT A NEW TOOTHBRUSH.
YOU TWO **SURE** YOU'VE BEEN GOOD ENOUGH?
DON'T EVEN **JOKE** ABOUT MY SOLSTICE CANDY.

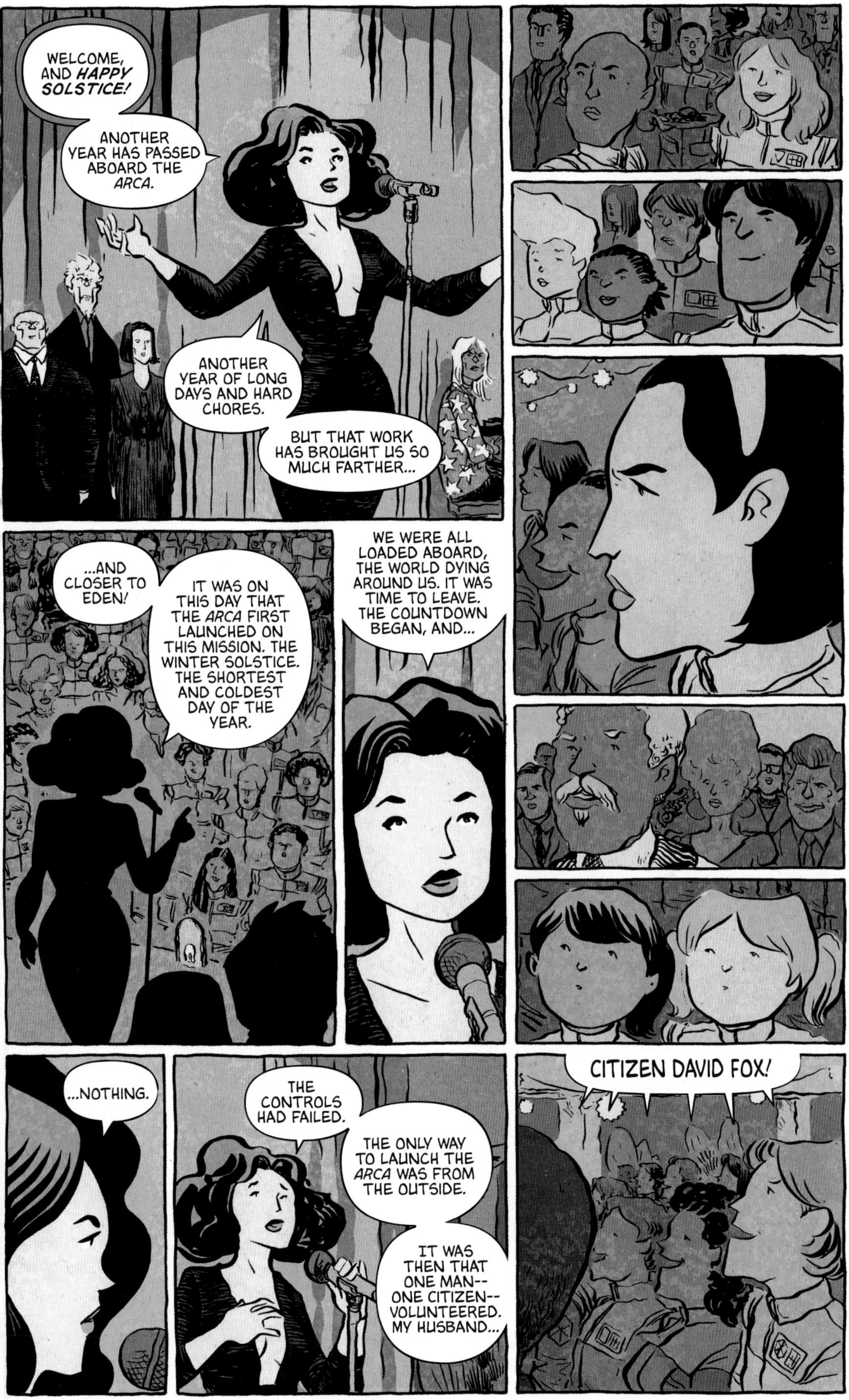
WELCOME, AND *HAPPY SOLSTICE!*
ANOTHER YEAR HAS PASSED ABOARD THE *ARCA.*
ANOTHER YEAR OF LONG DAYS AND HARD CHORES.
BUT THAT WORK HAS BROUGHT US SO MUCH FARTHER...
...AND CLOSER TO EDEN!
IT WAS ON THIS DAY THAT THE *ARCA* FIRST LAUNCHED ON THIS MISSION. THE WINTER SOLSTICE. THE SHORTEST AND COLDEST DAY OF THE YEAR.
WE WERE ALL LOADED ABOARD, THE WORLD DYING AROUND US. IT WAS TIME TO LEAVE. THE COUNTDOWN BEGAN, AND...
...NOTHING.
THE CONTROLS HAD FAILED.
THE ONLY WAY TO LAUNCH THE *ARCA* WAS FROM THE OUTSIDE.
IT WAS THEN THAT ONE MAN-- ONE CITIZEN-- VOLUNTEERED. MY HUSBAND...
CITIZEN DAVID FOX!

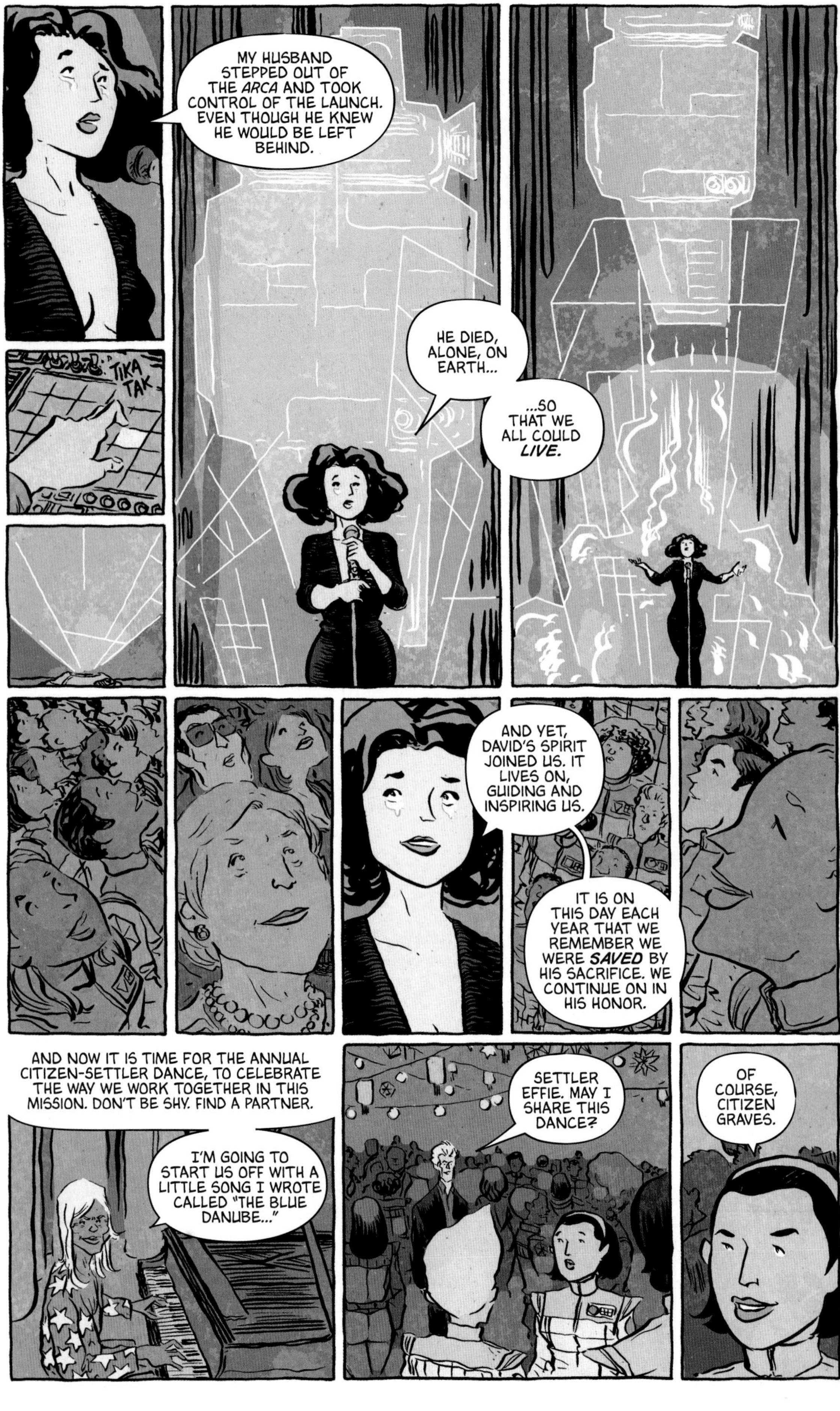
MY HUSBAND STEPPED OUT OF THE *ARCA* AND TOOK CONTROL OF THE LAUNCH. EVEN THOUGH HE KNEW HE WOULD BE LEFT BEHIND.
TIKA TAK
HE DIED, ALONE, ON EARTH...
...SO THAT WE ALL COULD *LIVE.*
AND YET, DAVID'S SPIRIT JOINED US. IT LIVES ON, GUIDING AND INSPIRING US.
IT IS ON THIS DAY EACH YEAR THAT WE REMEMBER WE WERE *SAVED* BY HIS SACRIFICE. WE CONTINUE ON IN HIS HONOR.
AND NOW IT IS TIME FOR THE ANNUAL CITIZEN-SETTLER DANCE, TO CELEBRATE THE WAY WE WORK TOGETHER IN THIS MISSION. DON'T BE SHY. FIND A PARTNER.
I'M GOING TO START US OFF WITH A LITTLE SONG I WROTE CALLED "THE BLUE DANUBE..."
SETTLER EFFIE. MAY I SHARE THIS DANCE?
OF COURSE, CITIZEN GRAVES.

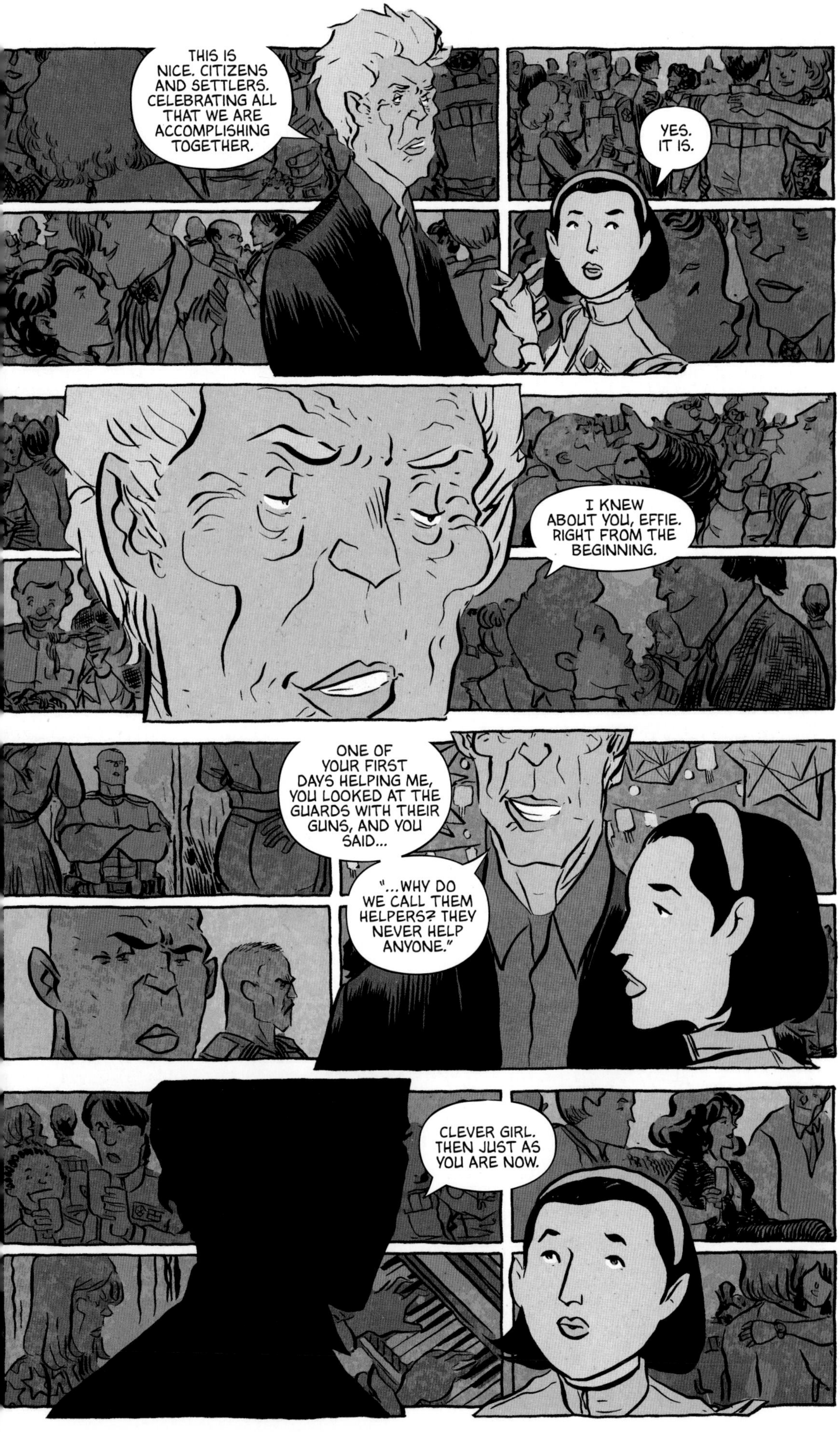
THIS IS NICE. CITIZENS AND SETTLERS. CELEBRATING ALL THAT WE ARE ACCOMPLISHING TOGETHER.
YES. IT IS.
I KNEW ABOUT YOU, EFFIE. RIGHT FROM THE BEGINNING.
ONE OF YOUR FIRST DAYS HELPING ME, YOU LOOKED AT THE GUARDS WITH THEIR GUNS, AND YOU SAID...
"...WHY DO WE CALL THEM HELPERS? THEY NEVER HELP ANYONE."
CLEVER GIRL. THEN JUST AS YOU ARE NOW.

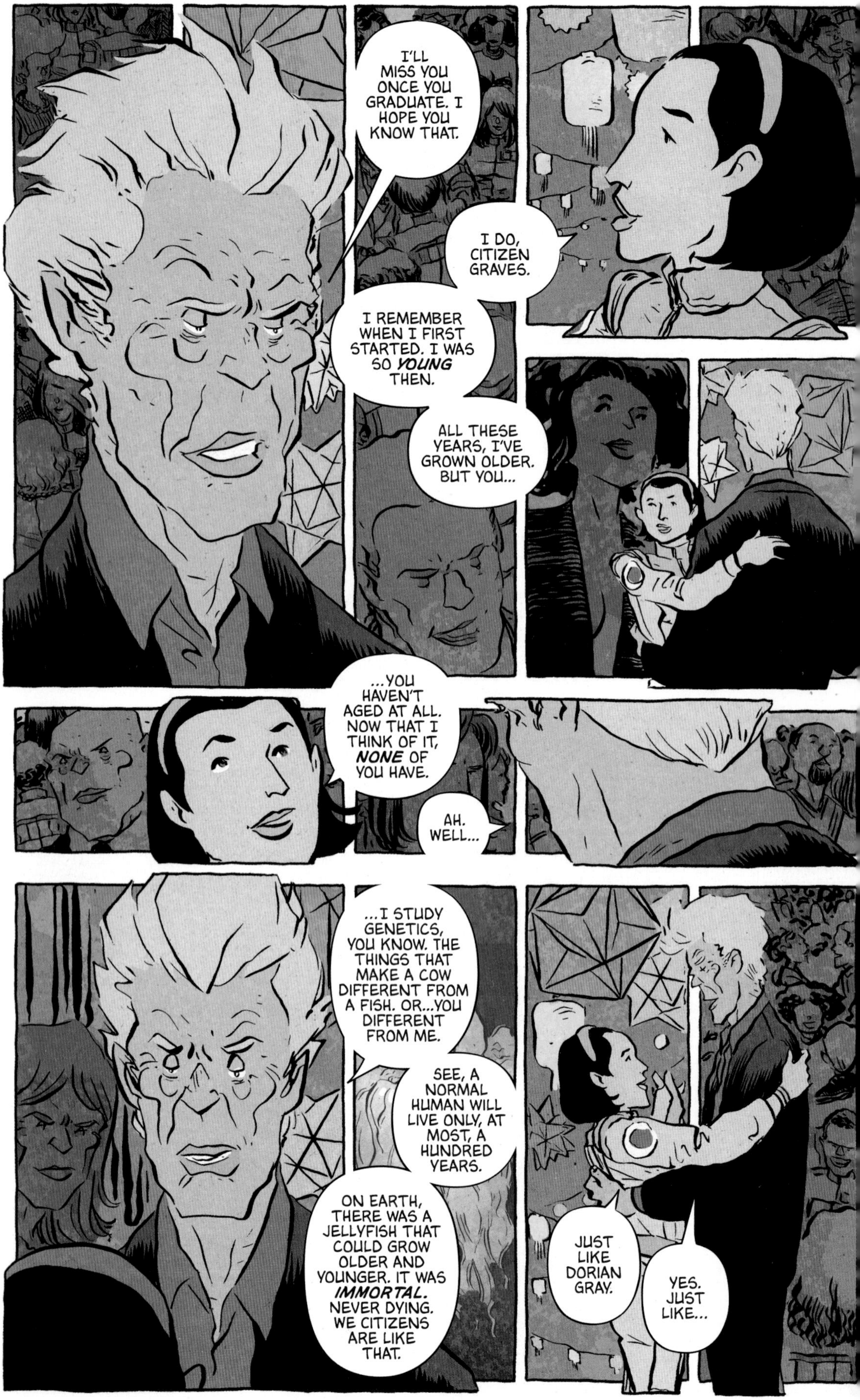
I'LL MISS YOU ONCE YOU GRADUATE. I HOPE YOU KNOW THAT.
I DO, CITIZEN GRAVES.
I REMEMBER WHEN I FIRST STARTED. I WAS SO *YOUNG* THEN.
ALL THESE YEARS, I'VE GROWN OLDER. BUT YOU...
...YOU HAVEN'T AGED AT ALL. NOW THAT I THINK OF IT, *NONE* OF YOU HAVE.
AH. WELL...
...I STUDY GENETICS, YOU KNOW. THE THINGS THAT MAKE A COW DIFFERENT FROM A FISH. OR...YOU DIFFERENT FROM ME.
SEE, A NORMAL HUMAN WILL LIVE ONLY, AT MOST, A HUNDRED YEARS.
ON EARTH, THERE WAS A JELLYFISH THAT COULD GROW OLDER AND YOUNGER. IT WAS *IMMORTAL.* NEVER DYING. WE CITIZENS ARE LIKE THAT.
JUST LIKE DORIAN GRAY.
YES. JUST LIKE...

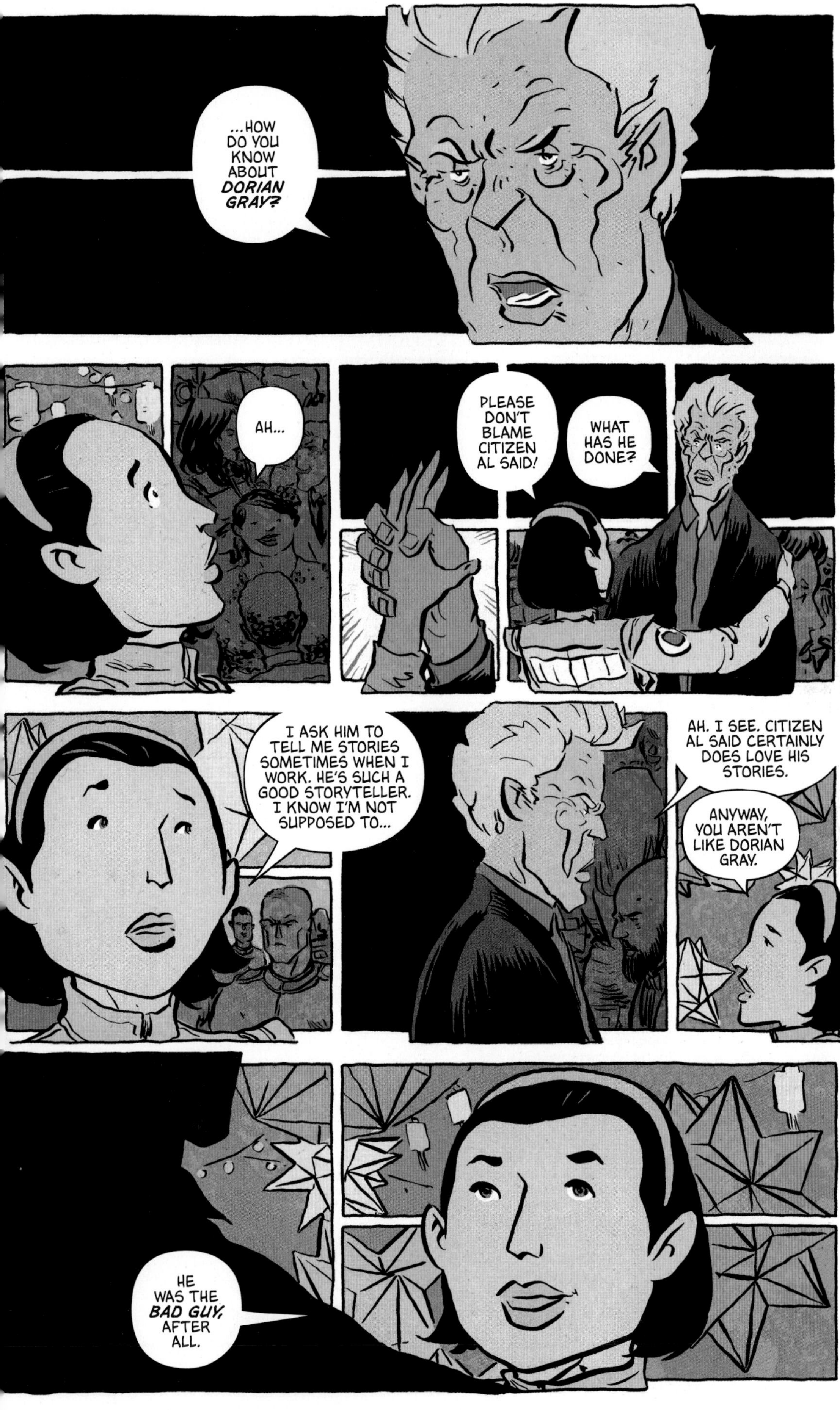
...HOW DO YOU KNOW ABOUT *DORIAN GRAY?*
AH...
PLEASE DON'T BLAME CITIZEN AL SAID!
WHAT HAS HE DONE?
I ASK HIM TO TELL ME STORIES SOMETIMES WHEN I WORK. HE'S SUCH A GOOD STORYTELLER. I KNOW I'M NOT SUPPOSED TO...
AH. I SEE. CITIZEN AL SAID CERTAINLY DOES LOVE HIS STORIES.
ANYWAY, YOU AREN'T LIKE DORIAN GRAY.
HE WAS THE *BAD GUY,* AFTER ALL.

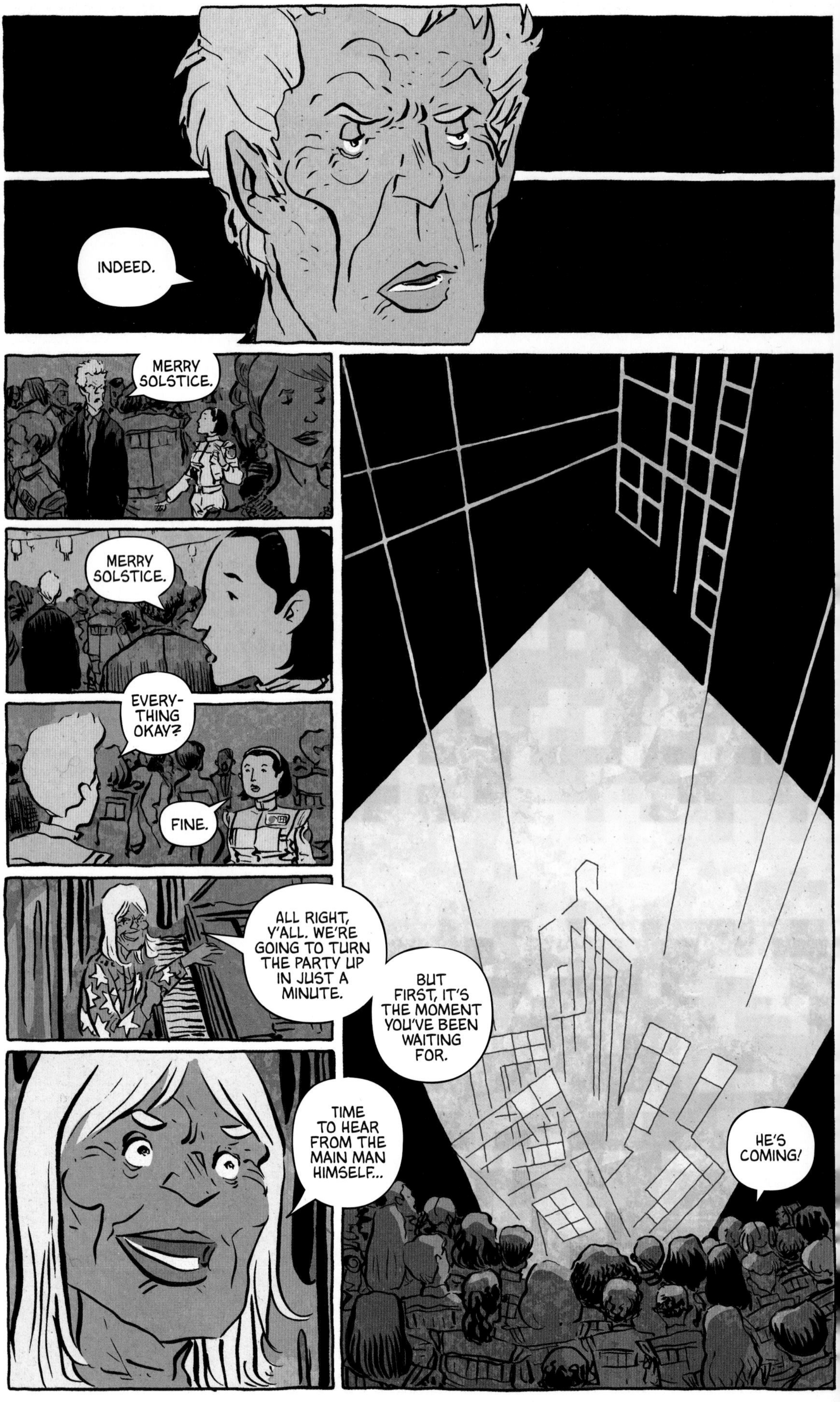
INDEED.
MERRY SOLSTICE.
MERRY SOLSTICE.
EVERY-THING OKAY?
FINE.
ALL RIGHT, Y'ALL. WE'RE GOING TO TURN THE PARTY UP IN JUST A MINUTE.
BUT FIRST, IT'S THE MOMENT YOU'VE BEEN WAITING FOR.
TIME TO HEAR FROM THE MAIN MAN HIMSELF...
HE'S COMING!

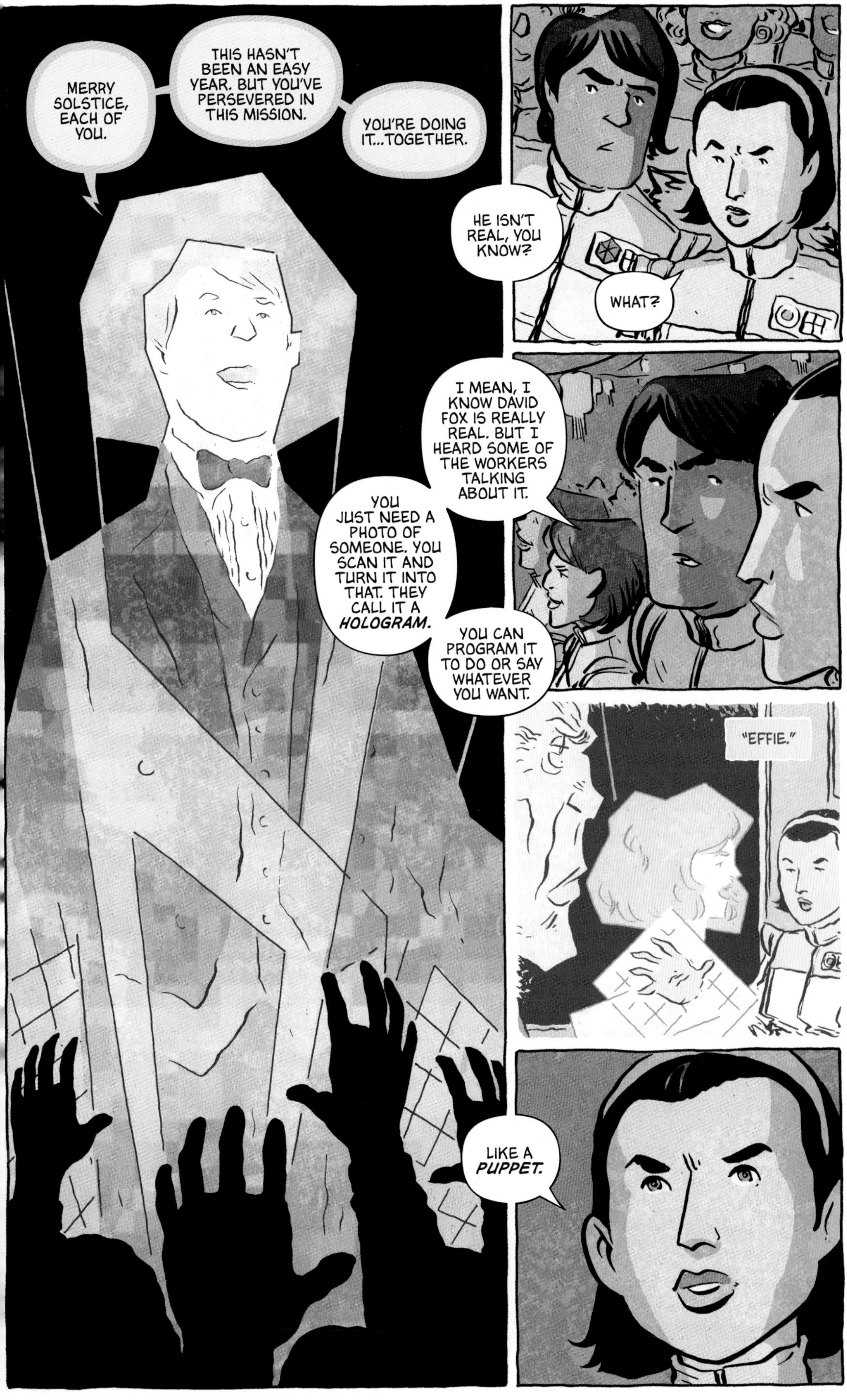
MERRY SOLSTICE, EACH OF YOU.
THIS HASN'T BEEN AN EASY YEAR. BUT YOU'VE PERSEVERED IN THIS MISSION.
YOU'RE DOING IT...TOGETHER.
HE ISN'T REAL, YOU KNOW?
WHAT?
I MEAN, I KNOW DAVID FOX IS REALLY REAL. BUT I HEARD SOME OF THE WORKERS TALKING ABOUT IT.
YOU JUST NEED A PHOTO OF SOMEONE. YOU SCAN IT AND TURN IT INTO THAT. THEY CALL IT A *HOLOGRAM.*
YOU CAN PROGRAM IT TO DO OR SAY WHATEVER YOU WANT.
"EFFIE."
LIKE A *PUPPET.*

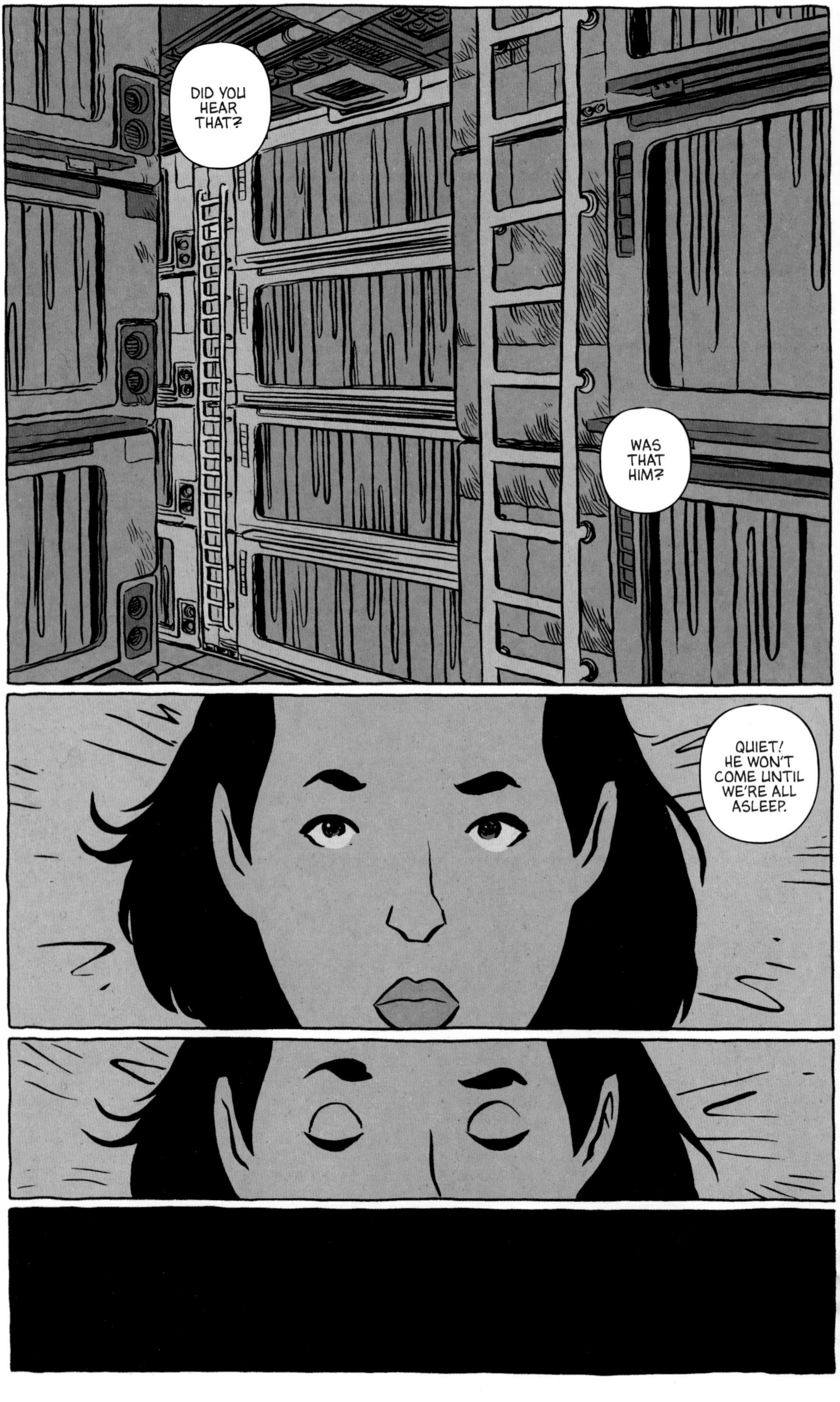

DID YOU HEAR THAT?
WAS THAT HIM?
QUIET! HE WON'T COME UNTIL WE'RE ALL ASLEEP.

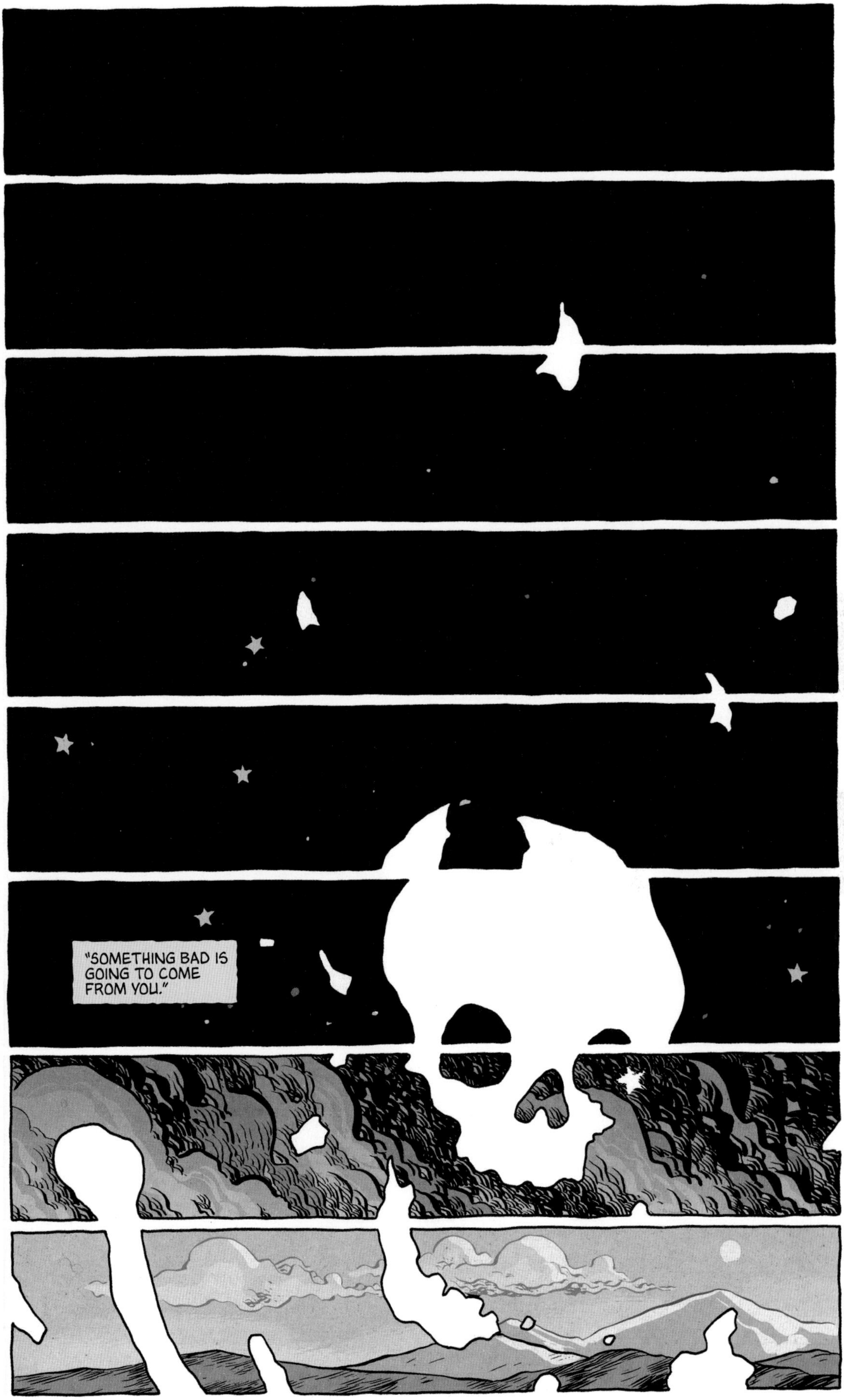
"SOMETHING BAD IS GOING TO COME FROM YOU."

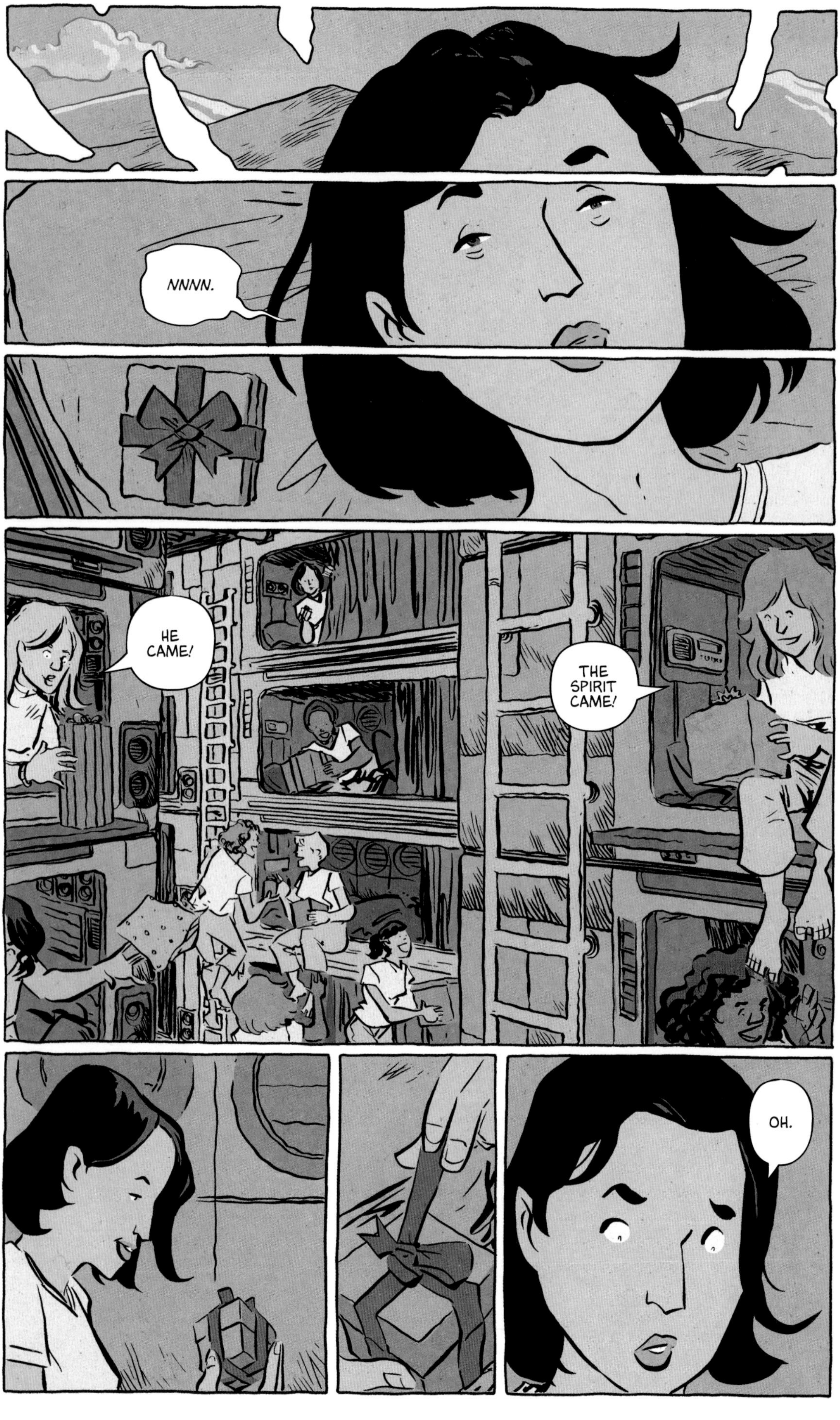
NNNN.
HE CAME!
THE SPIRIT CAME!
OH.

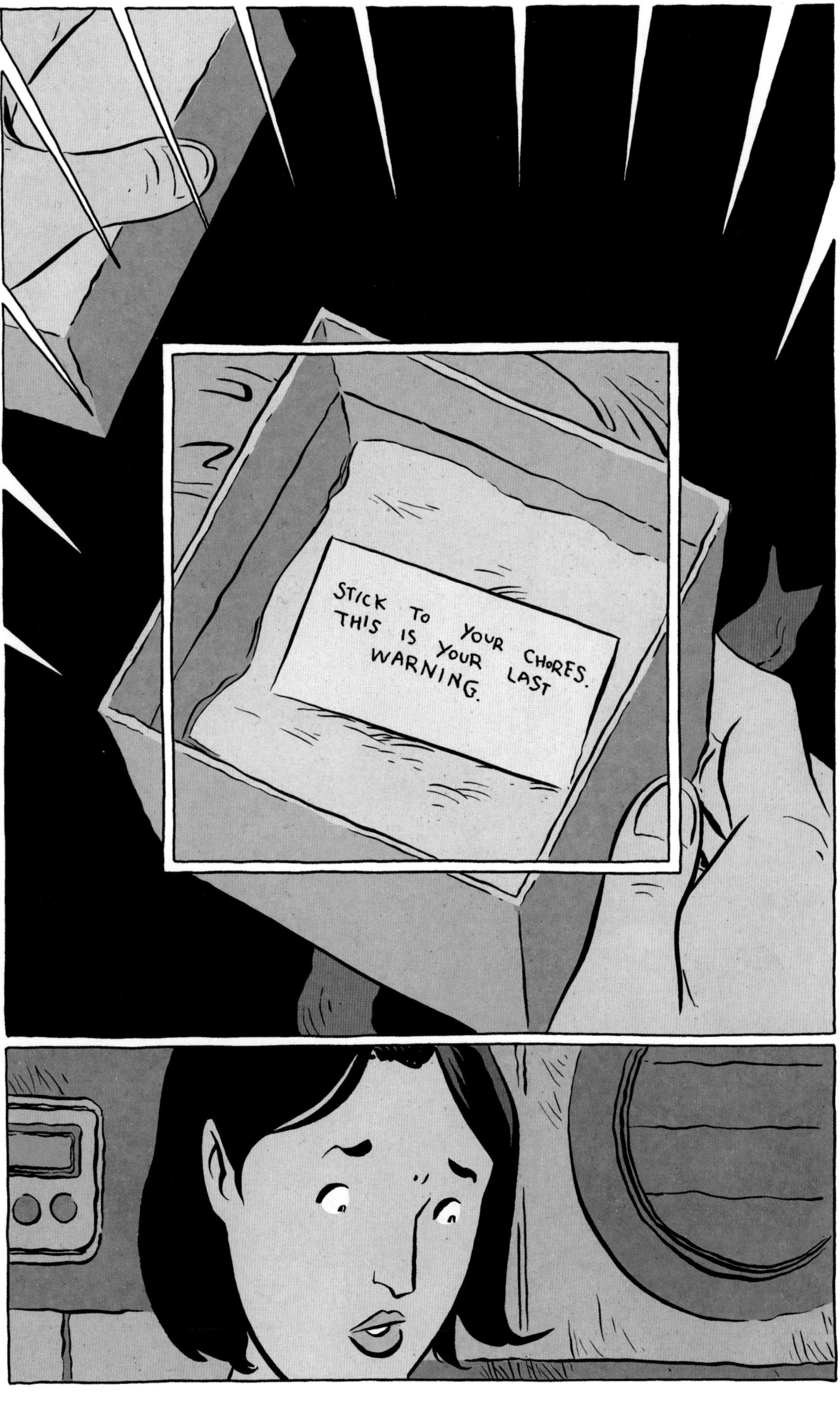
STICK TO YOUR CHORES. THIS IS YOUR LAST WARNING.

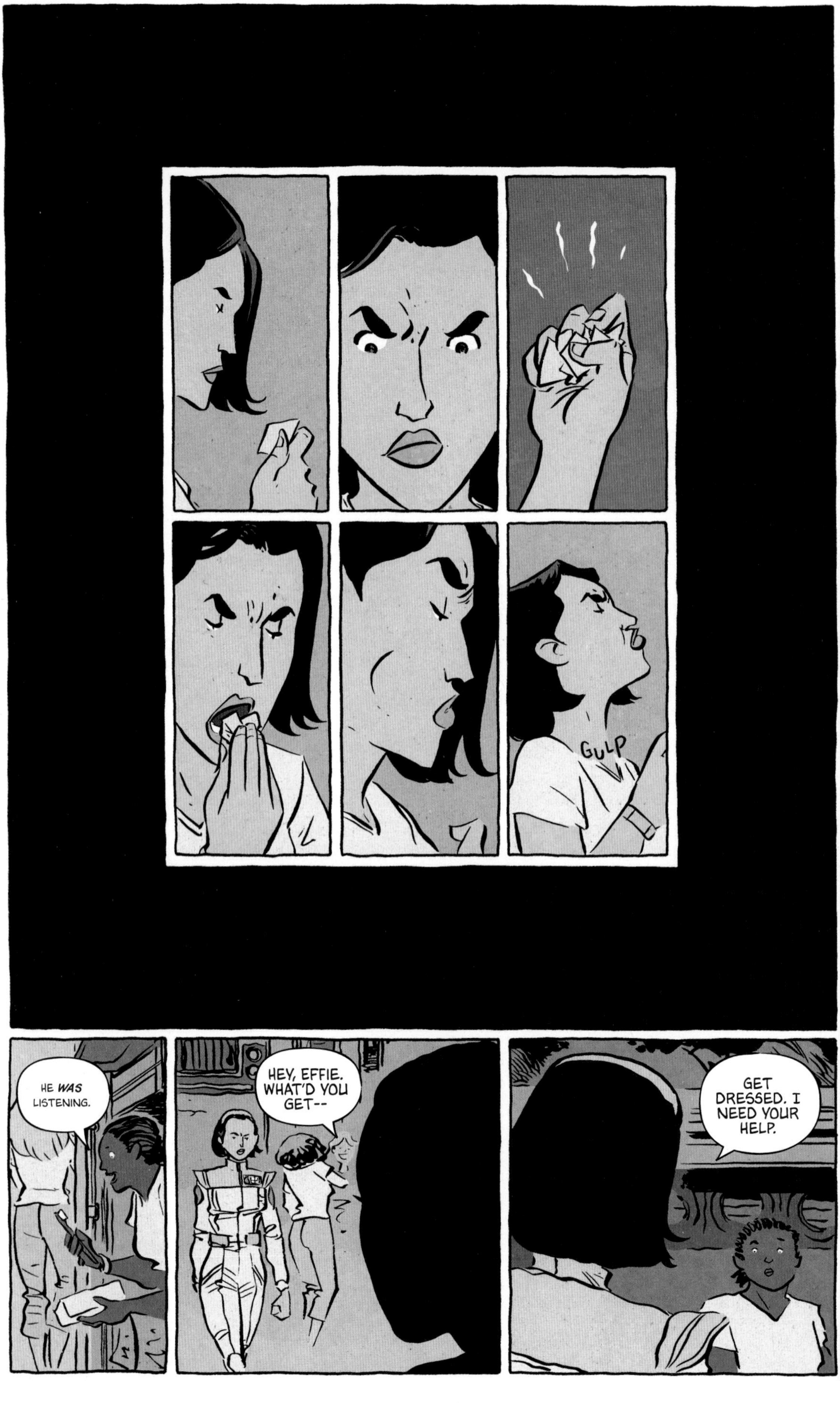
GULP
HE WAS LISTENING.
HEY, EFFIE. WHAT'D YOU GET--
GET DRESSED. I NEED YOUR HELP.

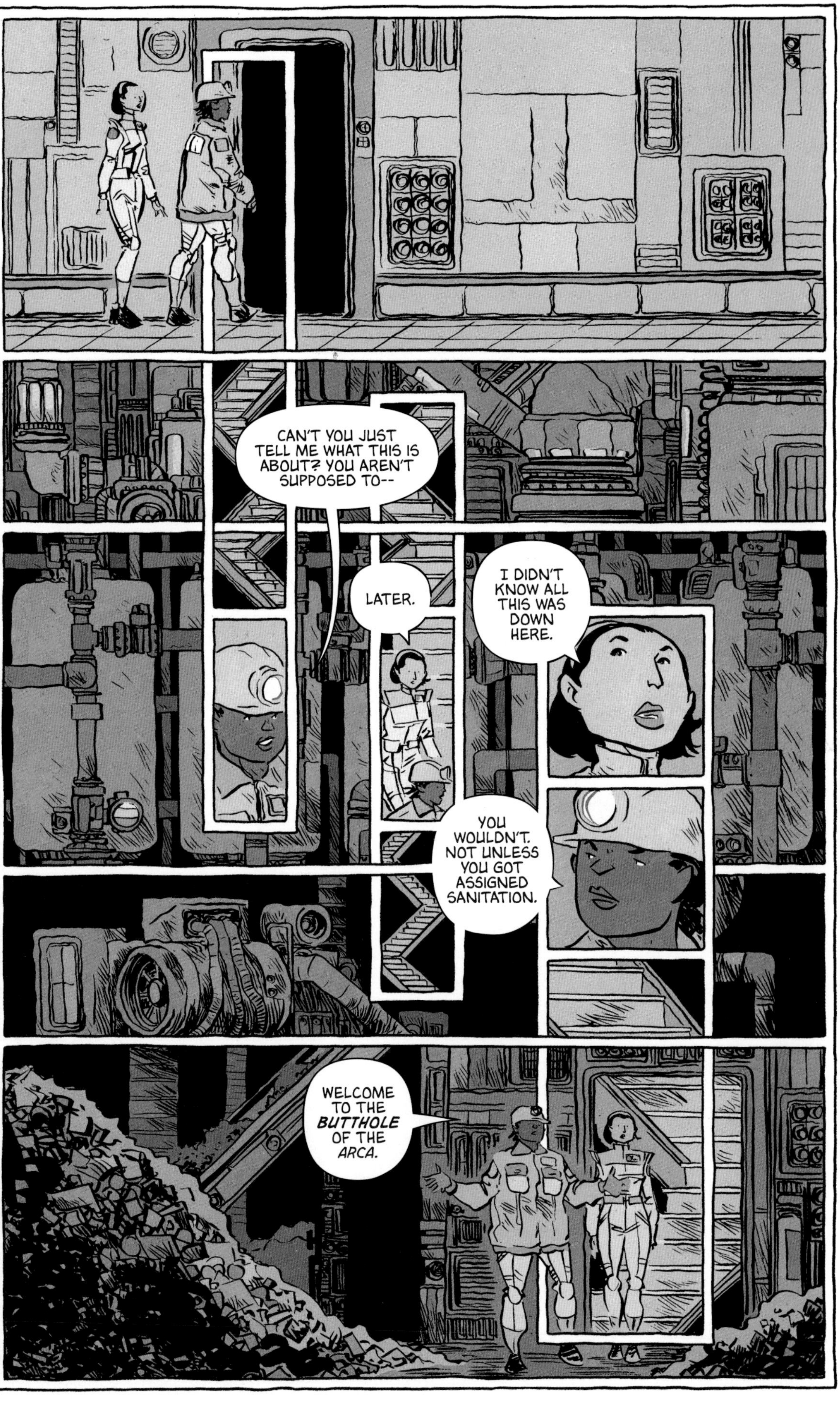
CAN'T YOU JUST TELL ME WHAT THIS IS ABOUT? YOU AREN'T SUPPOSED TO--
LATER.
I DIDN'T KNOW ALL THIS WAS DOWN HERE.
YOU WOULDN'T. NOT UNLESS YOU GOT ASSIGNED SANITATION.
WELCOME TO THE *BUTTHOLE* OF THE *ARCA.*

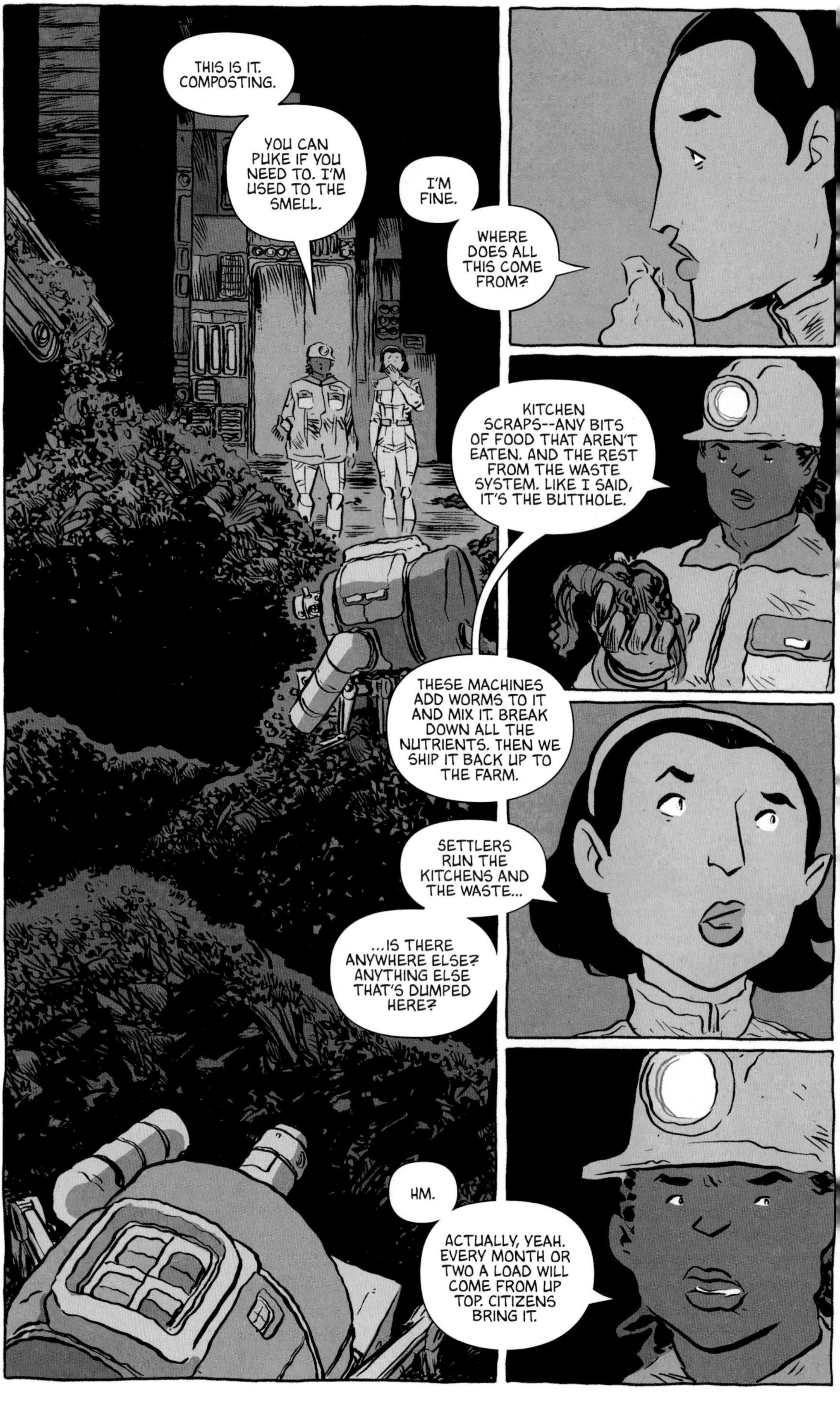
THIS IS IT. COMPOSTING.
YOU CAN PUKE IF YOU NEED TO. I'M USED TO THE SMELL.
I'M FINE.
WHERE DOES ALL THIS COME FROM?
KITCHEN SCRAPS--ANY BITS OF FOOD THAT AREN'T EATEN. AND THE REST FROM THE WASTE SYSTEM. LIKE I SAID, IT'S THE BUTTHOLE.
THESE MACHINES ADD WORMS TO IT AND MIX IT. BREAK DOWN ALL THE NUTRIENTS. THEN WE SHIP IT BACK UP TO THE FARM.
SETTLERS RUN THE KITCHENS AND THE WASTE...
...IS THERE ANYWHERE ELSE? ANYTHING ELSE THAT'S DUMPED HERE?
HM.
ACTUALLY, YEAH. EVERY MONTH OR TWO A LOAD WILL COME FROM UP TOP. CITIZENS BRING IT.

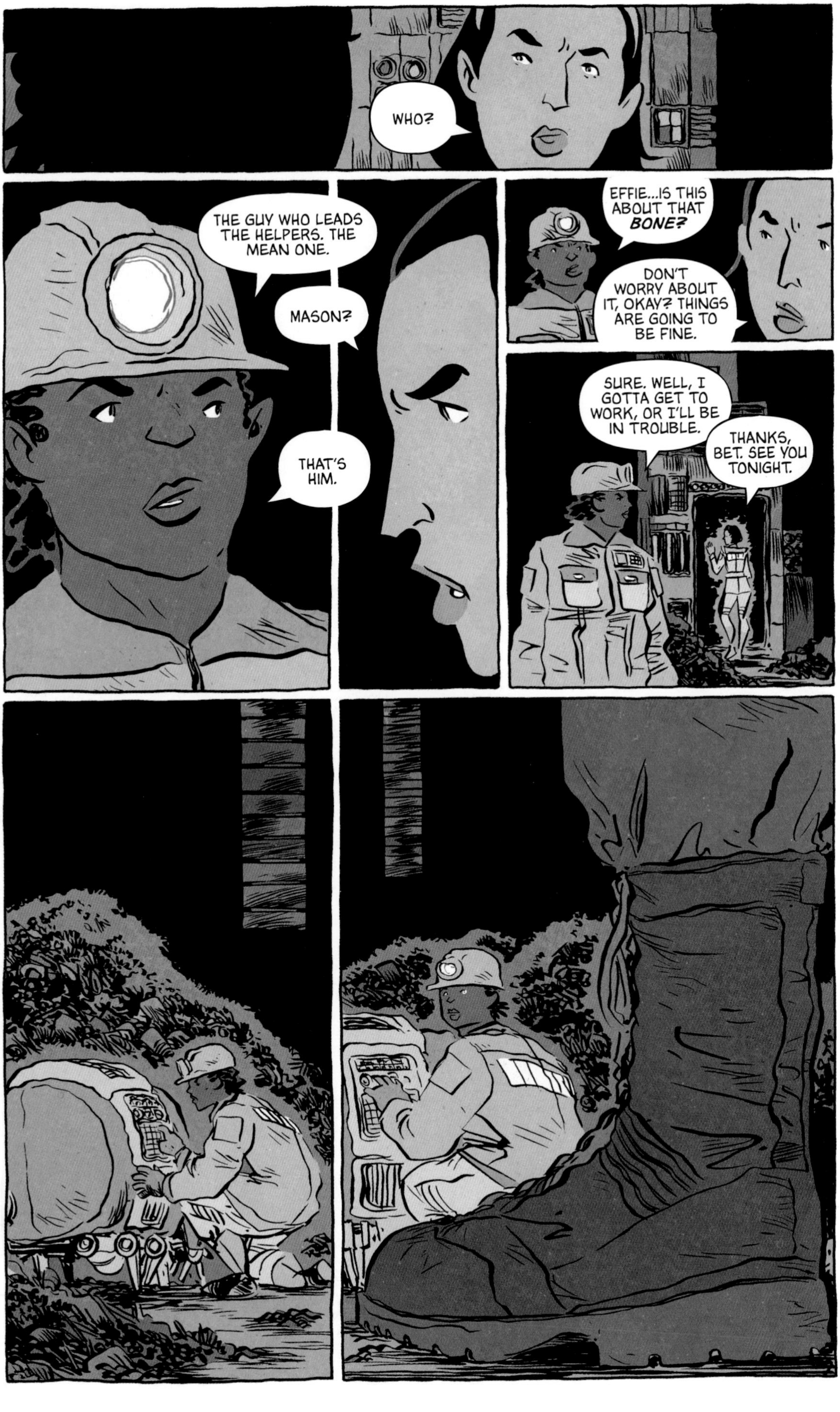

WHO?
THE GUY WHO LEADS THE HELPERS. THE MEAN ONE.
MASON?
THAT'S HIM.
EFFIE...IS THIS ABOUT THAT **BONE?**
DON'T WORRY ABOUT IT, OKAY? THINGS ARE GOING TO BE FINE.
SURE. WELL, I GOTTA GET TO WORK, OR I'LL BE IN TROUBLE.
THANKS, BET. SEE YOU TONIGHT.

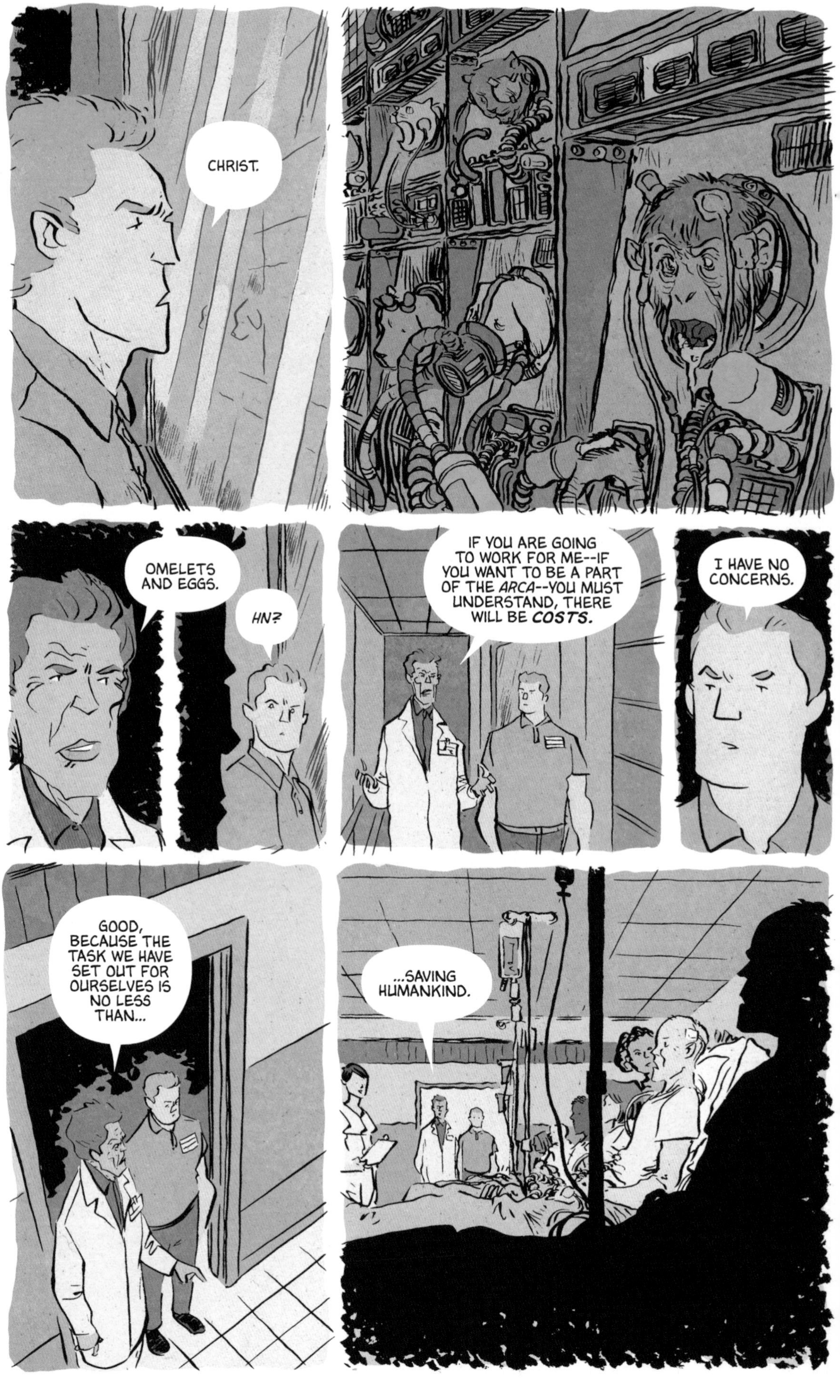
CHRIST.
OMELETS AND EGGS.
HN?
IF YOU ARE GOING TO WORK FOR ME--IF YOU WANT TO BE A PART OF THE *ARCA*--YOU MUST UNDERSTAND, THERE WILL BE ***COSTS.***
I HAVE NO CONCERNS.
GOOD, BECAUSE THE TASK WE HAVE SET OUT FOR OURSELVES IS NO LESS THAN...
...SAVING HUMANKIND.

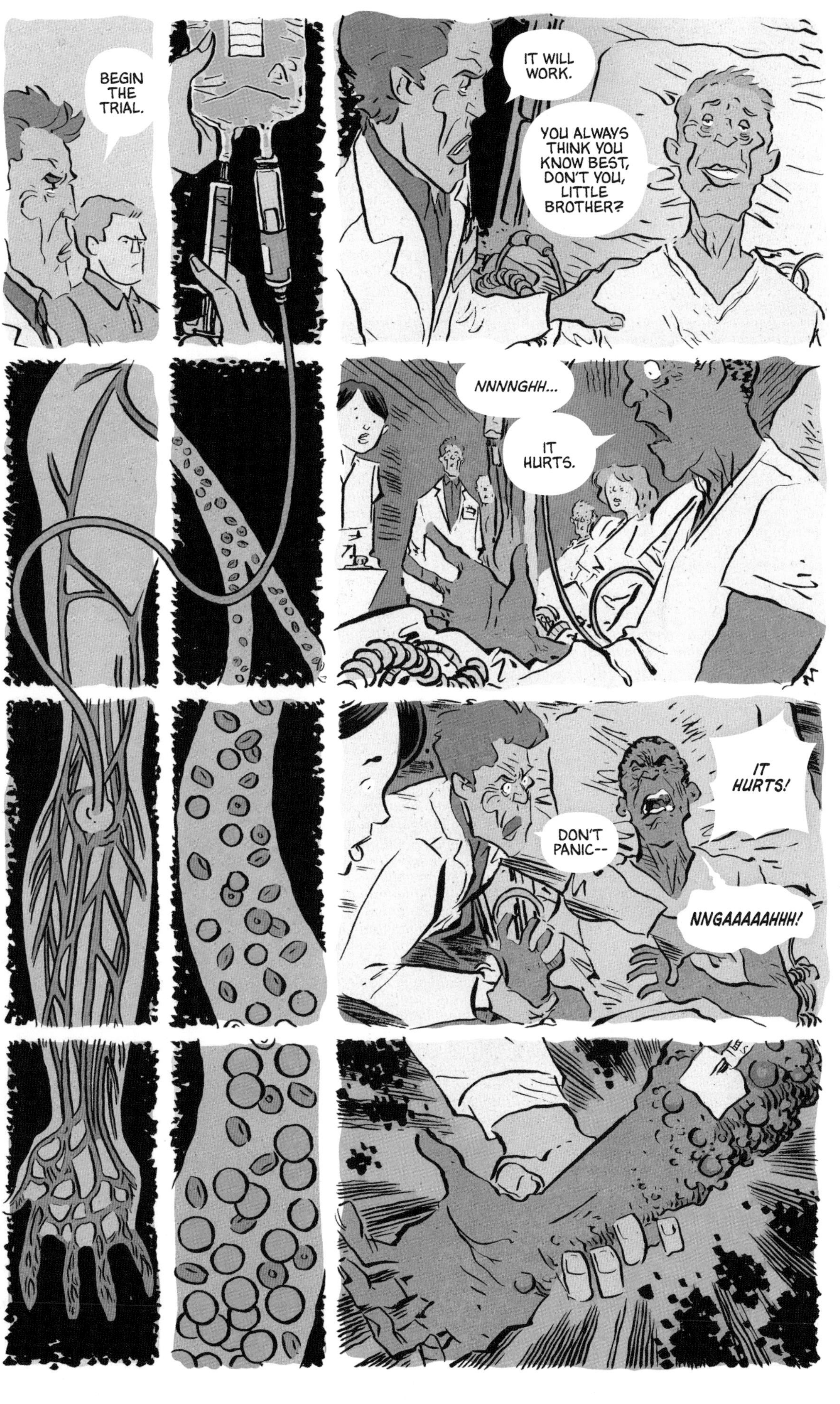
BEGIN THE TRIAL.
IT WILL WORK.
YOU ALWAYS THINK YOU KNOW BEST, DON'T YOU, LITTLE BROTHER?
NNNNGHH...
IT HURTS.
IT HURTS!
DON'T PANIC--
NNGAAAAAHHH!

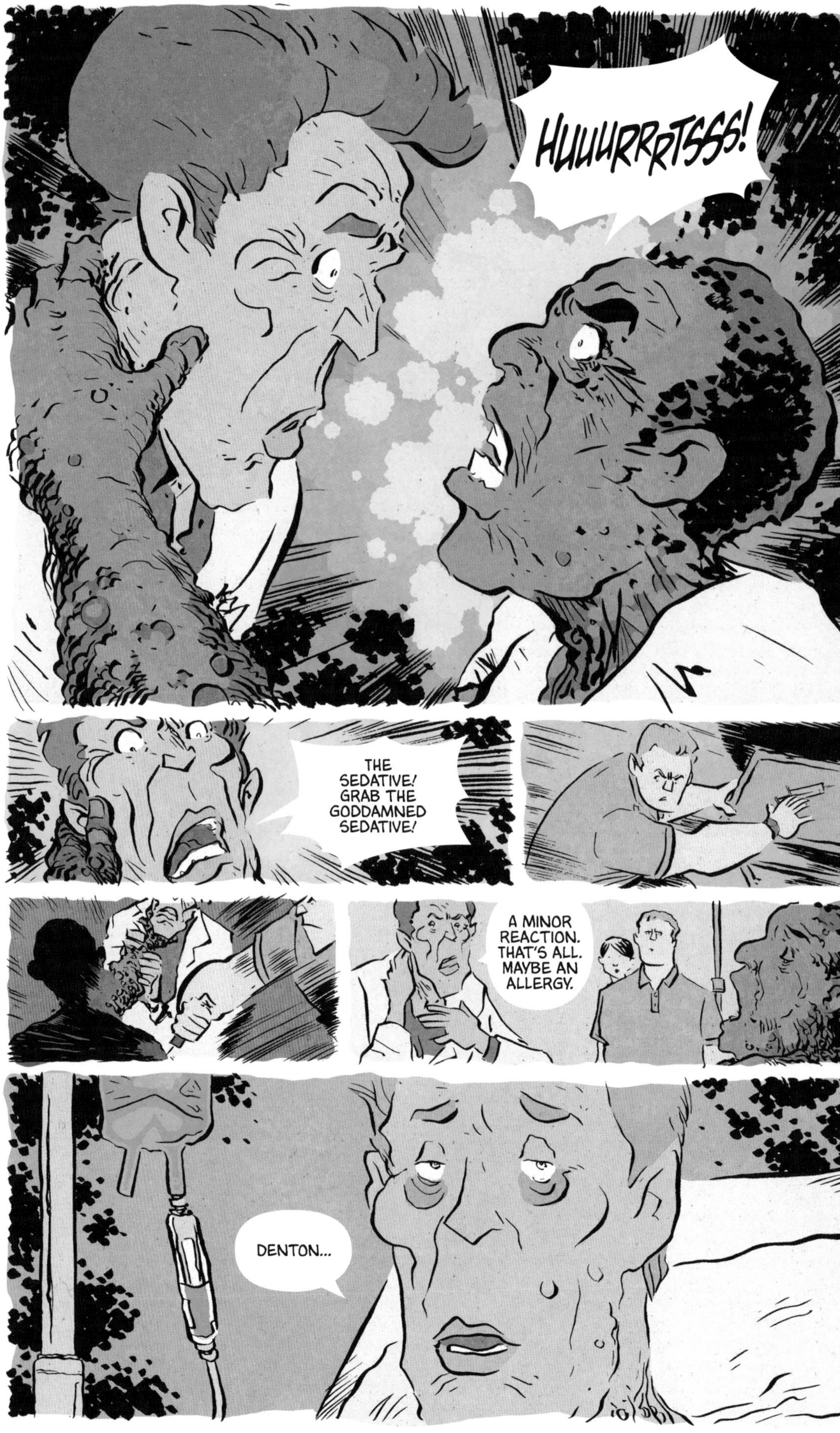
HUUURRRTSSS!
THE SEDATIVE! GRAB THE GODDAMNED SEDATIVE!
A MINOR REACTION. THAT'S ALL. MAYBE AN ALLERGY.
DENTON...

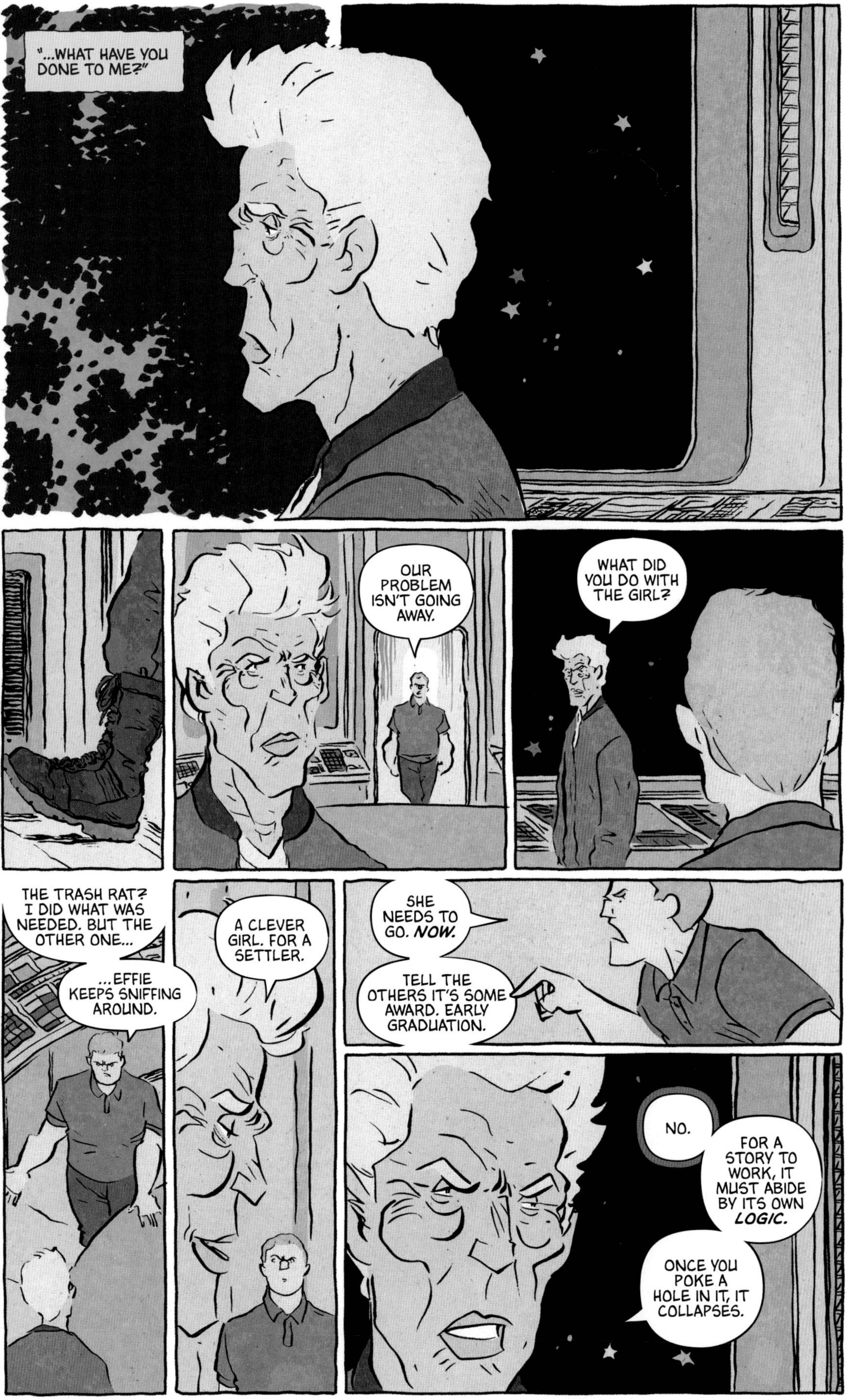
"...WHAT HAVE YOU DONE TO ME?"
OUR PROBLEM ISN'T GOING AWAY.
WHAT DID YOU DO WITH THE GIRL?
THE TRASH RAT? I DID WHAT WAS NEEDED. BUT THE OTHER ONE...
...EFFIE KEEPS SNIFFING AROUND.
A CLEVER GIRL. FOR A SETTLER.
SHE NEEDS TO GO. *NOW.*
TELL THE OTHERS IT'S SOME AWARD. EARLY GRADUATION.
NO.
FOR A STORY TO WORK, IT MUST ABIDE BY ITS OWN *LOGIC.*
ONCE YOU POKE A HOLE IN IT, IT COLLAPSES.

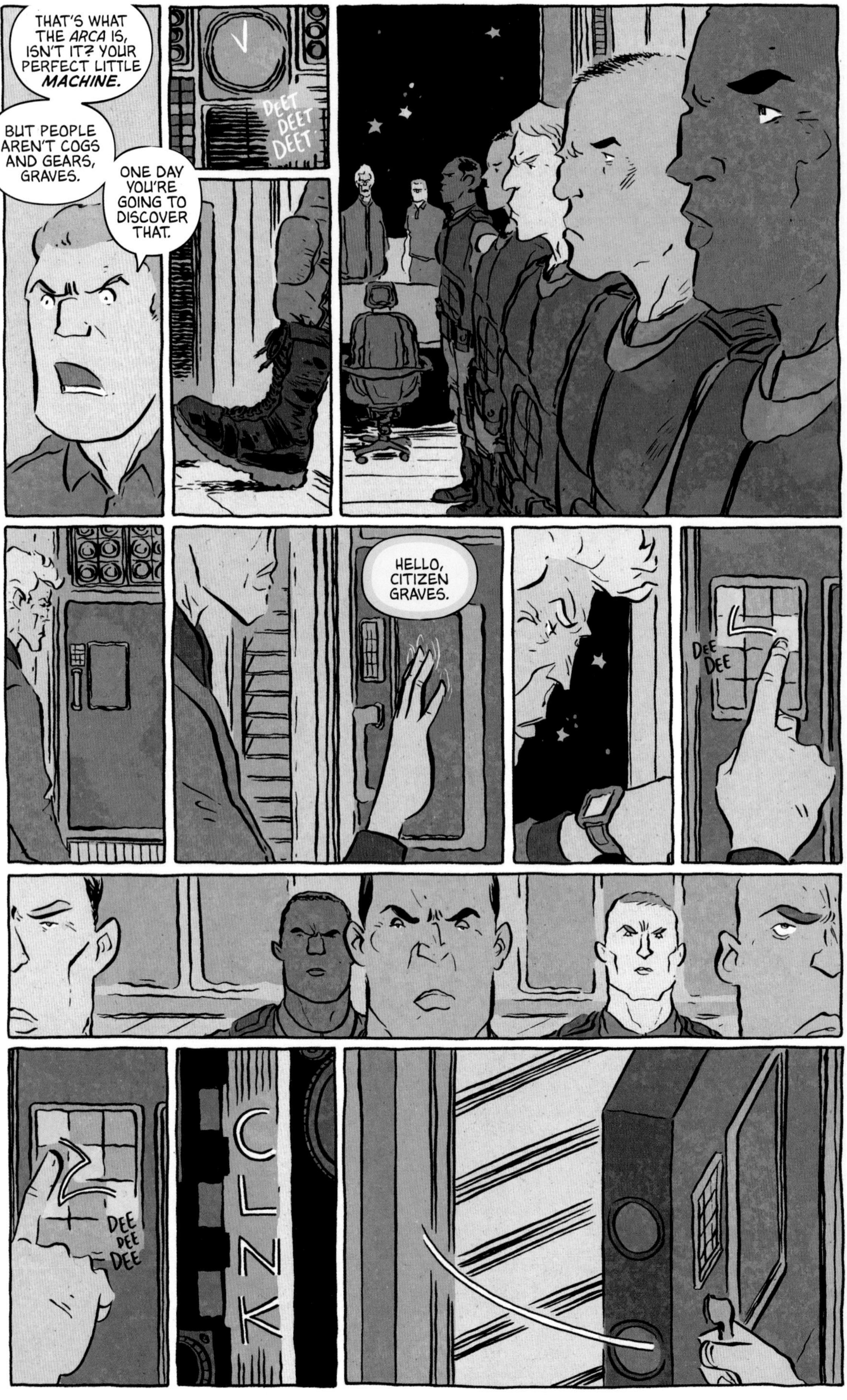
THAT'S WHAT THE *ARCA* IS, ISN'T IT? YOUR PERFECT LITTLE ***MACHINE.***
BUT PEOPLE AREN'T COGS AND GEARS, GRAVES.
ONE DAY YOU'RE GOING TO DISCOVER THAT.
DEET DEET DEET
HELLO, CITIZEN GRAVES.
DEE DEE
DEE DEE DEE
CLZK

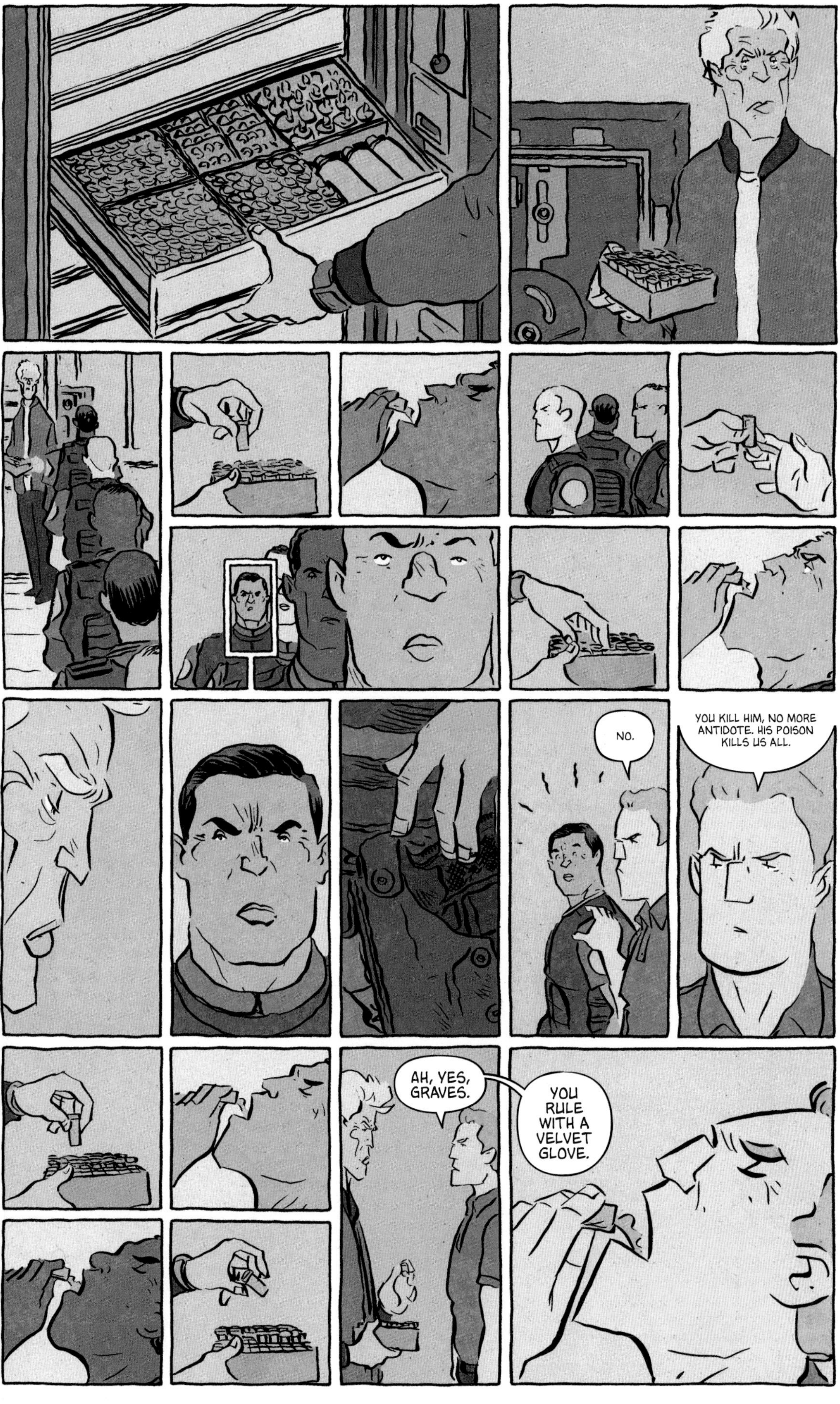
NO.
YOU KILL HIM, NO MORE ANTIDOTE. HIS POISON KILLS US ALL.
AH, YES, GRAVES.
YOU RULE WITH A VELVET GLOVE.

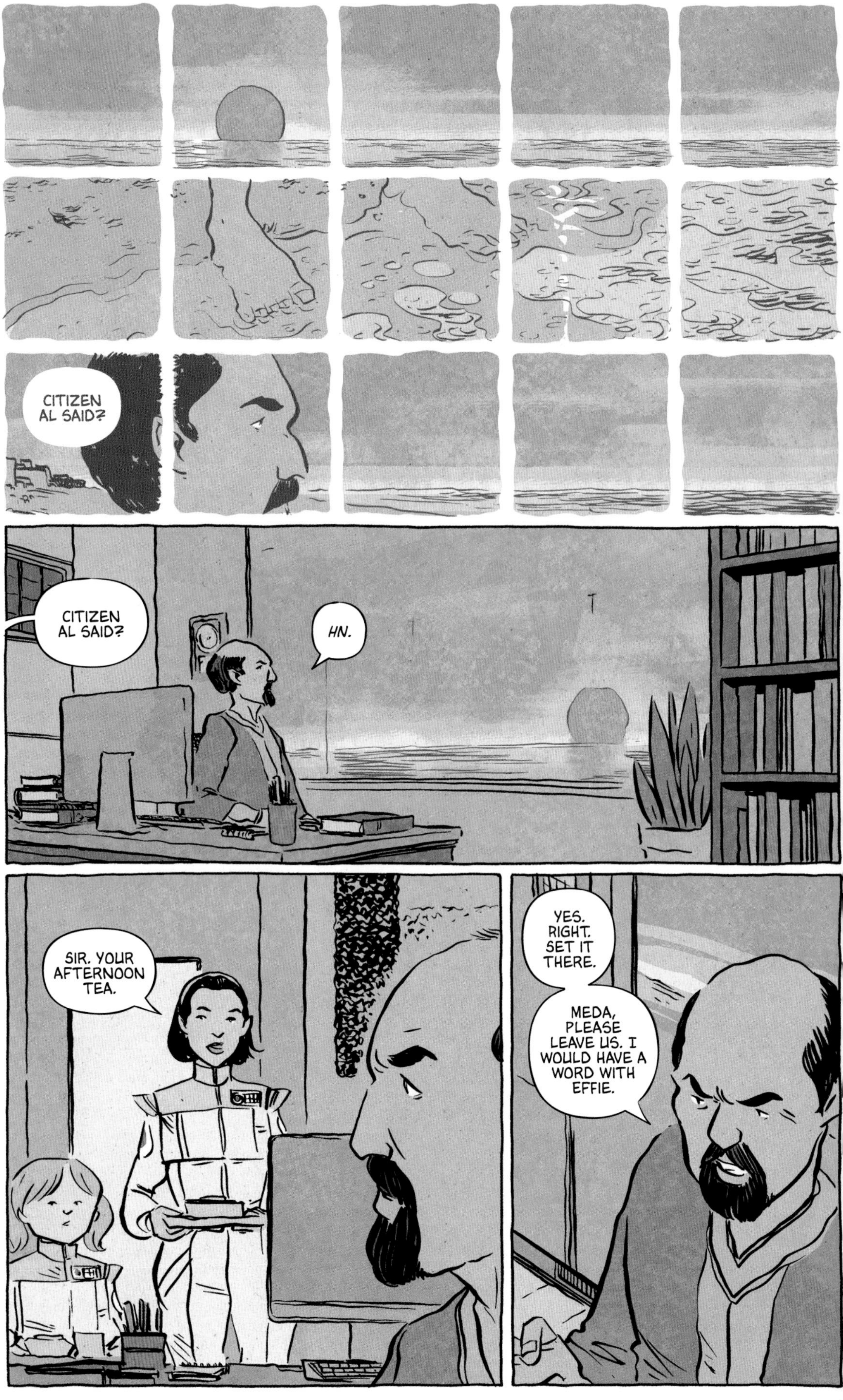
CITIZEN AL SAID?
CITIZEN AL SAID?
HN.
SIR. YOUR AFTERNOON TEA.
YES. RIGHT. SET IT THERE.
MEDA, PLEASE LEAVE US. I WOULD HAVE A WORD WITH EFFIE.

WHAT SHALL I READ TO THE CHILDREN TODAY?

NO. NO MORE. THEY ARE OLD ENOUGH TO READ TO THEMSELVES. TEACHING YOU...IT WAS A MISTAKE.

THE NOTE I RECEIVED ON SOLSTICE--THE *WARNING.* IT WAS FROM YOU?

I LIKE TO THINK I HAVE BEEN A...FRIEND. AND SO, AS A FRIEND, I HAVE THIS ADVICE.

ENJOY THESE DAYS. THEN BE FINISHED WITH YOUR WORK. ENJOY GRADUATION.

I KNOW YOUR FRIEND FRIEDA IS EAGER FOR YOU TO JOIN HER.

I WILL, CITIZEN AL SAID. I PROMISE.

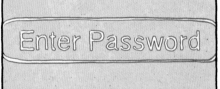

Enter Password

PASSWORD
FDBN7538

AFTERNOON PRIME

GYMNASTICS? M W F
SWIMM-F

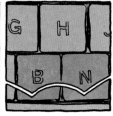

DOO
DOOT

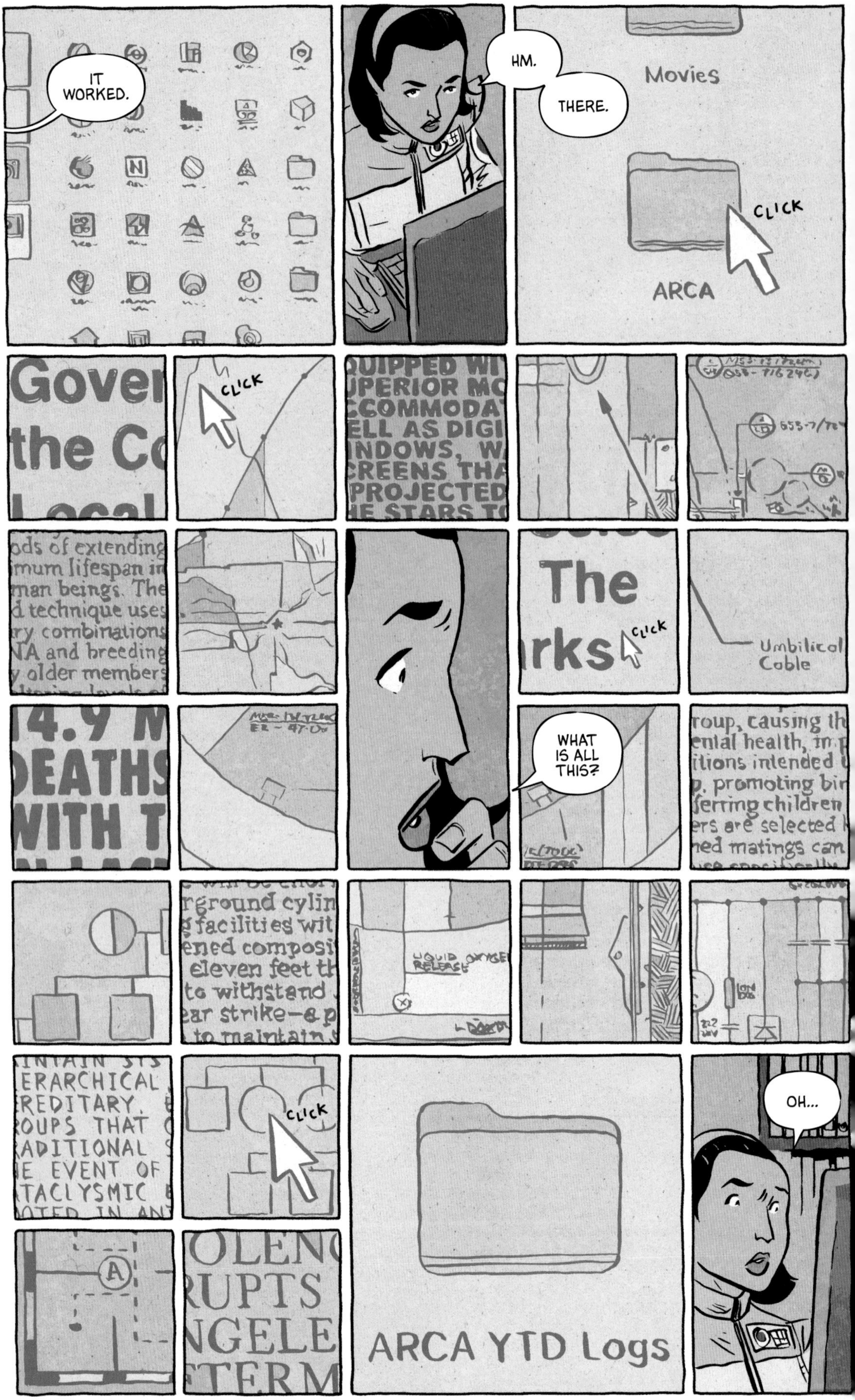

IT WORKED.
HM.
THERE.
Movies
CLICK
ARCA
Gover
the Co
CLICK
QUIPPED WI
UPERIOR MO
CCOMMODA
ELL AS DIGI
INDOWS, W
CREENS THA
PROJECTED
ods of extending
imum lifespan in
man beings. The
d technique uses
ry combinations
NA and breeding
y older members
The
rks
CLICK
Umbilical Cable
4.9 M
DEATHS
WITH T
WHAT IS ALL THIS?
roup, causing th
ental health, in p
ilions intended
p, promoting bir
ferring children
ers are selected
ned matings can
rground cylin
g facilities wit
ened composi
eleven feet th
to withstand
ear strike—a p
to maintain
LIQUID OXYGEN RELEASE
ERARCHICAL
EREDITARY
OUPS THAT
RADITIONAL
E EVENT OF
ATACLYSMIC
CLICK
OLEN
RUPTS
NGELE
TERM
ARCA YTD Logs
OH...

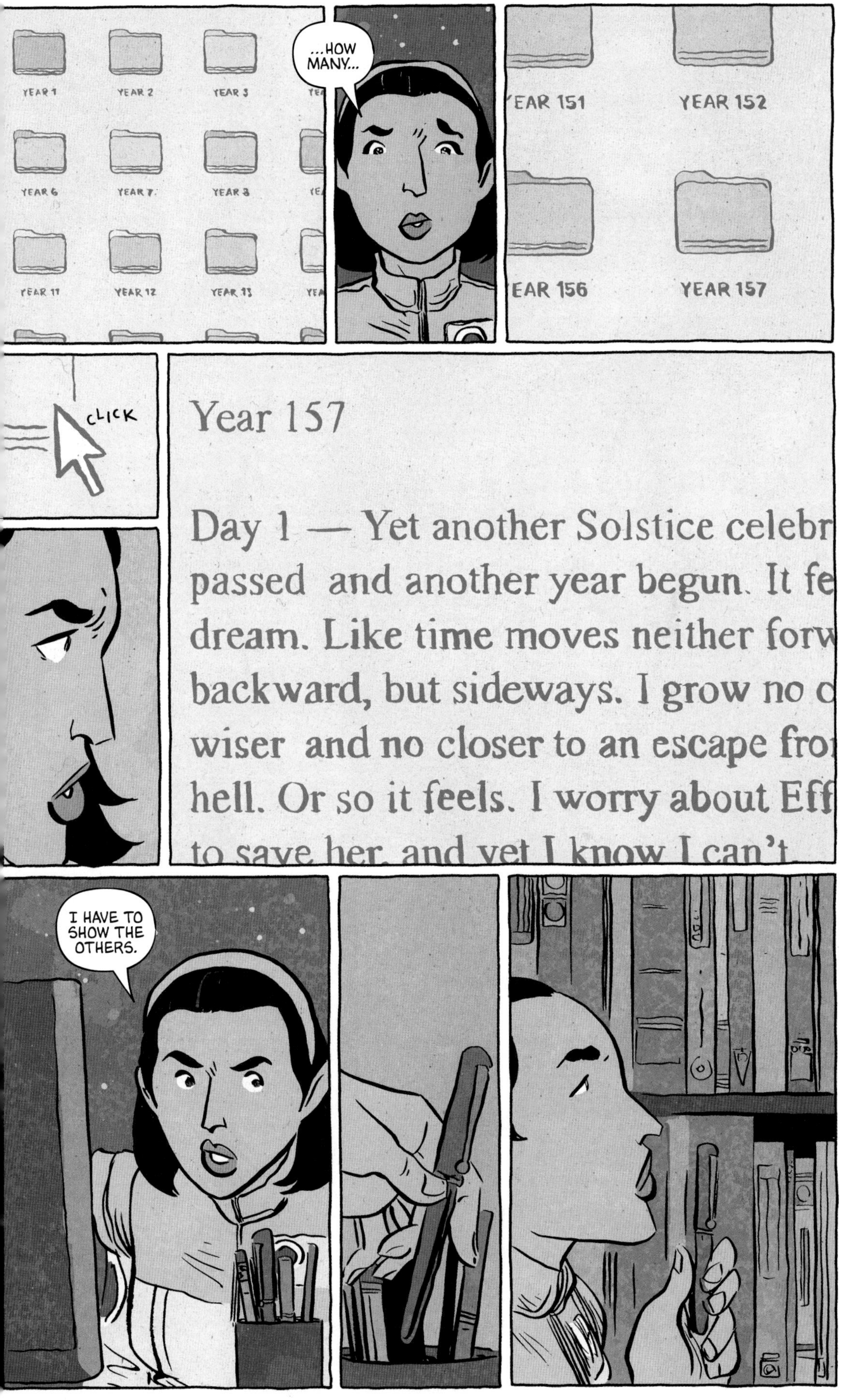
YEAR 1
YEAR 2
YEAR 3
YEAR 6
YEAR 7
YEAR 8
YEAR 11
YEAR 12
YEAR 13
...HOW MANY...
YEAR 151
YEAR 152
YEAR 156
YEAR 157
CLICK
Year 157
Day 1 — Yet another Solstice celebr
passed and another year begun. It fe
dream. Like time moves neither forw
backward, but sideways. I grow no o
wiser and no closer to an escape fro
hell. Or so it feels. I worry about Eff
to save her, and yet I know I can't.
I HAVE TO SHOW THE OTHERS.

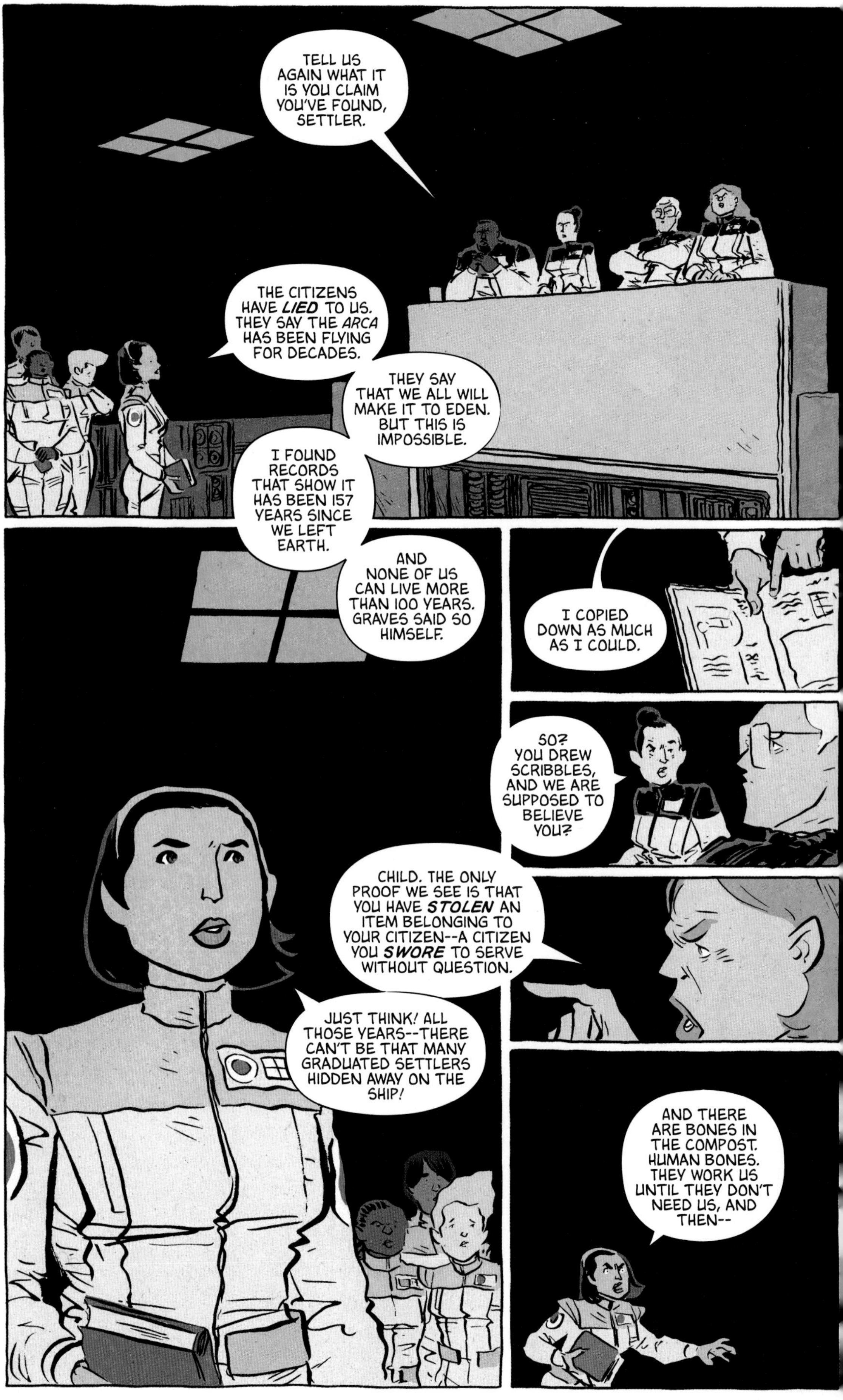
TELL US AGAIN WHAT IT IS YOU CLAIM YOU'VE FOUND, SETTLER.
THE CITIZENS HAVE *LIED* TO US. THEY SAY THE *ARCA* HAS BEEN FLYING FOR DECADES.
THEY SAY THAT WE ALL WILL MAKE IT TO EDEN. BUT THIS IS IMPOSSIBLE.
I FOUND RECORDS THAT SHOW IT HAS BEEN 157 YEARS SINCE WE LEFT EARTH.
AND NONE OF US CAN LIVE MORE THAN 100 YEARS. GRAVES SAID SO HIMSELF.
I COPIED DOWN AS MUCH AS I COULD.
SO? YOU DREW SCRIBBLES, AND WE ARE SUPPOSED TO BELIEVE YOU?
CHILD. THE ONLY PROOF WE SEE IS THAT YOU HAVE ***STOLEN*** AN ITEM BELONGING TO YOUR CITIZEN--A CITIZEN YOU ***SWORE*** TO SERVE WITHOUT QUESTION.
JUST THINK! ALL THOSE YEARS--THERE CAN'T BE THAT MANY GRADUATED SETTLERS HIDDEN AWAY ON THE SHIP!
AND THERE ARE BONES IN THE COMPOST. HUMAN BONES. THEY WORK US UNTIL THEY DON'T NEED US, AND THEN--

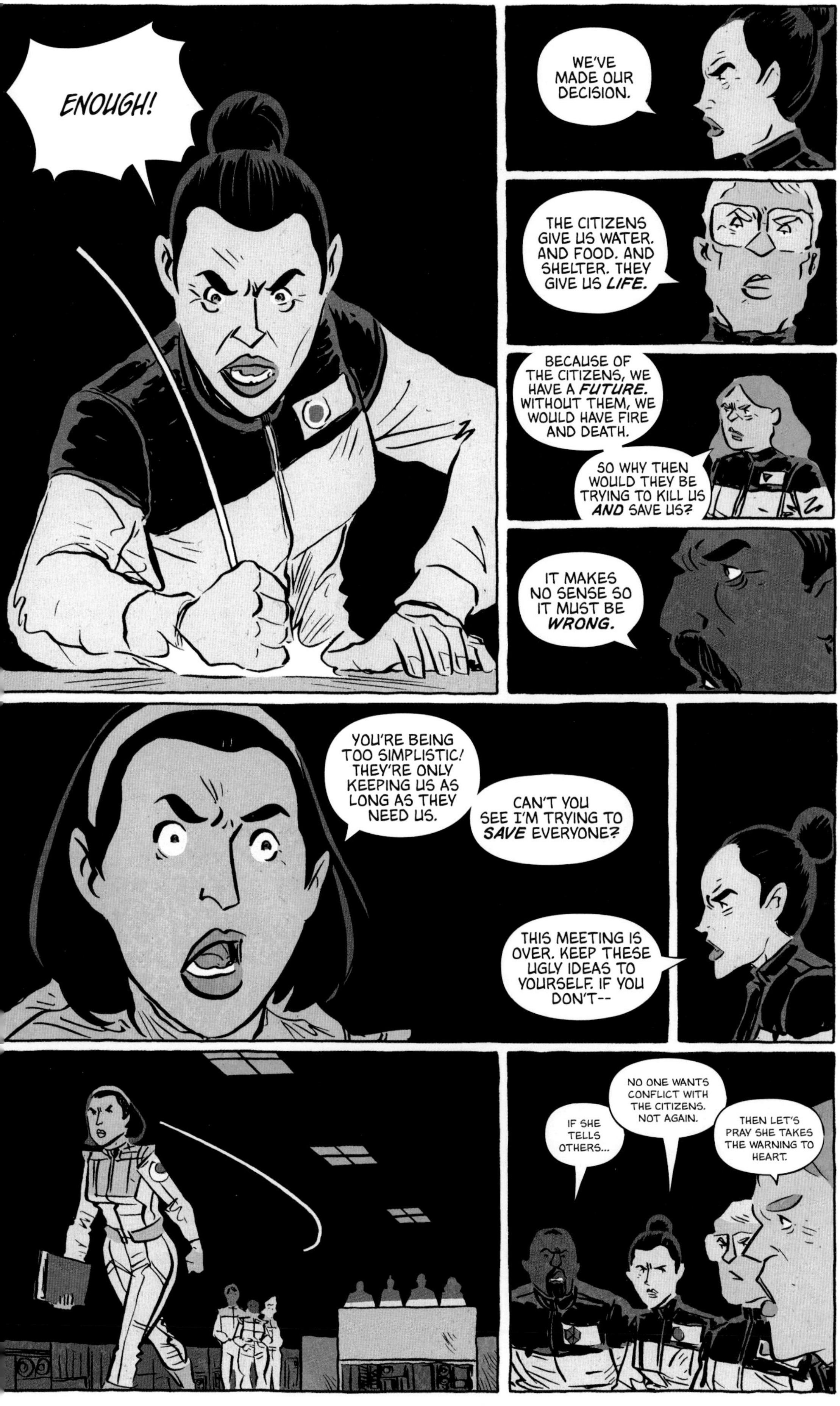
ENOUGH!
WE'VE MADE OUR DECISION.
THE CITIZENS GIVE US WATER. AND FOOD. AND SHELTER. THEY GIVE US *LIFE.*
BECAUSE OF THE CITIZENS, WE HAVE A *FUTURE.* WITHOUT THEM, WE WOULD HAVE FIRE AND DEATH.
SO WHY THEN WOULD THEY BE TRYING TO KILL US *AND* SAVE US?
IT MAKES NO SENSE SO IT MUST BE *WRONG.*
YOU'RE BEING TOO SIMPLISTIC! THEY'RE ONLY KEEPING US AS LONG AS THEY NEED US.
CAN'T YOU SEE I'M TRYING TO *SAVE* EVERYONE?
THIS MEETING IS OVER. KEEP THESE UGLY IDEAS TO YOURSELF. IF YOU DON'T--
IF SHE TELLS OTHERS...
NO ONE WANTS CONFLICT WITH THE CITIZENS. NOT AGAIN.
THEN LET'S PRAY SHE TAKES THE WARNING TO HEART.

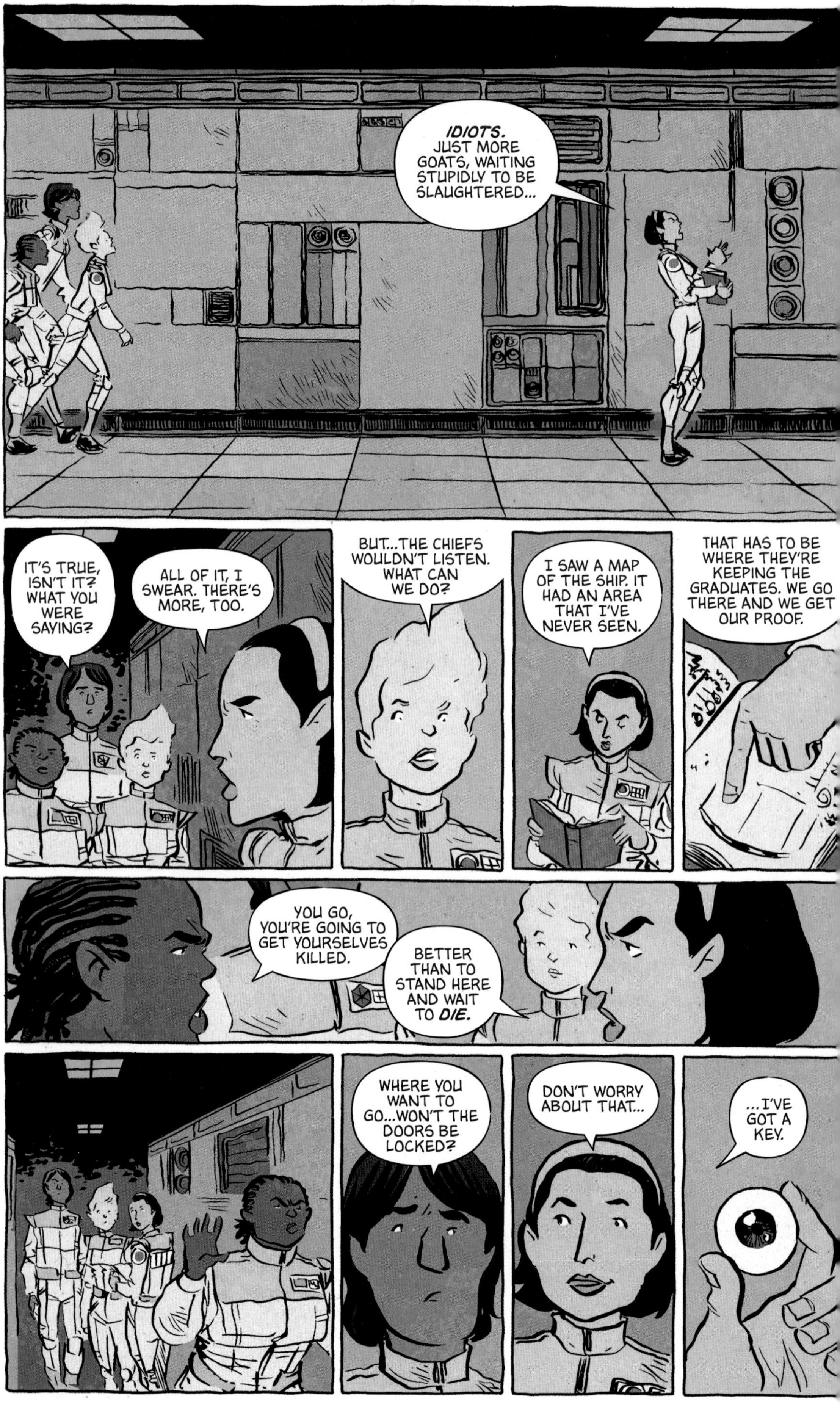
IDIOTS. JUST MORE GOATS, WAITING STUPIDLY TO BE SLAUGHTERED...
IT'S TRUE, ISN'T IT? WHAT YOU WERE SAYING?
ALL OF IT, I SWEAR. THERE'S MORE, TOO.
BUT...THE CHIEFS WOULDN'T LISTEN. WHAT CAN WE DO?
I SAW A MAP OF THE SHIP. IT HAD AN AREA THAT I'VE NEVER SEEN.
THAT HAS TO BE WHERE THEY'RE KEEPING THE GRADUATES. WE GO THERE AND WE GET OUR PROOF.
YOU GO, YOU'RE GOING TO GET YOURSELVES KILLED.
BETTER THAN TO STAND HERE AND WAIT TO *DIE.*
WHERE YOU WANT TO GO...WON'T THE DOORS BE LOCKED?
DON'T WORRY ABOUT THAT...
...I'VE GOT A KEY.

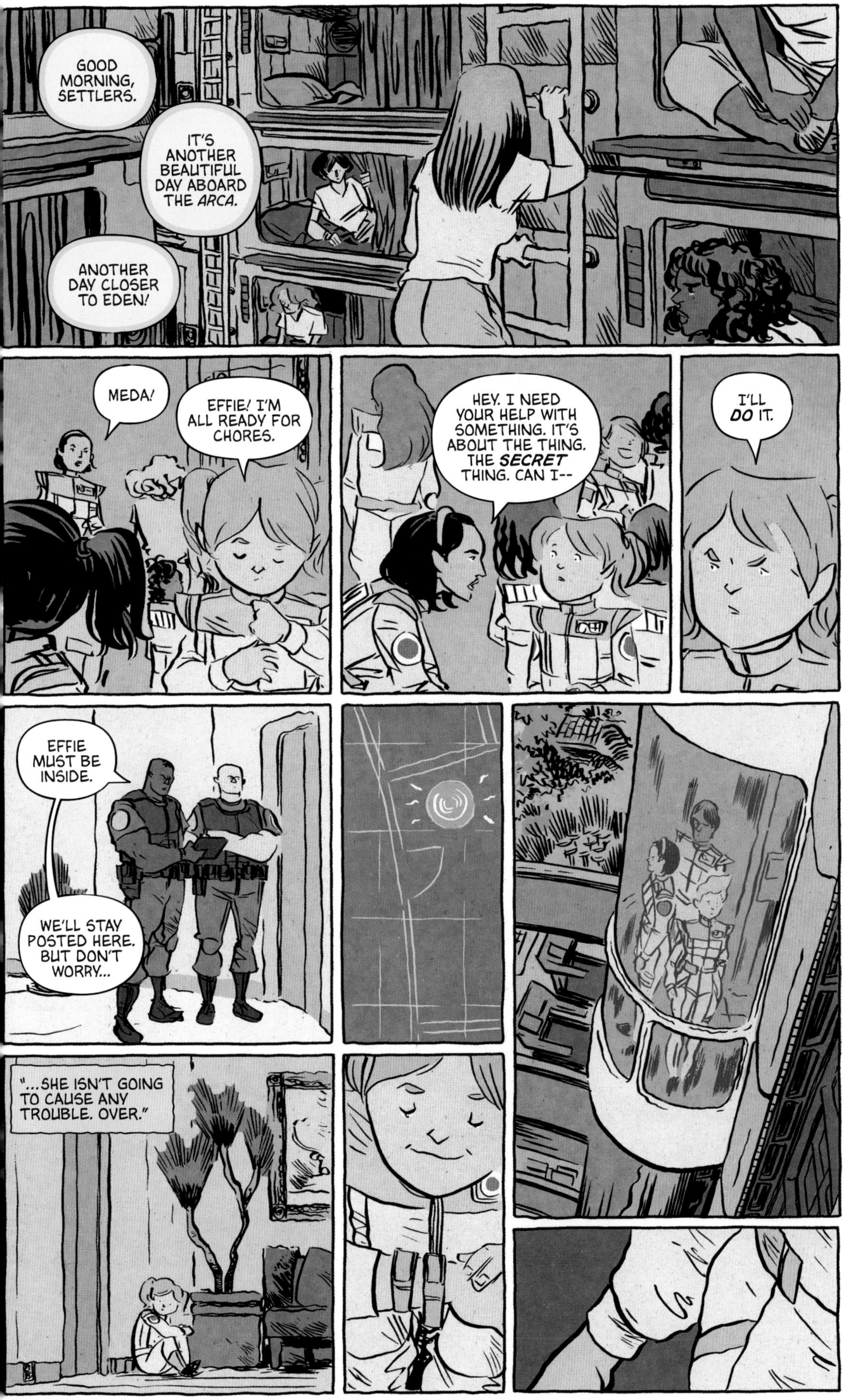
GOOD MORNING, SETTLERS.
IT'S ANOTHER BEAUTIFUL DAY ABOARD THE *ARCA.*
ANOTHER DAY CLOSER TO EDEN!
MEDA!
EFFIE! I'M ALL READY FOR CHORES.
HEY. I NEED YOUR HELP WITH SOMETHING. IT'S ABOUT THE THING. THE ***SECRET*** THING. CAN I--
I'LL ***DO*** IT.
EFFIE MUST BE INSIDE.
WE'LL STAY POSTED HERE. BUT DON'T WORRY...
"...SHE ISN'T GOING TO CAUSE ANY TROUBLE. OVER."

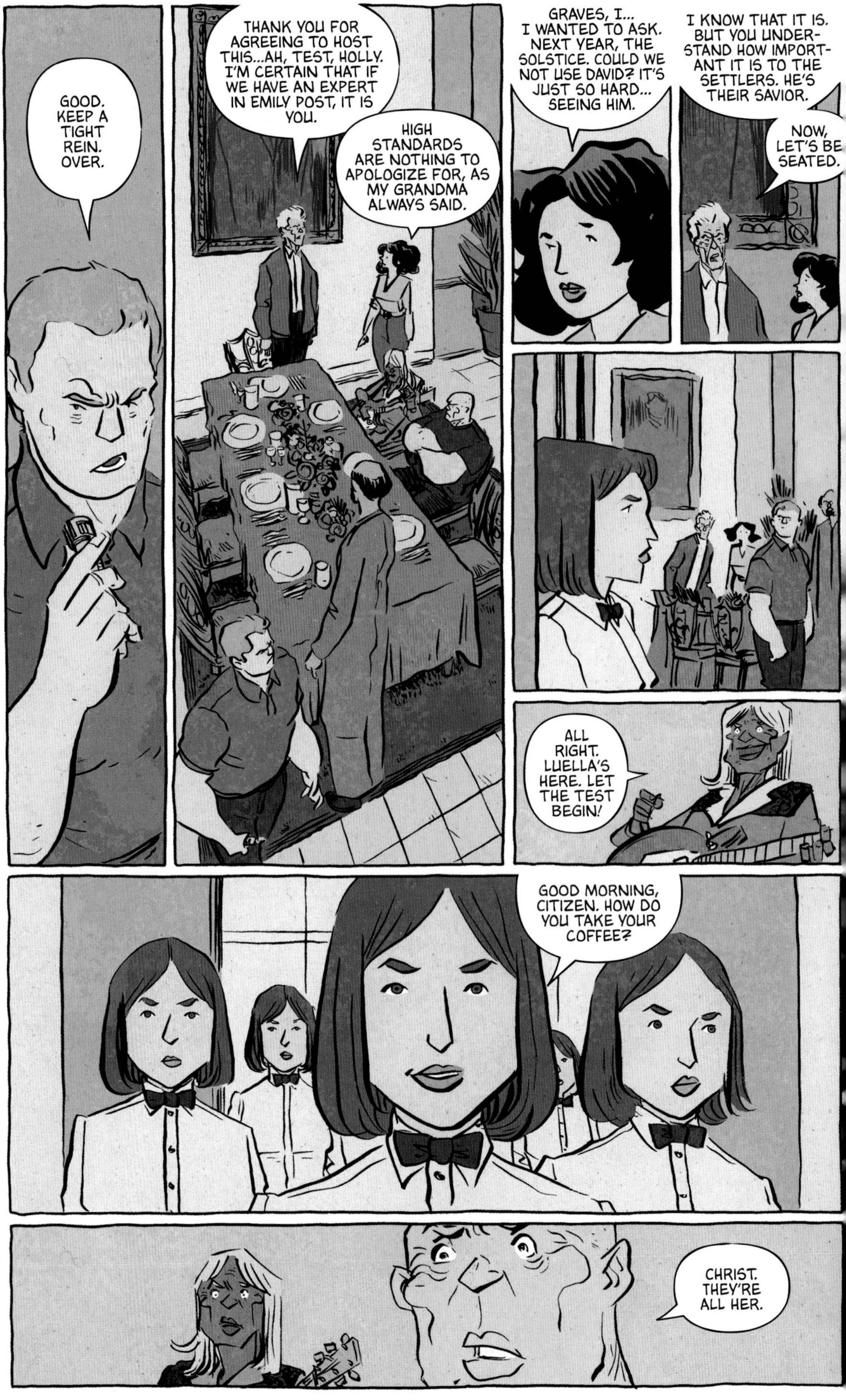
GOOD. KEEP A TIGHT REIN. OVER.
THANK YOU FOR AGREEING TO HOST THIS...AH, TEST, HOLLY. I'M CERTAIN THAT IF WE HAVE AN EXPERT IN EMILY POST, IT IS YOU.
HIGH STANDARDS ARE NOTHING TO APOLOGIZE FOR, AS MY GRANDMA ALWAYS SAID.
GRAVES, I... I WANTED TO ASK. NEXT YEAR, THE SOLSTICE. COULD WE NOT USE DAVID? IT'S JUST SO HARD... SEEING HIM.
I KNOW THAT IT IS. BUT YOU UNDERSTAND HOW IMPORTANT IT IS TO THE SETTLERS. HE'S THEIR SAVIOR.
NOW, LET'S BE SEATED.
ALL RIGHT. LUELLA'S HERE. LET THE TEST BEGIN!
GOOD MORNING, CITIZEN. HOW DO YOU TAKE YOUR COFFEE?
CHRIST. THEY'RE ALL HER.

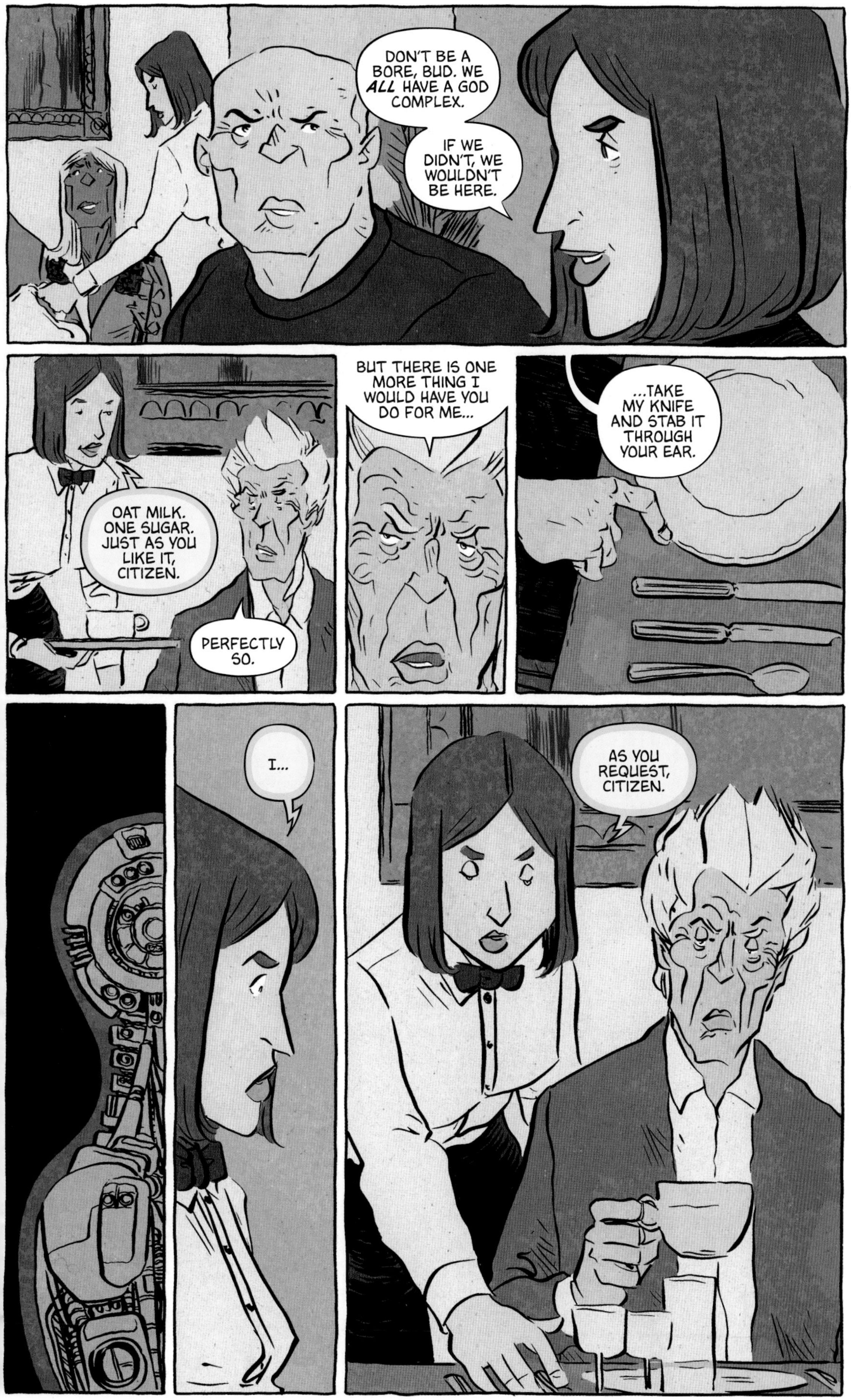
DON'T BE A BORE, BUD. WE *ALL* HAVE A GOD COMPLEX.
IF WE DIDN'T, WE WOULDN'T BE HERE.
OAT MILK. ONE SUGAR. JUST AS YOU LIKE IT, CITIZEN.
PERFECTLY SO.
BUT THERE IS ONE MORE THING I WOULD HAVE YOU DO FOR ME...
...TAKE MY KNIFE AND STAB IT THROUGH YOUR EAR.
I...
AS YOU REQUEST, CITIZEN.

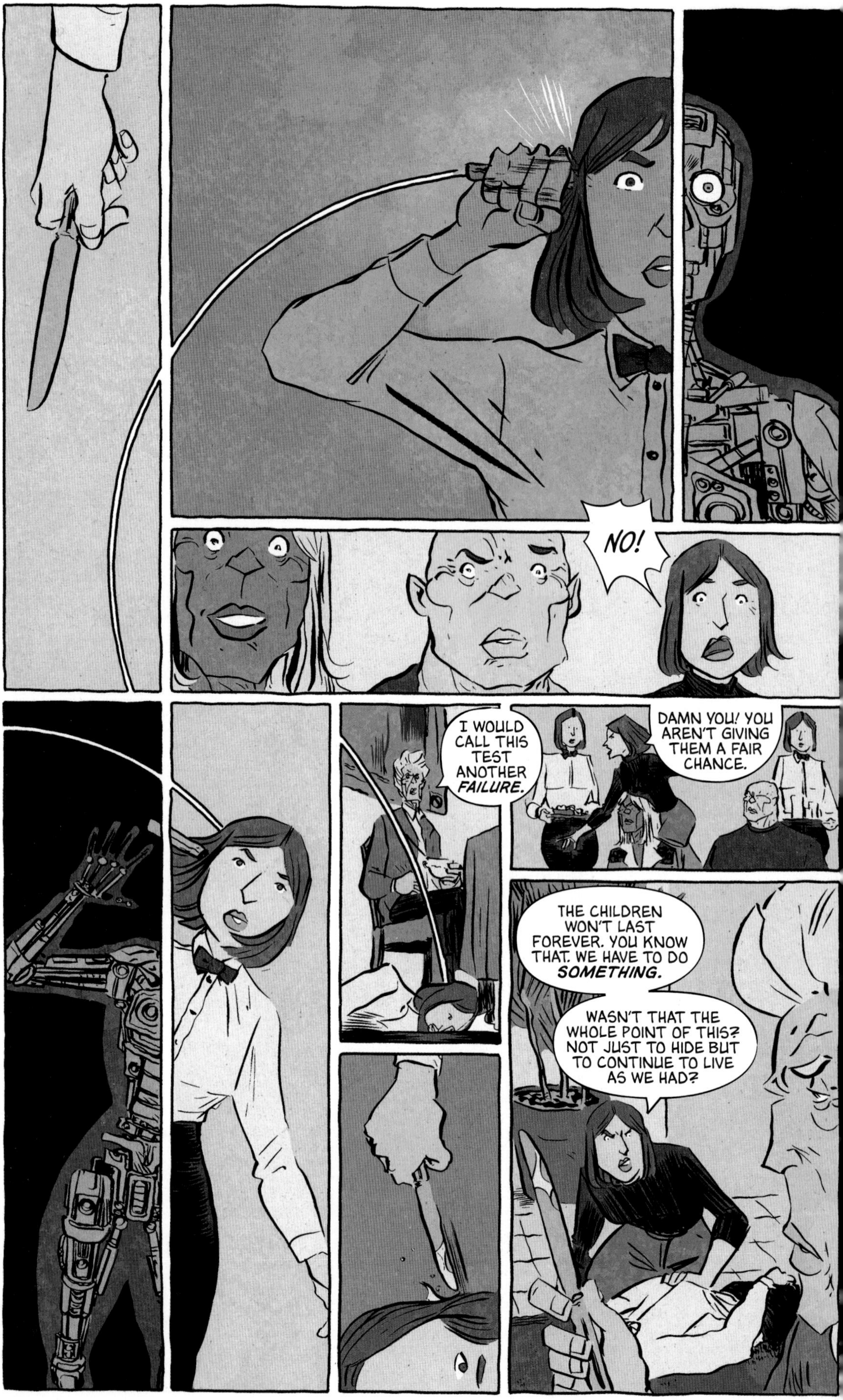
NO!
I WOULD CALL THIS TEST ANOTHER FAILURE.
DAMN YOU! YOU AREN'T GIVING THEM A FAIR CHANCE.
THE CHILDREN WON'T LAST FOREVER. YOU KNOW THAT. WE HAVE TO DO SOMETHING.
WASN'T THAT THE WHOLE POINT OF THIS? NOT JUST TO HIDE BUT TO CONTINUE TO LIVE AS WE HAD?

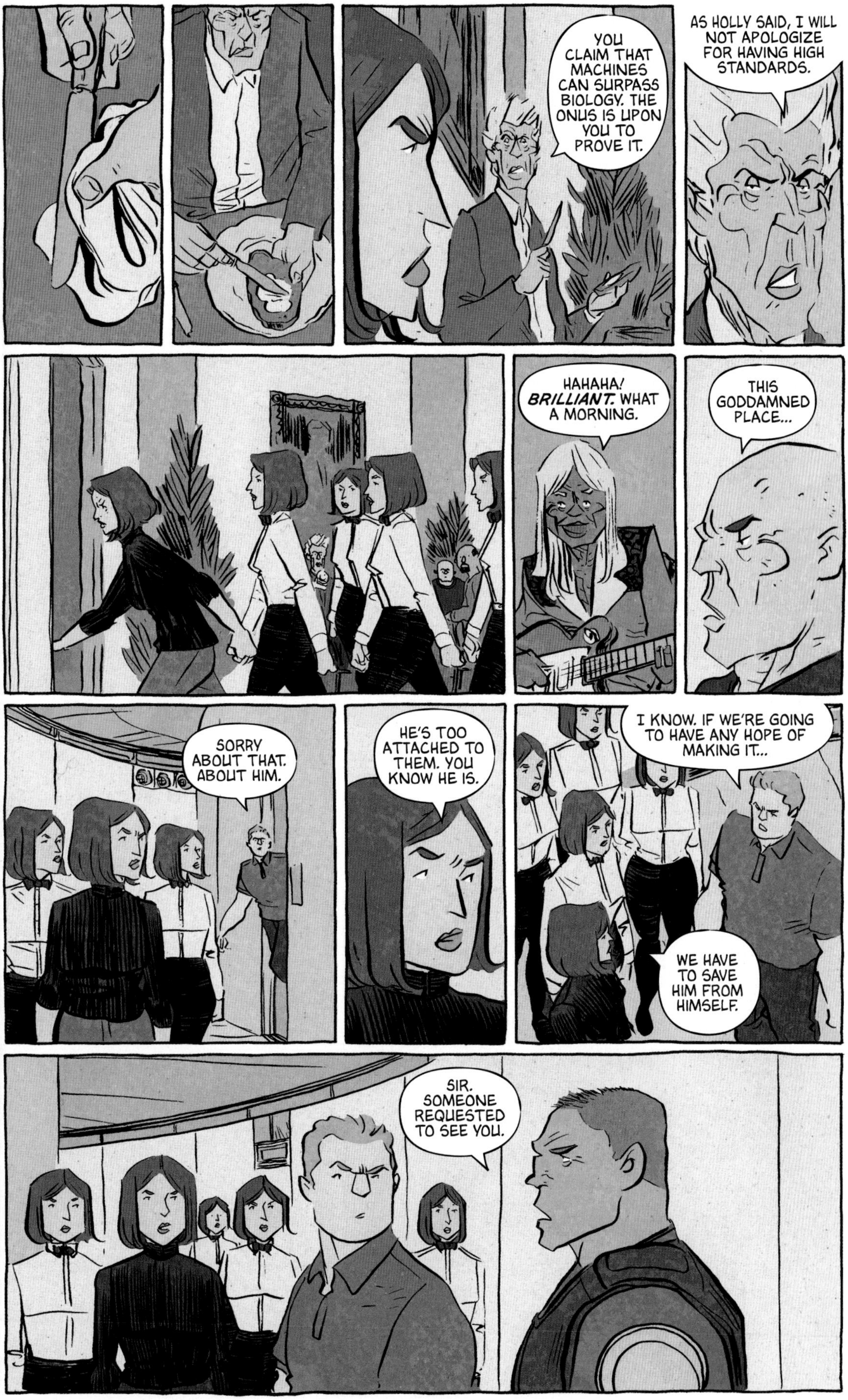
YOU CLAIM THAT MACHINES CAN SURPASS BIOLOGY. THE ONUS IS UPON YOU TO PROVE IT.
AS HOLLY SAID, I WILL NOT APOLOGIZE FOR HAVING HIGH STANDARDS.
HAHAHA! BRILLIANT. WHAT A MORNING.
THIS GODDAMNED PLACE...
SORRY ABOUT THAT. ABOUT HIM.
HE'S TOO ATTACHED TO THEM. YOU KNOW HE IS.
I KNOW. IF WE'RE GOING TO HAVE ANY HOPE OF MAKING IT...
WE HAVE TO SAVE HIM FROM HIMSELF.
SIR. SOMEONE REQUESTED TO SEE YOU.

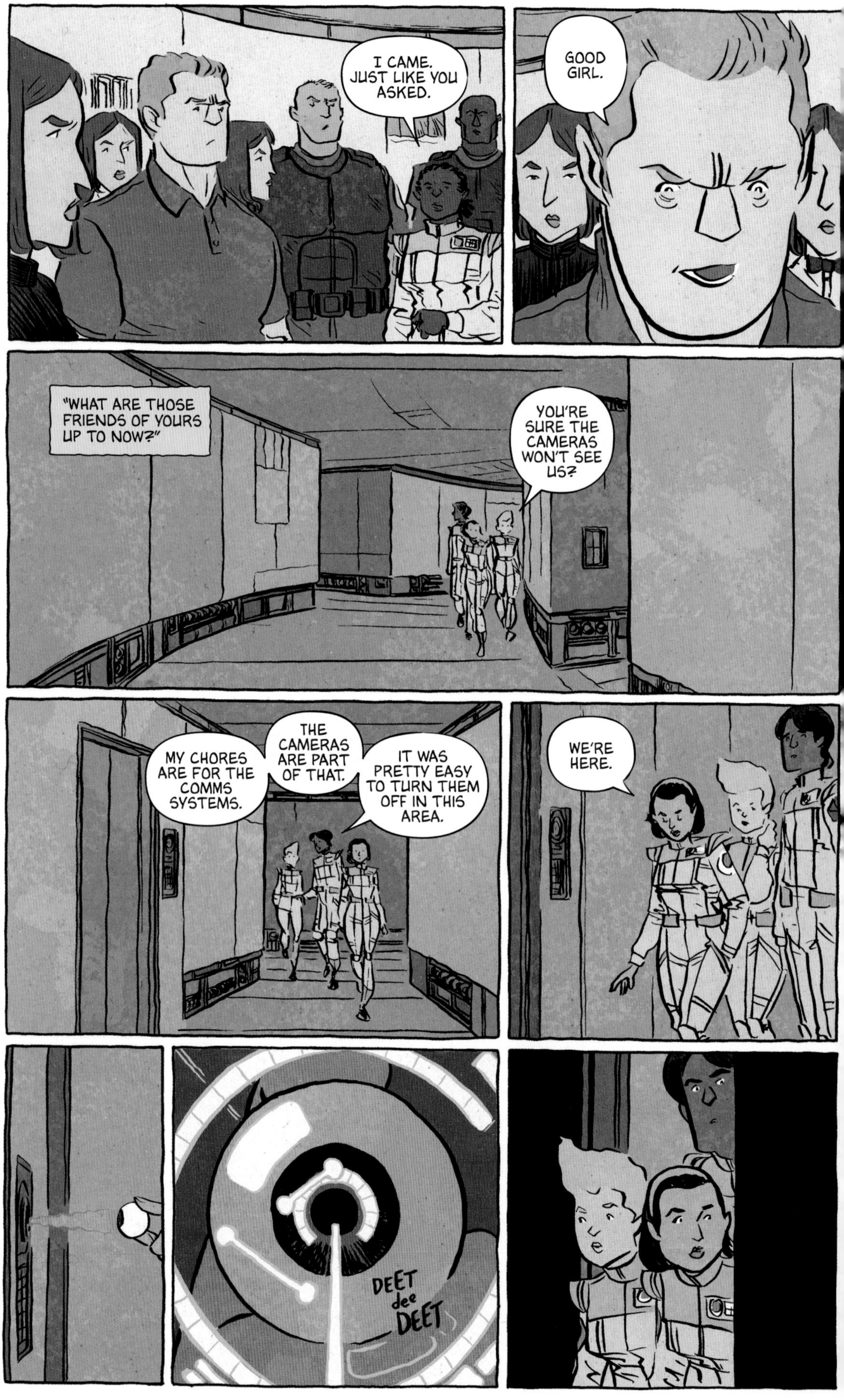
I CAME. JUST LIKE YOU ASKED.
GOOD GIRL.
"WHAT ARE THOSE FRIENDS OF YOURS UP TO NOW?"
YOU'RE SURE THE CAMERAS WON'T SEE US?
MY CHORES ARE FOR THE COMMS SYSTEMS.
THE CAMERAS ARE PART OF THAT.
IT WAS PRETTY EASY TO TURN THEM OFF IN THIS AREA.
WE'RE HERE.
DEET dee DEET

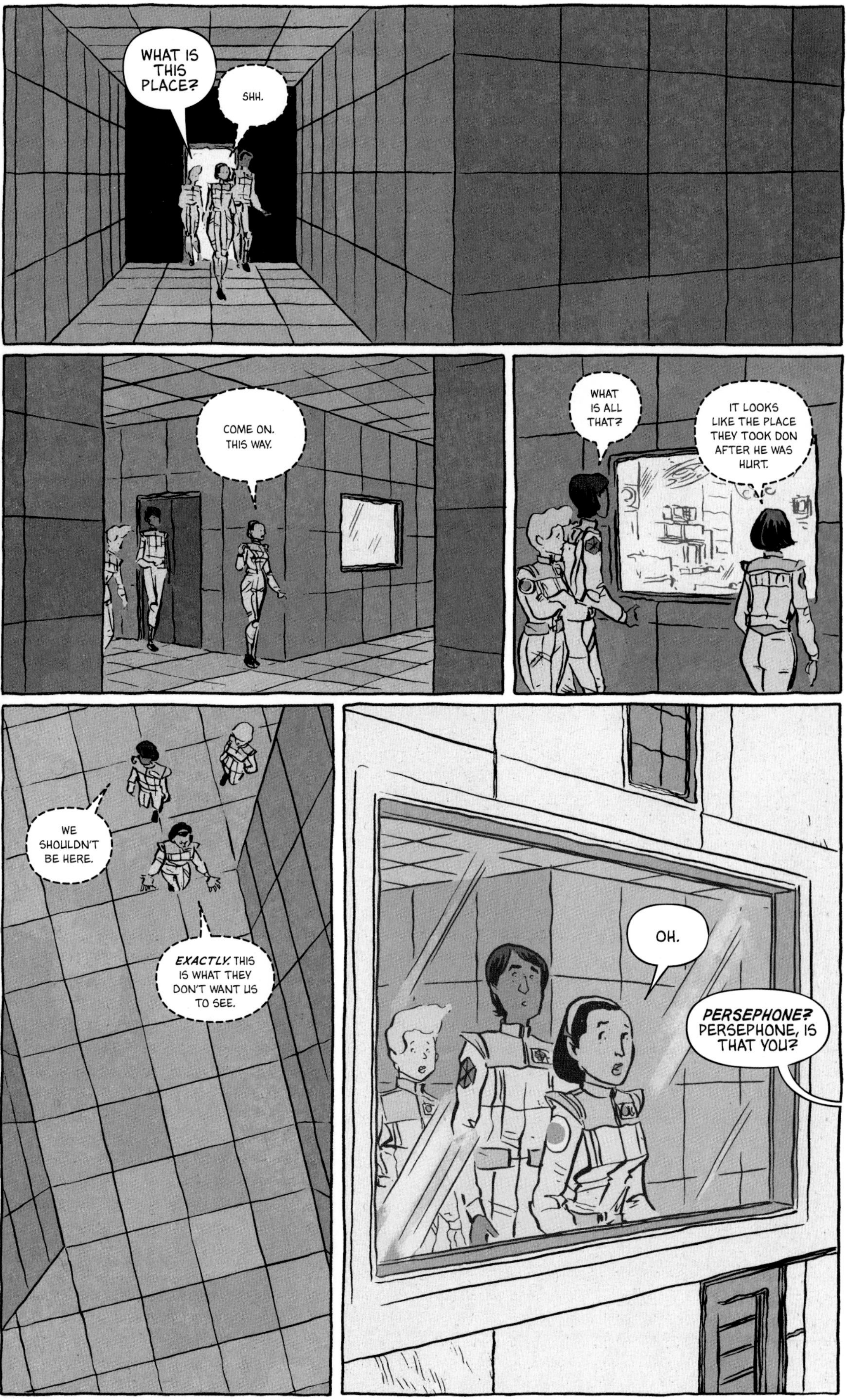
WHAT IS THIS PLACE?
SHH.
COME ON. THIS WAY.
WHAT IS ALL THAT?
IT LOOKS LIKE THE PLACE THEY TOOK DON AFTER HE WAS HURT.
WE SHOULDN'T BE HERE.
EXACTLY. THIS IS WHAT THEY DON'T WANT US TO SEE.
OH.
PERSEPHONE? PERSEPHONE, IS THAT YOU?

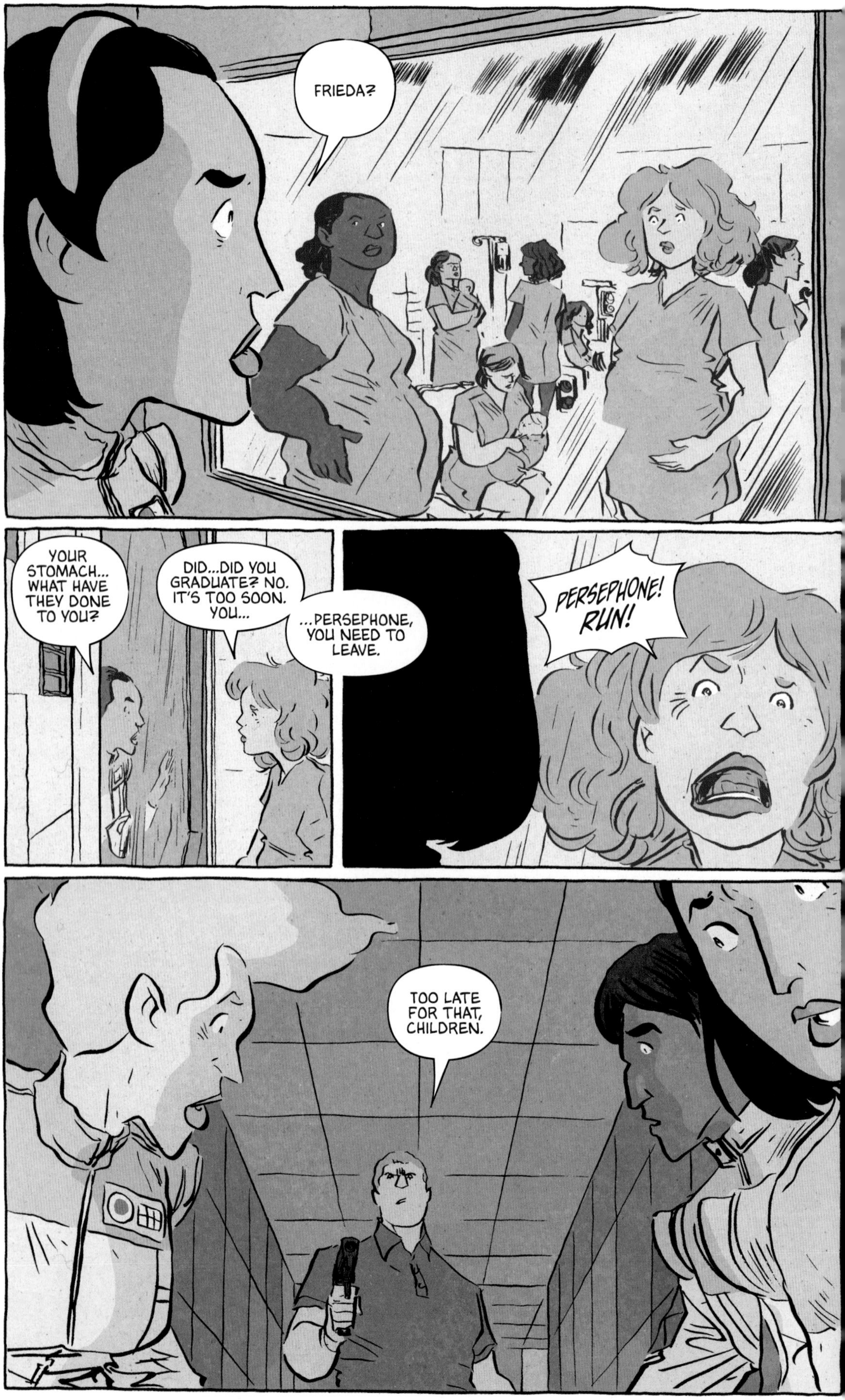
FRIEDA?
YOUR STOMACH... WHAT HAVE THEY DONE TO YOU?
DID...DID YOU GRADUATE? NO. IT'S TOO SOON. YOU...
...PERSEPHONE, YOU NEED TO LEAVE.
PERSEPHONE! RUN!
TOO LATE FOR THAT, CHILDREN.

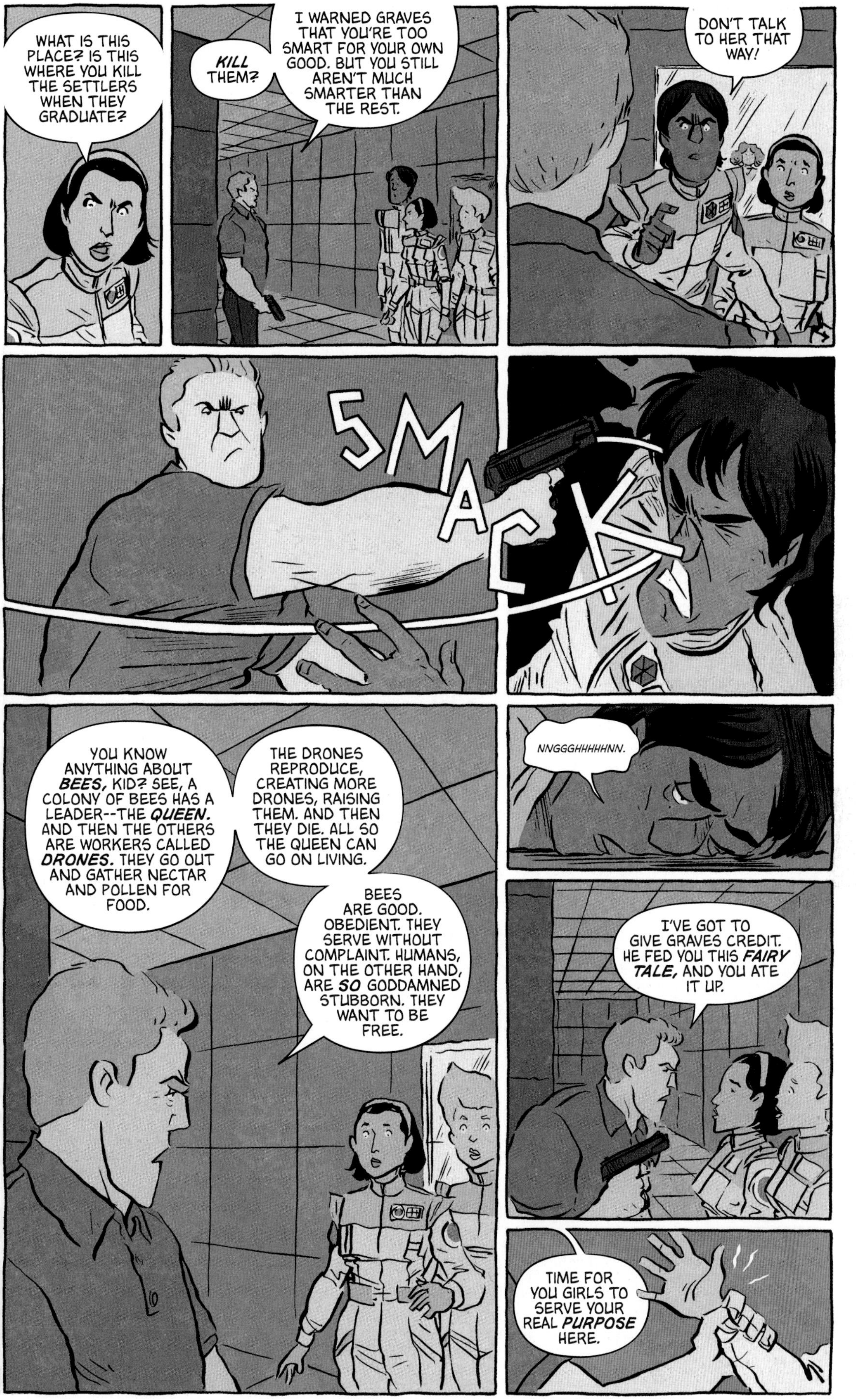
WHAT IS THIS PLACE? IS THIS WHERE YOU KILL THE SETTLERS WHEN THEY GRADUATE?
KILL THEM?
I WARNED GRAVES THAT YOU'RE TOO SMART FOR YOUR OWN GOOD. BUT YOU STILL AREN'T MUCH SMARTER THAN THE REST.
DON'T TALK TO HER THAT WAY!
SMACK
YOU KNOW ANYTHING ABOUT BEES, KID? SEE, A COLONY OF BEES HAS A LEADER--THE QUEEN. AND THEN THE OTHERS ARE WORKERS CALLED DRONES. THEY GO OUT AND GATHER NECTAR AND POLLEN FOR FOOD.
THE DRONES REPRODUCE, CREATING MORE DRONES, RAISING THEM. AND THEN THEY DIE. ALL SO THE QUEEN CAN GO ON LIVING.
BEES ARE GOOD. OBEDIENT. THEY SERVE WITHOUT COMPLAINT. HUMANS, ON THE OTHER HAND, ARE SO GODDAMNED STUBBORN. THEY WANT TO BE FREE.
NNGGGHHHHHNN.
I'VE GOT TO GIVE GRAVES CREDIT. HE FED YOU THIS FAIRY TALE, AND YOU ATE IT UP.
TIME FOR YOU GIRLS TO SERVE YOUR REAL PURPOSE HERE.

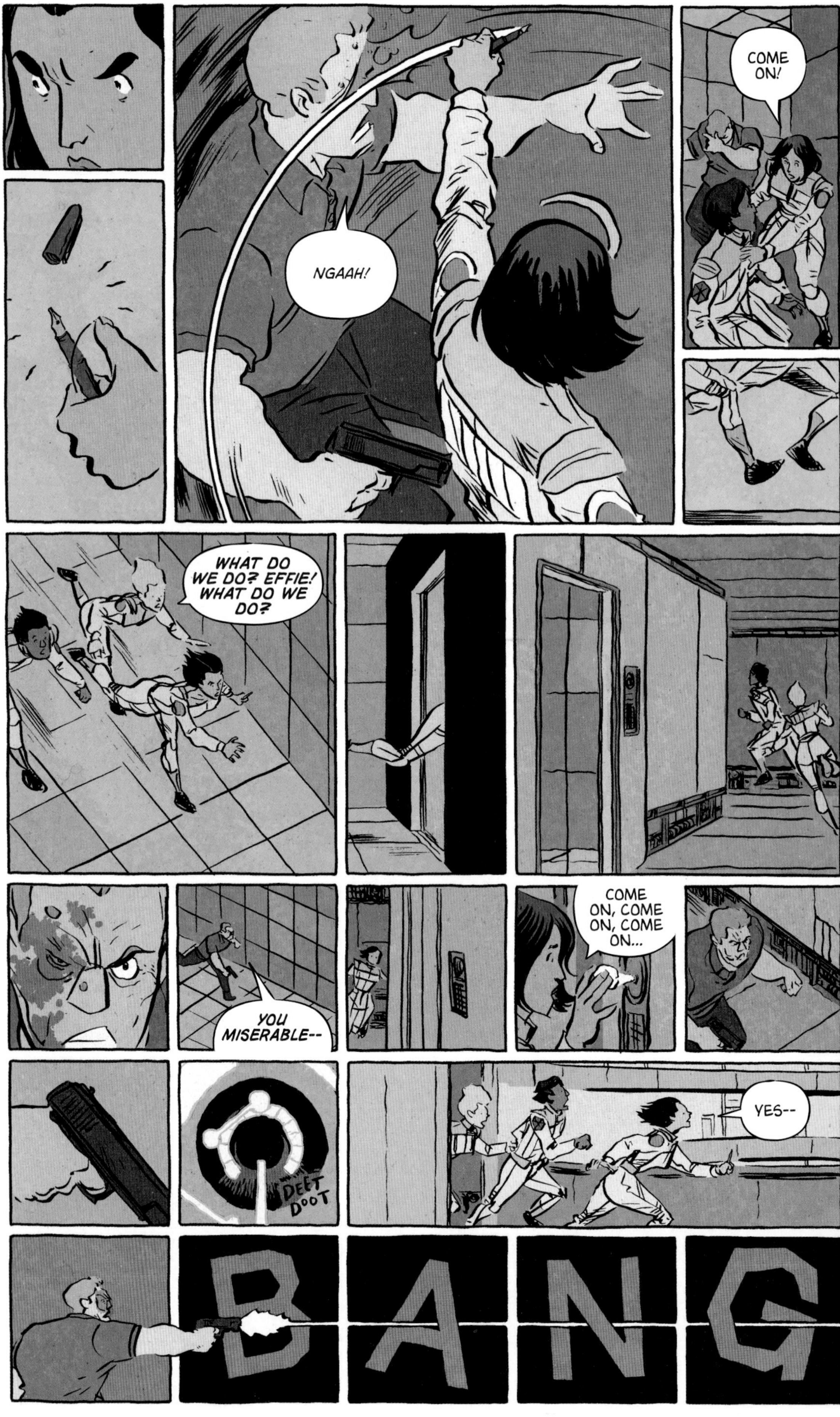
NGAAH!
COME ON!
WHAT DO WE DO? EFFIE! WHAT DO WE DO?
YOU MISERABLE--
COME ON, COME ON, COME ON...
DEET DOOT
YES--
BANG

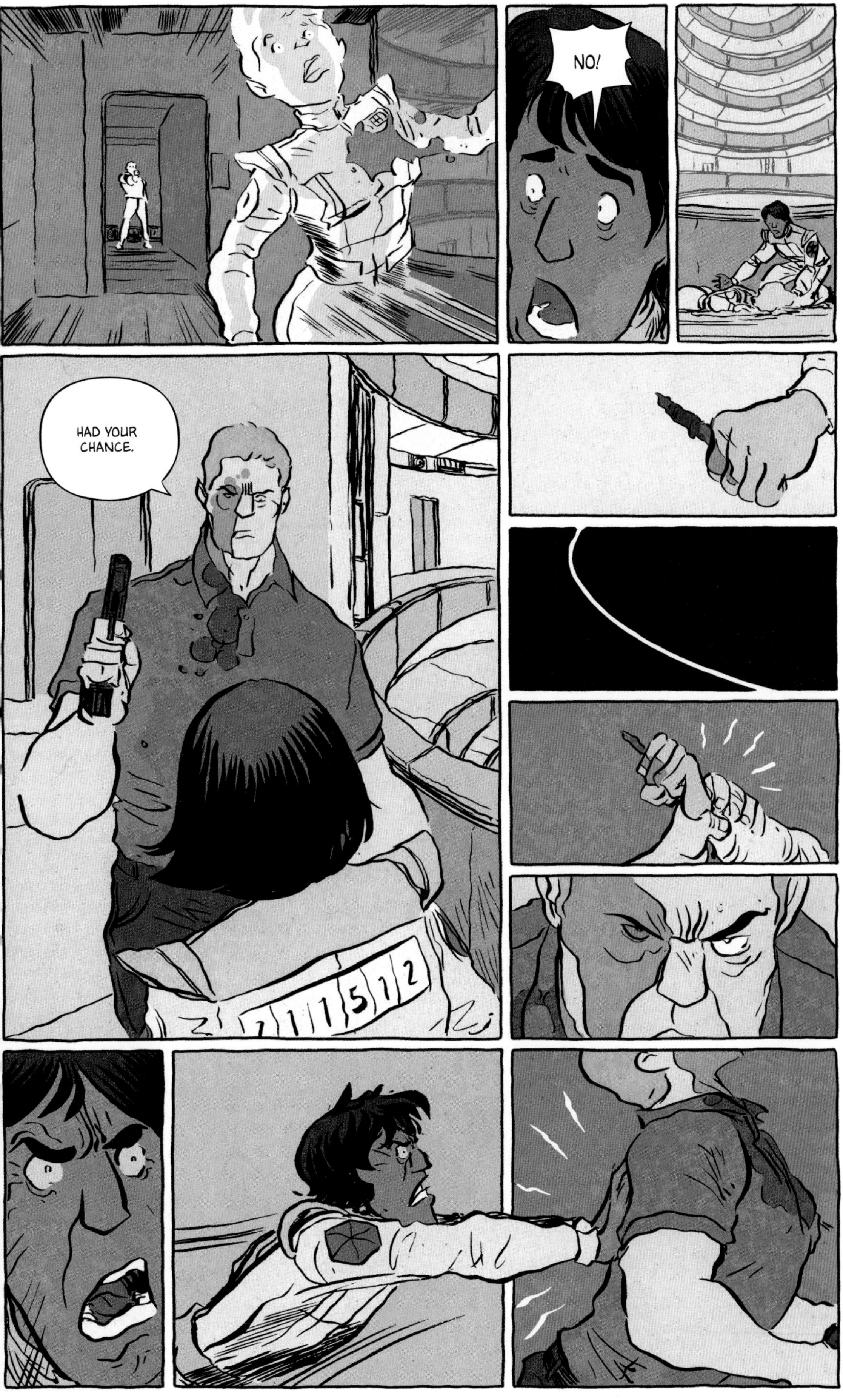
NO!
HAD YOUR CHANCE.
2 1 1 5 1 2

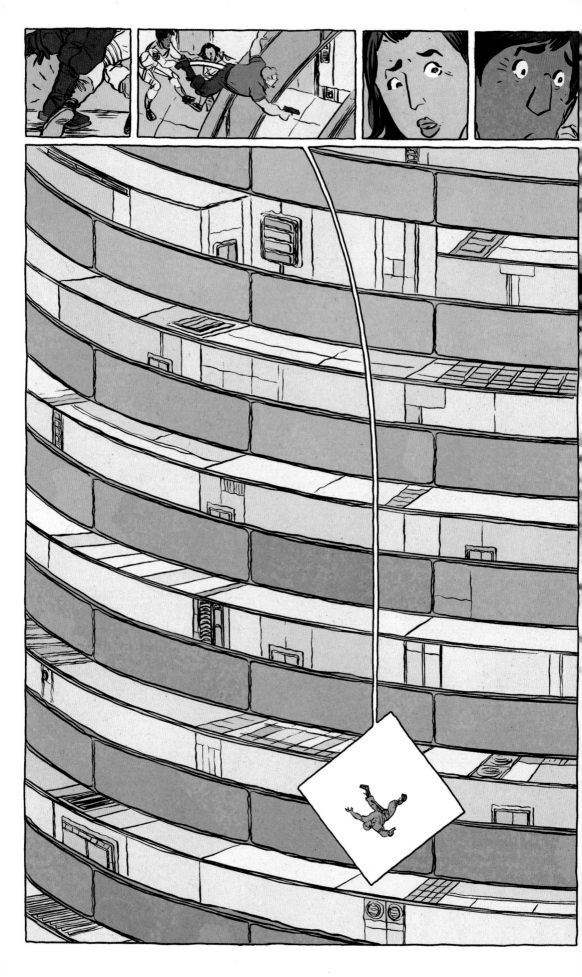

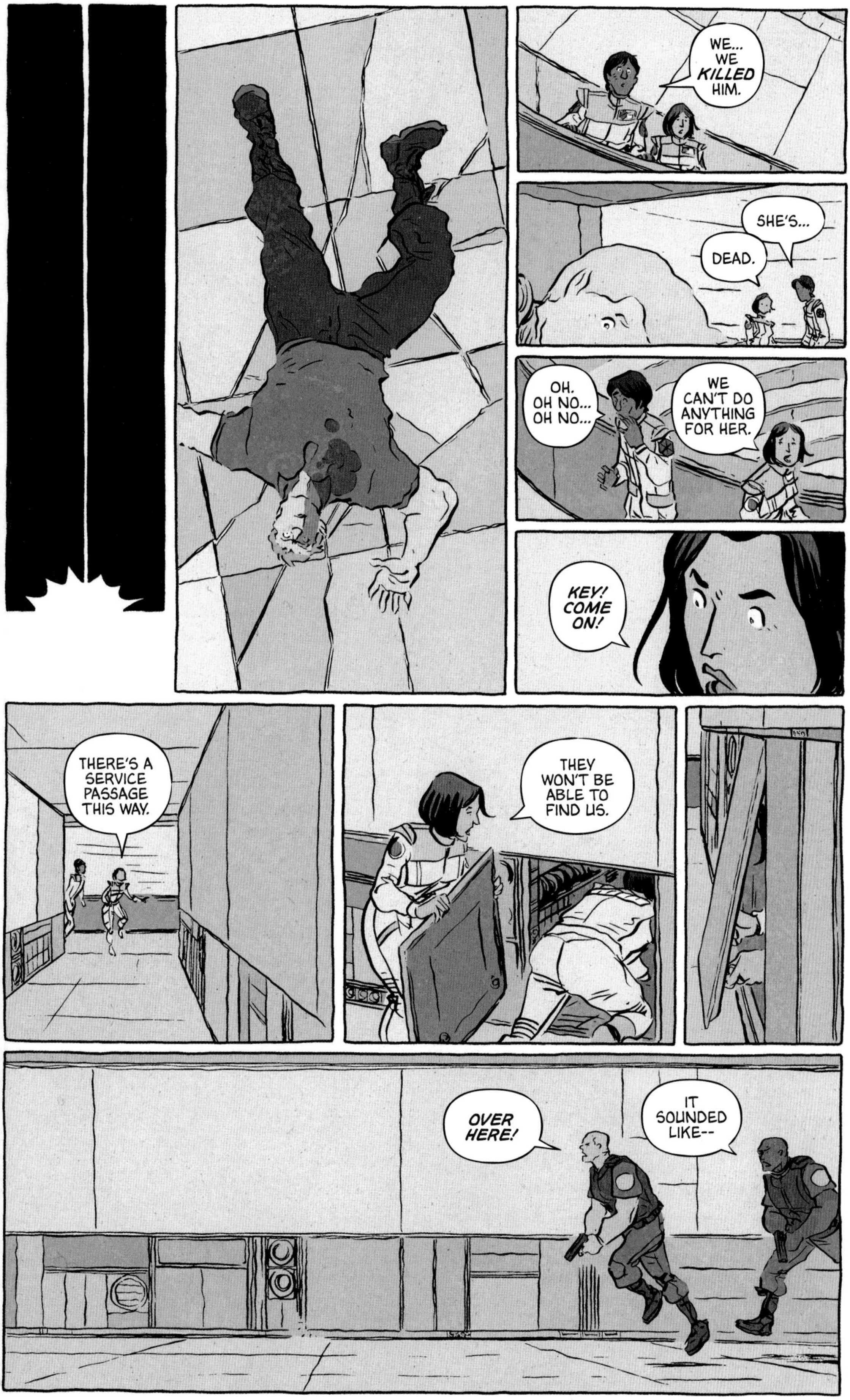
WE... WE *KILLED* HIM.
SHE'S...
DEAD.
OH. OH NO... OH NO...
WE CAN'T DO ANYTHING FOR HER.
KEY! COME ON!
THERE'S A SERVICE PASSAGE THIS WAY.
THEY WON'T BE ABLE TO FIND US.
OVER HERE!
IT SOUNDED LIKE--

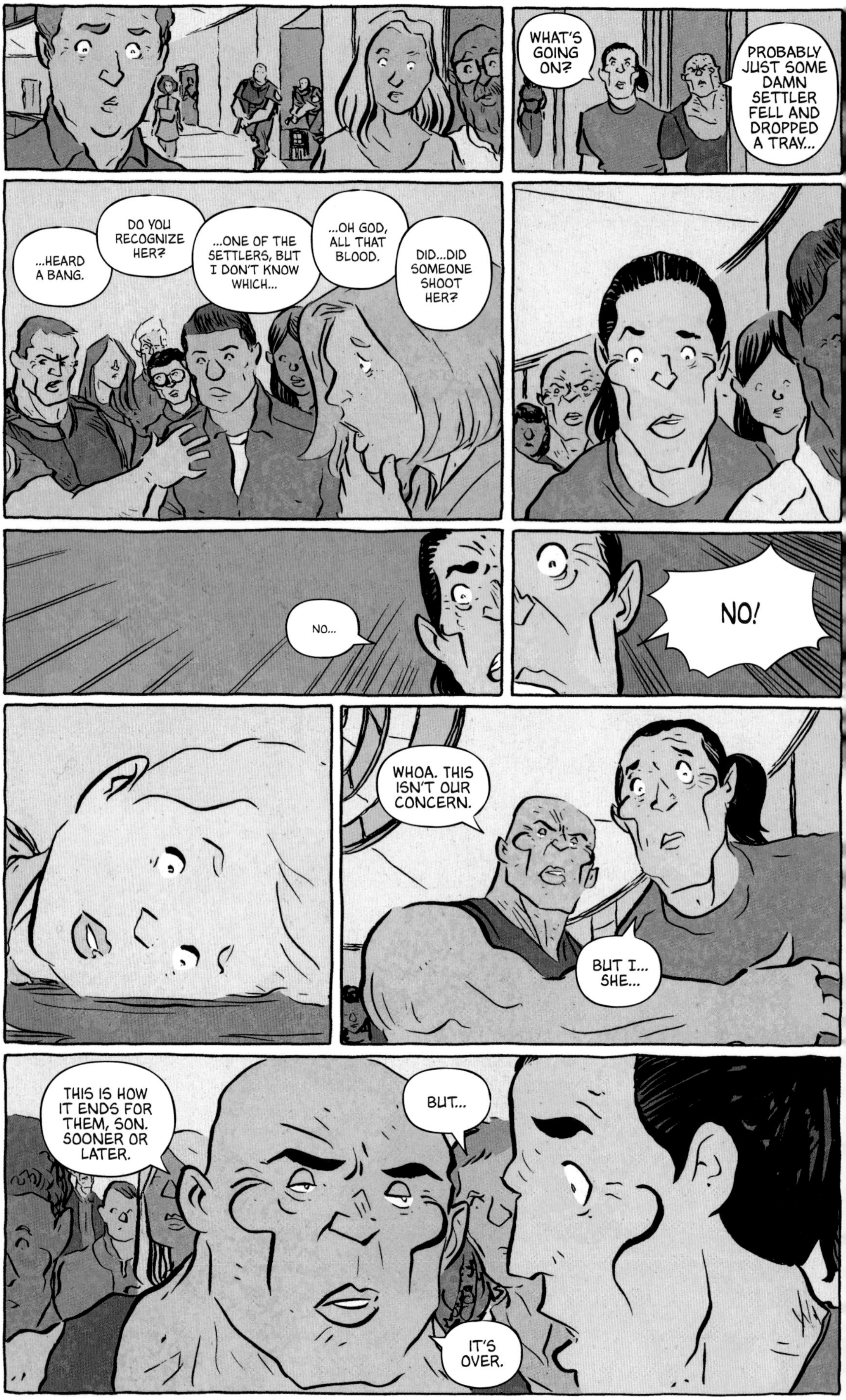
WHAT'S GOING ON?
PROBABLY JUST SOME DAMN SETTLER FELL AND DROPPED A TRAY...
...HEARD A BANG.
DO YOU RECOGNIZE HER?
...ONE OF THE SETTLERS, BUT I DON'T KNOW WHICH...
...OH GOD, ALL THAT BLOOD.
DID...DID SOMEONE SHOOT HER?
NO...
NO!
WHOA. THIS ISN'T OUR CONCERN.
BUT I... SHE...
THIS IS HOW IT ENDS FOR THEM, SON. SOONER OR LATER.
BUT...
IT'S OVER.

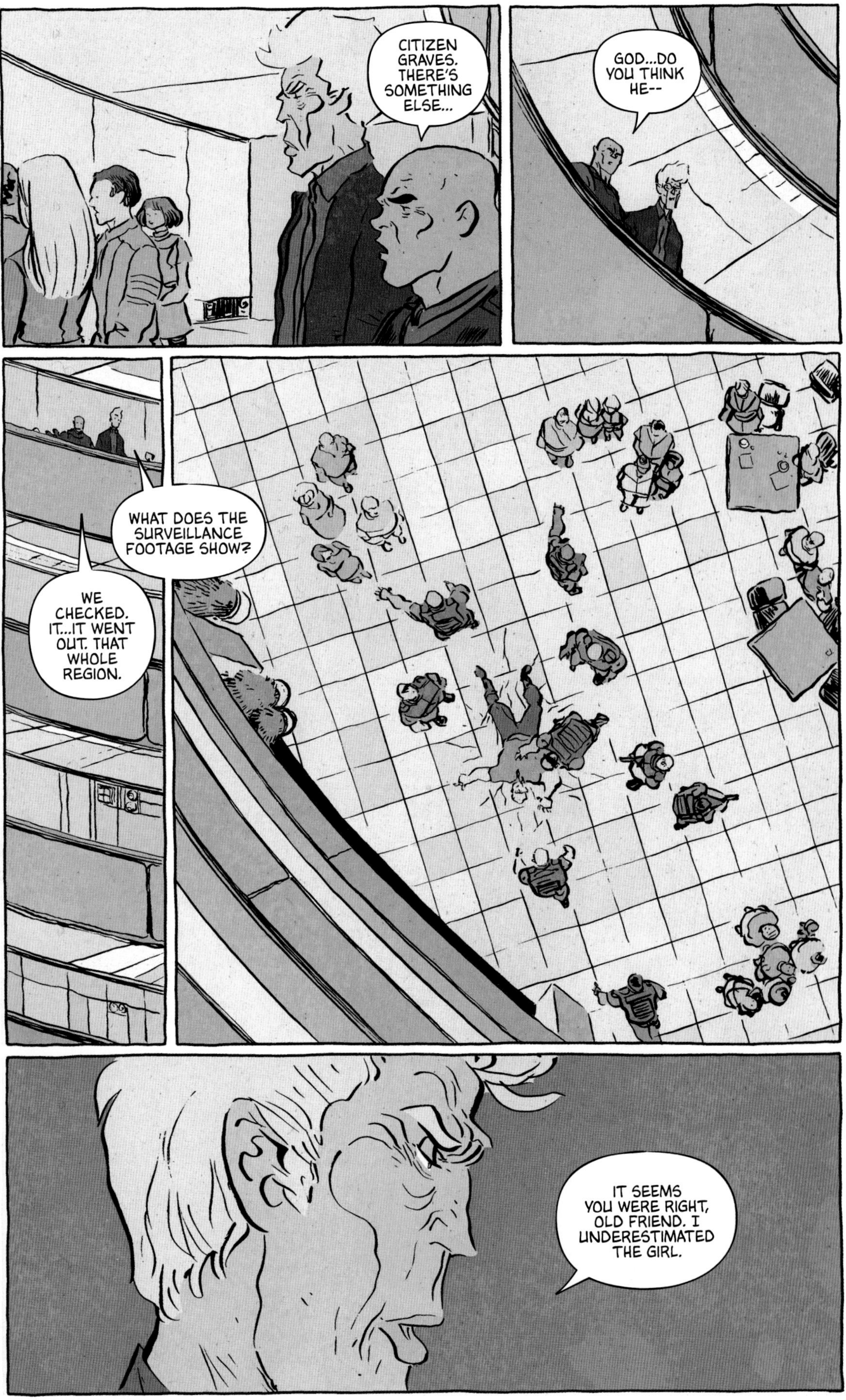
CITIZEN GRAVES. THERE'S SOMETHING ELSE...
GOD...DO YOU THINK HE--
WHAT DOES THE SURVEILLANCE FOOTAGE SHOW?
WE CHECKED. IT...IT WENT OUT. THAT WHOLE REGION.
IT SEEMS YOU WERE RIGHT, OLD FRIEND. I UNDERESTIMATED THE GIRL.

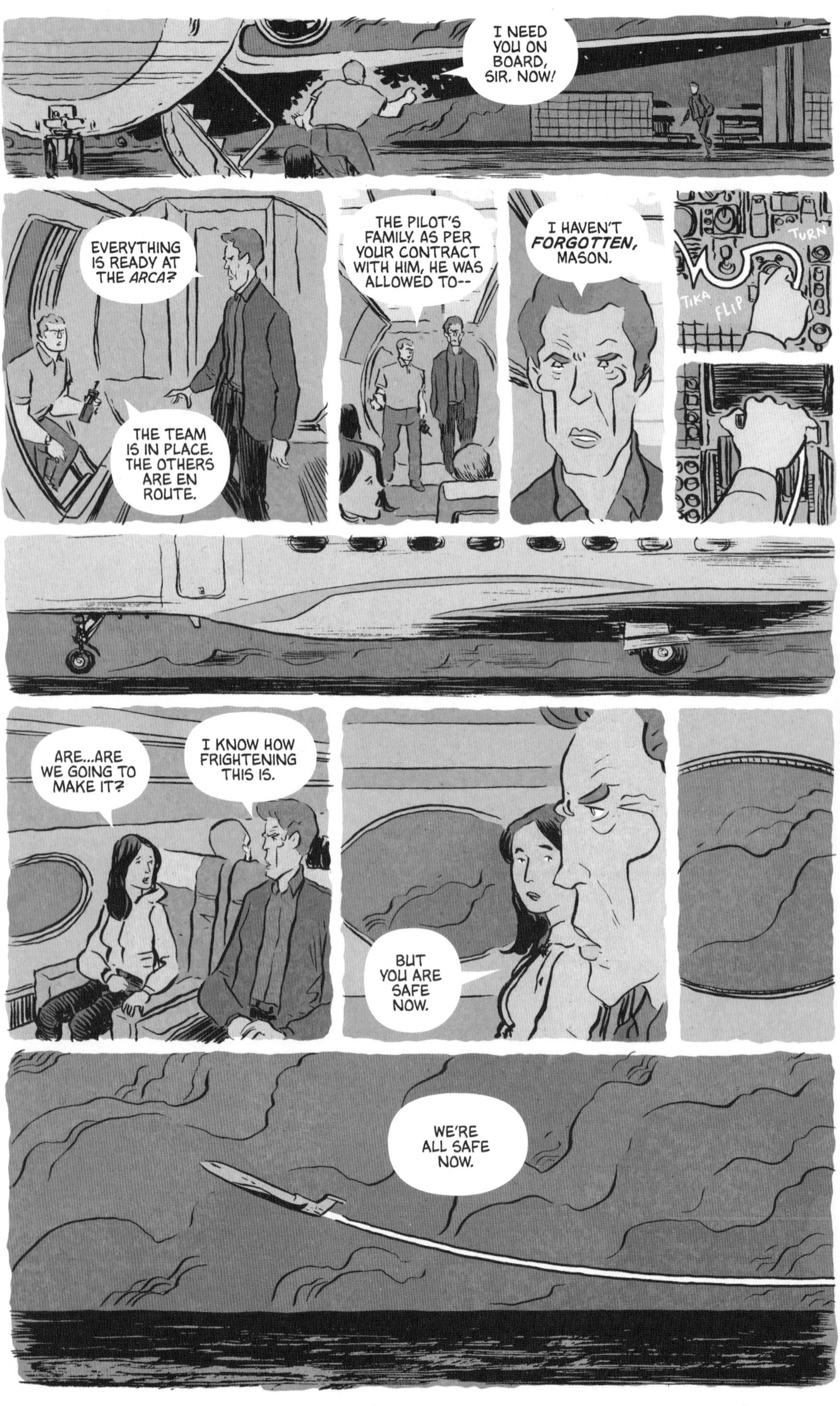

I NEED YOU ON BOARD, SIR. NOW!
EVERYTHING IS READY AT THE *ARCA*?
THE TEAM IS IN PLACE. THE OTHERS ARE EN ROUTE.
THE PILOT'S FAMILY. AS PER YOUR CONTRACT WITH HIM, HE WAS ALLOWED TO--
I HAVEN'T ***FORGOTTEN,*** MASON.
TURN
TIKA
FLIP
ARE...ARE WE GOING TO MAKE IT?
I KNOW HOW FRIGHTENING THIS IS.
BUT YOU ARE SAFE NOW.
WE'RE ALL SAFE NOW.

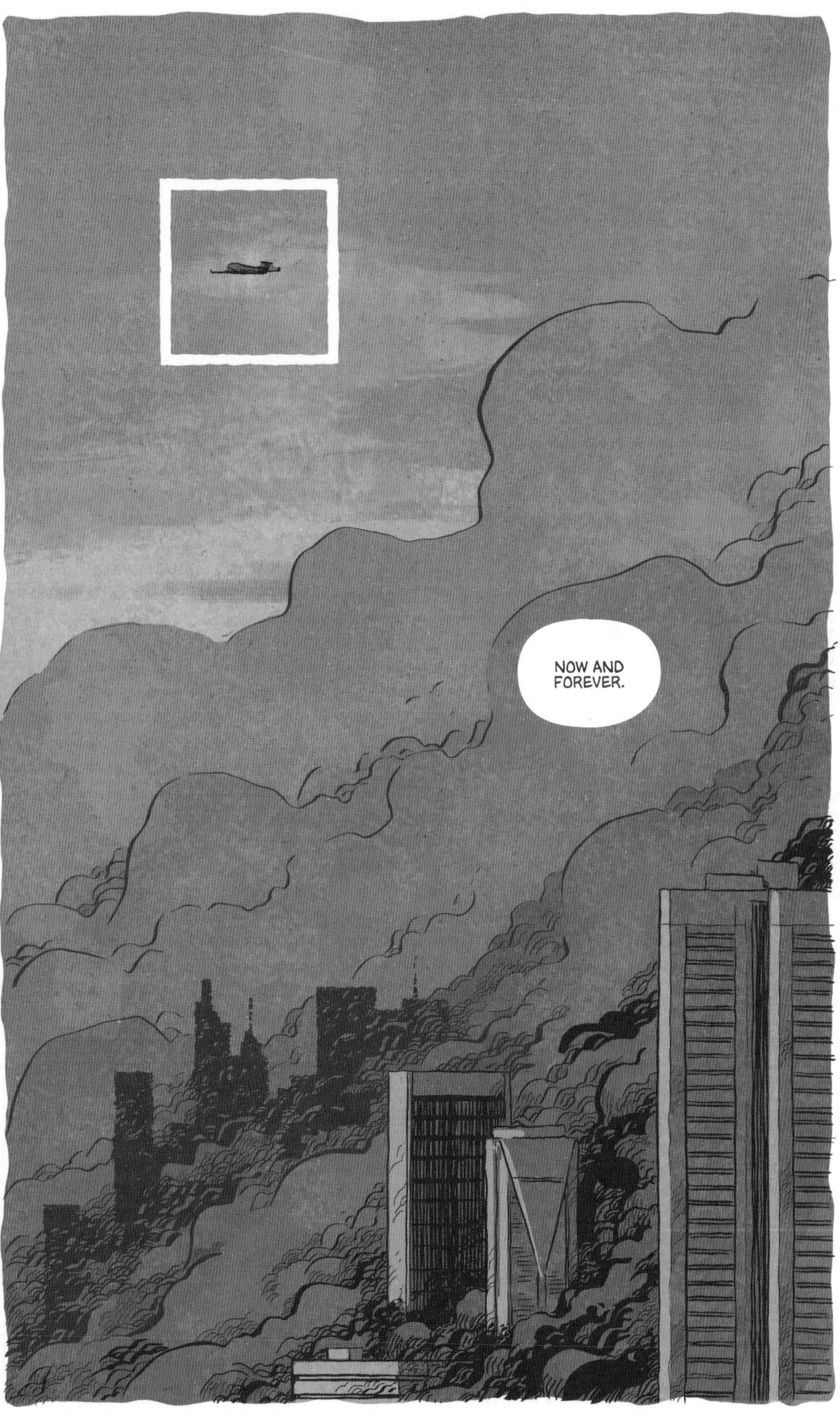
NOW AND FOREVER.

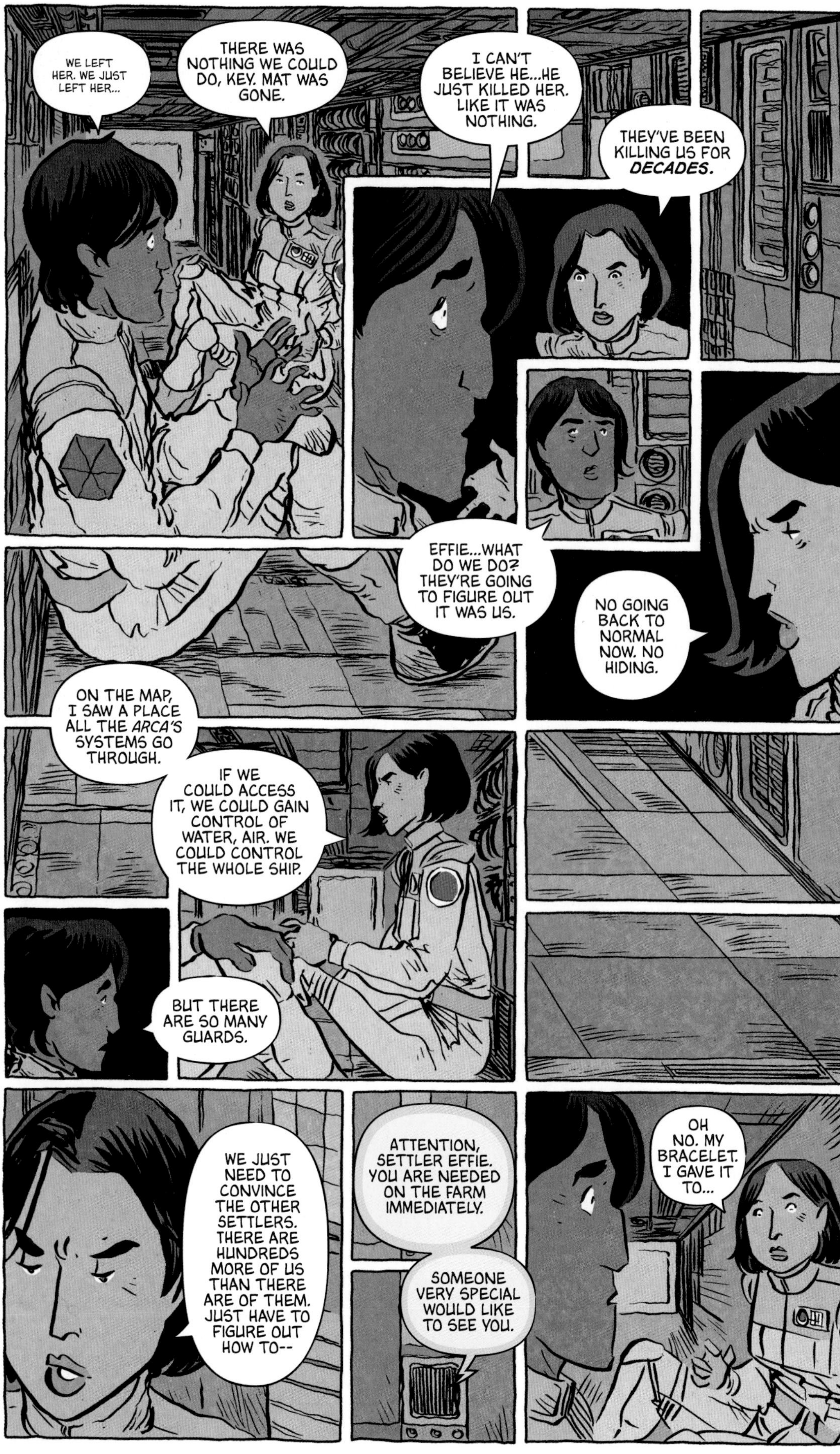
WE LEFT HER. WE JUST LEFT HER...
THERE WAS NOTHING WE COULD DO, KEY. MAT WAS GONE.
I CAN'T BELIEVE HE...HE JUST KILLED HER. LIKE IT WAS NOTHING.
THEY'VE BEEN KILLING US FOR *DECADES.*
EFFIE...WHAT DO WE DO? THEY'RE GOING TO FIGURE OUT IT WAS US.
NO GOING BACK TO NORMAL NOW. NO HIDING.
ON THE MAP, I SAW A PLACE ALL THE *ARCA'S* SYSTEMS GO THROUGH.
IF WE COULD ACCESS IT, WE COULD GAIN CONTROL OF WATER, AIR. WE COULD CONTROL THE WHOLE SHIP.
BUT THERE ARE SO MANY GUARDS.
WE JUST NEED TO CONVINCE THE OTHER SETTLERS. THERE ARE HUNDREDS MORE OF US THAN THERE ARE OF THEM. JUST HAVE TO FIGURE OUT HOW TO--
ATTENTION, SETTLER EFFIE. YOU ARE NEEDED ON THE FARM IMMEDIATELY.
SOMEONE VERY SPECIAL WOULD LIKE TO SEE YOU.
OH NO. MY BRACELET. I GAVE IT TO...

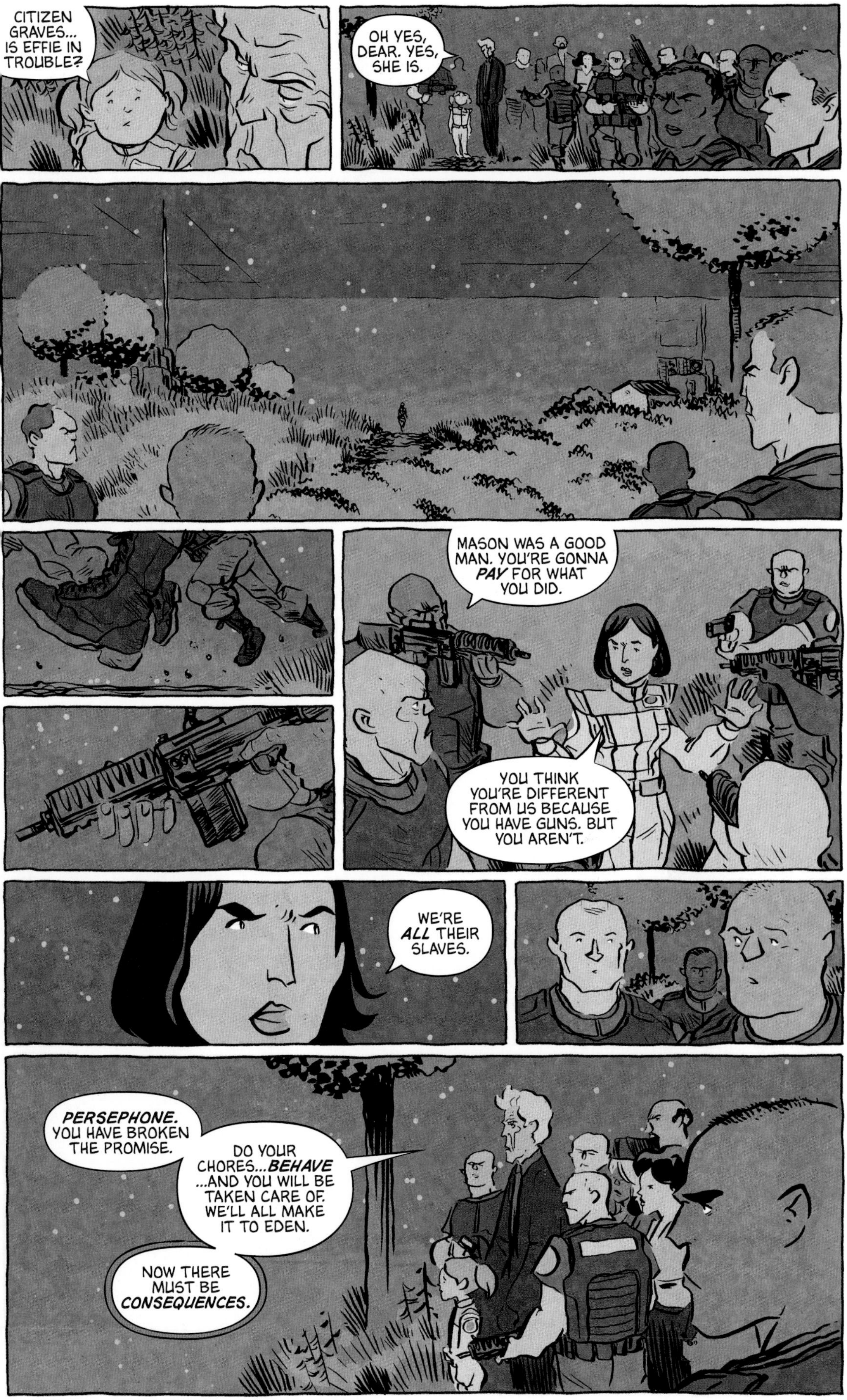
CITIZEN GRAVES... IS EFFIE IN TROUBLE?
OH YES, DEAR. YES, SHE IS.
MASON WAS A GOOD MAN. YOU'RE GONNA PAY FOR WHAT YOU DID.
YOU THINK YOU'RE DIFFERENT FROM US BECAUSE YOU HAVE GUNS. BUT YOU AREN'T.
WE'RE ALL THEIR SLAVES.
PERSEPHONE. YOU HAVE BROKEN THE PROMISE.
DO YOUR CHORES...BEHAVE ...AND YOU WILL BE TAKEN CARE OF. WE'LL ALL MAKE IT TO EDEN.
NOW THERE MUST BE CONSEQUENCES.

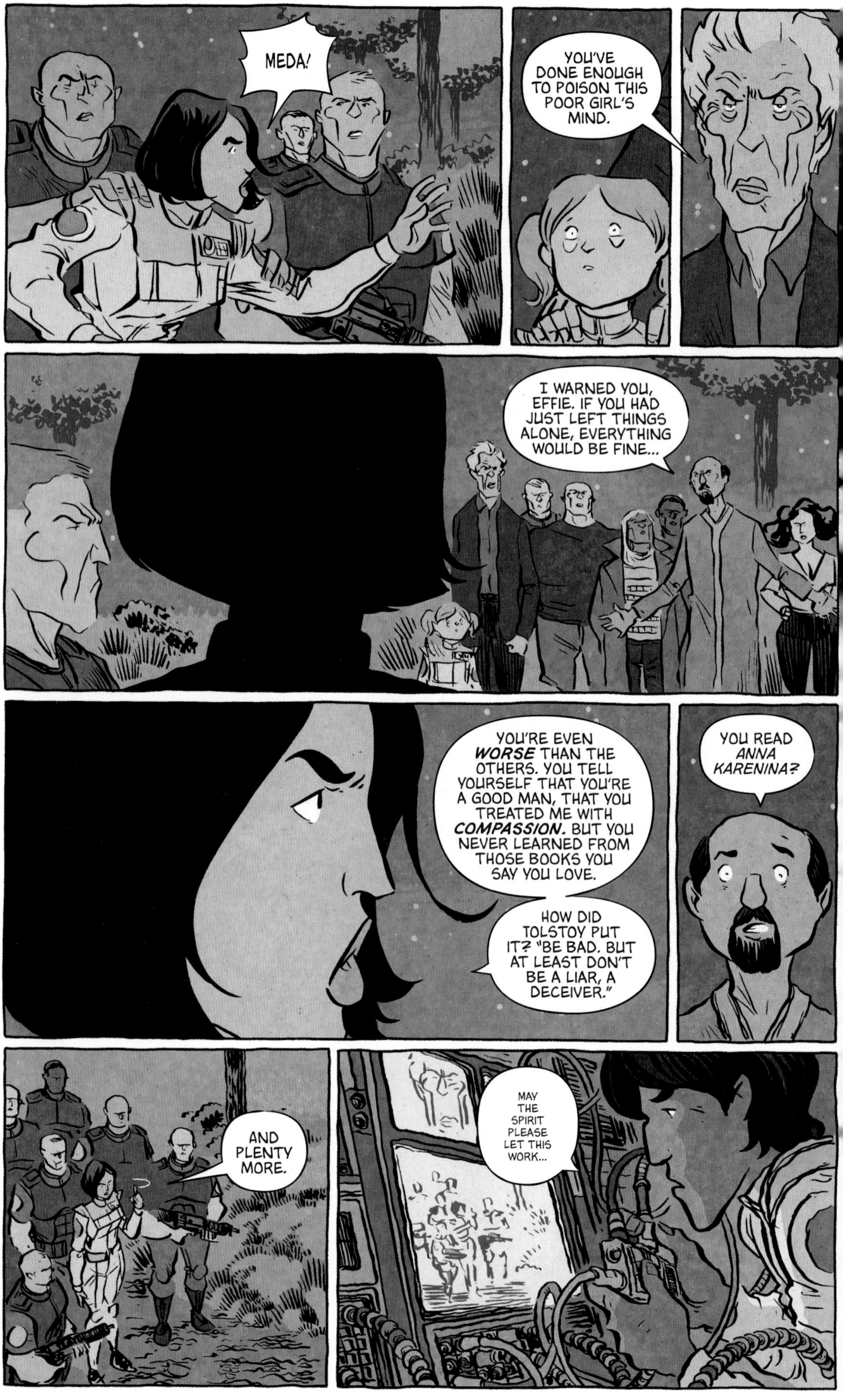
MEDA!
YOU'VE DONE ENOUGH TO POISON THIS POOR GIRL'S MIND.
I WARNED YOU, EFFIE. IF YOU HAD JUST LEFT THINGS ALONE, EVERYTHING WOULD BE FINE...
YOU'RE EVEN **WORSE** THAN THE OTHERS. YOU TELL YOURSELF THAT YOU'RE A GOOD MAN, THAT YOU TREATED ME WITH ***COMPASSION.*** BUT YOU NEVER LEARNED FROM THOSE BOOKS YOU SAY YOU LOVE.
HOW DID TOLSTOY PUT IT? "BE BAD. BUT AT LEAST DON'T BE A LIAR, A DECEIVER."
YOU READ *ANNA KARENINA?*
AND PLENTY MORE.
MAY THE SPIRIT PLEASE LET THIS WORK...

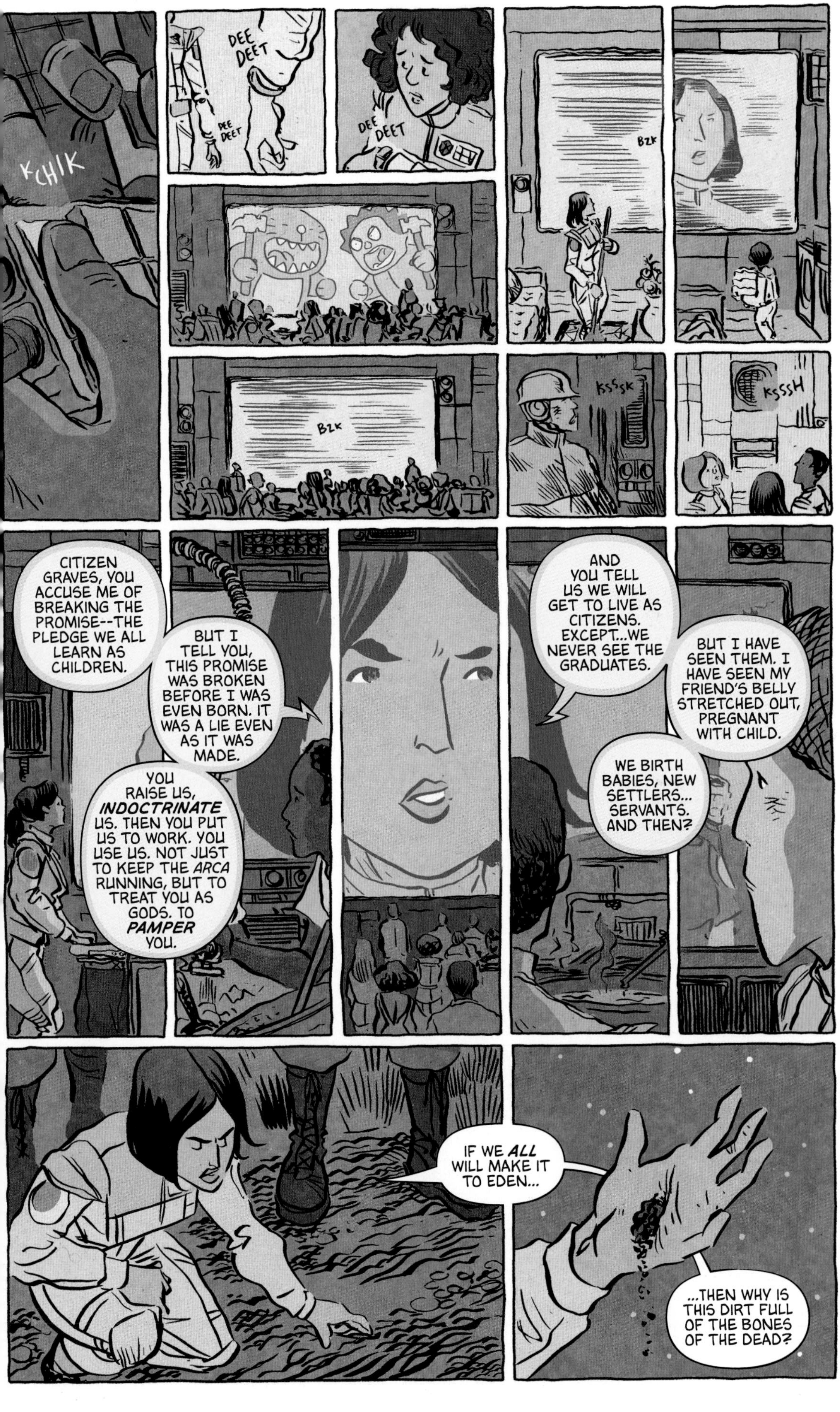
KCHIK
DEE DEET
DEE DEET
DEE DEET
BZK
BZK
KSSSK
KSSSH
CITIZEN GRAVES, YOU ACCUSE ME OF BREAKING THE PROMISE--THE PLEDGE WE ALL LEARN AS CHILDREN.
BUT I TELL YOU, THIS PROMISE WAS BROKEN BEFORE I WAS EVEN BORN. IT WAS A LIE EVEN AS IT WAS MADE.
YOU RAISE US, ***INDOCTRINATE*** US. THEN YOU PUT US TO WORK. YOU USE US. NOT JUST TO KEEP THE *ARCA* RUNNING, BUT TO TREAT YOU AS GODS. TO ***PAMPER*** YOU.
AND YOU TELL US WE WILL GET TO LIVE AS CITIZENS. EXCEPT...WE NEVER SEE THE GRADUATES.
BUT I HAVE SEEN THEM. I HAVE SEEN MY FRIEND'S BELLY STRETCHED OUT, PREGNANT WITH CHILD.
WE BIRTH BABIES, NEW SETTLERS... SERVANTS. AND THEN?
IF WE ***ALL*** WILL MAKE IT TO EDEN...
...THEN WHY IS THIS DIRT FULL OF THE BONES OF THE DEAD?

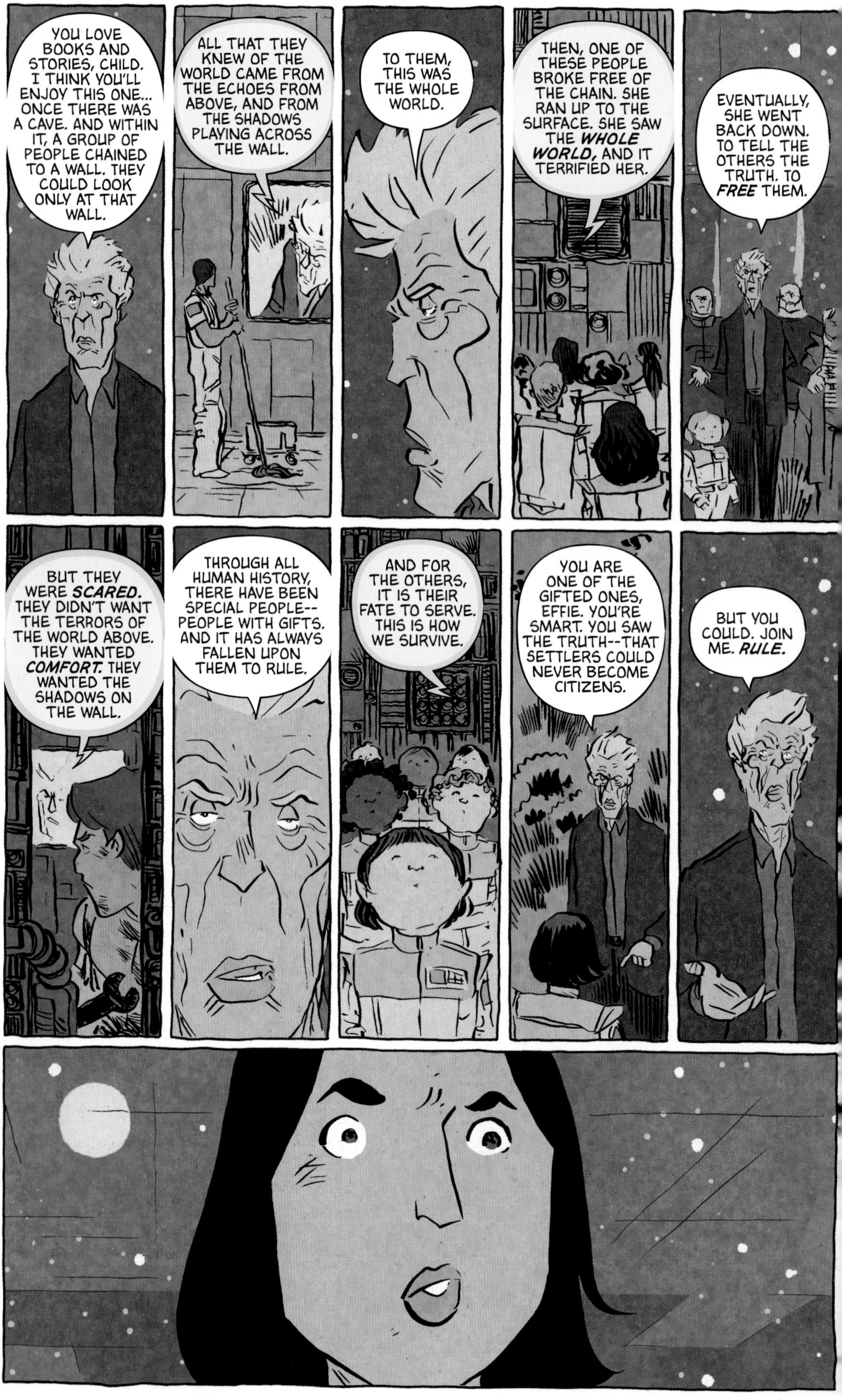

YOU LOVE BOOKS AND STORIES, CHILD. I THINK YOU'LL ENJOY THIS ONE... ONCE THERE WAS A CAVE. AND WITHIN IT, A GROUP OF PEOPLE CHAINED TO A WALL. THEY COULD LOOK ONLY AT THAT WALL.
ALL THAT THEY KNEW OF THE WORLD CAME FROM THE ECHOES FROM ABOVE, AND FROM THE SHADOWS PLAYING ACROSS THE WALL.
TO THEM, THIS WAS THE WHOLE WORLD.
THEN, ONE OF THESE PEOPLE BROKE FREE OF THE CHAIN. SHE RAN UP TO THE SURFACE. SHE SAW THE *WHOLE WORLD,* AND IT TERRIFIED HER.
EVENTUALLY, SHE WENT BACK DOWN. TO TELL THE OTHERS THE TRUTH. TO *FREE* THEM.
BUT THEY WERE *SCARED.* THEY DIDN'T WANT THE TERRORS OF THE WORLD ABOVE. THEY WANTED *COMFORT.* THEY WANTED THE SHADOWS ON THE WALL.
THROUGH ALL HUMAN HISTORY, THERE HAVE BEEN SPECIAL PEOPLE--PEOPLE WITH GIFTS. AND IT HAS ALWAYS FALLEN UPON THEM TO RULE.
AND FOR THE OTHERS, IT IS THEIR FATE TO SERVE. THIS IS HOW WE SURVIVE.
YOU ARE ONE OF THE GIFTED ONES, EFFIE. YOU'RE SMART. YOU SAW THE TRUTH--THAT SETTLERS COULD NEVER BECOME CITIZENS.
BUT YOU COULD. JOIN ME. *RULE.*

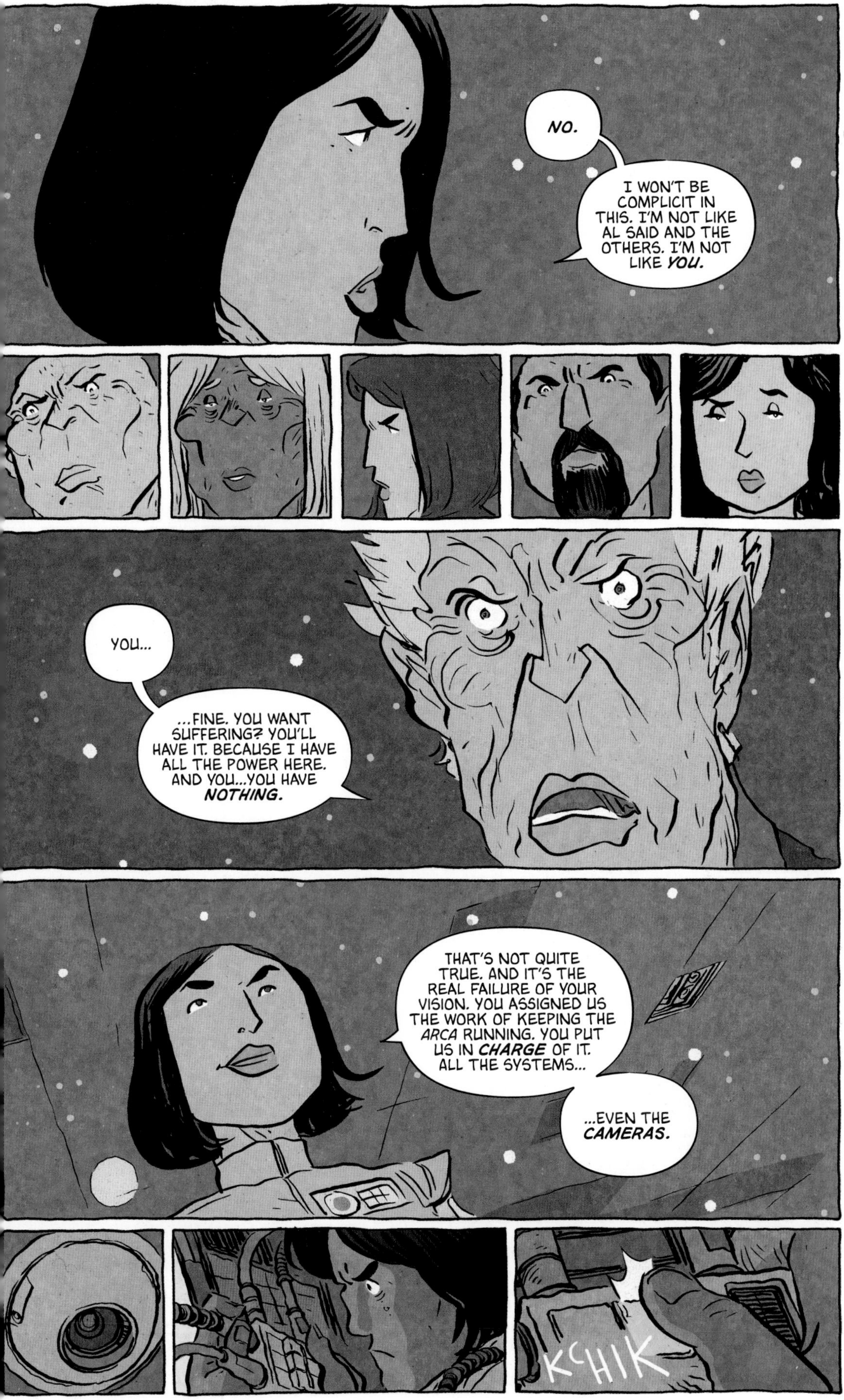
NO.
I WON'T BE COMPLICIT IN THIS. I'M NOT LIKE AL SAID AND THE OTHERS. I'M NOT LIKE *YOU.*
YOU...
...FINE. YOU WANT SUFFERING? YOU'LL HAVE IT. BECAUSE I HAVE ALL THE POWER HERE. AND YOU...YOU HAVE ***NOTHING.***
THAT'S NOT QUITE TRUE. AND IT'S THE REAL FAILURE OF YOUR VISION. YOU ASSIGNED US THE WORK OF KEEPING THE *ARCA* RUNNING. YOU PUT US IN ***CHARGE*** OF IT. ALL THE SYSTEMS...
...EVEN THE ***CAMERAS.***
K^CHIK

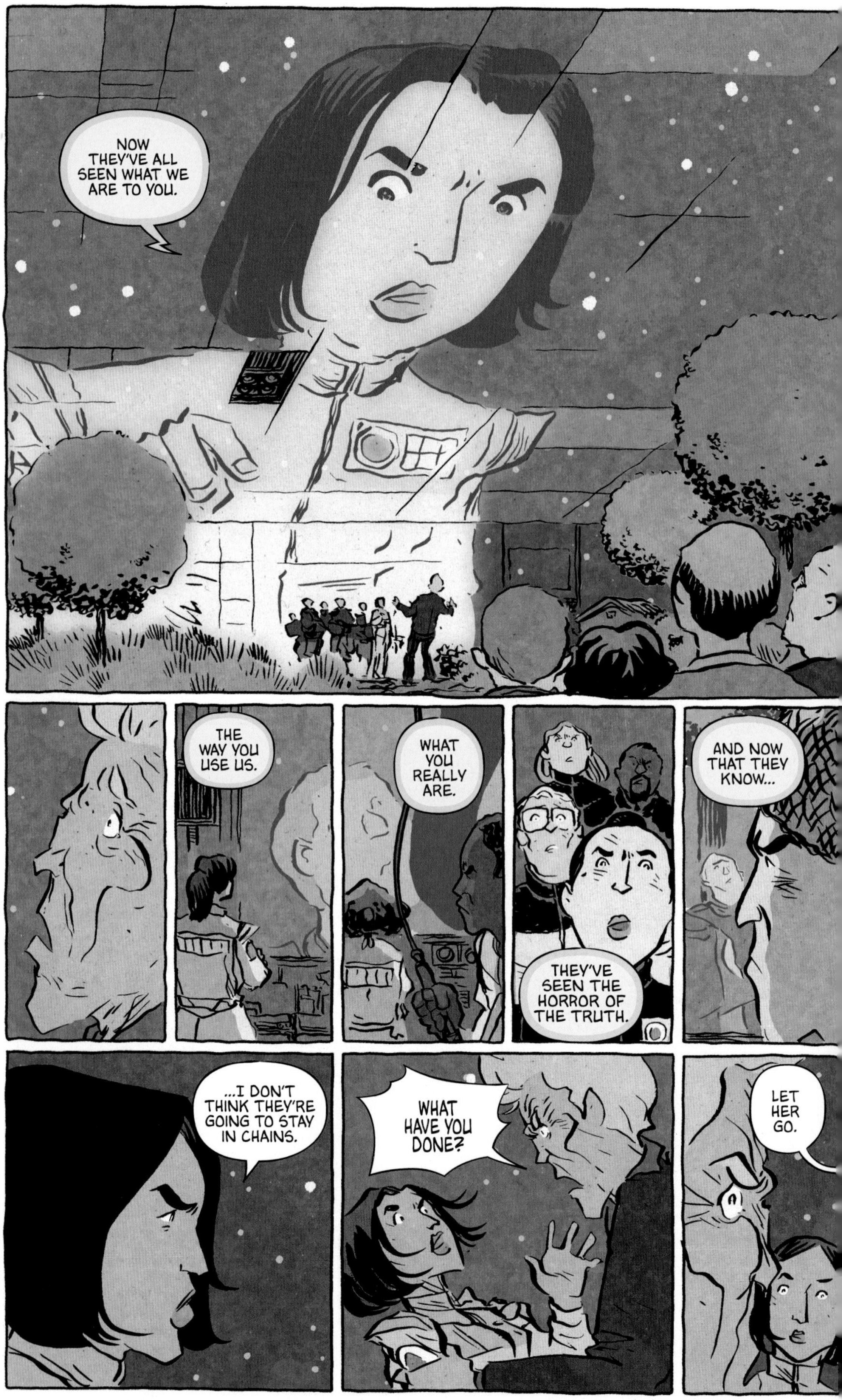
NOW THEY'VE ALL SEEN WHAT WE ARE TO YOU.
THE WAY YOU USE US.
WHAT YOU REALLY ARE.
THEY'VE SEEN THE HORROR OF THE TRUTH.
AND NOW THAT THEY KNOW...
...I DON'T THINK THEY'RE GOING TO STAY IN CHAINS.
WHAT HAVE YOU DONE?
LET HER GO.

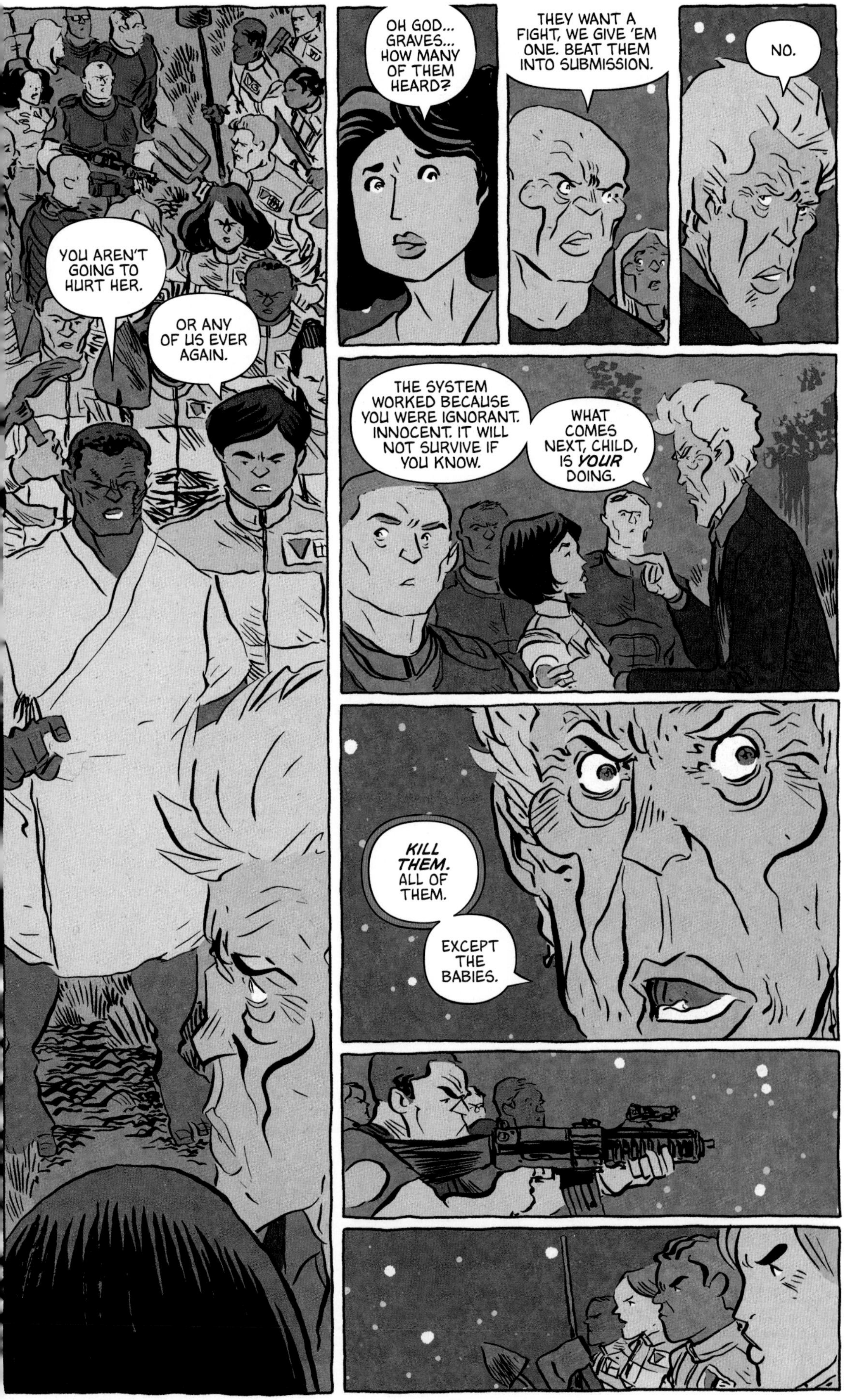
YOU AREN'T GOING TO HURT HER.
OR ANY OF US EVER AGAIN.
OH GOD... GRAVES... HOW MANY OF THEM HEARD?
THEY WANT A FIGHT, WE GIVE 'EM ONE. BEAT THEM INTO SUBMISSION.
NO.
THE SYSTEM WORKED BECAUSE YOU WERE IGNORANT. INNOCENT. IT WILL NOT SURVIVE IF YOU KNOW.
WHAT COMES NEXT, CHILD, IS *YOUR* DOING.
KILL THEM. ALL OF THEM.
EXCEPT THE BABIES.

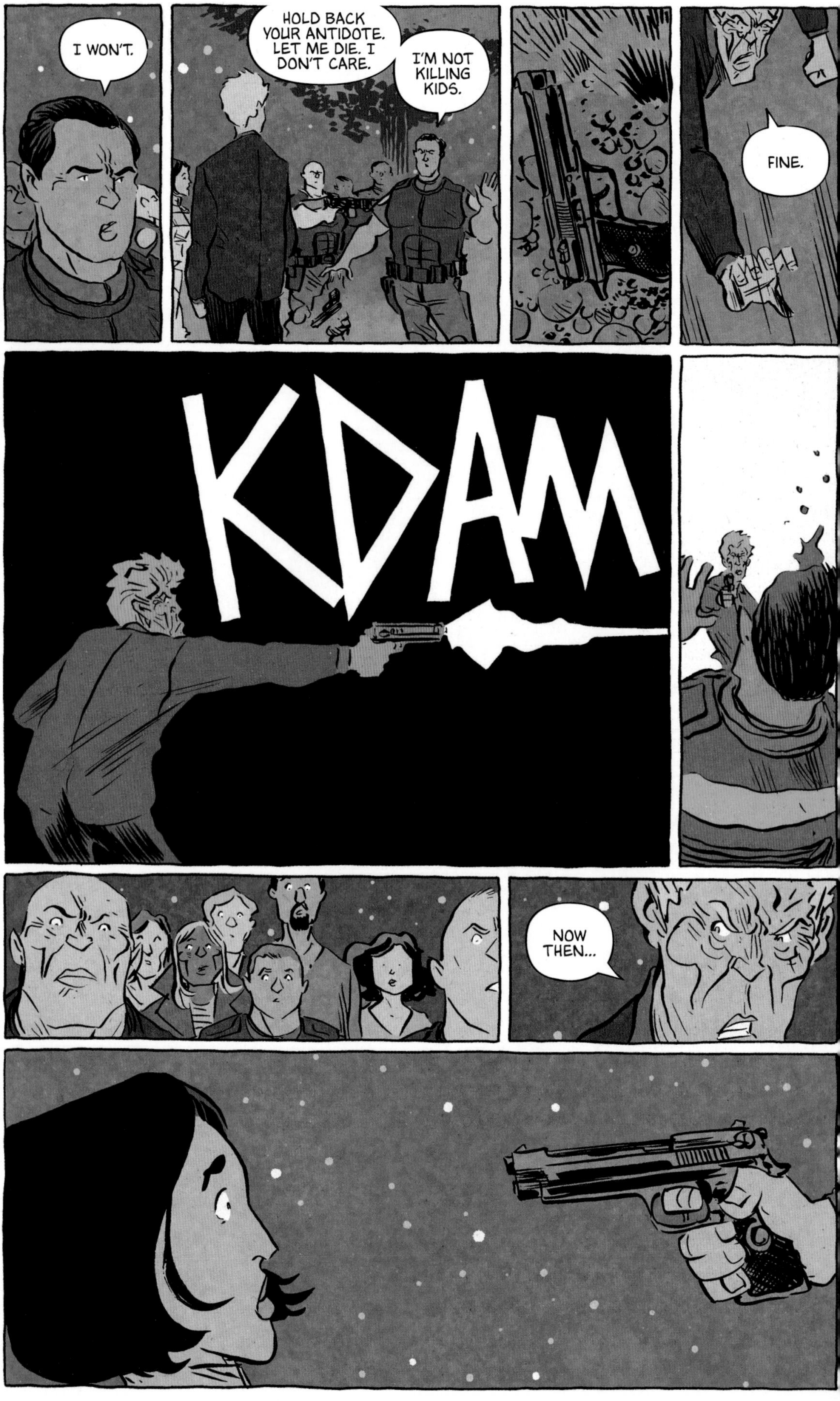
I WON'T.
HOLD BACK YOUR ANTIDOTE. LET ME DIE. I DON'T CARE.
I'M NOT KILLING KIDS.
FINE.
KDAM
NOW THEN...

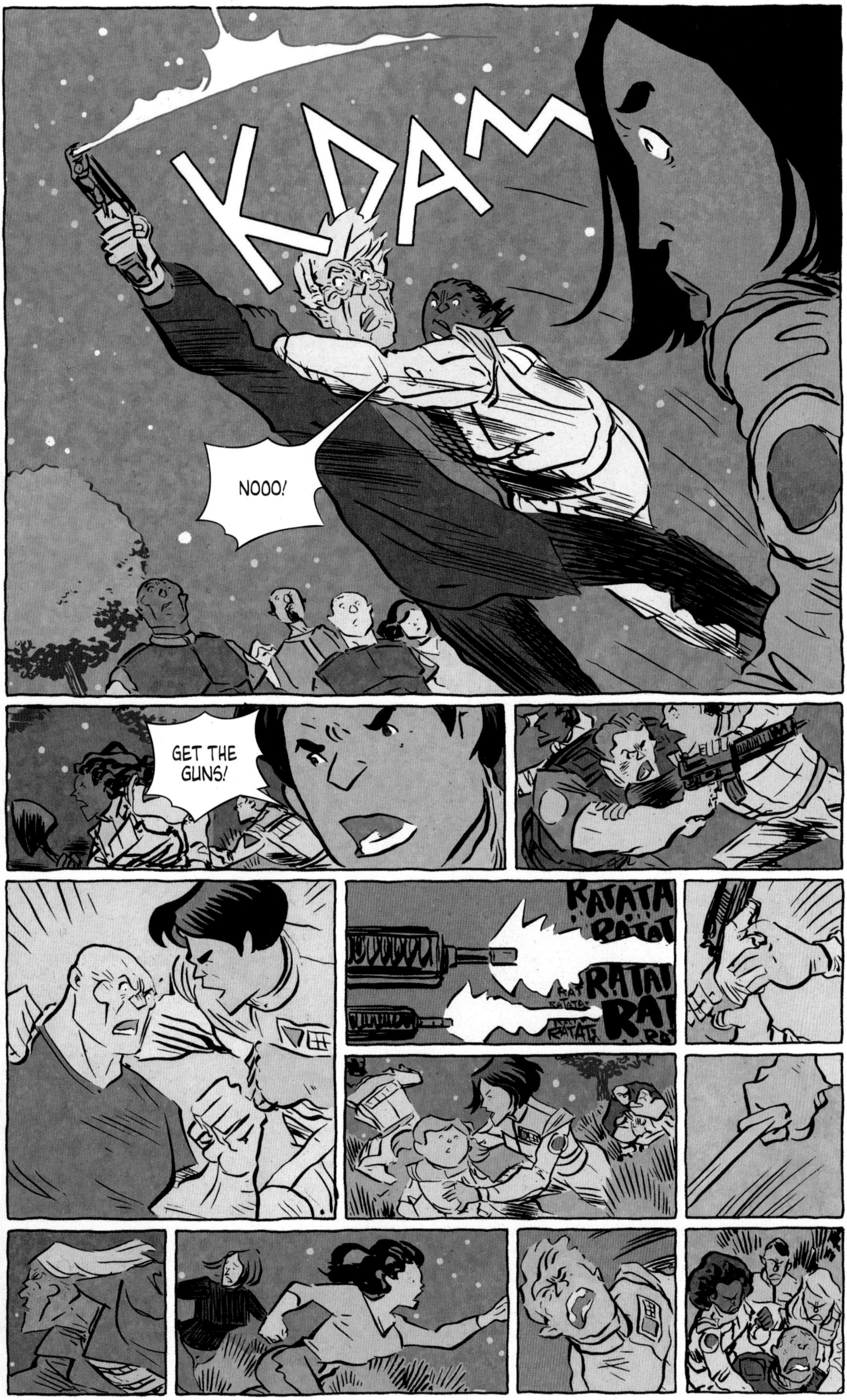
KDAM
NOOO!
GET THE GUNS!
RATATA
RATAT
RATAT
RAT
RATATA
RATAT

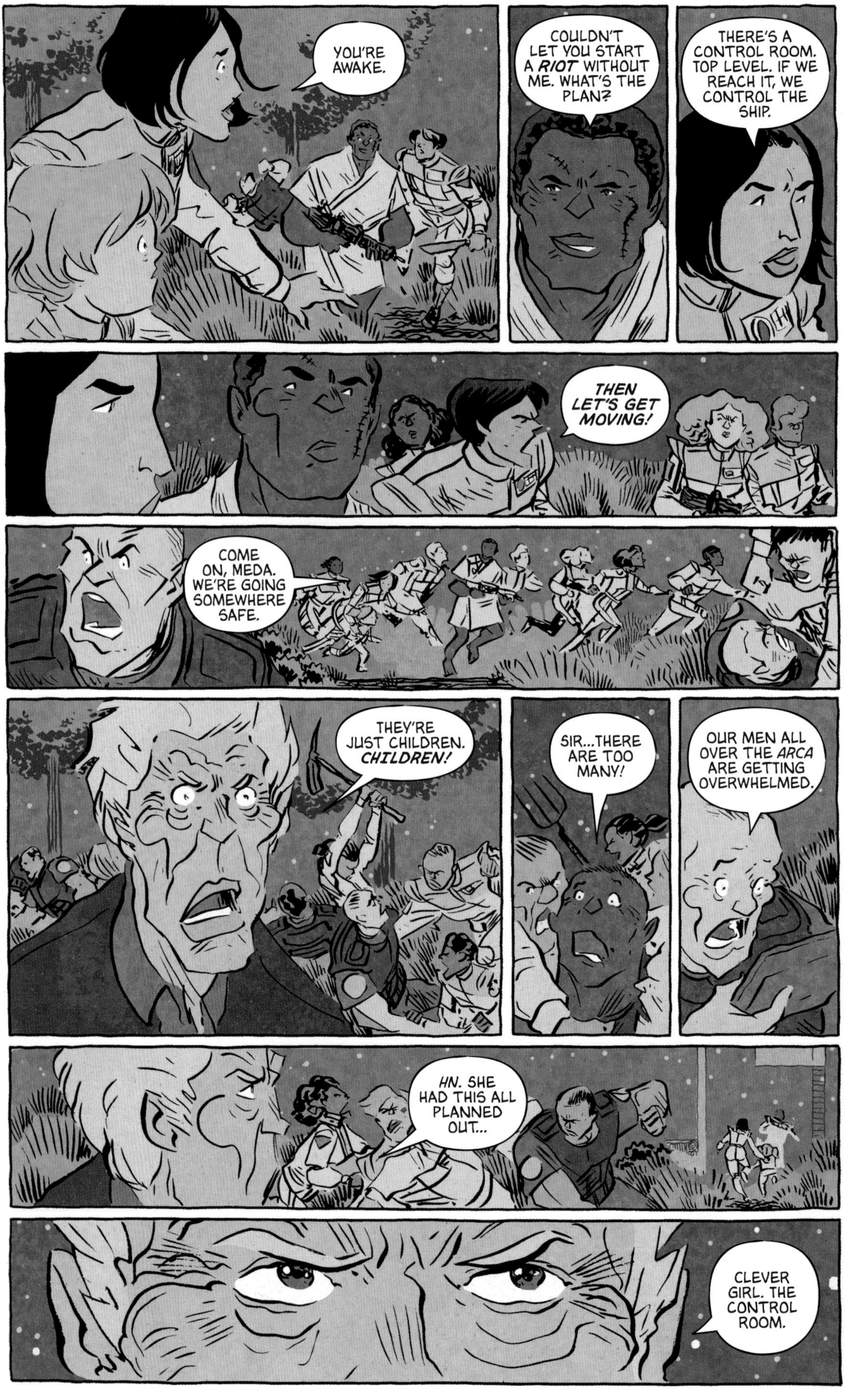
YOU'RE AWAKE.
COULDN'T LET YOU START A *RIOT* WITHOUT ME. WHAT'S THE PLAN?
THERE'S A CONTROL ROOM. TOP LEVEL. IF WE REACH IT, WE CONTROL THE SHIP.
THEN LET'S GET MOVING!
COME ON, MEDA. WE'RE GOING SOMEWHERE SAFE.
THEY'RE JUST CHILDREN. ***CHILDREN!***
SIR...THERE ARE TOO MANY!
OUR MEN ALL OVER THE *ARCA* ARE GETTING OVERWHELMED.
HN. SHE HAD THIS ALL PLANNED OUT...
CLEVER GIRL. THE CONTROL ROOM.

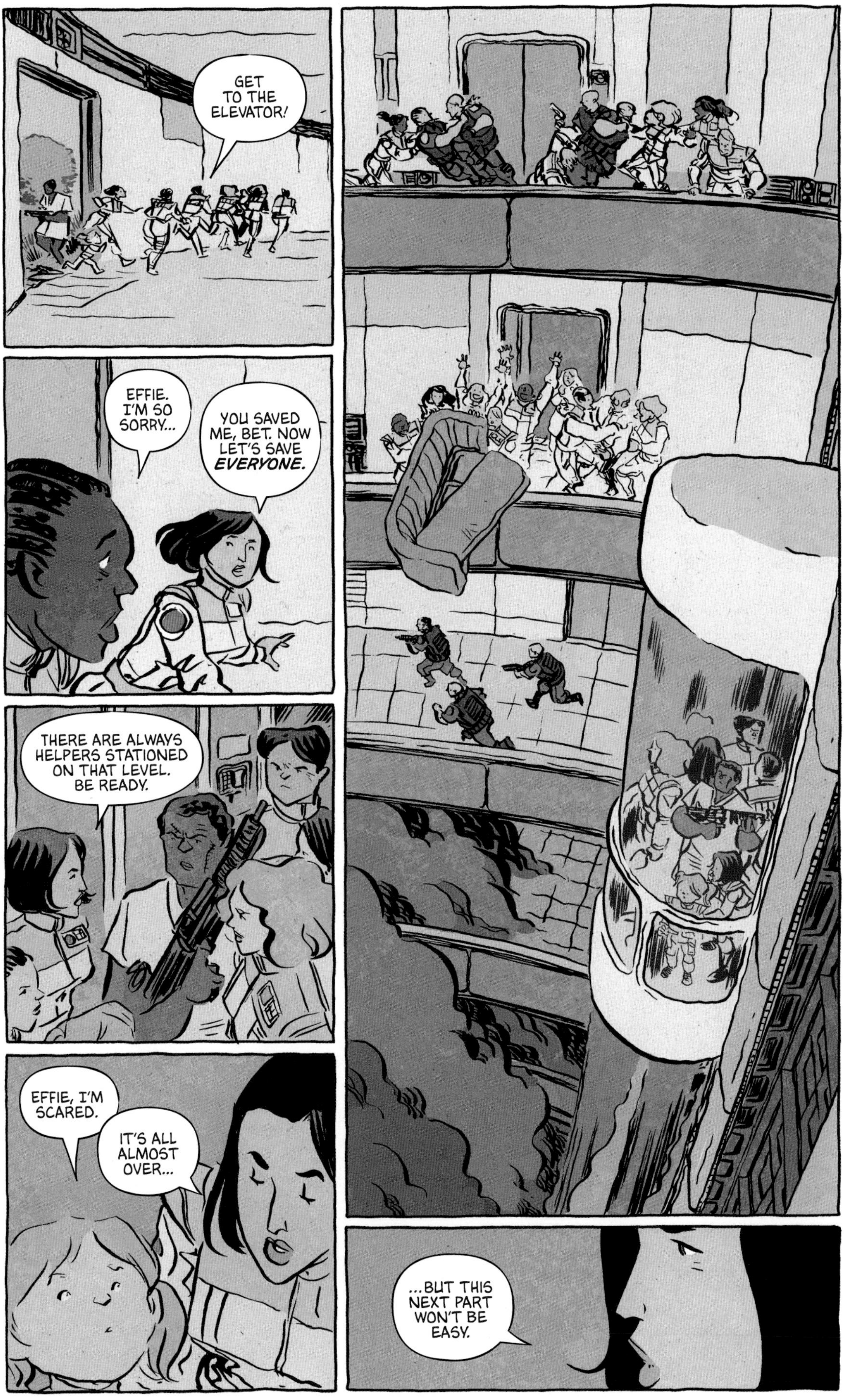
GET TO THE ELEVATOR!
EFFIE. I'M SO SORRY...
YOU SAVED ME, BET. NOW LET'S SAVE *EVERYONE.*
THERE ARE ALWAYS HELPERS STATIONED ON THAT LEVEL. BE READY.
EFFIE, I'M SCARED.
IT'S ALL ALMOST OVER...
...BUT THIS NEXT PART WON'T BE EASY.

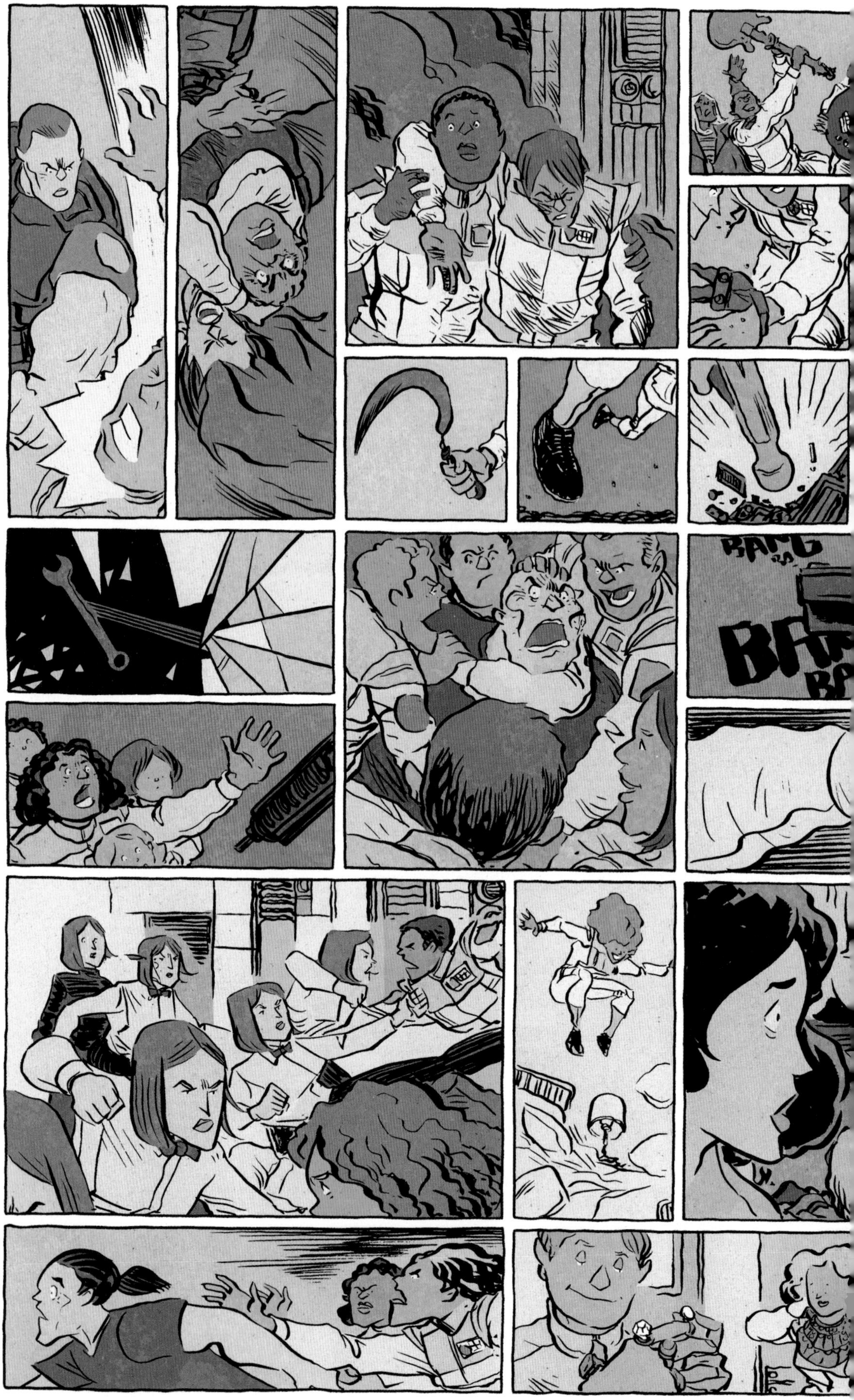
BANG

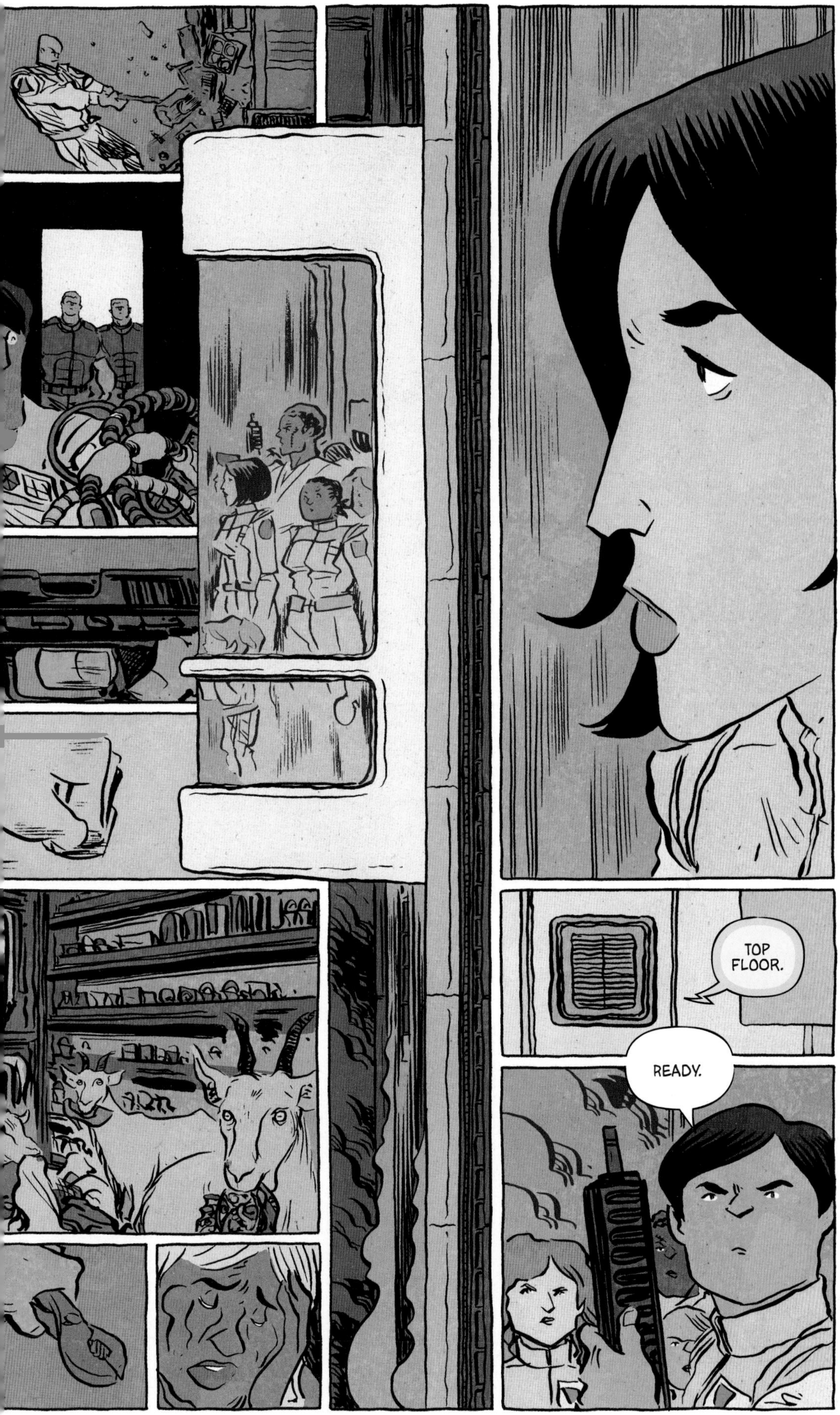
TOP FLOOR.
READY.

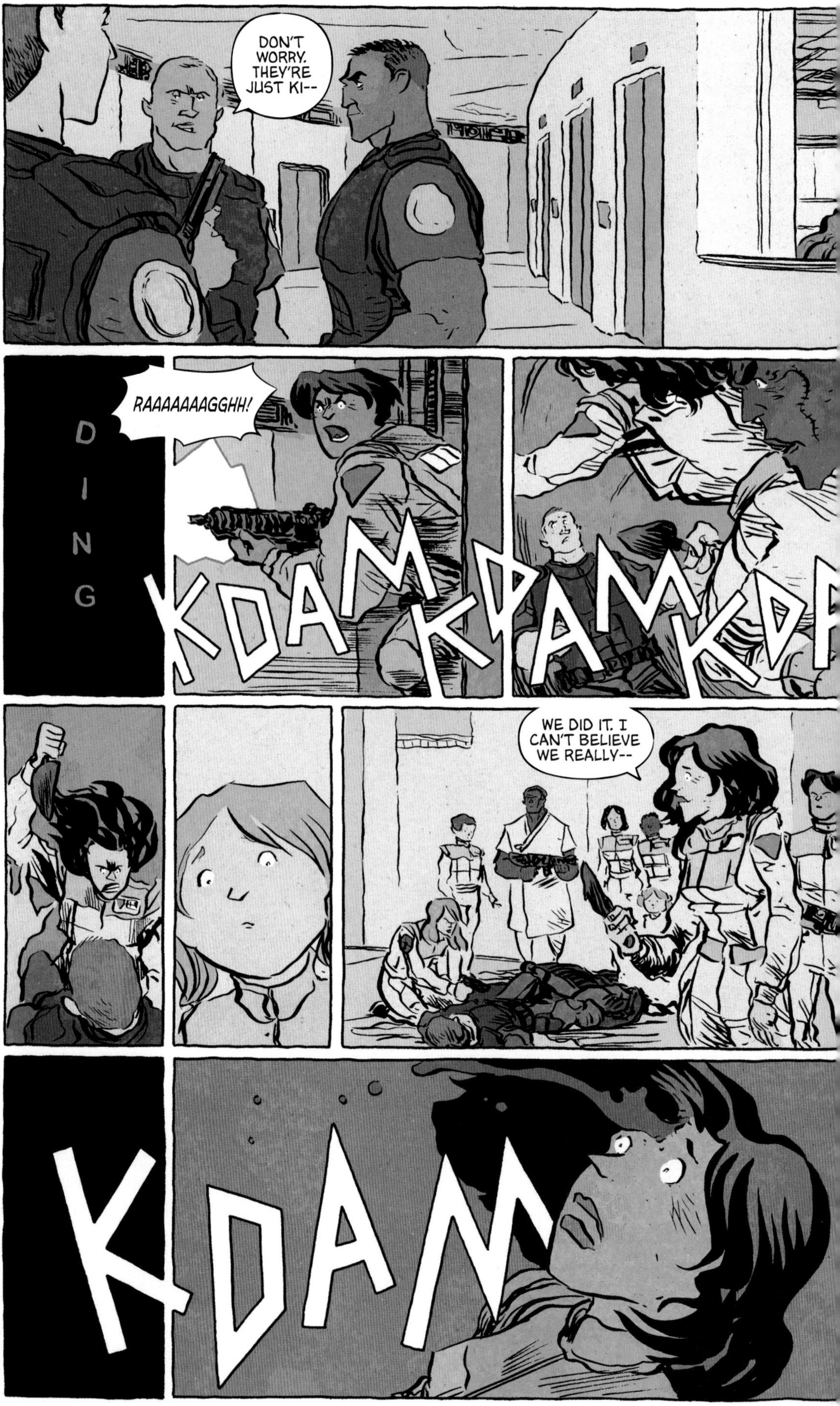
DON'T WORRY. THEY'RE JUST KI--
D
I
N
G
RAAAAAAAGGHH!
KDAM KDAM KDAM KDA
WE DID IT. I CAN'T BELIEVE WE REALLY--
KDAM

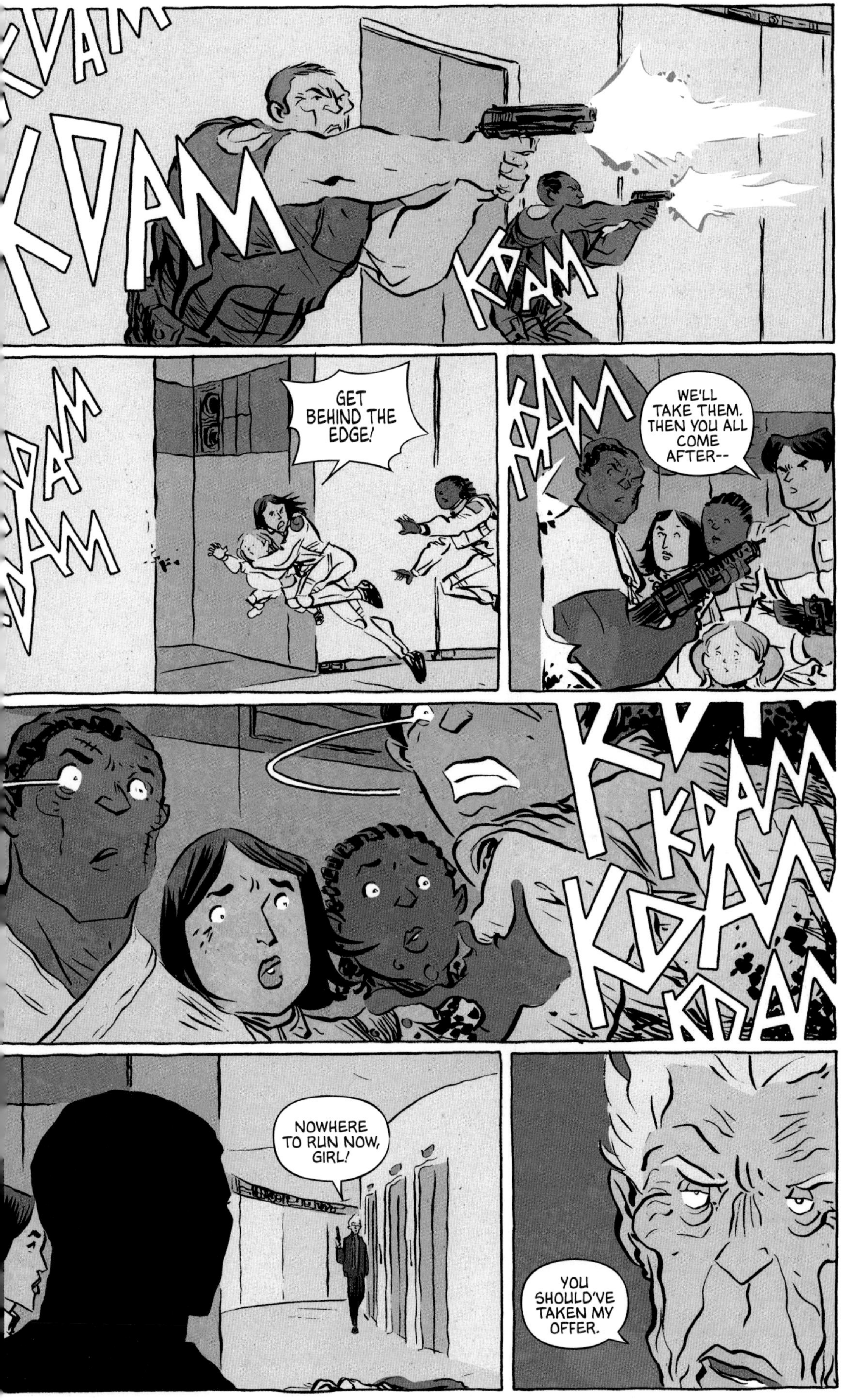
KDAM
KDAM
KDAM
KDAM
KDAM
KDAM
GET BEHIND THE EDGE!
KDAM
WE'LL TAKE THEM. THEN YOU ALL COME AFTER--
KDAM
KDAM
KDAM
KDAM
NOWHERE TO RUN NOW, GIRL!
YOU SHOULD'VE TAKEN MY OFFER.

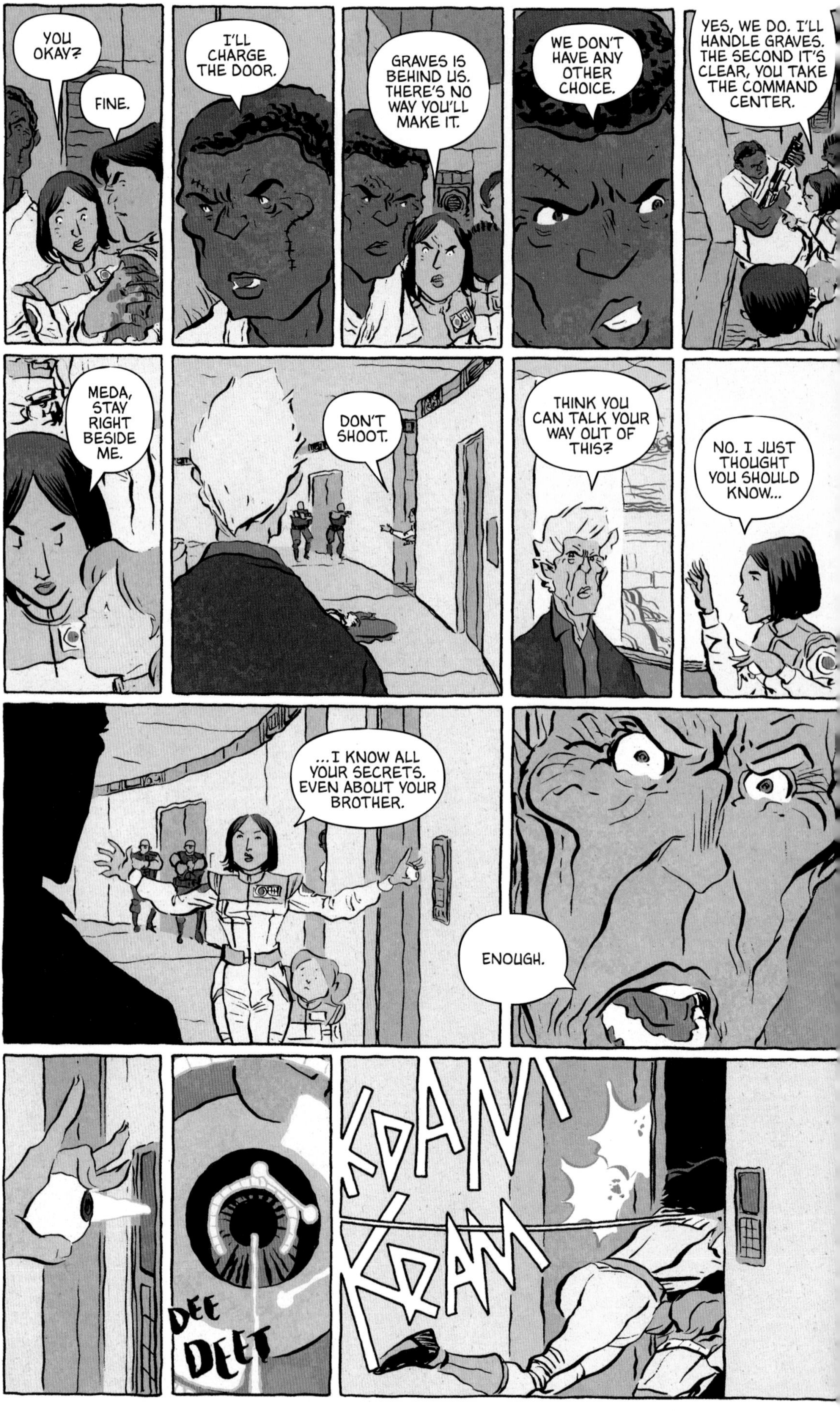
YOU OKAY?
FINE.
I'LL CHARGE THE DOOR.
GRAVES IS BEHIND US. THERE'S NO WAY YOU'LL MAKE IT.
WE DON'T HAVE ANY OTHER CHOICE.
YES, WE DO. I'LL HANDLE GRAVES. THE SECOND IT'S CLEAR, YOU TAKE THE COMMAND CENTER.
MEDA, STAY RIGHT BESIDE ME.
DON'T SHOOT.
THINK YOU CAN TALK YOUR WAY OUT OF THIS?
NO. I JUST THOUGHT YOU SHOULD KNOW...
...I KNOW ALL YOUR SECRETS. EVEN ABOUT YOUR BROTHER.
ENOUGH.
DEE DEET
KRAM KRAM

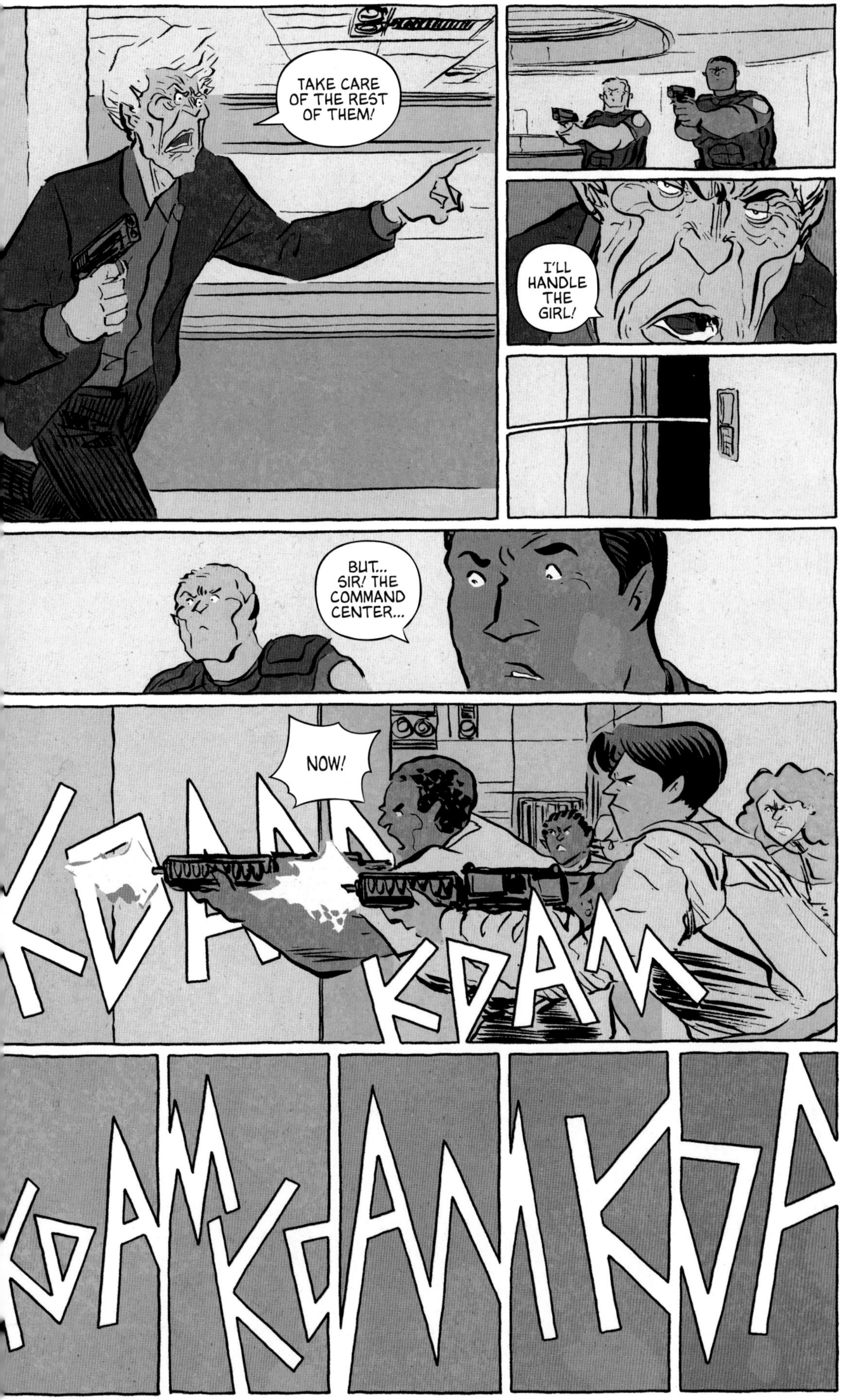
TAKE CARE OF THE REST OF THEM!
I'LL HANDLE THE GIRL!
BUT... SIR! THE COMMAND CENTER...
NOW!
KBAM
KBAM
KBAM
KBAM
KBAM
KBA

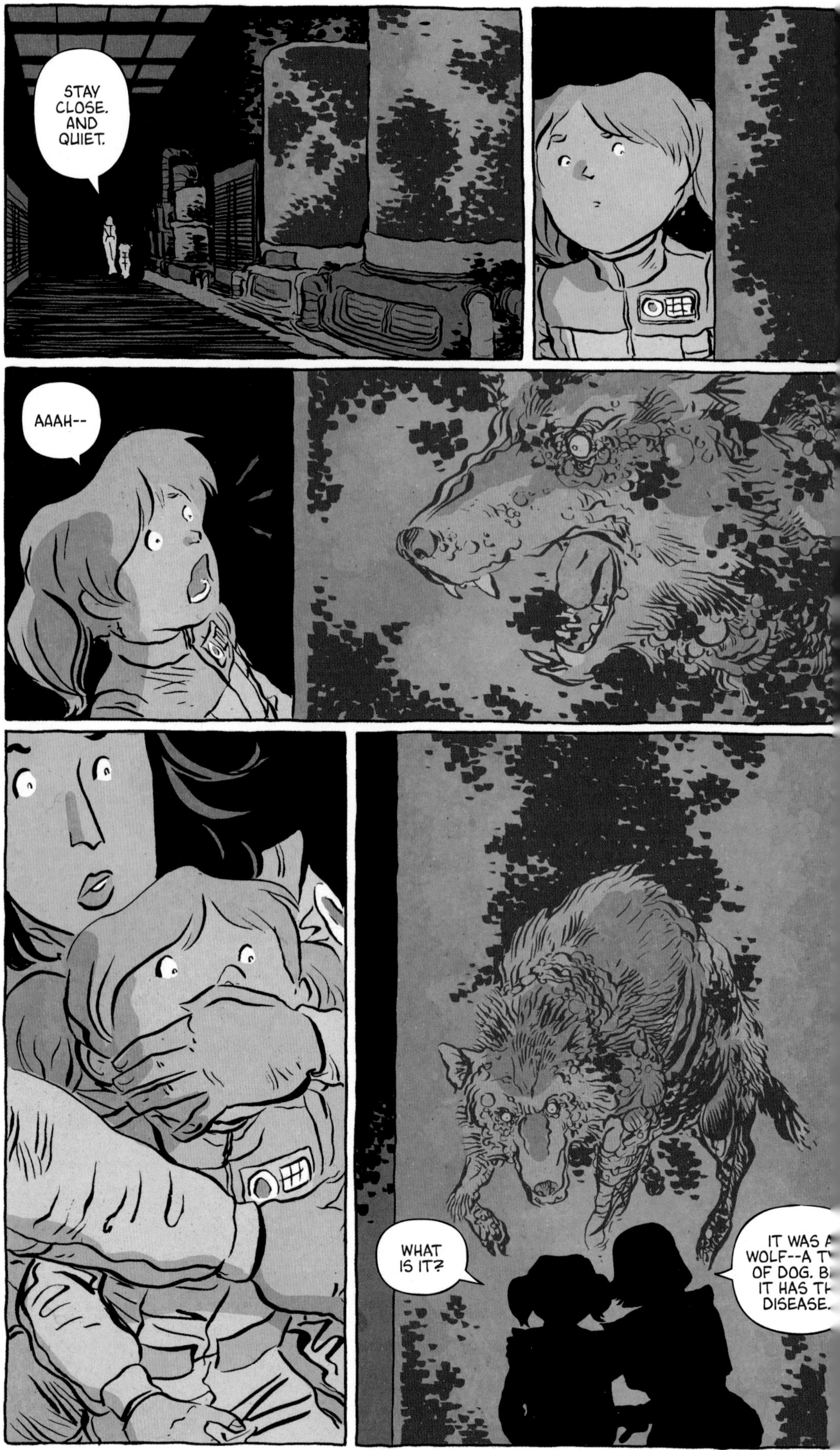
STAY CLOSE. AND QUIET.
AAAH--
WHAT IS IT?
IT WAS A WOLF--A T OF DOG. B IT HAS TH DISEASE.

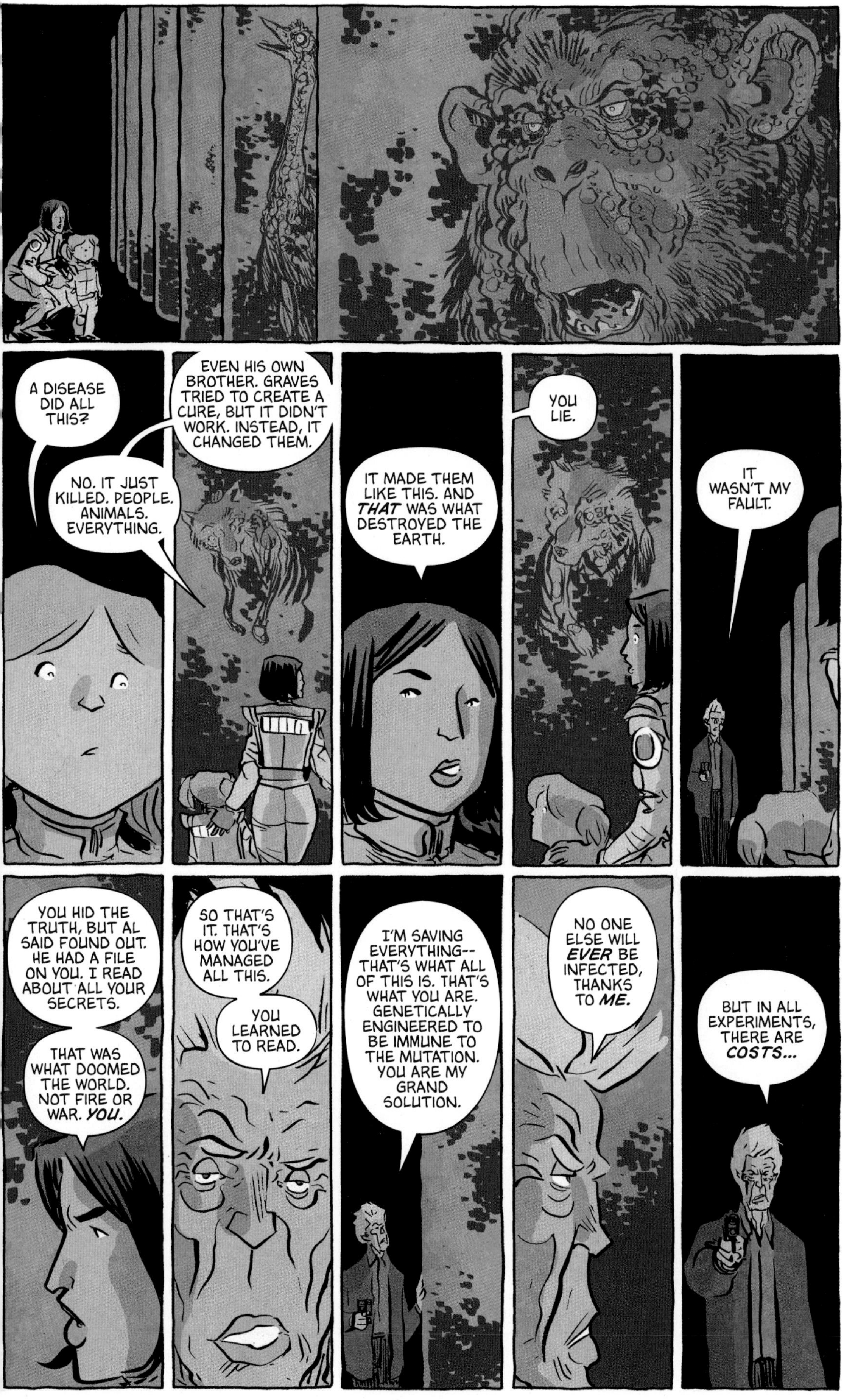

A DISEASE DID ALL THIS?
NO. IT JUST KILLED. PEOPLE. ANIMALS. EVERYTHING.
EVEN HIS OWN BROTHER. GRAVES TRIED TO CREATE A CURE, BUT IT DIDN'T WORK. INSTEAD, IT CHANGED THEM.
IT MADE THEM LIKE THIS. AND *THAT* WAS WHAT DESTROYED THE EARTH.
YOU LIE.
IT WASN'T MY FAULT.
YOU HID THE TRUTH, BUT AL SAID FOUND OUT. HE HAD A FILE ON YOU. I READ ABOUT ALL YOUR SECRETS.
THAT WAS WHAT DOOMED THE WORLD. NOT FIRE OR WAR. *YOU.*
SO THAT'S IT. THAT'S HOW YOU'VE MANAGED ALL THIS.
YOU LEARNED TO READ.
I'M SAVING EVERYTHING-- THAT'S WHAT ALL OF THIS IS. THAT'S WHAT YOU ARE. GENETICALLY ENGINEERED TO BE IMMUNE TO THE MUTATION. YOU ARE MY GRAND SOLUTION.
NO ONE ELSE WILL *EVER* BE INFECTED, THANKS TO *ME.*
BUT IN ALL EXPERIMENTS, THERE ARE *COSTS...*

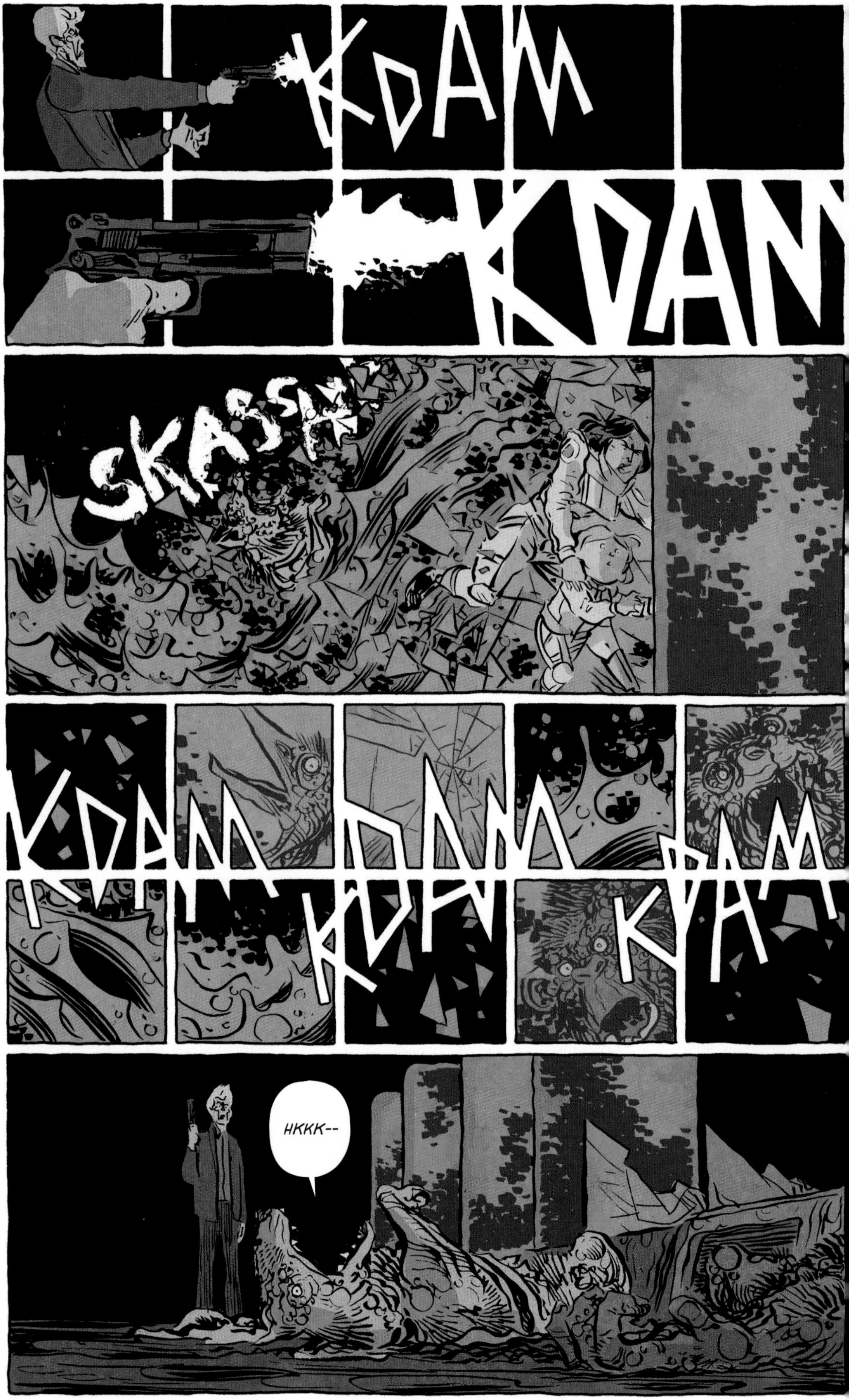
KDAM
KDAM
SKASH
KDAM
KDAM
DAM
KDAM
KDAM
HKKK--

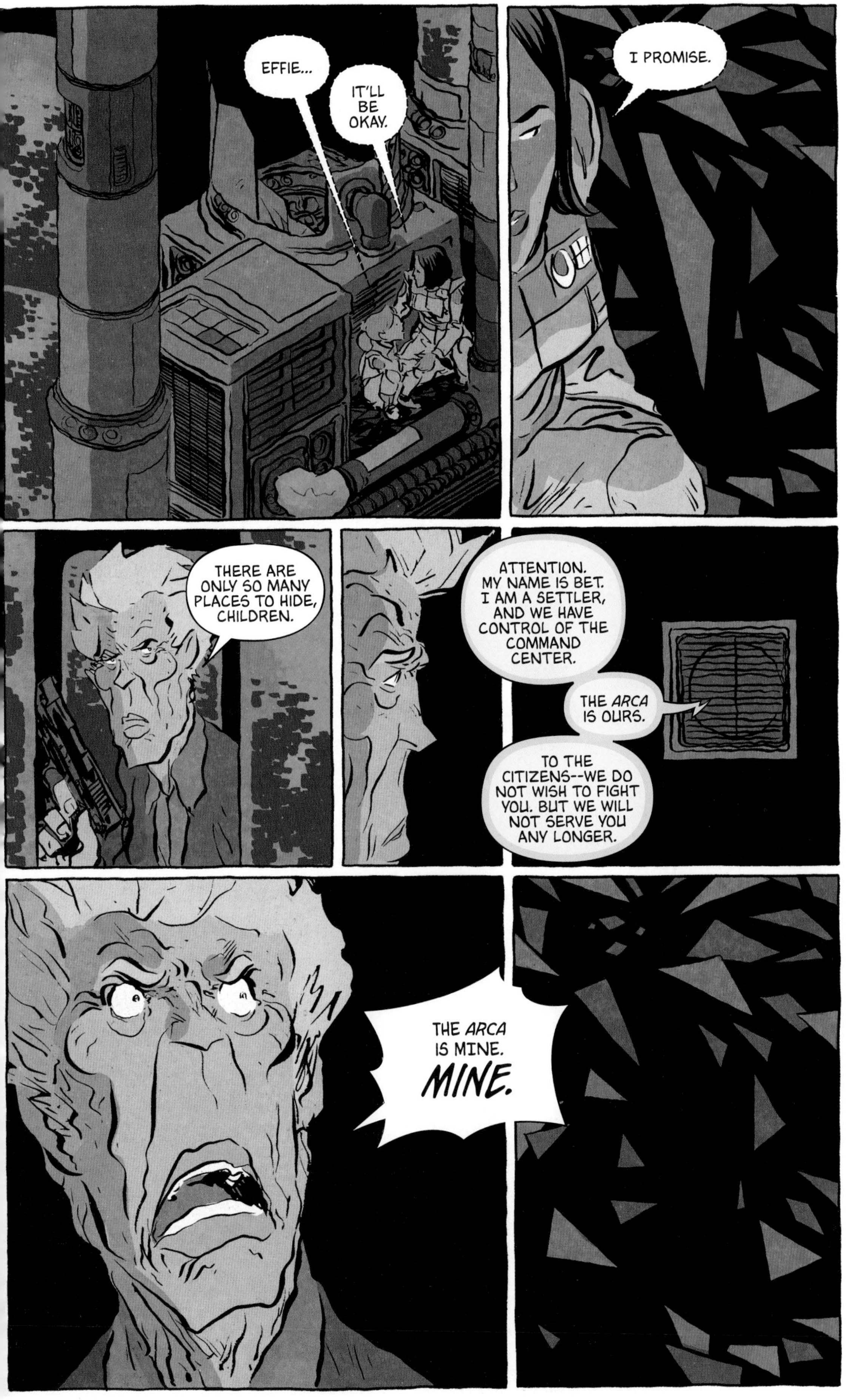
EFFIE...
IT'LL BE OKAY.
I PROMISE.
THERE ARE ONLY SO MANY PLACES TO HIDE, CHILDREN.
ATTENTION. MY NAME IS BET. I AM A SETTLER, AND WE HAVE CONTROL OF THE COMMAND CENTER.
THE *ARCA* IS OURS.
TO THE CITIZENS--WE DO NOT WISH TO FIGHT YOU. BUT WE WILL NOT SERVE YOU ANY LONGER.
THE *ARCA* IS MINE.
MINE.

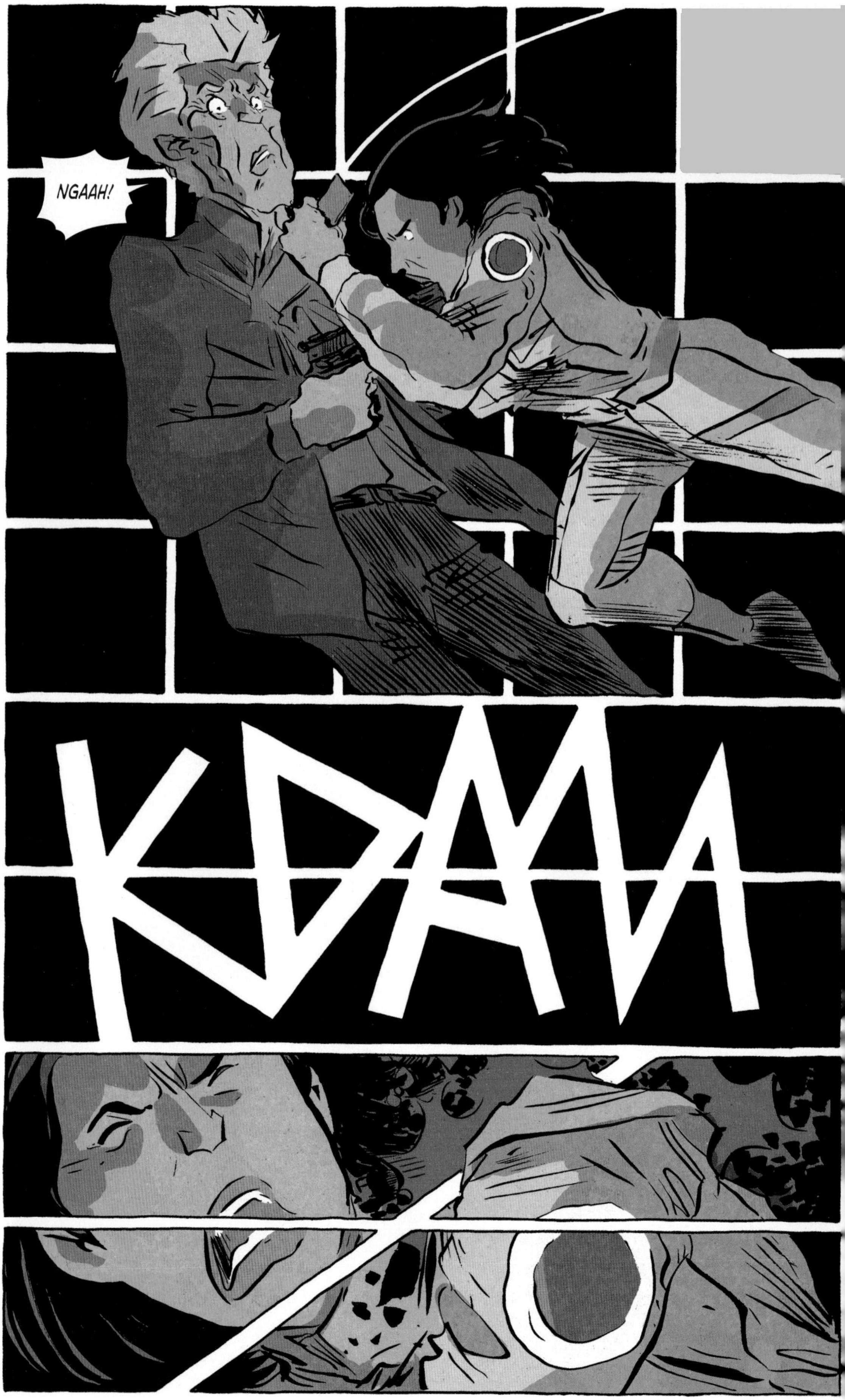
NGAAH!
KBAM

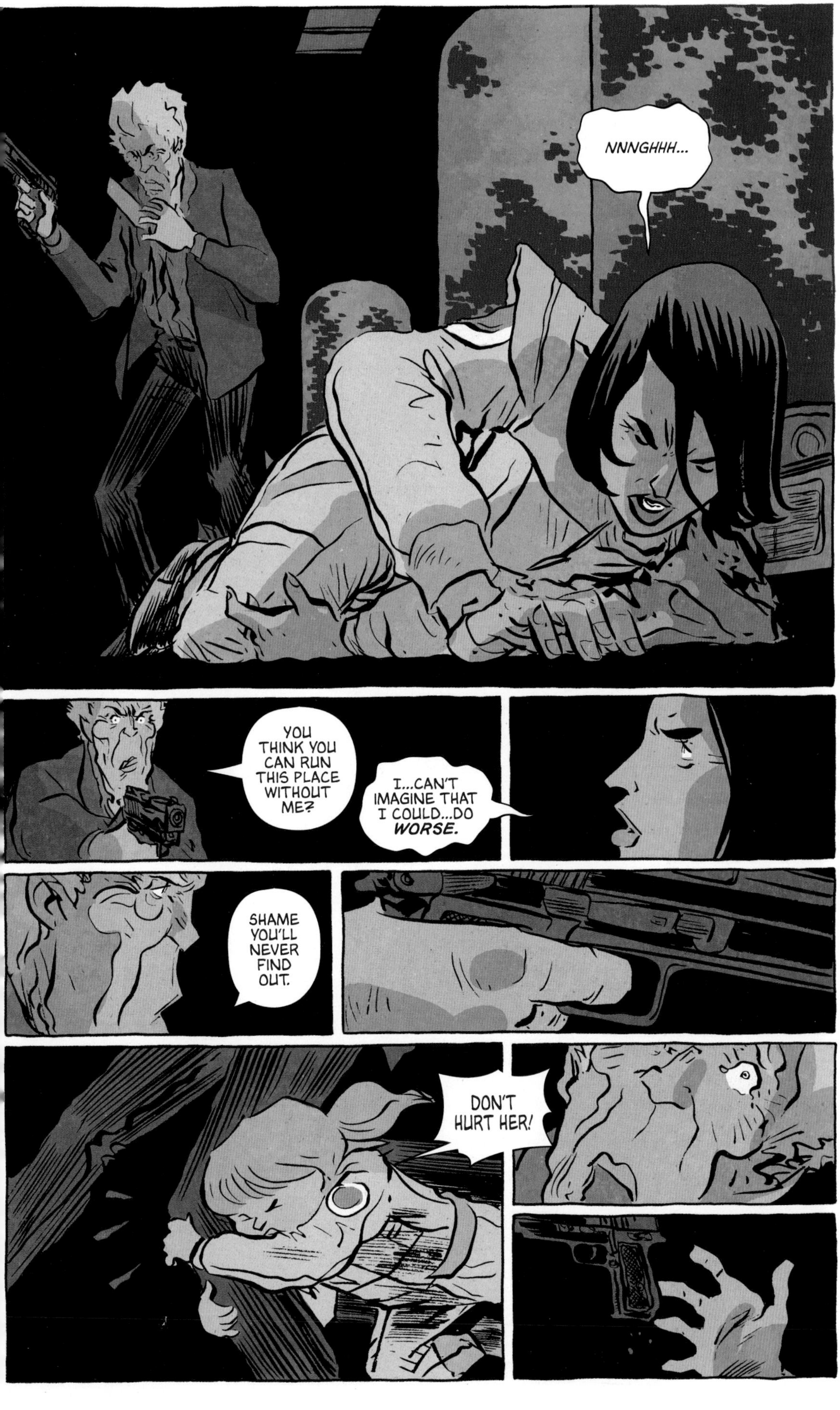
NNNGHHH...
YOU THINK YOU CAN RUN THIS PLACE WITHOUT ME?
I...CAN'T IMAGINE THAT I COULD...DO *WORSE.*
SHAME YOU'LL NEVER FIND OUT.
DON'T HURT HER!

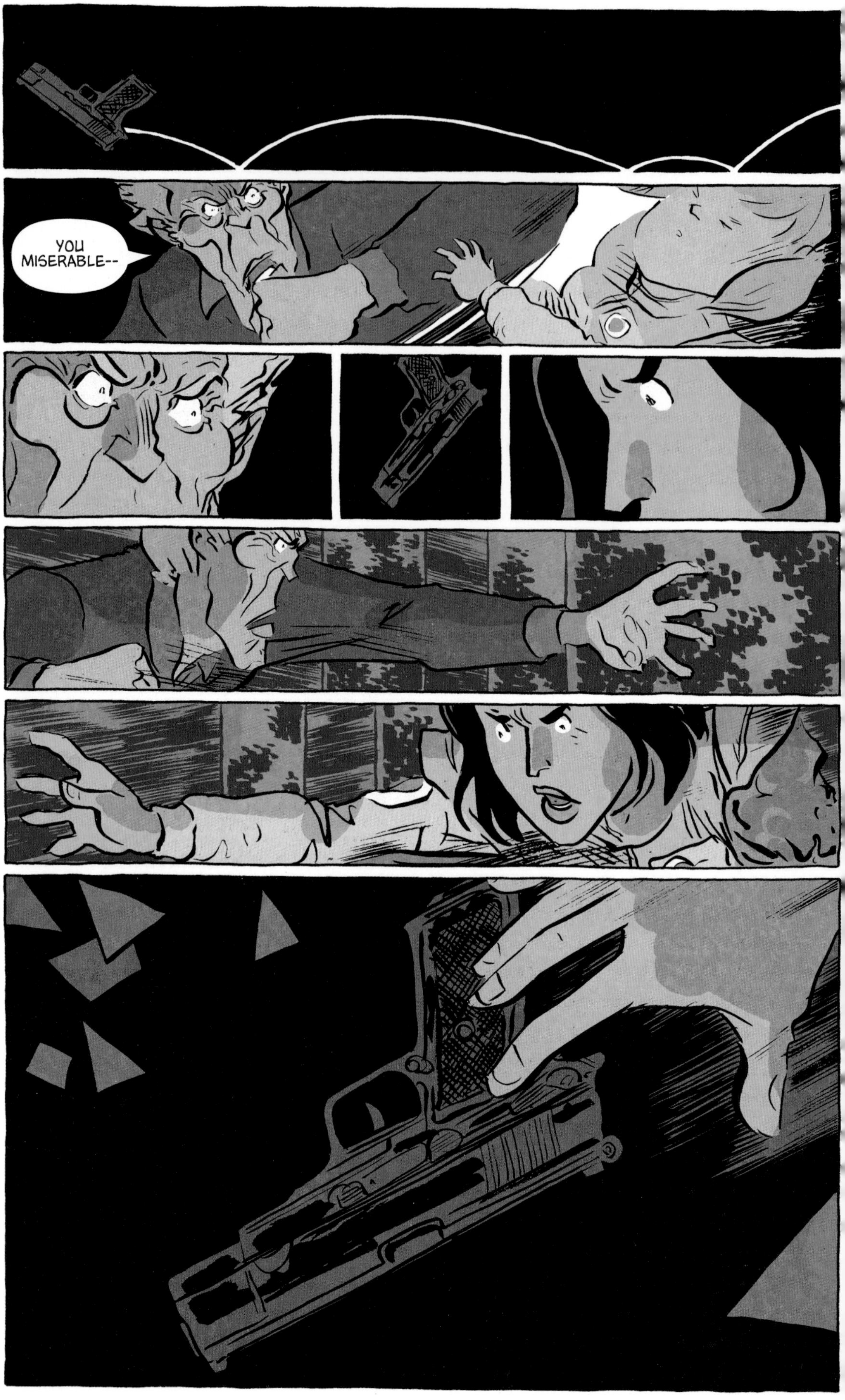
YOU MISERABLE--

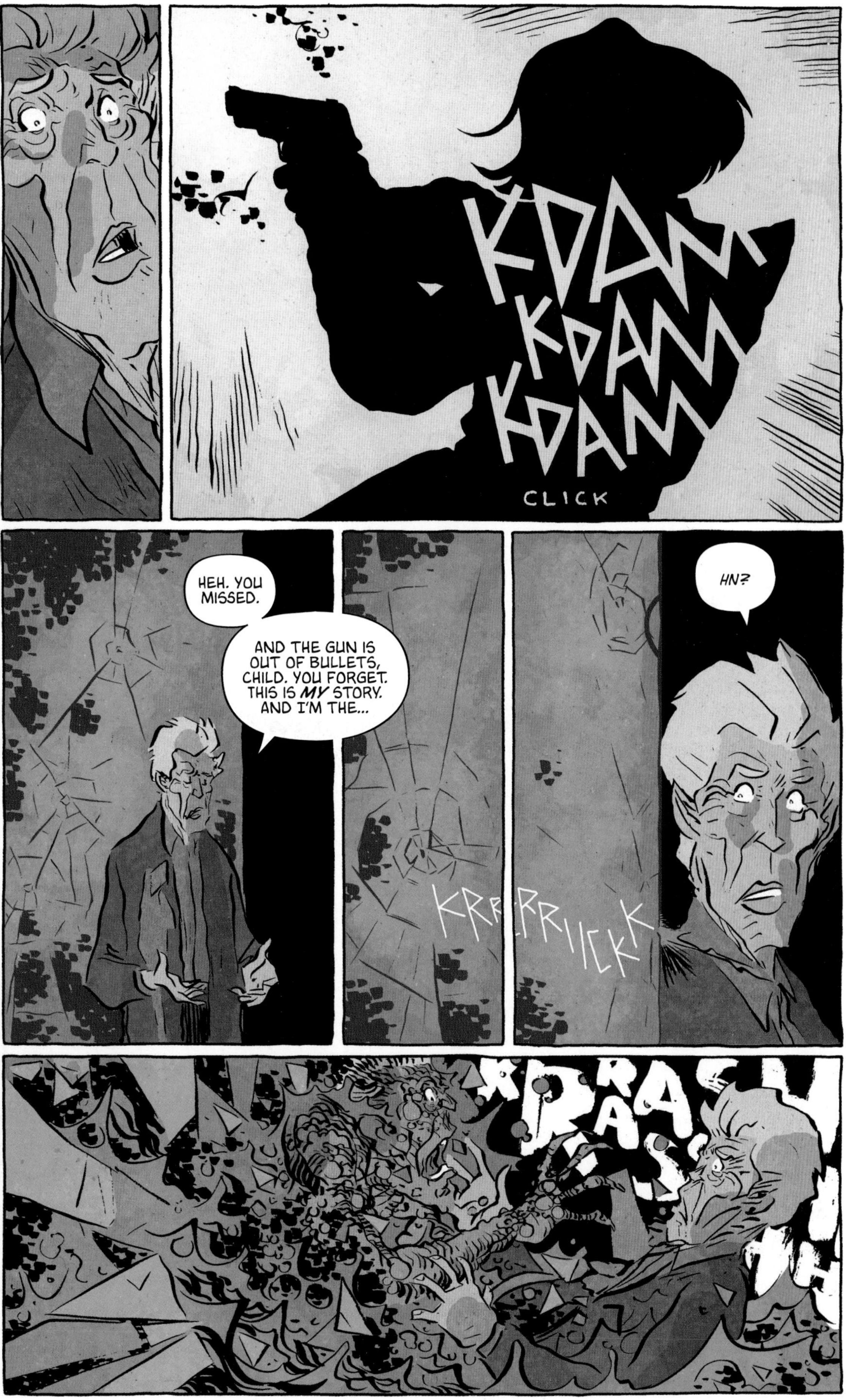
KDAM
KDAM
KDAM
CLICK
HEH. YOU MISSED.
AND THE GUN IS OUT OF BULLETS, CHILD. YOU FORGET. THIS IS *MY* STORY. AND I'M THE...
KRRRRRIICKK
HN?

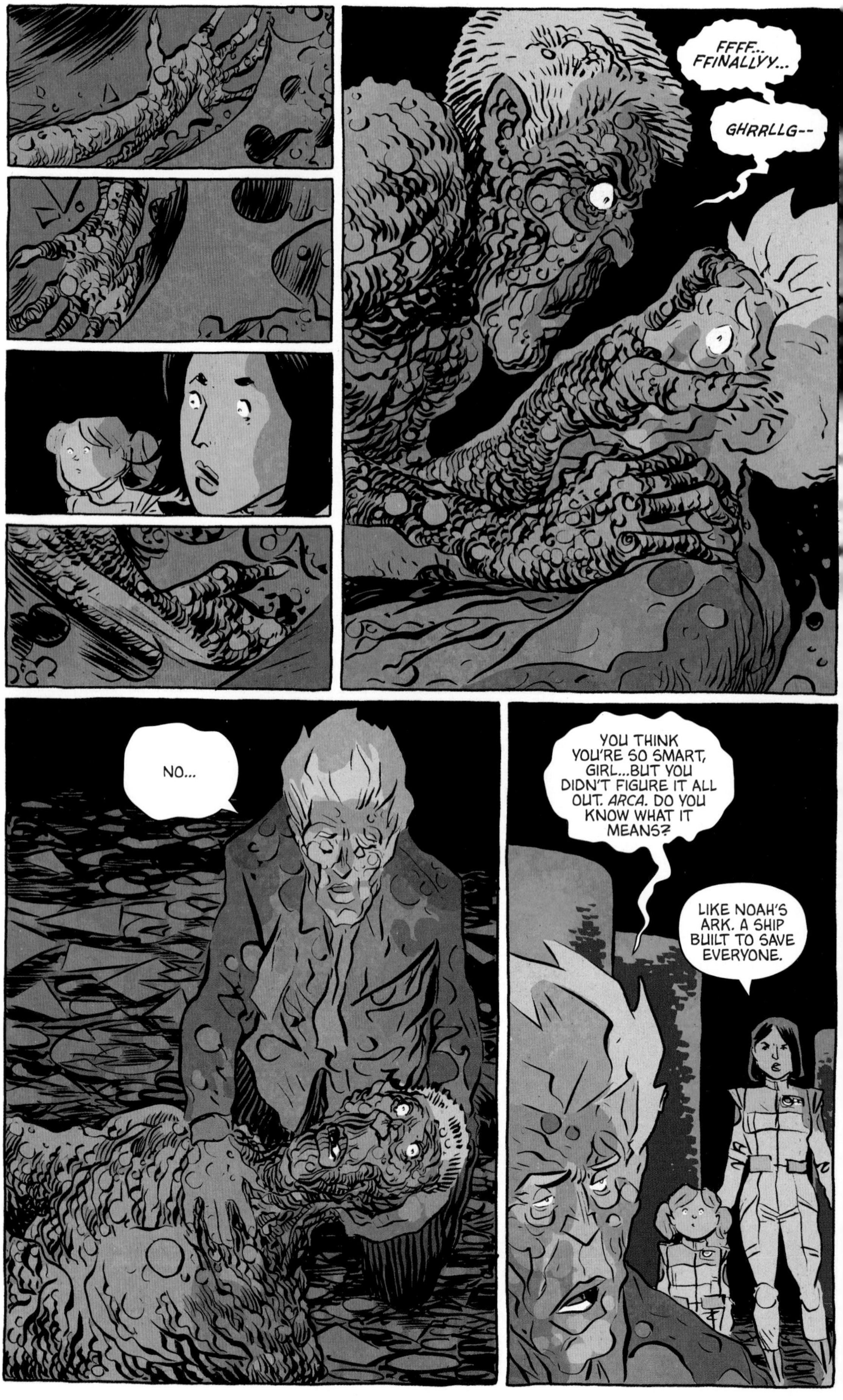
FFFF... FFINALLYY...
GHRRLLG--
NO...
YOU THINK YOU'RE SO SMART, GIRL...BUT YOU DIDN'T FIGURE IT ALL OUT. *ARCA.* DO YOU KNOW WHAT IT MEANS?
LIKE NOAH'S ARK. A SHIP BUILT TO SAVE EVERYONE.

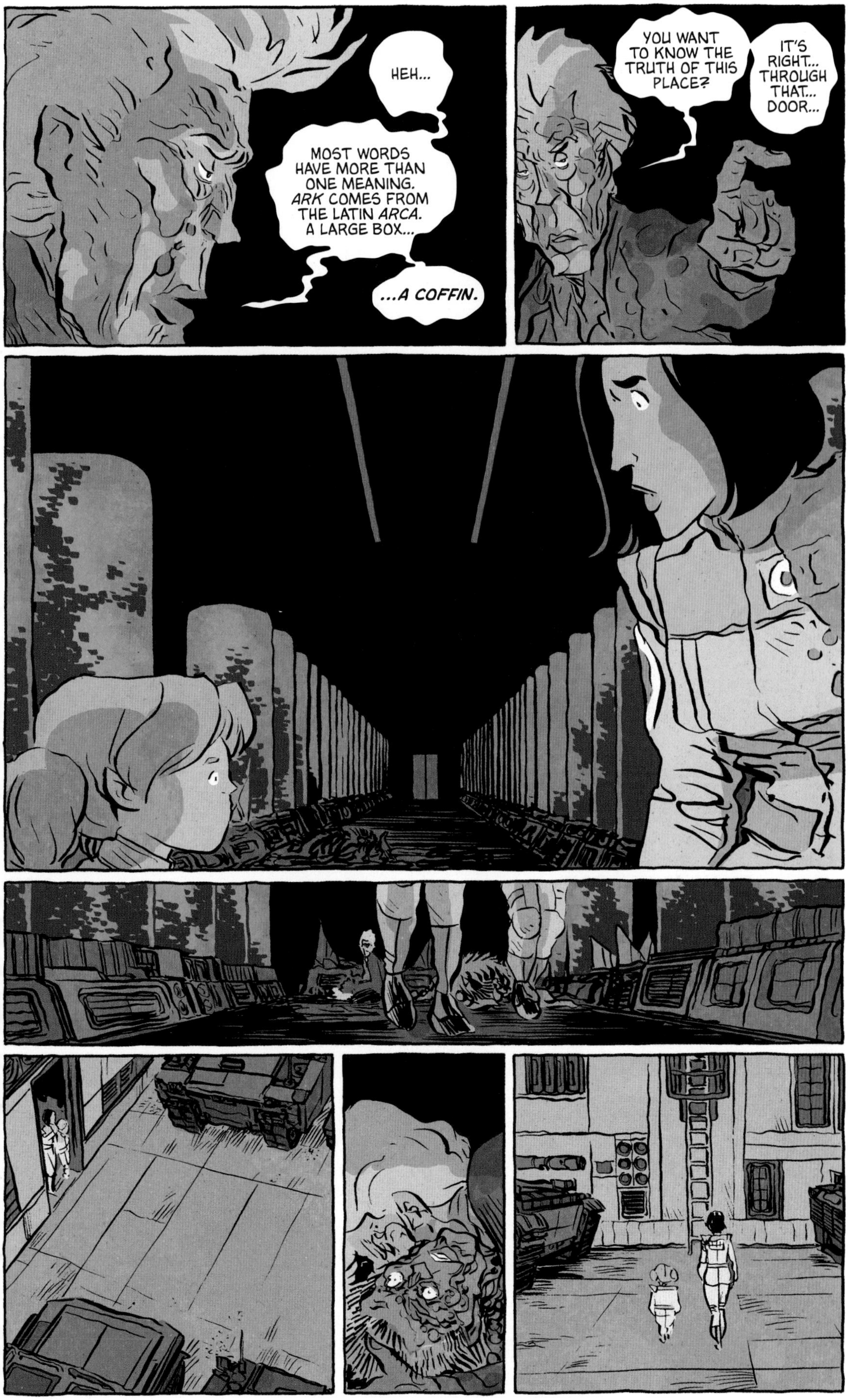
HEH...
MOST WORDS HAVE MORE THAN ONE MEANING. *ARK* COMES FROM THE LATIN *ARCA*. A LARGE BOX...
...A COFFIN.
YOU WANT TO KNOW THE TRUTH OF THIS PLACE?
IT'S RIGHT... THROUGH THAT... DOOR...

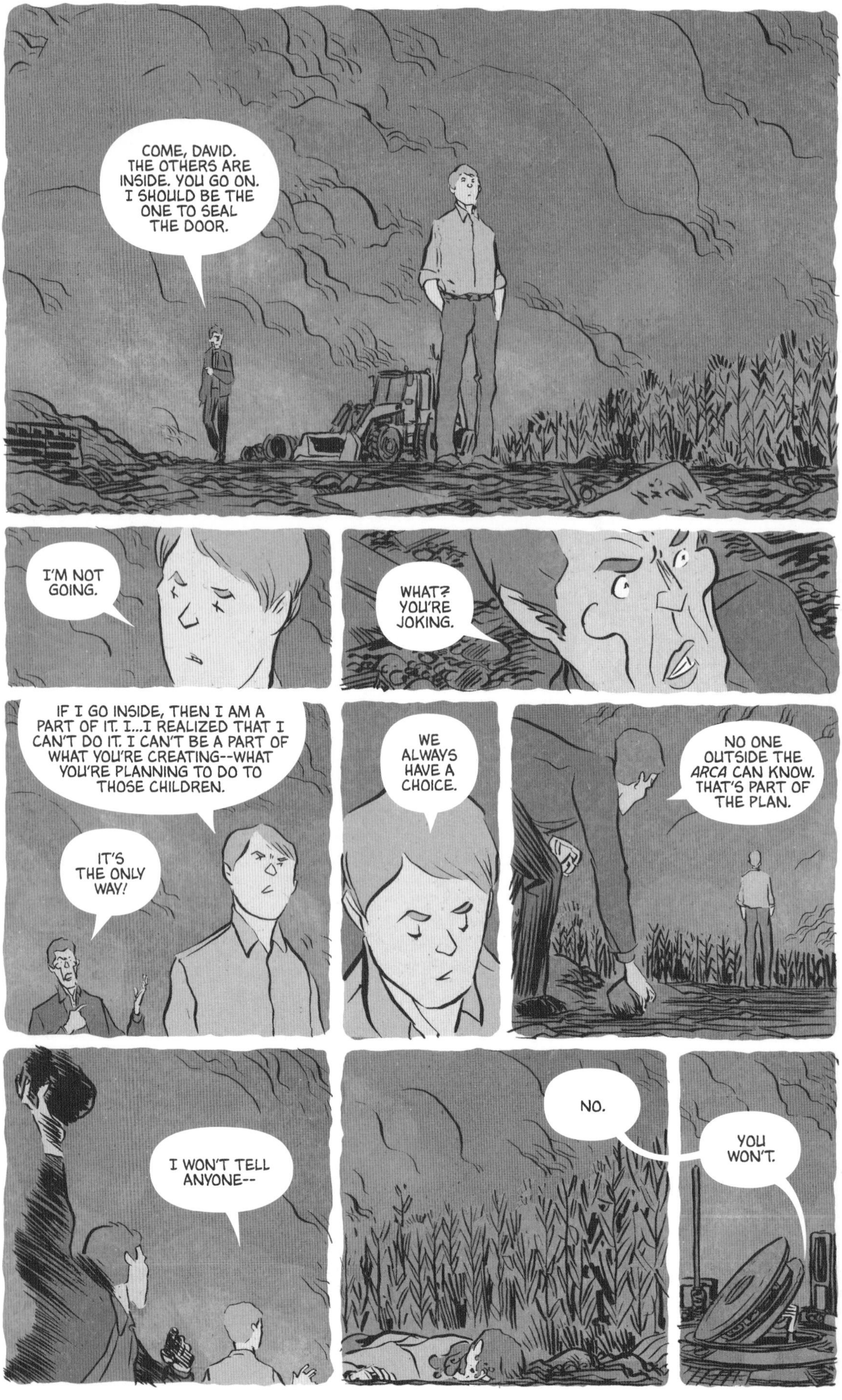
COME, DAVID. THE OTHERS ARE INSIDE. YOU GO ON. I SHOULD BE THE ONE TO SEAL THE DOOR.
I'M NOT GOING.
WHAT? YOU'RE JOKING.
IF I GO INSIDE, THEN I AM A PART OF IT. I...I REALIZED THAT I CAN'T DO IT. I CAN'T BE A PART OF WHAT YOU'RE CREATING--WHAT YOU'RE PLANNING TO DO TO THOSE CHILDREN.
IT'S THE ONLY WAY!
WE ALWAYS HAVE A CHOICE.
NO ONE OUTSIDE THE *ARCA* CAN KNOW. THAT'S PART OF THE PLAN.
I WON'T TELL ANYONE--
NO.
YOU WON'T.

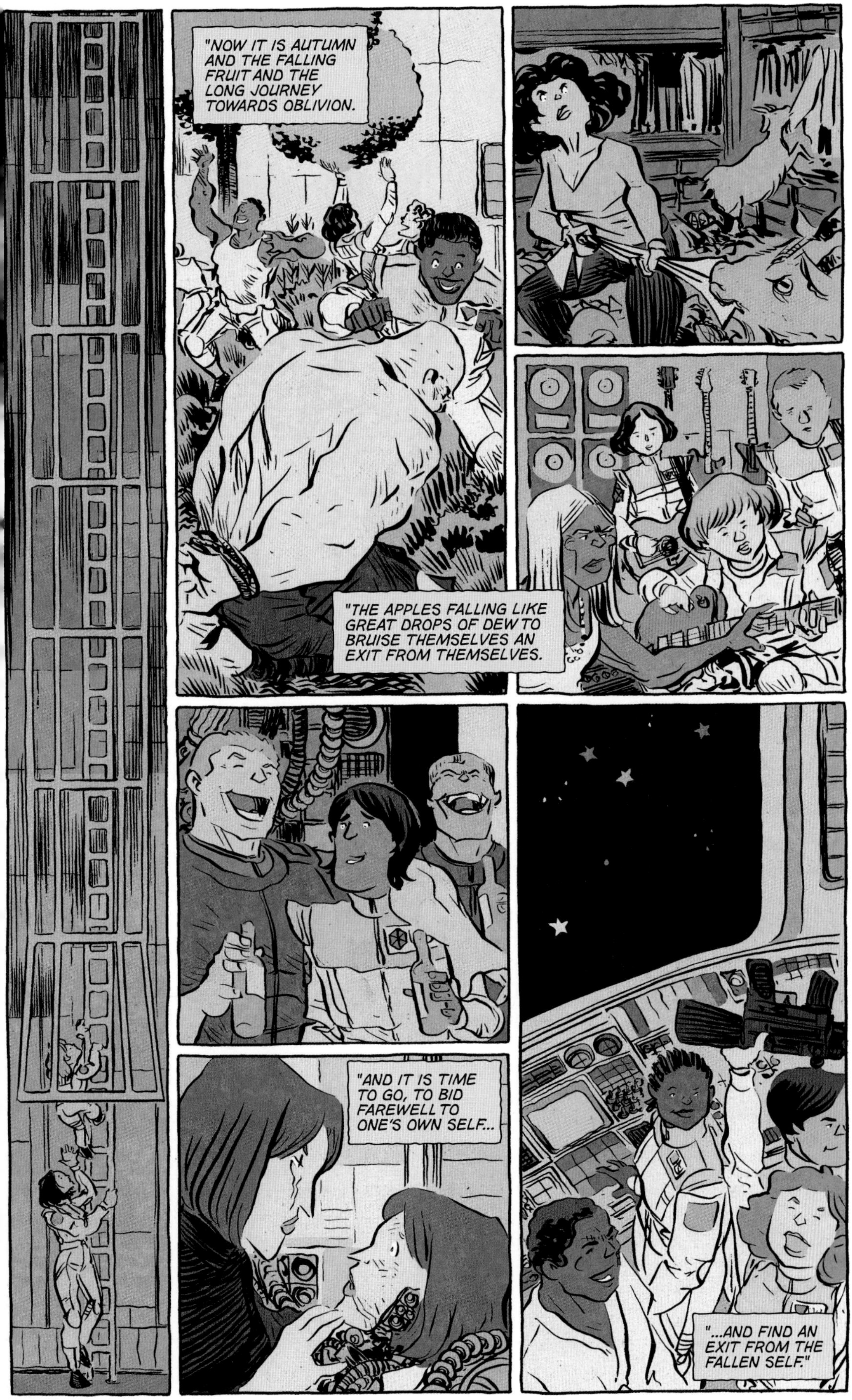
"NOW IT IS AUTUMN AND THE FALLING FRUIT AND THE LONG JOURNEY TOWARDS OBLIVION.
"THE APPLES FALLING LIKE GREAT DROPS OF DEW TO BRUISE THEMSELVES AN EXIT FROM THEMSELVES.
"AND IT IS TIME TO GO, TO BID FAREWELL TO ONE'S OWN SELF...
"...AND FIND AN EXIT FROM THE FALLEN SELF."

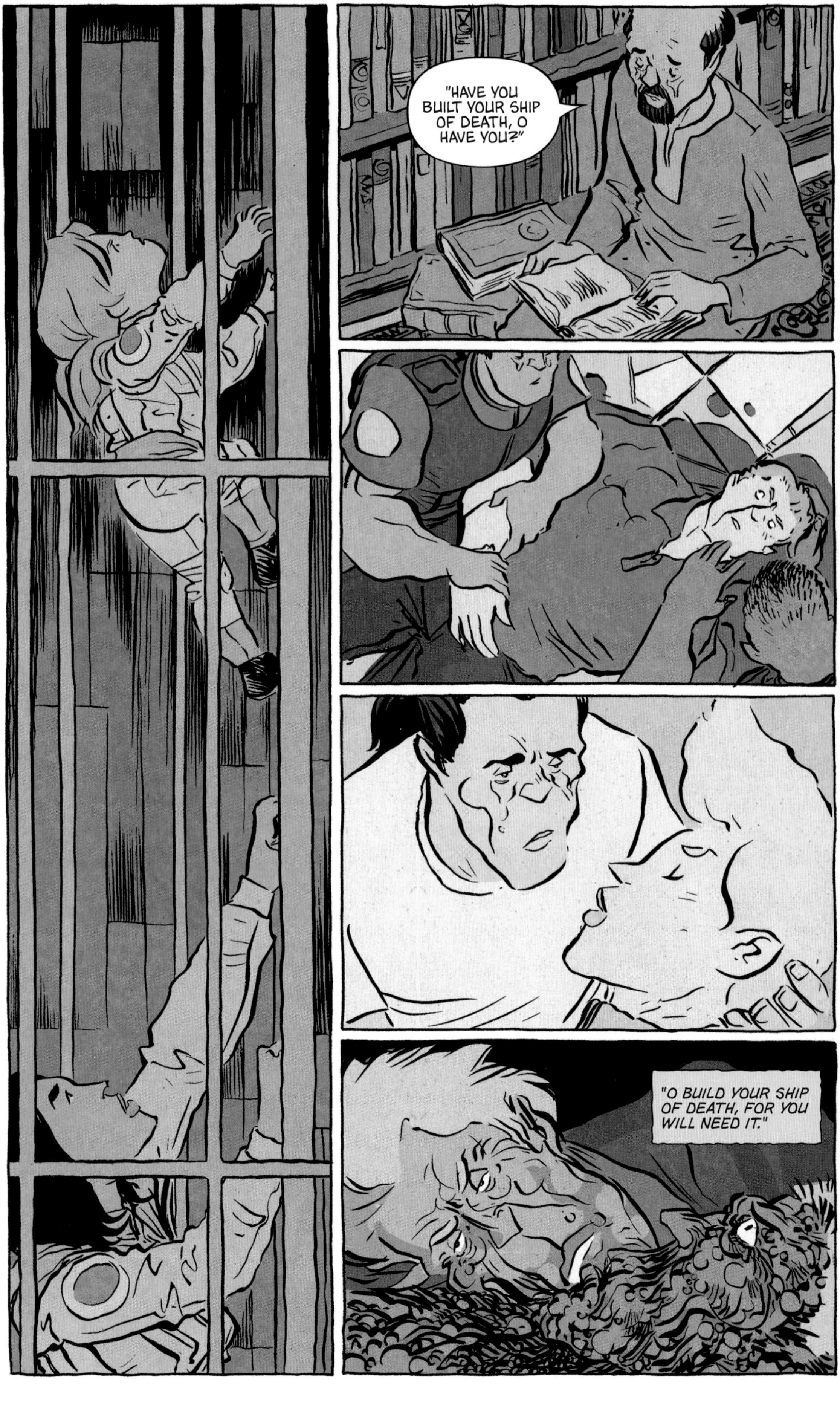
"HAVE YOU BUILT YOUR SHIP OF DEATH, O HAVE YOU?"
"O BUILD YOUR SHIP OF DEATH, FOR YOU WILL NEED IT."

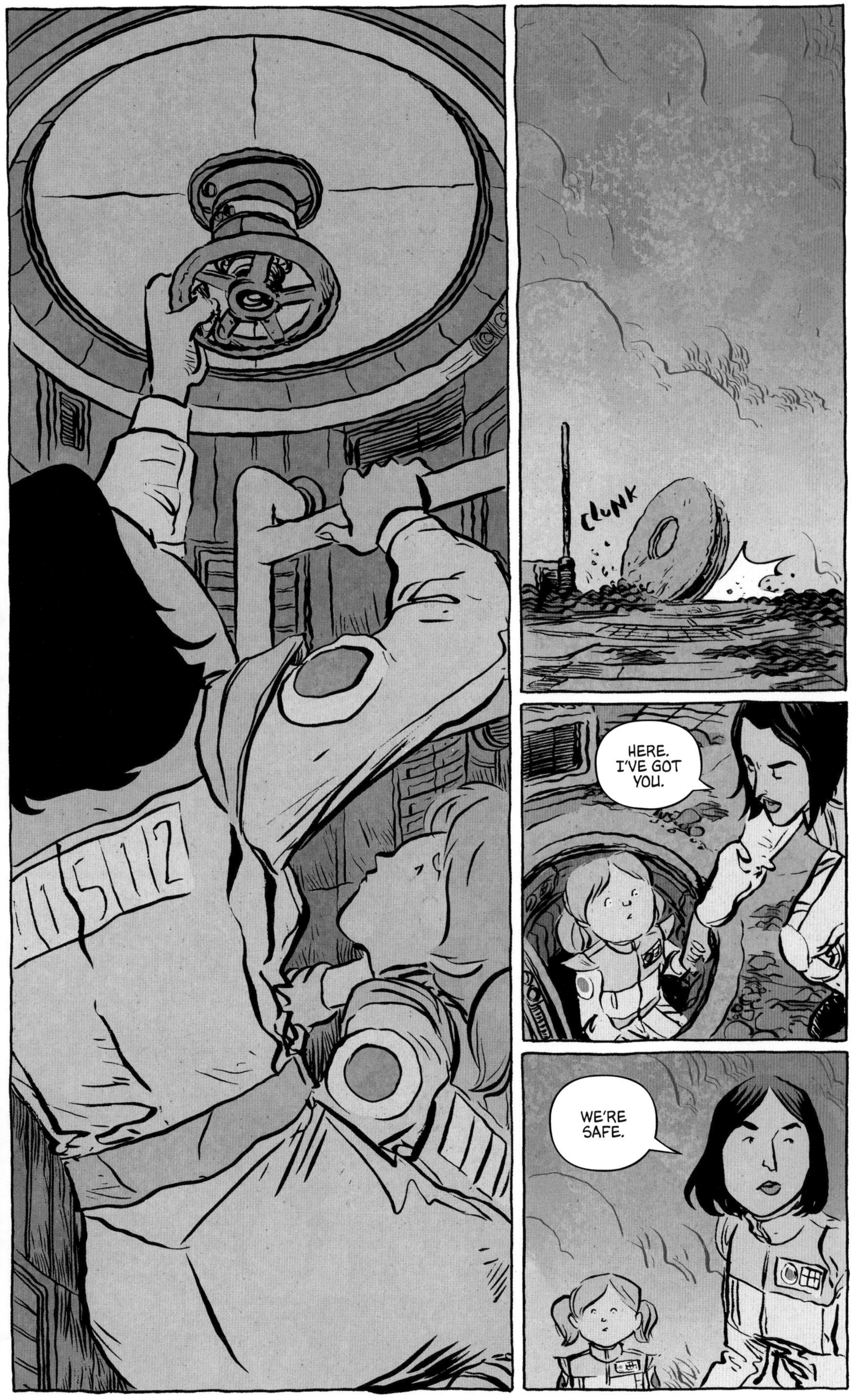
CLUNK
HERE. I'VE GOT YOU.
WE'RE SAFE.

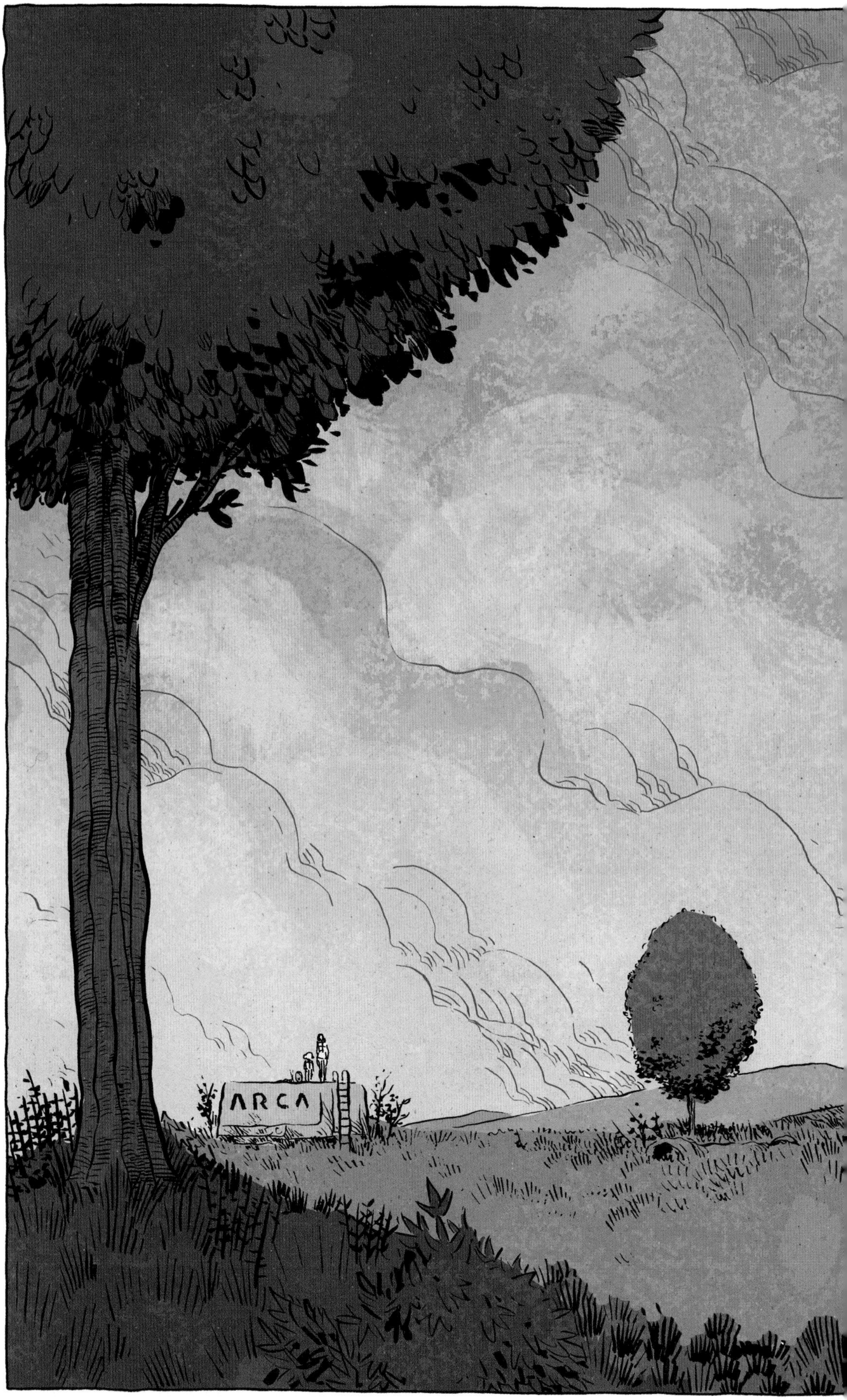
ARCA

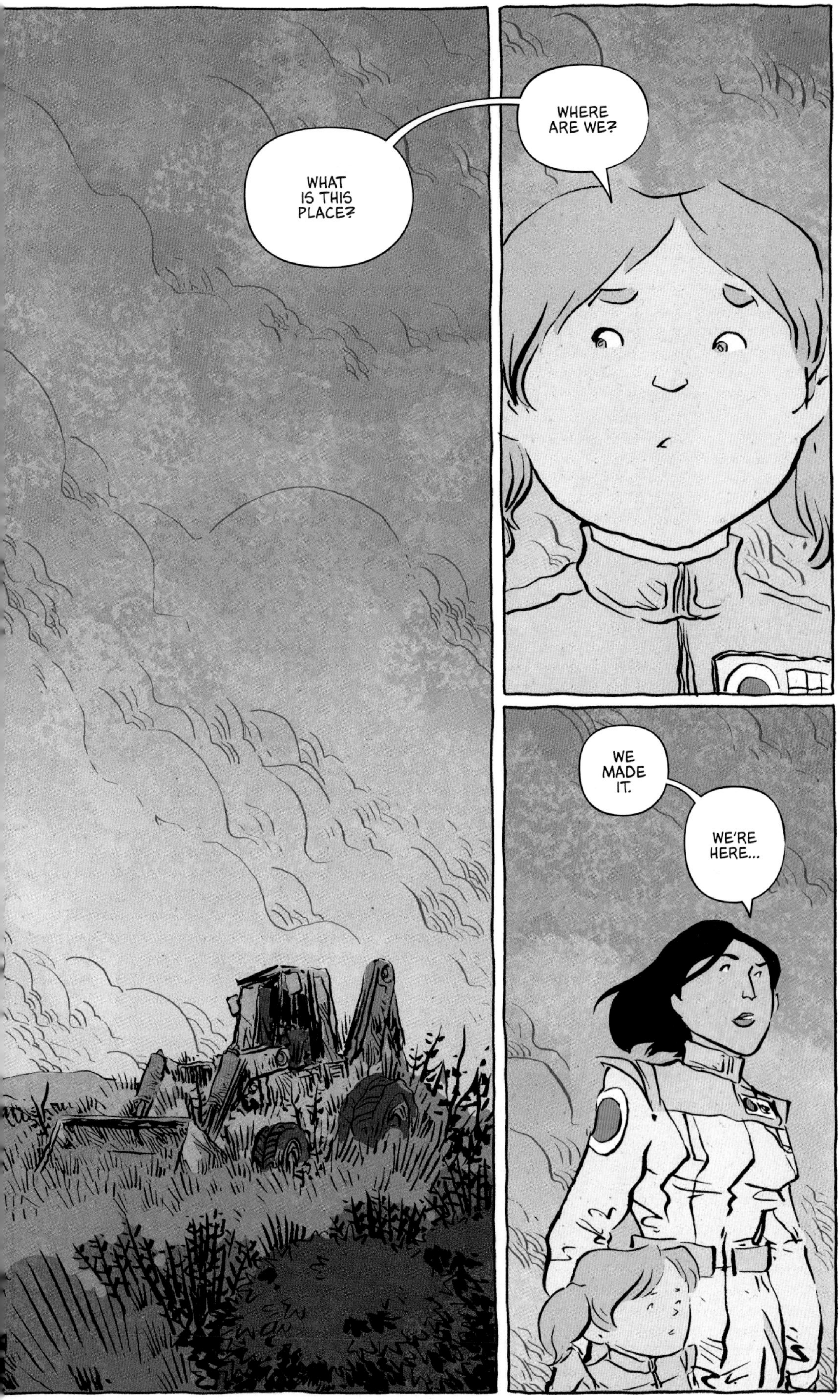
WHERE ARE WE?
WHAT IS THIS PLACE?
WE MADE IT.
WE'RE HERE...

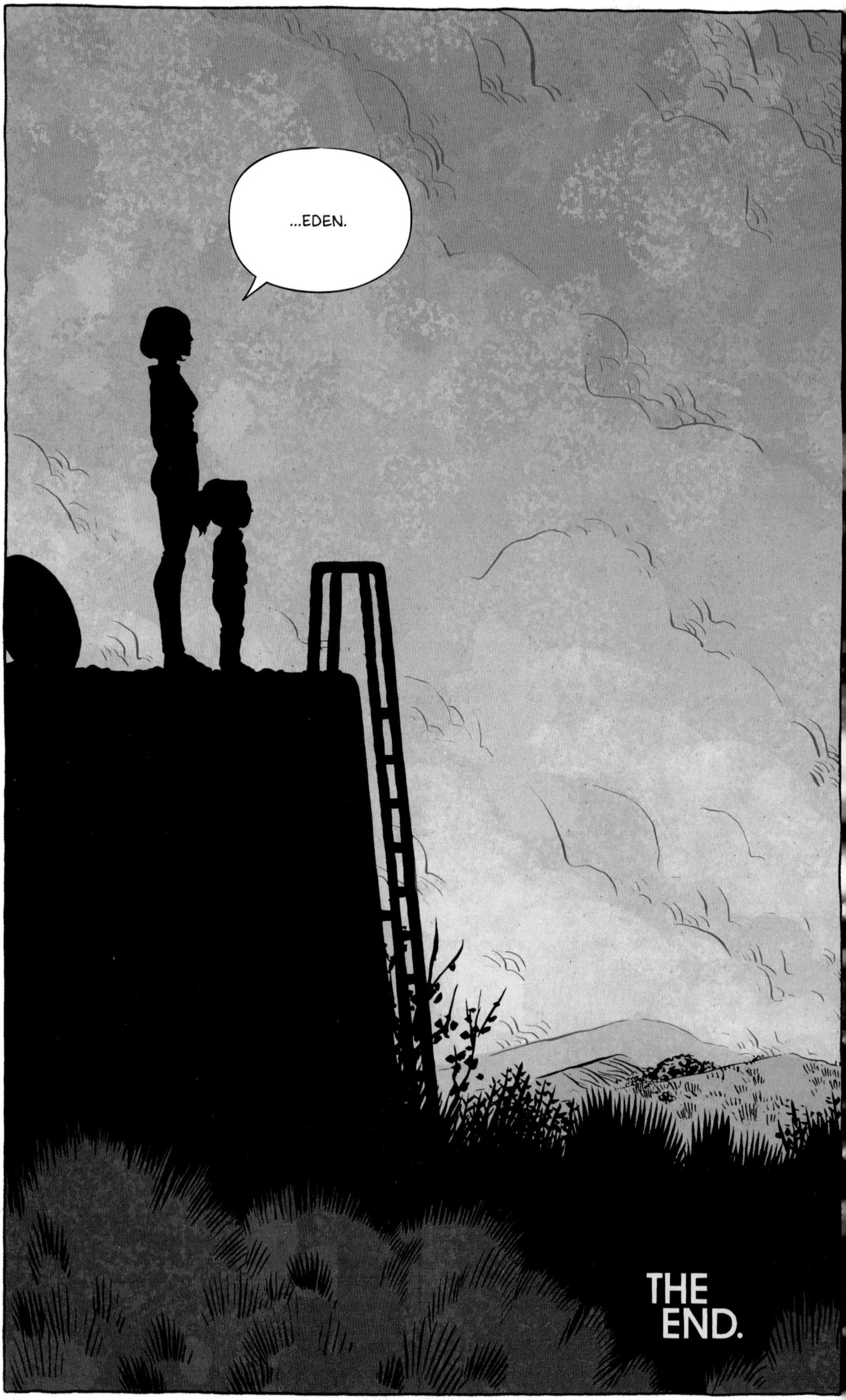
...EDEN.
THE END.

Van Jensen is the author of several comic books and graphic novels, including *Two Dead*, *Cryptocracy*, and *Pinocchio, Vampire Slayer*. He has written characters such as the Flash, Green Lantern, Superman, and James Bond. His debut novel will be released in 2023. Born and raised in rural Nebraska, he now lives in Atlanta.

Jesse Lonergan is a writer and artist (mostly an artist) with work published by IDW, Image, Dark Horse, Humanoids, and others. His first published work was *Flower and Fade* in 2007 from NBM ComicsLit. His wordless comic *Hedra* was nominated for an Eisner Award for best single issue in 2020.

Preliminary location and character sketches by Jesse Lonergan

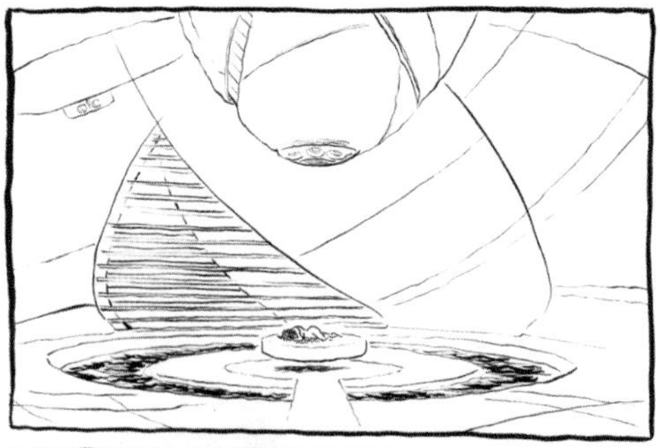
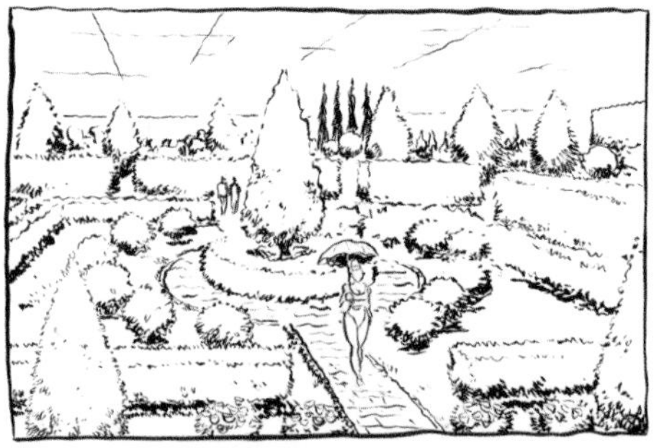
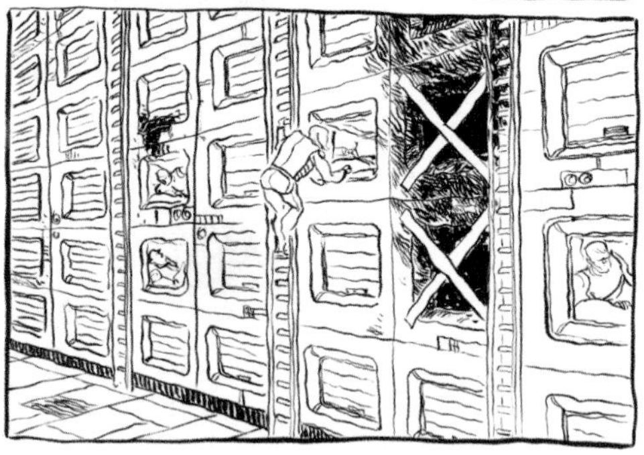
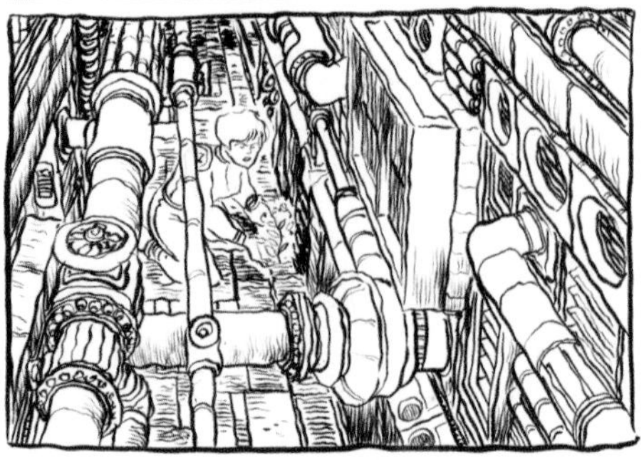
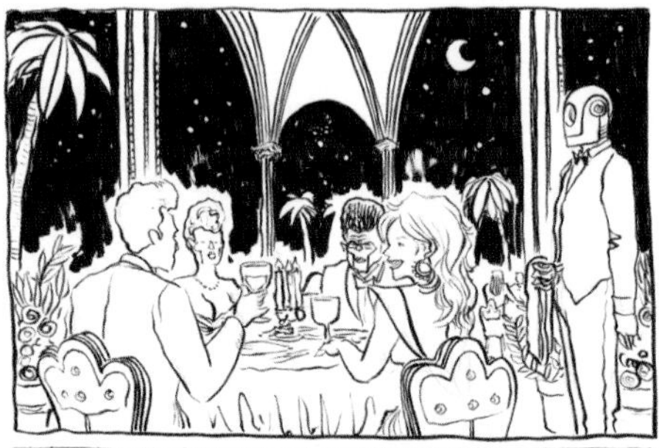
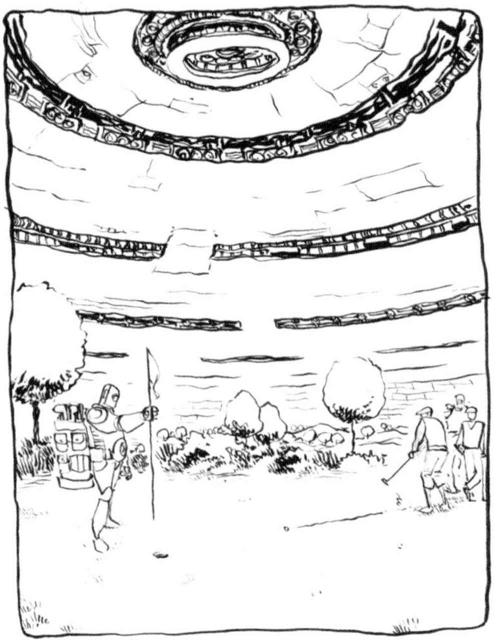
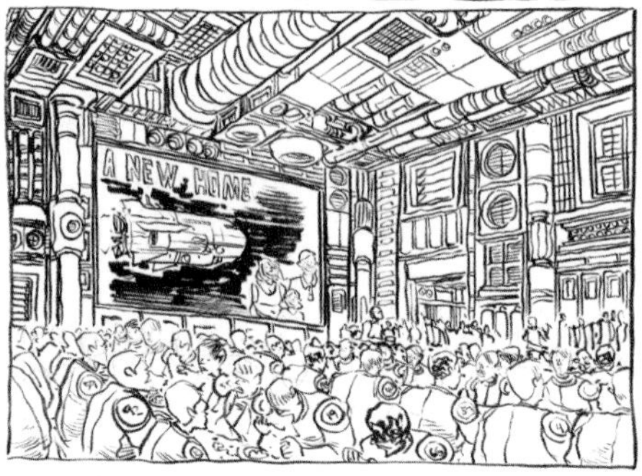
A NEW HOME
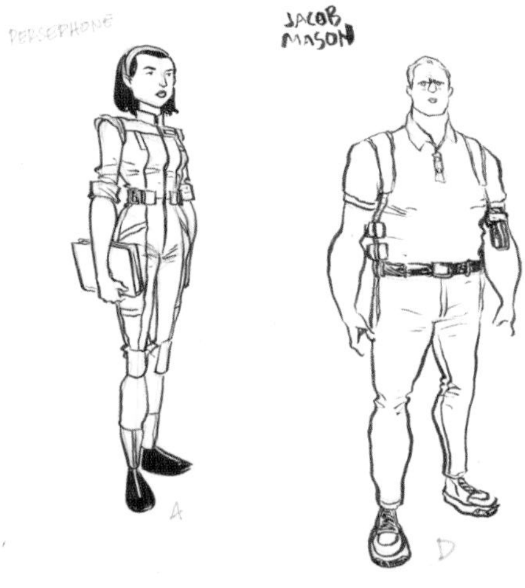
PERSEPHONE
JACOB MASON
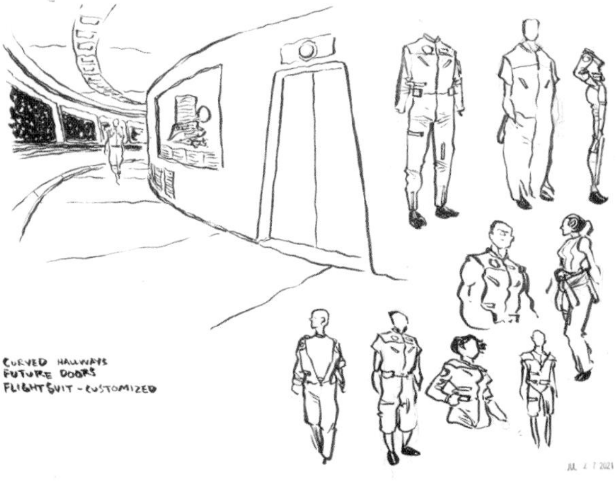
CURVED HALLWAYS
FUTURE DOORS
FLIGHTSUIT - CUSTOMIZED

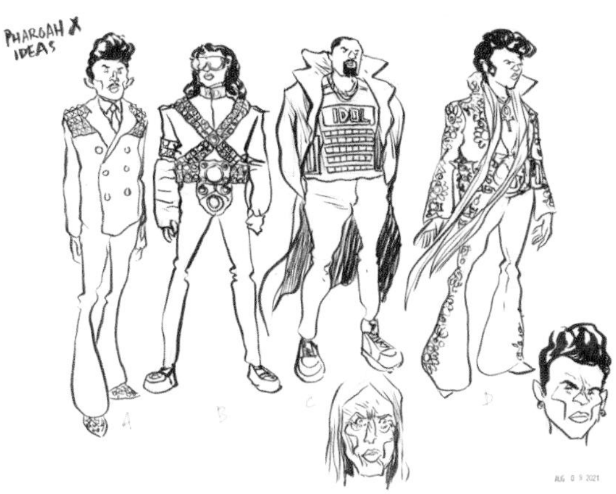
PHAROAH X
IDEAS
A
B
C
D
AUG 0 3 2021

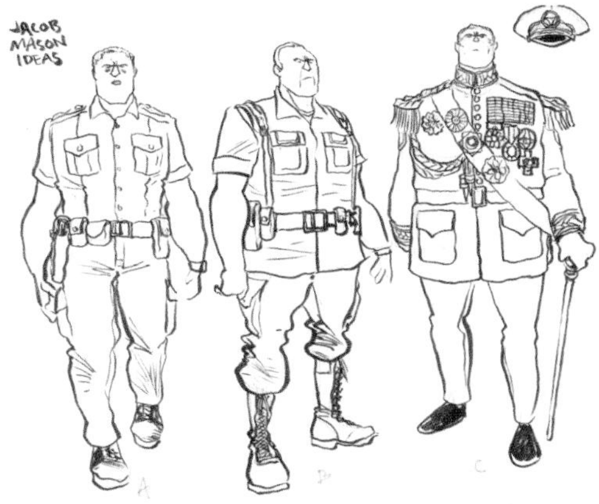
JACOB
MASON
IDEAS
A
B
C

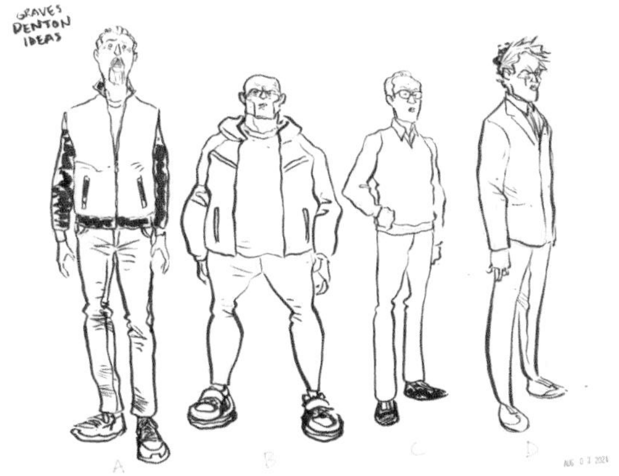
GRAVES
DENTON
IDEAS
A
B
C
D
AUG 0 3 2021

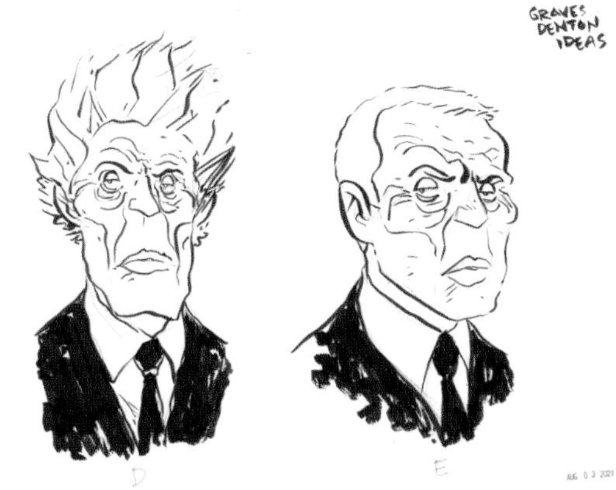
GRAVES
DENTON
IDEAS
D
E
AUG 0 3 2021

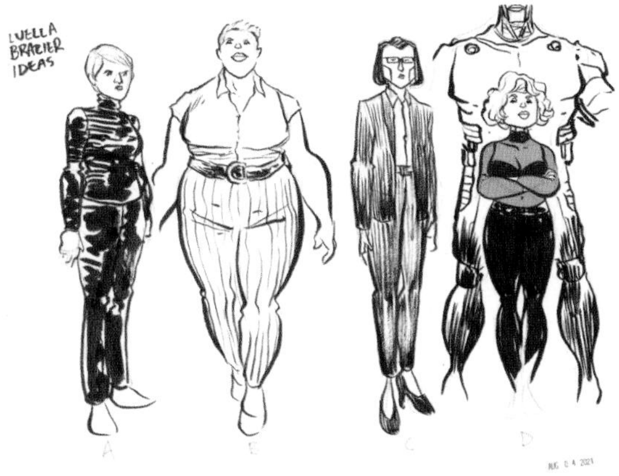
LUELLA
BRAZIER
IDEAS
A
B
C
D
AUG 0 4 2021

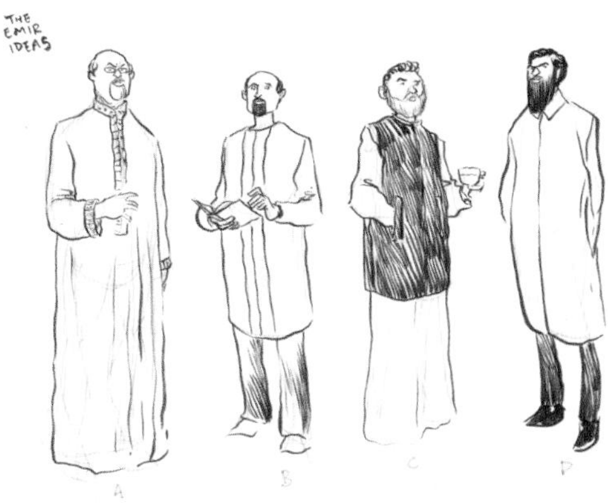
THE
EMIR
IDEAS
A
B
C
D

8 / 16 / 21

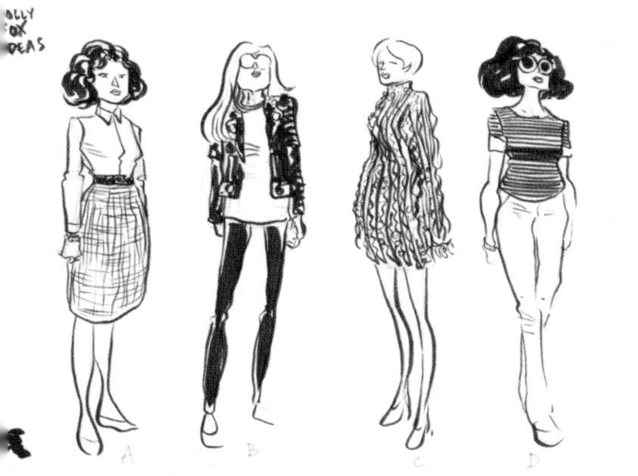
A
B
C
D

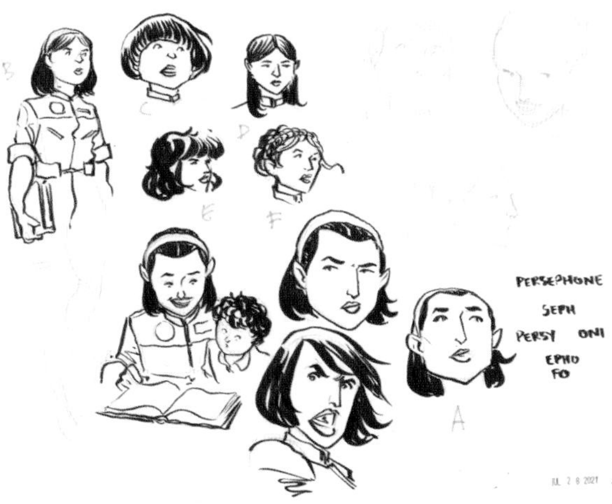
B
C
D
E
F
A
PERSEPHONE
SEPH
PERSY ONI
EPHO
FO
JUL 2 8 2021

/ 16 /21

Script to line art

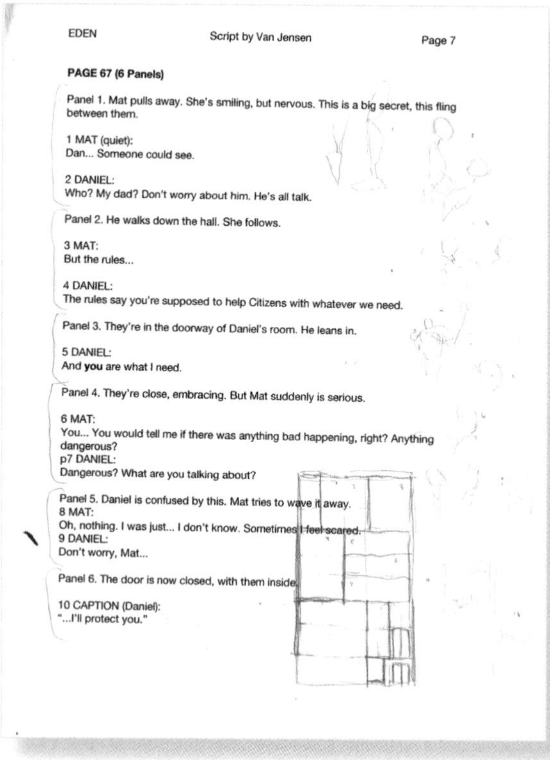
EDEN Script by Van Jensen Page 7

PAGE 67 (6 Panels)

Panel 1. Mat pulls away. She's smiling, but nervous. This is a big secret, this fling between them.

1 MAT (quiet):
Dan... Someone could see.

2 DANIEL:
Who? My dad? Don't worry about him. He's all talk.

Panel 2. He walks down the hall. She follows.

3 MAT:
But the rules...

4 DANIEL:
The rules say you're supposed to help Citizens with whatever we need.

Panel 3. They're in the doorway of Daniel's room. He leans in.

5 DANIEL:
And **you** are what I need.

Panel 4. They're close, embracing. But Mat suddenly is serious.

6 MAT:
You... You would tell me if there was anything bad happening, right? Anything dangerous?
p7 DANIEL:
Dangerous? What are you talking about?

Panel 5. Daniel is confused by this. Mat tries to wave it away.
8 MAT:
Oh, nothing. I was just... I don't know. Sometimes I feel scared.
9 DANIEL:
Don't worry, Mat...

Panel 6. The door is now closed, with them inside.

10 CAPTION (Daniel):
"...I'll protect you."

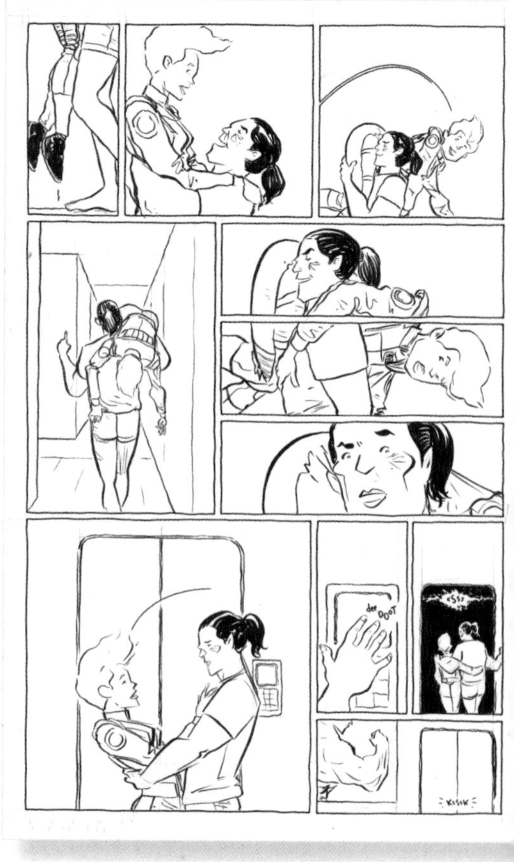
dee DOOT

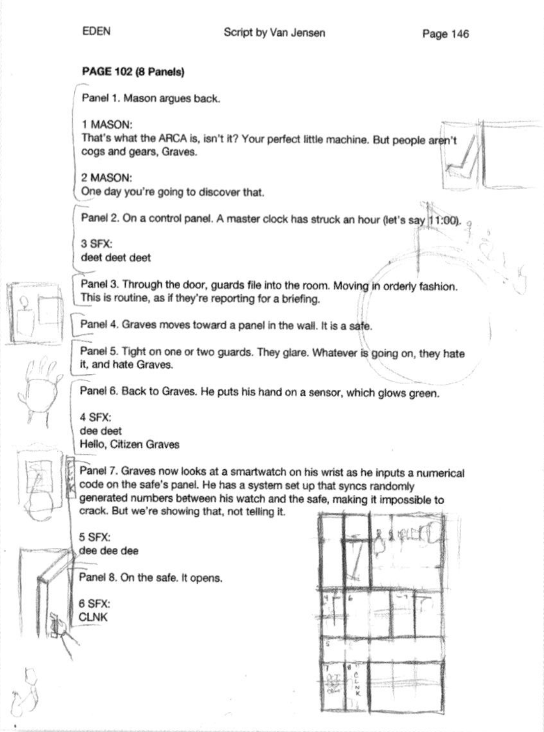
EDEN Script by Van Jensen Page 146

PAGE 102 (8 Panels)

Panel 1. Mason argues back.

1 MASON:
That's what the ARCA is, isn't it? Your perfect little machine. But people aren't cogs and gears, Graves.

2 MASON:
One day you're going to discover that.

Panel 2. On a control panel. A master clock has struck an hour (let's say 11:00).

3 SFX:
deet deet deet

Panel 3. Through the door, guards file into the room. Moving in orderly fashion. This is routine, as if they're reporting for a briefing.

Panel 4. Graves moves toward a panel in the wall. It is a safe.

Panel 5. Tight on one or two guards. They glare. Whatever is going on, they hate it, and hate Graves.

Panel 6. Back to Graves. He puts his hand on a sensor, which glows green.

4 SFX:
dee deet
Hello, Citizen Graves

Panel 7. Graves now looks at a smartwatch on his wrist as he inputs a numerical code on the safe's panel. He has a system set up that syncs randomly generated numbers between his watch and the safe, making it impossible to crack. But we're showing that, not telling it.

5 SFX:
dee dee dee

Panel 8. On the safe. It opens.

6 SFX:
CLNK

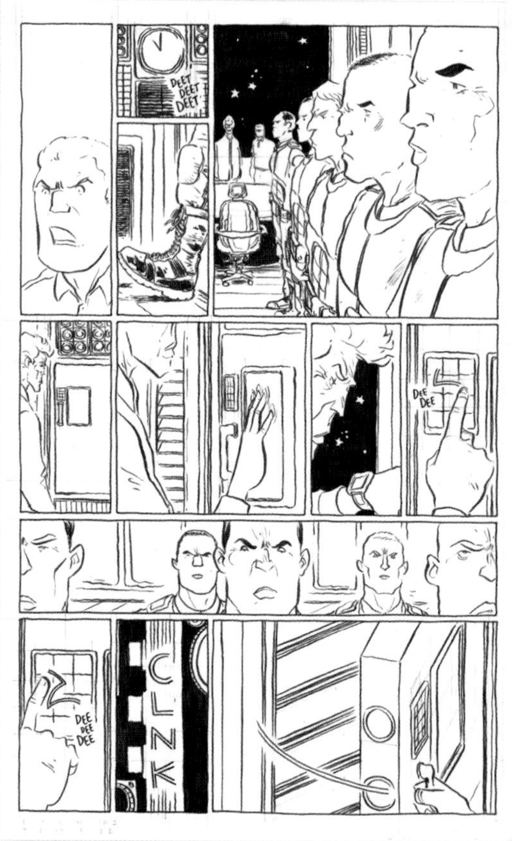
DEET DEET DEET
DEE DEE
DEE DEE DEE
CLNK

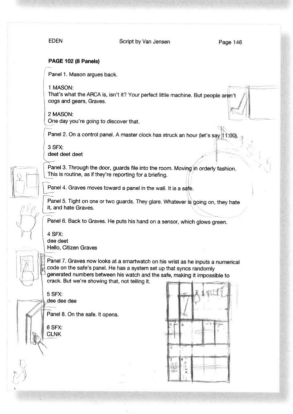

Script to line art

EDEN Script by Van Jensen Page 34

PAGE 87 (6 Panels)

Panel 1. Tight on Graves. His face turns harsh.

1 GRAVES:
How do you know about Dorian Gray?

Panel 2. Effie realizes the mistake she's made. Her eyes widen. Dorian Gray is from a book that she read. A book that she shouldn't know even exists.

2 EFFIE:
Ah...

Panel 3. And now ~~we're reversing the earlier beat. It's time for Effie to cover up the truth with a good story. Intellect vs. intellect.~~ Effie feigns being scared and does a good job of it.

3 EFFIE:
Please don't blame Citizen Nahyan!

4 GRAVES:
What has he done?

Panel 4. Effie gives a story. A convincing one.

5 EFFIE:
I ask him to tell me stories sometimes when I work. He's such a good storyteller. I know I'm not supposed to...

Panel 5. Effie watches Graves. He seems to buy it.

6 GRAVES:
Ah. I see. Citizen Nahyan certainly does love his stories.

7 EFFIE:
Anyway, you aren't like Dorian Gray.

Panel 6. Effie hits him with a hammer. The TKO of this battle of the minds.

8 EFFIE:
He was the bad guy, after all.

ARCA Script by Van Jensen Page 161

PAGE 112 (5 Panels)

Panel 1. Cut to a new location. This is Holly Fox's chambers. Inside a large, ornate formal dining room. Large table. Carved chairs. Old money trappings everywhere. Our core group of Citizens is here: Graves, Mason, Holly, Pharaoh, Bud and Nahyan (no Luella, yet). Some can be sitting and others standing. They're coming for a meal, though no food on the table yet. For now, let's open tight on Mason, to the side, talking via his radio.
1 MASON:
Good. Keep a tight rein. Over.

Panel 2. Widen to focus on the big group. There's a big portrait of Holly's husband hanging centered on the wall behind the table. He looms large over everything.
2 GRAVES:
Thank you for agreeing to host this...ah, test, Holly. I'm certain that if we have an expert in Emily Post, it is you.
3 HOLLY:
High standards are nothing to apologize for, as my grandma always said.

Panel 3. Graves and Holly stand beneath the painting of her husband. Holly is a bit timid.
4 HOLLY:
Graves, I... I wanted to ask. Next year, the solstice. Could we not use David? It's just so hard... Seeing him.
5 GRAVES:
I know that it is. But you understand how important it is to the settlers. He's their savior.
6 GRAVES:
Now, let's be seated.

Panel 4. They are seated. Luella enters. At least, we think it's Luella.
7 PHARAOH:
All right. Luella's here. Let the test begin!

Panel 5. Four or five Luella-bots enter the room, carrying trays of food and pitchers of drinks.
8 LUELLA-BOT:
Good morning, Citizen. How do you take your coffee?
9 BUD (grumbling):
Christ. They're all her.

Cover sketches by Jesse Lonergan
(The team considered several titles, including *Eden*, before landing on *Arca.*)

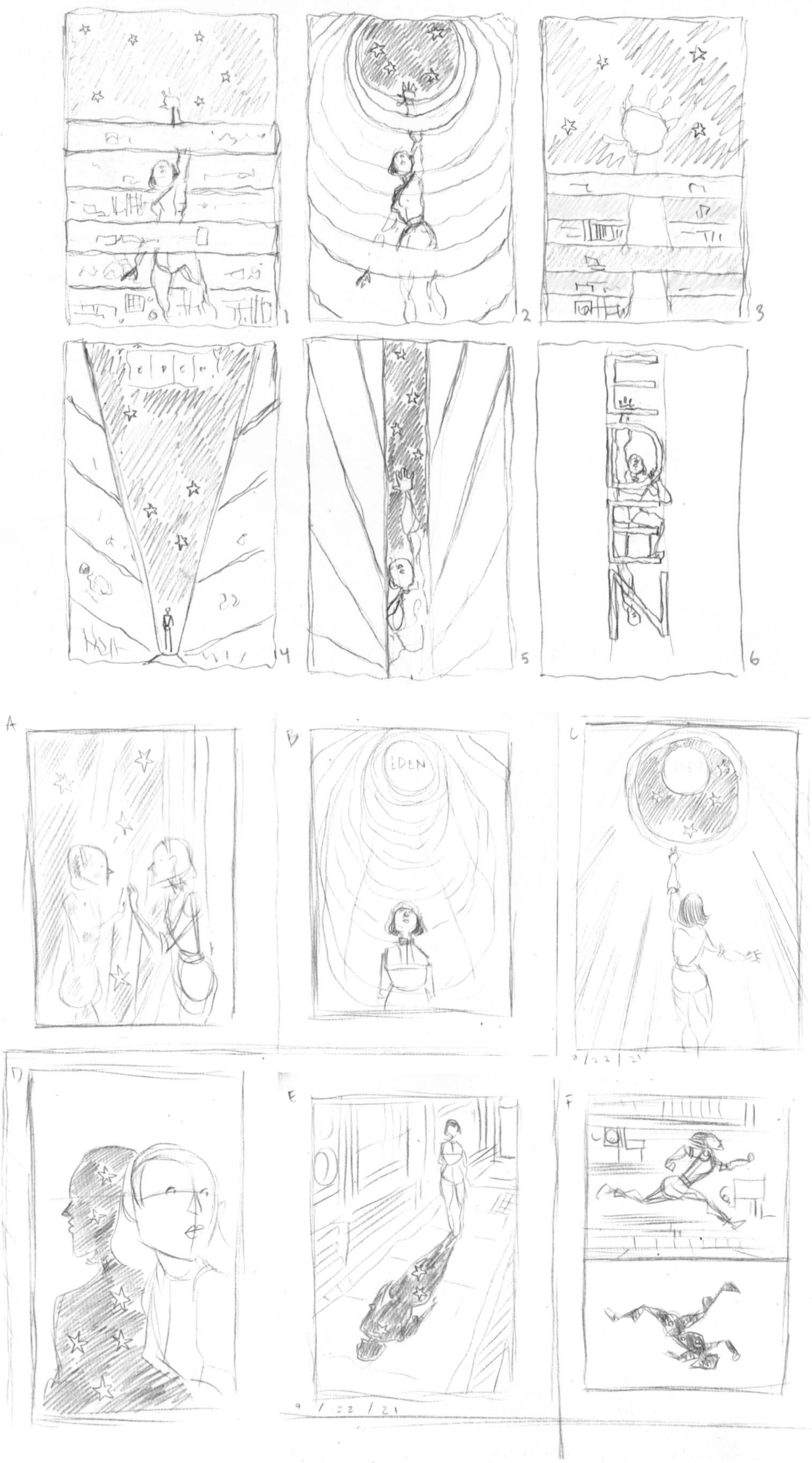
EDEN